HANDLER

TERRY WILKINSON

RIFTSWOOD PRINT

CHAPTER 1

Howard Wesley was only halfway down Augsburger-Strasse in Berlin on a drizzly autumn evening. He could already hear the music and laughter leaking through the doors and windows of the *Blauer Tiger* nightclub, even though it was still a hundred yards away. It was chilly and he had left his overcoat in his dressing room. He needed to get inside the club.

There was a buzz in the air tonight. He knew the place would be crammed. He noticed it in the theatre bar after the show. The 'chattering classes', as his father would have called them, were on fire. The British Prime Minister, Neville Chamberlain – the old man with the umbrella – had gone home. The *Führer* had assured him that the cession of the Sudetenland to the German *Reich* would be the end of his territorial ambitions. Nobody here was under any illusions.

The rest of the cast had moved on to their favoured post-show watering hole and he promised to join them later. He wanted to stay back and earwig while he mingled with those who had seen the show. Accept their plaudits and their praise. Sharing it with the rest of the actors was not his cup of tea.

He opened the door of the club and the noise hit him like an artillery barrage. It was loud at many decibels beyond safe and, from what he could see from the cavorting bodies, heavily alcohol fuelled. The joint was bursting with life. He stood on the edge of the gyrating throng and looked for his colleagues.

"Vesley. *Komm!*"

Wesley heard the shout. The dance floor to his right was a single writhing mass of sweaty humanity. There was music – jazz, he guessed, but it could have been anything. He looked over the sea of bobbing heads. A man beyond the swaying crowd was standing waving at him. He cupped his hands and shouted again.

"Vesley!"

He returned the wave and eased his way through the dancers. Now that they all knew his name, he was greeted by every single one of them as he forced his way past and slid through the warm, damp bodies – collecting slobbering kisses and squeezes of various parts of his lower anatomy on the way. There was a heady, moist cocktail of perspiration from the men, a nostril-twitching spectrum of perfumes from the ladies, and booze from all.

He emerged, drenched and exhausted – and probably bruised, when he had time to look.

"Jurgen"

He was hotly embraced. "Vesley. Glad you could make it." Wesley laughed. "It's Wesley, you oaf!"

Jurgen smiled. "I know. I like to tease you. Come. Drink."

He turned away and made a space for them in a booth on the back wall. The heat was oppressive. Already he was sweating heavily. The back of his shirt was sticking to the leather of the seat.

The German found him an empty glass from the detritus on the table and poured him a beer from a large stoneware jug. He held up his own.

"Bottoms up."

Wesley laughed. "You're learning". He had to shout. The noise level had not abated.

He noticed looks from the two uniformed officers who were sharing the booth. They were well sozzled but the use of the English language had obviously permeated their haze and piqued their curiosity. They smiled across at him.

One of them leant across. "*Engländer?*", he slurred.

Wesley replied in German and with a broad Berlin patois that shocked both of the officers and Jurgen. Introductions were made. The other German spoke. "So, you are bi-lingual, *ja?*"

Jurgen explained – it saved his friend straining his voice over the din – that Howard Wesley was a talented actor. English father and German mother whose family hailed from Wedding in Berlin. They smiled and nodded approval as he went on to explain that Wesley had chosen to move to the city a few years ago and made it his home. The first officer joined in and stabbed a podgy finger in Wesley's direction.

"I thought I knew your face. You were in . . ." He looked directly at Wesley while his synapses slowly made the connection. "*Faust*. Last year. At the . . . *Schauspielhaus. Der Tragödie.*"

The other officer yawned spectacularly. "Oh, fucking Goethe. We had to trawl through *Faust* at school. Bloody boring."

The first man punched his friend on the arm and turned

back to Wesley. "And you were Heinrich Faust himself. I never dreamt you were English!"

Wesley feigned embarrassment and nodded. He replied in his native tongue. "I'm afraid so, old chap." All three Germans laughed at that. At both the quintessential Englishness of the words and the lazy aristocratic drawl that delivered them.

"I didn't see your face up close but I would recognise your . . . your build anywhere."

Jurgen laughed and leant over to clap Wesley's leg. "He's like a tank! Shoulders of an ox!"

They were all laughing now. Wesley knew he struck an imposing figure. Wearing a topcoat, it always looked as if he had left the coat hanger in there. "And what else have you been in?"

Jurgen and Wesley smiled. The German responded. "Were you at the Olympic opening ceremony in 36?"

The others groaned at the memory. That day had been long and boring, and not made any more bearable by the searing heat of what had come to be known as *Hitlerwetter*. One of them pointed a wavering arm towards the Englishman. "You were the Titan! In that big production at the end."

He turned to the others. "What a triumph that was for the *Reich*, don't you think? The *Führer* must have been so pleased." Wesley was uneasy. The focus of attention had suddenly turned away from him – to Hitler. He had to nip this in the bud. "The finale was better than the overture." All three looked at him blankly. "Did you see the release of the pigeons at the beginning? They released thousands of the buggers and then . . ."

The other officer laughed. "Oh yes, I think they were doves, who knows? But when they fired the cannon, the birds got such a fright that they shat all over the crowd. Bird shit everywhere."

Wesley had just lost his punchline. He took control again. "They had been in their baskets for almost a full day. I don't remember seeing it on the newsreels though."

Jurgen spoke up. "I saw Göbbels' wife, Magda. Her outfit was covered in it. And her hat. She was wiping it off her cheek."

They all laughed at the memory. Wesley leant across and, in his best grandiose theatrical style, declared, "*Ein Scheissesturm.*" He had made the word up but the meaning was clear. A shitstorm.

After half an hour or so of mainly Wesley-centric chat, the club started to quieten. Those who had joined the revelling earlier in the evening were now drifting off. A few of those seated had started to doze.

Jurgen leaned across to Wesley and whispered. "This place needs waking up. Why don't you do your Chamberlain, Vesley? I'll get you an umbrella and a hat." He walked across to the cloakroom.

Over the previous few days, Wesley had been regaling anyone who cared to watch, with his impression of the British Prime Minister. It never failed to amuse. He looked at those still sitting around. Many of them looked bored rigid. Perfect. Jurgen returned a few minutes later. He had excelled himself. Across his arm was a black overcoat and he was holding a Homburg and a gent's black umbrella. He dropped them into Wesley's lap.

"I need one more thing, Jurgen."

The German looked puzzled. "What?"

"A piece of paper. Anything will do."

Jurgen fished through his pockets, unfolded a letter and passed it to Wesley. He looked at it. The German grabbed it back. "No, Wesley. Do not read it. It's . . . it's from a friend. It's personal."

They both laughed. Wesley put on the hat and coat and stuffed the letter into the pocket. He knew he looked nothing like the man without one of his collection of wigs and a moustache but the mannerisms, accent and supercilious smile would be flawless. He was usually able to grab a copy of *The Times* once or twice a week, so he had read the speeches Chamberlain made both on his return to Heston aerodrome and on the steps of Number Ten. He edited and merged them together for his little routine, focussing on the extracts which he knew would get a reaction. He picked up the umbrella and stood. Jurgen moved ahead of him and spoke to those assembled. His uniform and his authoritative tone rendered the band silent. All eyes were now on Jurgen and Wesley.

"*Meine Damen und Herren* . . . tonight, we have a special guest with us. He has come all the way from the British parliament in London. He . . ."

Wesley took the floor. There were puzzled looks and Jurgen was building his part. The Englishman eased him aside. The umbrella was now open. He addressed the audience.

"We, the German *Führer* and Chancellor . . ."

Everyone cheered. Wesley smiled the PM's smile and continued. ". . . and the British Prime Minister . . ." There were boos. Chamberlain smiled nervously. ". . . have had a further meeting today and are agreed in recognising that the question of Anglo-German relations is of the first importance for our two countries and for Europe."

He took the letter out of his pocket and held it up. He read it loudly in measured tones. "We regard the agreement signed last night as symbolic of the desire of our two peoples never to go to war with one another again. We are determined to continue our efforts to remove possible sources of difference, and thus to contribute to assure the peace of Europe."

He waved the paper timidly. "My good friends, for the second time in our history, a British Prime Minister . . ." More booing. ". . . has returned from Germany bringing peace with honour. I believe it is peace for our time."

Laughter erupted. Wesley made to turn away and then faced them again.

"So . . . go home and get a nice quiet sleep."

To signal the end of this *pièce de résistance*, he bowed clumsily – just enough for the hat to fall off. Then he comically closed the umbrella and walked away.

The reaction was better than he had dared hope. He had started with an audience that was practically comatose, and turned them into a baying mob. Well, not quite, but it was certainly up there with the best of receptions he had ever had for the piece. The cheers abated. The band took their cue and struck up with something jauntier.

Wesley returned to the booth and graciously received the expected plaudits from Jurgen and the other two. One of them told him that if he had closed his eyes, he would have sworn it was the Umbrella Man himself.

Wesley demurred. "Apart from the body shape, of course!"

Jurgen piped up. "But you haven't seen his Hermann Göring, gentlemen."

Looks of expectation appeared from the other two. "Go on, Vesley. Don't be shy!"

Wesley was not sure of this. He had only ever done his Hermann in chosen company but such was the pressure from these three that he stood, pushed his belly out and started pontificating in Göring's distinctive Bavarian drawl. Jurgen and the other two were almost on the floor laughing. Although it was a more intimate performance than his Chamberlain *tour de force*, others had noticed and there was a smattering of applause.

As he sat back down and acknowledged those who had been clapping, his eyes fell on those of a uniformed officer sitting on his own in a booth diagonally across from theirs. The man smiled with thin lips and stood. He walked across to Wesley and bent down to him. His English was impeccable.

"Very good, Mr Wesley. I would like you to meet me here, tomorrow morning at ten o'clock sharp."

With that, the man walked away and left the club. Wesley started to sweat. Maybe his Hermann had been a step too far.

CHAPTER 2

The oak-panelled manager's office of the Westminster Bank branch in Euston Road was not for the faint-hearted. Remittance clerk, Albert Stokes, could remember very few occasions when he was summoned through its august portals. The first was on his induction day and it was the usual one-way traffic of 'stick in, do your job, keep your nose clean and you will go far, young man'.

That was almost ten years ago when he was, indeed, a young man. Now, as a superannuated thirty-three year old, he was not sure. He had stuck in. He had certainly done his job. He had kept his nose clean. But he did not feel as if he had gone very far. He was still a clerk, albeit Grade Two, and only one step above the crop of fresh-faced grammar school sprogs that arrived every autumn.

The job was extremely boring. Once he had got to grips with it, he could have done it with his eyes closed. It involved inspecting every customer cheque for correctness of date, checking the signature or absence thereof, and whether or not the words and figures agreed. Another clerk then checked the amount against cleared funds and was equally bored by the process. At times, to relieve the monotony, they would swap jobs. Without approval, without official sanction and without notice by anyone who mattered.

The work was stultifying. It was turning his brain to mush.

Then came the day when he detected a fraudulent practice which was slowly siphoning funds from one of the branch's larger accounts. If it were allowed to continue, the reputation of the Westminster Bank itself was under threat. He had done his own investigation and laid a trap for the perpetrators. With some help from the Metropolitan Police, the miscreants were nabbed. The only mistake that Stokes had made was in not informing his manager of what he was doing.

The occasion of the second summons to visit the oak and leather of Mr Charlesworth's office was when two members of the Fraud Squad called in to inform the manager that the fraudsters had been apprehended, and to thank Stokes for his help and co-operation. The manager was dumbfounded and patently embarrassed. It was all news to him. Stokes was called in.

For appearance's sake, the boss had gone along with it, doled out faint praise while the police officers were there and then gave him a right bollocking once they left.

The story got to the newspapers. No glory photo for Stokes but a beaming shot of Charlesworth. In fact, he used it to his advantage at his club. It was he and 'a subordinate' who had fettled the criminals. He had dined out on it for weeks.

Stokes had no idea why he was being called in for this,

the third time. The bank had formally acknowledged his help with a cheque for £50 and a promise that he was being seriously considered for promotion. That was a couple of weeks ago. He was not expecting any further reward. He was right. He could tell by the look on Charlesworth's face as he stormed in through the door.

"This is your last day here, Stokes."

There were a few seconds silence while he tried to make sense of what he had just heard. Was he actually being sacked after he had saved the bank thousands? "I'm sorry, sir. I don't understand."

A letter was waved in front of him. "I've just had this from Brigadier Harker." The name meant nothing to Stokes. "Who's Brigadier Harker?"

Charlesworth leant forward across the desk. "He's a member of my club, Stokes. He's one of the big chiefs in MI5." He detected petulance from his boss. And he had not finished.

"I am being told. *Told*, mark you, to hand you over to them."

"Me? To MI5. I . . ." "My fault, of course. I was singing your praises about how you foiled that cheque fraud thing." He paused. "What the hell do they see in you, Stokes, eh? A run of the mill bloody bank clerk."

Stokes felt his face getting warm. What a silly old bugger this man was.

He had not finished. "I'm short of staff as it is with almost every able-bodied man being called up. I'm not happy about this, Stokes"

"I gather that, sir." Stokes had not finished either. "Perhaps they see something in me that the bank has failed to recognise."

Charlesworth looked as if he had just been slapped in the face. Stokes had had enough. He stood.

"Do you have instructions for me there." He did not bother with the niceties of a 'sir' this time. He had had enough of this small man's ire.

"Erm, yes." He handed the letter over. "It's all in there. I suppose this is effectively your call-up, Stokes."

"Good. I'll bid you goodbye then. I take it this month's salary will be in my account as usual."

"Yes, of course." Stokes held out his hand. Charlesworth shook it limply. "Well . . . erm, good luck, Stokes." "Thank you."

By the time Stokes drew the letter from his pocket, he was sitting on the tube on his way to Waterloo to catch the train home to Epsom. He had calmed down from his anger against Charlesworth and was now starting to wonder what was facing him in his new life. The piece of paper was an introduction to Maxwell Knight, head of Section B5(b) at MI5. He was to present himself to the man at Hood House in Dolphin Square, Pimlico.

He told his wife, Susan, that he had been called up but that she was not to worry. He was very careful in what he told her as he was certain that one of the first things required of him in his new job would be to sign the Official Secrets Act. He fell back on vagueness and told her it was a new admin post at the Ministry of Defence. She did not ask him to elaborate and was especially relieved that he would be neither wearing the khaki nor bearing arms. He was not exactly sure about the latter but he kept his doubts to himself.

Stokes telephoned the number on the letter. It was a strange conversation. Knight seemed genuinely pleased to hear from him. He called him his new *Wunderkind*. If that was a test of his German, it was pretty feeble, Stokes felt, but he played along with a *vielen Dank*. He was to meet Knight at Hood House at ten the following morning.

KNIGHT'S OFFICE in Pimlico was just far enough away from the various seats of power in Westminster to be divorced, to some degree, from close scrutiny. Stokes found the place without any trouble and was shown to a small waiting room. Knight came to collect him and they chatted merrily about the weather as he led him up the two flights to his office.

"Albert Stokes. Your reputation goes before you. Without any further ado though, I need to sign you up." He opened a drawer and slid the Official Secrets Act in front of Stokes. "Please make sure you read every bloody syllable before you sign."

He did as he was told. It took a full ten minutes. He signed and handed the papers back across the desk.

"Good. Attention to detail is important in this game, Albert."

"I'm sure. There's a typing error on page fourteen."

Knight looked surprised and flicked through to the page. "Where?"

"About a third of the way down. 'Prohibited' has the second 'i' missing." The man's index finger moved down and stopped at the offending word. "By George, you're right. Well done, old boy!" He laughed. "Thank you. I'll have fun with that."

"It wasn't a test then?"

"Not at all. But at least you've proved you have a sharp eye."

Knight sat back in his chair and folded his arms. "Now

then, let me clue you up, old chap. Section B5(b), of which I am chief bottle washer, is responsible for infiltrating agents into potentially subversive groups."

Stokes nodded.

"And I have read the police files of the little racket you uncovered. I gather from what they say that you employed more than a little infiltration yourself. That sounds right up our alley. Care to tell me about it?"

Stokes related how he had followed one of the individuals who had deposited one of the questionable cheques. He had actually left his desk several times with help from one of his fellow clerks who covered his work for him while he trailed the man. It was a big branch. Nobody noticed.

In time he made contact with his quarry and posed as a disgruntled clerk who had rumbled them and wanted a cut for his silence. He also hinted about further deceptions they could operate. Then Stokes visited the Metropolitan Police who rounded them all up at a meeting which he himself had called. It was a long and detailed tale but Knight was obviously rapt. He let Stokes finish without interruption.

"Well, thank God we got you out of the Westminster Bank, my dear fellow. You were wasted there. Well done. I'm impressed." He looked closely at Stokes. "You're a very ordinary looking chap, if you don't mind me saying so. Unusually unremarkable, in fact."

Stokes laughed. "Is that not a good thing?"

"It's absolutely perfect. I doubt I would be able to pick you out in a police identification parade."

Both men laughed.

"Let's hope you never have to. Now, I insist on tea. It's like cat's piss but at least it's hot. Have a look at this while I go and find the char wallah. It's your first project, old man."

Knight took a thick manila file from a filing cabinet and thumped it on the desk in front of Stokes. He left and Stokes heard him pounding down the stairs. He picked up the file and read the label. Siemens-Schuckert. It already looked like a lifetime's work.

CHAPTER 3

The *Blauer Tiger* was virtually empty when Wesley entered it the following morning for his appointment with the German officer.

He did not normally see the first ten o'clock of the day, especially after a hectic night of performances, drinking and carousing. The club was weakly lit and still felt strangely warm from the previous night's body heat. He had a headache and felt strongly that those restocking the bar and the crew clearing up the litter-strewn shambles of the dance floor should be doing so with less gusto – and certainly less noise. Where was their sympathy?

He spotted the officer very quickly. It was not difficult. He was the only customer in the place and had selected a booth that had obviously already been serviced. He was the archetypal Aryan. Blonde hair. Chiselled looks. A poster boy for the Germanic race. It was obvious the man looked after himself. On the table in front of him was a pot of coffee and two cups. He waved the Englishman over.

Wesley's guts took a lurch. He remembered, suddenly, the less than respectful impression of Göring that he had done the previous night, following which he had received this summons. How could he have been so stupid?

The German stood. He was smiling. "You look as if you need a coffee, Mr Wesley."

The Englishman tried to return the smile, failed and sat opposite the officer. "Yes. Thank you." As the coffee was poured from pot to cup, the smell hit Wesley's senses. He did need it.

"You look slightly the worse for wear, my friend." He pushed the cup across the table and waited for Wesley to take his first sip.

The memories of the night before were slowly dribbling back into his consciousness. Drip by painful drip. Could this be the last coffee he would taste before his liberty was removed? Nazi Germany was swiftly becoming a place where you could neither speak nor act without at least a modicum of self-censorship.

He looked across at the German and regarded him while his mind raced. He was immaculately dressed in his uniform. And it was *Luftwaffe*. Wesley had not noticed that the previous night but he had been well lubricated by the time he came on the scene. He was not sure of the man's status but he seemed distinctly patrician in appearance. He guessed senior rank. His fear subsided gently as the man smiled again and looked back at him curiously.

The actor relaxed and smiled back. "I'm fine, thank you. This is quite an early morning for me. I do apologise for my . . . erm, dazed state."

"I'm sorry, too. I have to get back to Hamburg by this afternoon but I wanted to speak to you first."

Wesley thought about his Göring *faux pas* again. He needed to know if he was in the shit or not, although it was looking better by the second. He wanted to clear the air.

"Can I apologise for my dreadful impression of Göring. The . . ." He paused. He could not remember the *Luftwaffe* chief's rank.

The German laughed. "I don't think the *Generalfeld-marschall* would lose any sleep over it. Please, do not worry. When you're as big a target as Hermann, it happens all the time. Just be careful in whose company you do it. Best I've seen though! And steer clear of including the *Führer* in your repertoire – that would ruffle too many feathers. Anyway, you're the wrong build for him."

Wesley's relief must have been very evident to the man facing him.

"It was really good. As was your earlier portrayal of Mr Chamberlain. You have talent, Mr Wesley."

The Englishman could feel the anxiety and the stress evaporating. The officer leant across the table and lowered his voice. "But again, I must warn you. Be very careful where you do it and who is watching. There were at least two offi-cers in here last night who would have taken exception to it."

He pointed across to a booth a few metres away.

"They would have been amused, I am sure, by your 'Umbrella Man'. Your *Generalfeldmarschall* came later so they had probably left by then."

Wesley was starting to realise how lucky he had been.

"Of course, it would not have been because they were genuinely offended by it, but it would have given them the opportunity to curry favour with the *Gestapo*. And you would have spent last night in secluded accommodation in Prinz-Albrecht-Strasse."

The actor knew that was the address of the *Gestapo* HQ in Berlin. He shuddered.

The German looked at his watch. "We have less than an

hour. Let me order more coffee." He held the coffee pot aloft, signalled across to the bar and then returned his attention to Wesley. "Before we start, allow me to introduce myself." He handed over a card.

Major Dieter Grosskopf, *Luftwaffe*. It said nothing more.

The *Major* proceeded to ask Wesley about his background. Why was he living in Germany? What did he think about life in the *Reich*? What were his politics? What was his domestic background? Any relationships? Given that he was born and educated in Great Britain, where did his allegiances lie?

He made no notes of the Englishman's answers and Wesley got the distinct impression that most of them were already known. He also felt that it had very quickly taken on the mantle of an interrogation. Although that was perhaps too strong a word, he reflected. It was more like what he imagined a job interview to be. Not that he had ever had one. Auditions were more his stock in trade. He was very careful to give replies that he thought the man wanted to hear.

The fresh coffee arrived during the questioning. Wesley took a drink before replying.

He was half-German by birth - father English, mother German. He travelled from his native Coventry to visit his mother's family in Berlin after she died too soon. He stayed because he loved what was happening here. He was not a Party member but not opposed to it should the need arise. No relationships, no encumbrances. And no love of Great Britain.

That seemed to clinch it. Grosskopf released the tension and relaxed back into his seat. "Good. Then I think I may have some work for you. How would you like to tread a bigger stage?"

"But I . . ."

"Oh, don't worry, you can still employ your undoubted talents to the utmost."

Once again, the actor was struck by the man's excellent command of English. Only a slight guttural tone to it and it would not pass muster north of Watford, but it was very good nevertheless. Grammatically perfect and a seemingly extensive vocabulary.

Grosskopf went on to explain that he worked with the *Abwehr* in Hamburg. Military intelligence. They needed agents in Britain. He saw Wesley as a perfect candidate.

The German looked at his watch and stood.

"All I want is a provisional 'yes', Mr Wesley. I would like to see you in Hamburg soon so that we can tell you more about what would be required. When does your current run end?"

The Englishman stared up at him. "It ended last night. Hence the unbridled frivolity. I am free for the foreseeable future. So, I passed the audition, then?"

The German laughed. He threw some *Reichsmarks* on the table. "Don't go anywhere, Wesley. I will be in touch. Your training will also be in Hamburg."

"Erm . . . do I get to wear a uniform? I am a good friend of Hugo Boss."

Grosskopf laughed again.

"I don't think it will help you where you're going, do you? You might look rather conspicuous."

At that, he bent closer to Wesley and, in a stage whisper, said, "Spies would be too easy to spot if they wore uniforms. We find it counter-productive."

He laughed and clapped the Englishman on the shoulder. "Now . . . I must go. We will be in touch."

"But you don't know where I live."

"Oh, believe me, we do. *Auf Wiedersehen* and . . . *Heil Hitler*"

Wesley raised his hand and repeated the mantra. It was the first time he had ever used the words. He sensed it would not be the last.

Grosskopf left quickly. Wesley poured another coffee from the still warm pot. The cleaning had stopped. Silence enveloped him. Suddenly, he was back in that worst nightmare that all actors have from time to time. You are on stage and everyone but you knows the lines and the moves. But this time it would be for real.

CHAPTER 4

By the time Maxwell Knight returned with a tray bearing two cups of tea, Stokes had only had a brief chance to skim through the weighty tome that was the MI5 file on Siemens-Schuckert. The MI5 man placed the tray carefully on the desk between them.

Knight laughed. "It's not a light read, is it? No sugar, I'm afraid." He placed one of the cups in front of his new employee.

Stokes closed the file. "It certainly isn't. Just one question."

"Fire away."

"Siemens-Schuckert. Subsidiary of a German company, operating in Brentford."

Knight took a sip of his tea. "And Dublin, by the way. But Eire is neutral, so beyond our reach – officially anyway."

"But why? Why weren't all German companies operating in Britain immediately closed down and staff repatriated as soon as war was declared?"

"That, old son, is a good question."

"And what's the answer?"

Knight put his cup to one side and rested his forearms on the desk. "The enemy within, you mean. A viper at our bosom, so to speak?"

"Yes."

"It does seem somewhat contradictory, I'll admit, but there is method to what appears to be our madness."

Stokes allowed silence to reign as Knight began to explain that madness. "Siemens' business is basically in the manufacture and supply of electrical goods. It has subsidiaries all over the world. But we are under no illusions. There is *no* employee of *any* German company operating *anywhere* in the world who is not under strict obligation to work also for the *Reich*."

He paused and looked at Stokes. "What would *you* do?"

Stokes sighed. "I'm obviously missing something . . ."

"Let me put it this way. You discovered that little racket going on in the bank all on your own."

"Yes."

"Good work. But you didn't go straight to your manager . . . or the police. Why not?"

Knight saw Stokes smiling. He pointed at him.

"Exactly. We know that the factory in Brentford is a hotbed of espionage. We suspect – in fact it's a tad more than mere suspicion - that it may also have tentacles all over the country."

"The Fifth Column?"

"Well, I don't think what you read in the papers these days is in any way exaggerated."

"So, let them continue to do their stuff but infiltrate them."

"Like you did, my boy. But I prefer to see it as containment. Keep your friends close but your enemies closer."

Stokes took a sip of his tea. It was cold. He grimaced. He

looked back at Knight. "But you didn't take that tack with Mosley's mob. The British Union of Fascists. You disbanded them and interned the lot last month."

Knight frowned. "Yes. Not entirely my decision. That came from upstairs. I think they were just too bloody obvious to be ignored. They wore uniforms for God's sake. Not difficult to spot."

"And I suppose your fear there is that Mosley's octopus may have had more tentacles than the standard eight."

"Precisely. Although the Standard Eight is a very nice car. My sister has one."

Stokes smiled politely at the joke. Knight continued. "But yes, Stokes. That's the danger. Many of those who were not full BUF members but just camp-followers are still out there. There may be hundreds of Nazi sympathisers across our great nation, forming themselves into little cells as I speak. Filling the BUF vacuum, as it were."

Knight went on to tell Stokes of his own wide experience of investigating Communist affiliated groups. It had been difficult and he had been left with a sense that they had missed a lot. The enemy was of a different stripe now and he was convinced there was another, better way of doing it.

THE TWO MEN talked for hours about how to tackle the two main problems facing them. The first was infiltration and how to do it; the second, constant containment. As far as the former was concerned, Stokes felt he would need to assume another identity.

"I have to make those who wish to convey information to the *Reich* believe that I can do it for them."

"That you're a German spy, you mean?"

"No, that's too obvious. It would not give me any great

credibility. It would not put me above their level to any degree."

Maxwell looked puzzled. "So . . . what do you suggest?"

The other man smiled. "I need to be . . . Hitler's man in London. These people have to be convinced that there is a direct and uninterrupted channel between me and Berlin. In fact, they must believe that the *Führer* himself will see everything that they pass to me."

Knight did not speak for half a minute. Stokes could see that he had taken the idea on-board and was already playing around with it. He could see the lights going on.

"Yes. That has legs, old chap. You would have to have the proper papers, of course."

"Essential. I need two lots of documents – German and English, but in different names. There may well be times when I have to prove who I really am. That Albert Stokes is on the right side."

Knight paused to mull that over. "You're right. We can do that."

Stokes added to the concept. "One other thing. They have to have some kind of proof that their efforts are being appreciated by the *Führer*."

"Of course. And *there's* your containment. We identify them and keep them in some sort of . . . active limbo. Little bubbles of evil."

Both men laughed. Stokes provided another suggestion. "And certificates of appreciation and medals for our . . . clients."

"Badges that they can show to the invading forces when they land . . ."

Stokes laughed. He was pleased that they were singing from the same hymn sheet. "Of course. All of which can also serve for identification once we've won the war."

"If they are stupid enough to hold onto them."

"It doesn't matter, does it? We will know exactly who and where they are."

Both laughed again. It was a wondrous wheeze. Knight opened a drawer in his desk and liberated a packet of custard creams.

"I think this calls for another cup of tea flavoured boiled water."

He stamped downstairs again, taking the empty cups with him.

While he was away, Stokes opened the biscuits and extracted one. He bit into it and walked across to the window. He stared at the view. Life was going on. There were sandbags around doorways, tape across window panes and signs of blackout curtains behind the glass. Nothing had changed from yesterday.

Albert Stokes, however, had gone from the relative safety of Westminster Bank remittance clerk, to the role of an MI5 agent, impersonating an employee of the *Führer* and digging out Fifth Columnists. All within twenty-four hours.

He had an inkling his life would never be the same again.

CHAPTER 5

Howard Wesley heard nothing from the *Abwehr* officer, *Major* Dieter Grosskopf, for nearly a year after their meeting in Berlin's *Blauer Tiger* nightclub. He was beginning to think he had been forgotten, when a package arrived. It bore a Hamburg postmark and contained his appointment to the rank of *Leutnant* in the *Luftwaffe.*

In a handwritten covering letter, Grosskopf explained that this rank was the lowest commission in the service. He went on to say that he had noted Wesley's penchant for dressing-up but that the uniform was 'for display purposes only'. He would not be allowed near any aeroplanes and, from henceforward, his 'Hermann routine' was never to be repeated. There was a business card for a military outfitter in Berlin, where he was to be measured for his uniform. A warrant for one-way rail travel to Hamburg was the only other enclosure.

He put all of the papers back together, piled them on the pillow and sat staring at the wall. It seemed he was held in high regard already but, for once, the expectation bothered him. He sensed also that he had passed the point of no return. He had, after all, been receiving the Nazi penny for several months of doing nothing.

The purpose of his new role was not to entertain, nor was it to receive applause from a live audience. However, he knew exactly nothing of what *was* required of him.

He shivered. He looked to see if he had left a window open. They were all closed.

THE WALK to Berlin's *Hauptbahnhof* to catch the train to Hamburg, was short but illuminating. His pristine uniform seemed to generate great respect from the general populace. Not for the first time in his life, he felt the power of costume. The ecstasy of authority.

The train journey was entertaining. Wearing his uniform felt splendid but he should really have asked about the saluting protocol. But whom would he have asked without a raising of eyebrows?

He found a seat toward the rear of the carriage and settled down to watch. Lower ranks were expected to snappily flick the right palm upward and outward with a perfunctory *Heil Hitler*. It sounded more like the English word 'littler'. Almost as if he was apologising that he was too big and that he wished he was 'littler'.

He was picked up at the station by a young man who introduced himself, in passable English, as Otto Ziegler. He also greeted him with a 'littler', though not with any enthusiasm. Ziegler was to be training Wesley in wireless use and protocol.

Wesley watched him negotiate the traffic. He was in his thirties, he guessed, good-looking in a lean and interesting kind of way and, so far, quite engaging. They chatted but he had obviously been instructed not to divulge anything until it had been more officially imparted.

"That will come soon enough, *Leutnant* Vesley.", Ziegler said with a grin as he flicked one of the Englishman's epaulettes.

Wesley laughed nervously.

ZIEGLER DROVE them through a majestic gateway and announced that they had arrived at the *Stadthöfe*. It was rather grand, even by German standards. He explained that it housed *Gestapo* HQ. The top two floors at the rear of the building were occupied by *Abwehr Luft* – Military Intelligence Air. He apologised that the view from the windows was not so grand, unless you had a penchant for dockyards.

After showing his pass and a temporary permit for Wesley, Ziegler ignored the lifts and led the Englishman up six flights of stairs to the *Abwehr.* His uniform felt suddenly very hot and restricting. He thanked God for the breeches where at least a little air could circulate.

"No wonder it's called *Abwehr Luft.*"

Ziegler laughed. "Yes, I'm sorry about that. We try to avoid the *Gestapo.*"

"Doesn't everybody?"

The German was suddenly serious. "It is better to keep that in your head, *Leutnant.* I am taking you straight to *Major* Grosskopf. He is looking forward to meeting you again."

The smiling officer greeted them and ushered both into his office. Wesley thought it best to stick to convention and raised his right hand. "Littler"

The *Major* returned the hand gesture in a blur of uniformed sleeve. The accompanying words were rushed and meaningless. "Please, sit. Your uniform suits you."

"Yes, thank you. It was a kind thought."

Grosskopf sat behind his desk. Wesley took one of the two seats opposite him. Ziegler remained standing expectantly. "Yes, Ziegler. Please arrange coffee and come straight back. I need you here." Ziegler left with a chirpy *'Herr Major'*. Grosskopf looked across the desk at Wesley and pointed at the retreating man. "You will get to know Ziegler very well. The relationship between you will be essential to your work. The better you get on and understand each other, the happier we will all be. Which is why this meeting is a three-way exchange. Do you understand?"

Wesley was slightly taken aback. The *Major* noticed. "Don't worry. Your training will be second to none. I will confess to you that you are an experiment, Wesley. And the buck, as you English say, will stop with me. If it were widely known that we were employing a foreign national as an agent in the field, there would be questions."

"Oh."

Grosskopf laughed. "So, no pressure, *Leutnant!* You will soon get used to the politics around here. That's one thing that Ziegler can fill you in on. But . . . I would advise you to speak German when you are anywhere else in the building. You speak it well but we need to fill you in on the content."

"*Verstanden,* Herr *Major.*"

"Excellent. That's a good start."

Ziegler returned with a tray of coffee which he placed on the desk.

WHAT FOLLOWED over the next hour did nothing to ease Wesley's discomfiture. He was to be placed 'in the field' – in England. The view taken by Grosskopf was that his essential Englishness, acting abilities and gift of mimicry would allow him to assimilate very easily and quickly. They were placing him, after all, in the country of his birth.

"Germans stick out like a sore thumb Wesley. They are too . . . stiff. Nobody knows how to relax like an upper class Englishman. No German agent could possibly replicate that."

Both Germans stared at him as if the last sentence was a cue. Wesley hated to disappoint. He stretched his legs out languidly. He laughed a lazy laugh and flapped a hand about.

"Well, I couldn't possibly comment."

That hit the spot. Both men applauded.

ALL THREE ADJOURNED to the wireless room. Wesley had absolutely no experience with a wireless set. Not even a domestic set. The family had never owned one. His father thought they were the work of the devil.

"This is where Ziegler will train you." Grosskopf looked at his watch. "Now, I must go. You will start today with how these things work." He pointed to the array of wireless sets around the room. "I will meet you both tomorrow when I will tell you more about your duties in the field, Wesley."

That phrase again. Wesley was beginning to feel like a sheep. The officer turned smartly and swept out of the room. Ziegler took him to a booth in a corner of the room. It was a two-seater specially made for training purposes.

He looked at his pupil. "Any questions so far?"

"Erm, yes. Just about timing, really. When do I go?"

"Well, not until you are up to speed with everything. And then you'll go by steamer from here."

Wesley was relieved. The German clapped him on the back.

"I'm joking. We have a few people there already. They were parachuted in under cover of darkness."

Wesley gasped. "But . . . look at my build. I'll drop like a brick and leave a hole like a bomb crater!"

Ziegler laughed so loudly that one of the operators behind them turned and shushed. The very thought of jumping out of a plane, in the dark, his face probably covered in animal excreta as if he were some kind of Commando, filled Wesley with dread.

"Come on, Wesley, be brave. You're in the *Luftwaffe* now."

The Englishman wondered, not for the first time, why he had never learned to stop showing off. He could not yet see an upside to this job but he was already in it up to his neck. But then, as he watched Ziegler deftly manhandling the wires, plugs and leads, then slipping the headphones over his ears, another thought entered his head. He had never, ever performed a role without the three 'A's – Aplomb, Acclaim, Applause. This was just another role and the stage was his.

THE FOLLOWING day was his first session of serious training. Ziegler was waiting for Wesley when he arrived. Grosskopf had told them the day before that he required the pair of them to develop a very close relationship. A bond that was to transcend the machinery and mechanics of the wireless set itself.

Wesley was to educate Ziegler in the idiosyncracies of English culture and to use this shared knowledge in their communications, in order that both of them could read between the lines of anything transmitted.

The German was to ensure that Wesley knew the practicalities of wireless operating. The nuts and bolts, valves and wires. He should be able to take it to bits and put it back together again with his eyes closed.

GROSSKOPF SAT at his desk painstakingly adding to the notes he had so far made on his 'experiment'. It had been expected that Britain would not enter the war. They had assumed that peacemakers like Chamberlain would prevail, but it transpired that even he could not tolerate the invasion of Poland. The *Abwehr* man had worked tirelessly to ensure that they were ready for this eventuality. He was dedicated to the role of military intelligence and keen to push the boundaries of espionage. This experiment was a calculated risk but he was sure that he had found the right man as his 'guinea pig' in Howard Wesley.

He reflected on the agents whom the *Abwehr* had been assiduously planting in Britain for the past few years. The quality was poor. Some of them did not even speak English. Those who had managed to evade detection were operating in the type of *Kriegsnetz* that existed in every neutral European country. Britain was included but she was now an enemy state. This agent 'rump' was either German, or of Germanic origin, and would be easily detected in any British pub.

His colleagues were not thinking laterally in this respect. Grosskopf was determined to make a difference. He called Ziegler and Wesley through to his office. The pair sat facing him across the desk. He looked at them and smiled.

"Gentlemen. My hopes are invested in you. I have every faith in the mission upon which you are embarking."

The two men looked at each other, trying to gain confidence from Grosskopf's obvious enthusiasm. To Wesley, it sounded very much like the 'giddy up, boys, I know you'll be absolutely wonderful' directorial exhortation on an opening night. Ziegler was nodding but there was nothing in the eyes.

"Wesley. Your wireless will be your only means of communication between you – the man in the field – and us here in Hamburg. Ziegler, in fact, will be the conduit for everything you have to tell us."

Wesley looked at Ziegler. They both smiled.

"But it is no good just telling us, in plainspeak, that you have discovered that the RAF are planning to destroy a flak installation . . . or bomb the *Messerschmitt* works in Leipzig."

He laughed.

Wesley nodded but without understanding a word of what Grosskopf meant. Ziegler was the one brave enough to ask.

"Herr *Major*, can you explain, please?"

"Of course. Your mode of communication will be a double code. Even if the first level is cracked, the key to the layer beneath must be impenetrable."

That helped neither man. They looked at each other in total bemusement.

The *Major* laughed. "I apologise, gentlemen. I am not being clear." He paused. "This may sound totally irrelevant but be patient. My wife, Heike, and I have been married for over twenty years. We are very close. I don't just mean physically. That, to some extent, comes down to knowing each other's bodily needs and desires . . ."

Ziegler smiled. Grosskopf noticed.

"Yes . . . Ziegler! A good lover gets to know well what their partner likes, what they do not like. How to flick their switches."

Both men laughed.

"But the physical is superficial. You can touch it, feel it . . . stroke it."

Wesley laughed again and pulled at his uniform collar. "I'm sorry, Herr *Major*! Is it me, or is getting warmer in here?"

Grosskopf laughed. Ziegler was not sure whether or not to join the hilarity.

"There is a point to all of this. I do not want you to be left with the image, compelling though it may be, of my wife and myself . . . flicking switches. No. Let's move away from the physical. A long relationship also brings with it a meeting of minds. It can be - almost telepathic."

The two listeners were now back in their earlier state of confusion.

"Let me give you an example. A few months ago, Heike and I were at a dinner party. Twelve of us there. Six couples. We knew only the host and hostess, so there were eight people around the table whom neither of us had ever seen before. When we got back home, we compared notes."

Ziegler and Wesley were now re-engaged.

"We were able to say, with unerring accuracy, what the other one thought about the other ten in the room. What they were wearing, how they spoke, the manner of their eating, how they related to their partner . . . everything of the evening."

Wesley spoke. "There is nothing more fascinating than people-watching."

"Exactly so, *Leutnant*. Although people-watching is generally a solitary occupation. Basic observation. But I want your skills to be developed. I want more than the basic. Much more. Heike and I were both astounded about how much we were able to read from the mind of the other. I from her and she from me."

Grosskopf was warming to his subject. "There were two or three occasions when a simple glance between us spoke volumes. A simple glance, Ziegler. No words, Wesley. She was even able to tell me which of the ladies present most appealed to my, erm . . . tastes."

Wesley needed more. "Herr *Major*. Are you saying that you want Ziegler and myself to develop some kind of telepathy in our communications?"

The *Major* smiled broadly. "Exactly right, *Leutnant*."

"But you and Frau Grosskopf have had twenty years or more of practice."

"Indeed. And it would take you and Ziegler here a similar length of time to get to that level."

"So how can we do it? I don't understand."

Grosskopf leant across the desk and bridged the space between the three of them. He explained to Wesley first of all that there were a few months before he would be placed into the field. In that short time, the two of them were to embark upon a programme of experiences together. There would be social outings, visits to art galleries, cafés and restaurants, the theatre, even the zoo. In addition to that, Grosskopf explained, Wesley was to educate Ziegler in English idioms, literature, culture.

"There is a scientific word for what I want from the pair of you. From the animal kingdom. *Symbiotisch*." He let this sink in. "I know it's a tall order for you both. But I have faith in you."

Grosskopf looked at his watch. He passed a few sheets of heavily typed paper to each of them.

"Your schedule, gentlemen. It starts tonight. You will see also that there is extremely comfortable accommodation allotted to you for the duration. I think you should live up each other's arses for the next few weeks."

The two men laughed.

The *Major* smiled. "But not literally, obviously."

He withdrew another file from his briefcase. Clearing his throat, he addressed them both, "And this is hot off the press, gentlemen."

Wesley was suddenly nervous. He glanced across at Ziegler. As he continued, the *Major* seemed have gone into storytelling mode, almost.

"During the course of our secession of Czechoslovakia – now the Protectorate of Bohemia and Moravia, of course – and our acquisition of Poland, we have acquired a certain number of pilots from their respective air forces. Only the best have been selected. We are facilitating their escape down from Krakow, Poland and into France. The hope is that they will end their journey in Britain and be warmly greeted by the Royal Air Force. Once there, they will feed us with information relating to the RAF. And these pilots have an incentive to co-operate."

Wesley was curious. "Do I need to ask what incentive they have been given?"

Grosskopf looked at him crossly. "No, Wesley. You do not need to know that."

The Englishman realised that, despite his obvious bonhomie, there was steel in this man that he had not detected before.

Grosskopf continued. "Aside from providing us with information, these pilots have also been tasked with stealing a fighter aircraft and delivering it to the *Reich*. In that way, their debts to us will be expunged."

Ziegler gasped.

Grosskopf laughed. "Yes, I know it sounds like the plot of a cheap novel but think about it. How difficult can it be? They are, after all, on their own in these aircraft."

Wesley was also astounded by the sheer audacity of the plan. That faded when he began to think of how it might impinge on his own mission. He was still searching for a connection to himself.

"And what is my involvement with these pilots, Herr *Major*?"

"Hopefully very little. Let me show you this . . ." The officer handed him the file. "These are the two men. Please read the digest at the top of each page. For obvious reasons, you will not be taking these papers with you."

Wesley opened the file. There were only two pages. The first related to Czech airman Augustin Preucil, captured in Prague, codename MOTORRAD; the second was Polish pilot, Tomasz Gierczak, captured at his Rakowice base, code-name STANGE. Both now known to have been recruited into the RAF. It seemed that both had been diligent in sending information back to their *Abwehr* masters while travelling through France. The Pole had continued in the same vein when he entered RAF service but the Czech, MOTORRAD, had gone under the radar. There had been no contact at all.

He handed the file back to Grosskopf. There was not a lot to remember. Basically, it seemed to be 'good guy, bad guy', Pole and Czech respectively. "So, there is nothing from MOTORRAD?"

"No. He may be dead, of course. There is no way of knowing."

Wesley was coming to the conclusion this was all 'much ado about nothing'. He had another question. "But the Pole is active and still in play. I assume neither of them came up with the goods."

"In terms of delivering a fighter, no. So, at some point, we may need you to try to contact them both and exert a little pressure."

"How do they - or the Pole anyway - pass their information to the *Abwehr*? I'm assuming neither of them has a wireless. I can imagine they would be a little obtrusive in a barrack room."

Grosskopf smiled. "Indeed. No, we felt that some of the information would be too technical anyway. A cutout is used."

Wesley looked at Ziegler. The look on his face implied that the term meant nothing to him either. The Englishman spoke up.

"Cutout?"

The officer explained. "A cutout is basically an individual, friendly to the *Reich* obviously, who accepts mail from an agent, sticks it unopened into another envelope and forwards it on to our Embassy in Dublin. For the appropriate remuneration."

"And who is this individual? Is it safe?"

Grosskopf took a piece of paper from his pocket. "It's Mrs Ada Wigglesworth of Sackville Street in Barnsley. In Yorkshire. North of England - which is also good."

Ziegler tried speaking the surname as it would be pronounced by most Germans. "Vigglesvort. Viggles . . . vort."

Grosskopf laughed. Ziegler and Wesley joined in. They tried it together several times. The officer finally brought them both to order. "Yes, I know. Not a name you will ever forget. I am sure she is a lovely woman. She has apparently been doing it for some time."

Ziegler was still smiling. "So how did these two airmen know how to get in touch with her."

"They were told to send her a letter. Just a single piece of blank paper inside. She will open it, obviously. Its lack of content is simply a signal to her that she must retain the envelope. Any subsequent letters with the same handwriting will be properly actioned and forwarded, unopened, to Dublin. From there it will come to us by diplomatic bag."

Wesley could see that Ziegler did not see the significance of Dublin. He leant across to him. "Dublin is the capital of Eire, so it's a neutral city."

Ziegler was impressed. "That is clever. And so simple."

Grosskopf leant across the desk. "Apparently, Mrs Vigglesvort runs a . . ." He referred again to the scrap of paper. "A lonely hearts club."

The *Major* saw Ziegler's perplexed expression. "Don't worry. It had to be explained to me too. It's an agency for those who are seeking love, Ziegler. Mostly older people, those who have lost a partner and now want companionship. She . . . erm, brings them together."

Ziegler sniggered. "For companionship?"

The officer laughed. "Yes, I know. I could give her your name if you're interested? 'Otto of Hamburg' seeks friendship leading to possible relationship'"

"No, thank you!"

"The point is, Ziegler, that she is very successful. She gets hundreds of letters a week so any monitoring of her incoming mail would be pointless. Needle in a haystack. As long as we don't start getting requests from lovelorn widows."

The other men laughed.

"But deal with them as you wish, Ziegler."

He turned to Wesley. "It occurs to me that it might be useful to have the address of wherever you stay. We could use the cutout to send you papers. Information too bulky for a wireless transmission. Please let Ziegler have it as soon as you are settled."

Wesley nodded. It made sense.

"Now, I must go. I suggest that you start on the wireless training immediately, Ziegler. Once Wesley is even halfway proficient, you can drop that to mornings. You must start on the outings tonight."

GROSSKOPF LEFT. The two stood and looked at each other. Ziegler stuck his hand out and smiled. "*Mein Bruder.*"

Wesley shook the proffered hand and clapped Ziegler on the back. "The only one I have. I'm looking forward to it."

The German grinned. "Yes, me too."

"Only one thing worrying me."

Ziegler looked puzzled. "What?

"I haven't actually been told what my mission is when I get over to this damned 'field' everyone talks about."

Ziegler laughed. "That will be revealed nearer the time. Things are moving very quickly now. I can tell you the first thing you *must* get right though."

Wesley looked at him. Keen for any clue. "What?"

"Don't break your bloody leg when you land in that 'damned field'."

Wesley drew no comfort from his partner's levity.

CHAPTER 6

Augustin Preucil had just turned twenty five years old. The Czech's life was not going according to plan but he was fervently hoping that the next half hour would change that.

He was sitting in the very well-appointed reception area of the Brazilian Embassy at no. 5 Panskà in Prague where he had come to apply for a visa. The walls were covered with images of Rio de Janeiro's Copacabana and Ipanema beaches, the cable cars up to the stupendous Sugar Loaf mountain, the awe-inspiring Christ the Redeemer statue and . . . beautiful women. Lots of them. Would they all be as breath-taking in the flesh?

He stood to look more closely at an advert for the national airline, Varig. A plane sat on a sun-drenched tarmac apron. He smiled as he imagined himself in the cockpit, at the controls. As he turned to go back to his seat, two men entered. They walked to the counter and rang the bell. Preucil felt himself starting to sweat.

The same pretty girl who had asked him to take a seat

just a few minutes earlier, came through and smiled at the two men. One of them spoke to her. He could not hear what was being said but could not help but discern the man's harsh guttural tones.

They were German.

Preucil was the only one in the waiting room. The girl was speaking to the men in broken German, while glancing at him. Decision made. He did not return to his seat. As they turned to look at him, he was already on the move. He exited the room before they were able to react. They were both heavy-set and did not look that athletic.

He was down the short corridor before they left the room. What Preucil had not been expecting was a third man outside the street door. It was open and he stood in the gap, facing him. The Czech froze. His two pursuers were shouting. A few seconds later, all four met in an unseemly scrum. Passers-by turned away.

Preucil's right arm was painfully wrenched between his shoulder blades. He was bundled across the pavement. The third man opened the rear passenger door of a car while the other two unceremoniously lifted him off his feet and threw him roughly onto the back seat. One of the men got in behind him while his colleague walked around and got in the other side. He was wedged between them. The other drove them away at high speed.

The whole operation had taken less than a minute. It seemed like a well-practised manoeuvre.

THE JOURNEY WAS SHORT. Probably no more than a few hundred yards. In a straight line. Fast, furious and not a word spoken.

As the car came swiftly to a halt, both men on the back seat got out. One pushed him towards the door, while the other pulled him out by his feet. He slid across the leather. So swift was the action that he had no chance to stop his head from meeting the door sill on its way down to the paving stones.

From the fleeting glimpse he got of his surroundings, he suspected that he was being taken into Petschek's Palace on Wenceslas Square. He had heard what went on within these walls. He wondered if he would survive the stay. The two men lifted him by the arms again and pulled him backwards through the main entrance. He now knew for sure where he was. The large framed picture of the *Führer* on the wall was the only clue he needed. This was *Gestapo* Headquarters.

They dragged him down two flights of stairs and along a corridor to the left. He was roughly released into a room which was no more than six feet square. It was dank, unlit and contained only a narrow bench against the far wall. There was a strong stink of piss. Some small vestige of pride prevented him falling as they released him.

One of the men stepped into the corridor and threw a small wooden chair into the space.

"*Setzen Sie*"

He turned to see the men for the first time. They were dressed in identical long black coats. Both heavily built. One of them sported a boxer's nose and was clearly no stranger to the pugilistic arts. Both were ugly. They removed their coats and laid them in a neat pile on the wooden bed plank.

The request to sit was repeated – this time with a shove. Preucil landed hard and the chair fell backwards, its trajectory only halted by the wall behind it. He eased the chair back upright. His head was spinning. He could feel blood running into his eyes. The one with the nose strode behind him and yanked his arms backwards, almost out of their sockets. Tape was wound around his wrists. He pulled Preucil's head backwards by his hair. The other approached and put his face into his. He smelt the stale smell of cigarettes.

"Augustin Preucil, ja?"

He tried to nod but the enforced angle of his head prevented any movement.

"Ja."

"Son of Augustin Preucil?"

"Ja."

"Are you Czechs so stupid you can't even think of a different name for each family member? It must be very confusing."

Both men laughed as if it was the most original comment that either of them had ever heard.

"Do you love your father, Augustin?"

"J . . . ja"

"So why do you steal money from him? Is that the action of a loving son?"

The one with the breath walked over to his coat and extracted something from a pocket. He walked back to Preucil, hiding his hands behind his back. He thrust a wallet into the Czech's face. He withdrew it and grabbed the wad of notes that it contained, slapping Preucil across the face several times with them.

"Is this the way a son shows love for his father?"

The Czech could see that the leading notes were now covered in his blood and sweat.

The one with the nose held the wad up and said "Blood money". They repeated their laughter. These two could give Laurel and Hardy a run for their money.

"Your father is bereft. He told us you had stolen his life

savings."

Preucil tried to shake his head. He could not manage that either. It was wrong of him to 'borrow' his father's money. He fully intended to repay it from Brazil once he started earning. He had only called in briefly the previous evening to tell his parents of his plans. Why would his father do that?

"No"

"Is that – no, he's not bereft; no, you didn't steal his money; or no, it's not his life savings?"

The laughing started again then face was back in face. "He told us where you would be and why. His son stole his life savings and wants to go off to Brazil to spend it."

The ensuing laughter stopped abruptly as an officer entered the room, file in hand. He stood in the doorway and the ugly pair backed off. He allowed a few seconds silence as he looked at all three of them, as if they had suddenly been caught with their hands in the till.

"Bring him a towel for his cut and then bring him down to my office."

With that, he strode out of the door and out of sight. Breath man exited behind him and turned in the opposite direction down the corridor. Boxer nose released Preucil's head from his iron grip and the Czech slumped forward.

When the towel arrived, the pair pulled him back upstairs to the first floor, passing the grand entrance on their way. He was escorted to an office further down a corridor and one of the pair knocked on the door.

A voice bellowed from within. "*Rein!*" His two captors opened the door and stood back to allow him to enter. They closed the door as they left and the officer gestured to a chair in front of his desk. He sat down facing the Czech. The German opened the file and read from it. A minute later, he put the file back on the desk and looked at the man opposite.

"I am *Kriminalinspektor* Oskar Fleischer. You know nothing about me. I, however, know everything about you." He tapped the file.

Preucil said nothing. He assumed it was his air force service file that the man had in front of him.

"So, you have been working in a tailoring business here in Prague since you left the air force as a pilot?"

It was not just his services file, then. "Yes."

"And how was that?"

Preucil found Fleischer's use of the past tense somewhat disturbing. "It is boring, Herr *Kriminalinspektor*."

"I expect so. After a career as a fighter pilot."

The Czech laughed politely and nodded.

"Do you know how much trouble you are in, *Flieger*?"

"*Nein.*"

"Then you are remarkably stupid. But that is perhaps not surprising given your nationality."

Fleischer stood and walked around the room as he spoke. "You steal your father's life savings. You come to the Brazilian Embassy in an illegal attempt to leave the Protectorate. Oh . . . and you stole a *Praga* motorcycle from one of your *Kameraden* while you were in post at Cheb. You are a habitual criminal."

The officer sat back down and flicked through the file again, stopping once or twice to read a particular section. His facial expressions varied from mild amusement to frowns of disapproval. He stood again - his back to the door. Preucil had to turn to join the conversation.

"Your disciplinary record is not good."

Preucil said nothing. The man was right.

"Gambling, absent without leave, theft."

"I did not steal the *Praga*. I won it fair and square. He . . ."

Fleischer waved away his defence. "Do you confess to your sins, *Flieger* Preucil?"

The Czech was struggling to know what to say. He now had a serious headache and his vision was blurred. The only thought he could muster was to wonder if he would ever fly again.

Fleischer came closer and spoke. "Are you telling me you deny these accusations? Let me tell you, if I had left you any longer with my colleagues, then you would willingly have confessed to fucking the Pope."

Preucil conjured a smile from somewhere.

"I can see you are confused. I save you from further, shall we say, embarrassment and inconvenience – not to mention much pain - for one reason only."

Fleischer returned to his seat. "Can I get you a coffee?"

This was incongruous. Preucil mumbled a 'yes, please' as the German picked up the phone and ordered two coffees.

"I have a proposition for you, *Flieger*. If you agree to it then I have the power to absolve you of all your crimes and misdemeanours."

The coffees arrived before Preucil could answer. Fleischer did not waver, merely placing one cup in front of the airman and gesturing for him to drink. The Czech was shocked at the quality of the brew. He had not tasted coffee as good as this for a very long time. The blurring of vision started to ease.

Fleischer explained that it was illegal to leave the Protectorate without specific permission from his office. He went on to describe similar incidents where fliers like himself had tried illicit departures. He had to admit though that Preucil's chosen destination of Brazil was the most exotic he had heard so far.

"But I believe that some of them have made it through. I am unhappy about that. Can you understand why?"

"Yes, but I don't understand what you want me to do?"

"I want you to work for me. And if you fulfil the tasks I allot to you, then you will be able to repay your father's life savings a few times over. Always providing that you wish to, of course." He smiled.

"How can I work for you? I was already refused entry to the *Luftwaffe* because I was not ethnic German."

He told Fleischer the tale of six Czech airmen whom the *Luftwaffe* had taken on as ferry pilots to transport aircraft back to bases in the *Reich*. None of them had made it and it was suspected that they had flown the planes straight to a then-unoccupied Poland. That put an end to any further offers of employment by the *Luftwaffe*.

Fleischer nodded gravely. "Then they were very stupid, Preucil. I hope you will be more sensible. The vacancy I have in mind can only be filled by a Czech flier. And you fit the bill perfectly."

The officer suddenly stood and looked closely at his guest's forehead. "I think you need medical attention for that cut above your right eye. Let us deal with that first."

He made a call and asked for a medical orderly. As the medic arrived, Fleischer asked him to let him know when he had finished, and left the room.

. . .

FLEISCHER LEFT Augustin Preucil in the tender care of one of the resident medical team. It was felt appropriate to have such a team within easy reach. The number of 'accidents' that occurred in Prague's *Gestapo* headquarters on any given day was appallingly high.

The Czech's treatment for his minor injuries was cursory. They were, he supposed, not particularly life-threatening. When the first aid had been administered, he was left alone. He wondered what the *Gestapo* had planned for him. He could not see what he had to offer them. Before he had time to mull anything over, Fleischer returned.

"Your criminality is of no importance to us, Preucil. We are not expecting character references for the work you will be doing. What matters is that your duties are performed to the utmost of your ability. When you return to us - as indeed you will - then you will be rewarded."

The Czech was still none the wiser. "And what if I don't?"

"Have no fear. Your family and friends will feel our wrath." Fleischer picked up the file and found the page he was looking for. He read out a list of names and addresses. Preucil was staggered. Not only did they have the details of all his immediate family members, but also those of one or two male drinking companions - and several ladies with whom he had been especially friendly.

Fleischer closed the file. "If you fail to satisfy your job requirements, then these people will be relentlessly rounded up and rehoused in one of our camps."

Preucil was still reeling from the extent of their knowledge about him and his immediate circle.

The German laughed. "And I'm afraid the survival rate is not high."

The Czech, although surprised by the revelation, was

not especially alarmed. His family was far from a close knit unit and the discovery that his father had virtually turned him in to the *Gestapo* had done nothing to help that situation. The loss of any member of his bloodline would there fore be momentarily regrettable but no more than that. Nor had he found friendships of either gender any closer. He was a loner and completely self-sufficient. That was the way he preferred it but he felt that it might be better to feign some vestige of concern to the German officer. The opening of his mouth, the hand on his brow and the dropping of his head were all practised moves and designed to deceive.

"But . . .", he stuttered, looking as panicked as he was able.

Fleischer leant across the table. The next fifteen minutes were taken up with him explaining to the airman what his 'allotted tasks' were to be. He would be reissued with a Czech Air Force uniform from the stock that the Germans had accumulated. He would be taken to Frystat on the Czech/Polish border and allowed to escape with directions to Krakow.

This discourse took place without much space for Preucil to assimilate all that he was being told. He was given no opportunity to question anything. When Fleischer was finished, he simply stood and told the Czech to follow him. He led him out of the office and downstairs again.

Preucil noticed very quickly that he was not being taken back to his earlier cell. The room he was finally ushered into was better appointed. There were obviously different classes of accommodation here at Petschek's Palace. This one had a toilet and a handbasin.

Fleischer left and locked the door. The Czech looked around at the comparative opulence. A proper bed as opposed to a plank, a small cupboard and a stool completed the inventory. He pulled the stool across to the high barred window, stood on it and looked out. The earlier sunshine had evaporated. Dark, heavy clouds were gathering.

Not thirty minutes earlier, he had been so confident that his life was about to be changed. He was right.

CHAPTER 7

F lying Sergeant Tomasz Gierczak of the Polish 2nd Air Regiment needed to land desperately. The fabric of his P-11 was punctured with holes from Me109 machine gun hits, black smoke billowed from the engine and he still had a German on his tail.

The Fritz had stopped firing. That could mean, of course, that he had run out of ammo and was waiting for the Polish plane to crash. He could see the full extent of the damage to the P-11, so knew it was soon to hit the earth. He was saving ammunition.

Gierczak had now lost power and control. He was gliding into Rakowice, his squadron's home. The runway was pockmarked with craters. Aircraft at different stages of burning and disintegration lay everywhere. Other Me109s were strafing the buildings and hangars. It was a scene from Hell.

He spotted an unencumbered area of grass close to a hangar, took off as much speed as he could and wrenched the yoke across. The P-11 grudgingly responded and pointed itself in the right direction. When he was twenty feet up, he lifted the nose as hard as he could. The plane bounced reluctantly and thumped the earth, gouging furrows as it went.

The P-11 tipped violently to the left. The wing tip hit the deck and the craft slewed, tossing Gierczak out of his seat as he tried to unbuckle his harness. The left undercarriage had either collapsed or been shot away.

As he tumbled onto the grass, he looked back at his plane. The left half of the structure had snapped under the impact and the machine was gently rolling onto its back. The Pole scrambled to his feet and ran. He looked over his shoulder but there was no sudden blaze from the fuel tank. It was empty.

He sank to his knees and gave himself a quick recce. No blood. All limbs intact. He could hear. He could see. He instinctively ducked as the 109 swept over him in a welter of noise and fumes. Four German soldiers were racing toward him, rifles raised.

Gierczak had been in the air, on and off, for three days. He had lost count of the number of times he had been forced to ditch whichever plane he was in, and commandeer another. The German *Blitzkrieg* had completely overwhelmed all Polish armed forces. What he had witnessed from above was a relentless orgy of death and destruction. He had ridden his luck as far as he could take it.

He stumbled as swiftly as he could under the not so gentle guidance and rifle-butt encouragement of his German escort. They took him to the main hangar and pushed him inside.

It was full of Polish airmen – some slumped against the walls, others lying on the oil-patched ground. All were exhausted. Many badly injured. He recognised only a small number from his own squadron.

He was looking at what remained of the Polish air force. It had been decimated. Overwhelmed and crushed by a force with more modern, more powerful machines. Their weaponry and speed were far superior. Even the German bombers were faster than the P-II.

Luftwaffe officers were moving around the hangar, taking names, ticking them off on lists. Each individual was ushered to either of the two long sides of the building. All the seriously injured seemed to be in the group opposite him, alongside able-bodied men. Gierczak recognised a lot of them as Rakowice's groundcrew and technical staff.

Gradually, the space in the centre emptied and both walls were lined with men. After a conflab in the centre between German officers, the men on the opposite side – all dishevelled and clearly non-combatant - were led from the back wall and out through the door. It took a long time. Men fell and had to be picked up by comrades. The shambling crowd gradually disappeared from view.

Little was heard for the next twenty minutes or so. Some trestle tables had been found from the canteen and placed in the centre of the space. The Germans sat and compared lists, now and again looking around at the remaining line of men. There was quiet laughter.

Three trucks lumbered up outside the hangar doors. The group of men on the opposite wall were marshalled three abreast into a platoon of sorts, and marched outside.

Five minutes passed and Gierczak's group were ushered out in similar fashion. As they saw the sight before their eyes, a communal gasp rippled down the column. The order of "*Silenz!*" was barked at them. They were ordered to halt and face left.

The men who had exited the hangar earlier were lined up against a wall. They were bound hand and foot. Facing them, just a few feet in front of Gierczak's group, knelt three machine gunners, each aiming his weapon at the section of assembled men immediately in front of him.

The pilot could hear sobbing and groaning. One of the officers shouted "*Feuer!*".

The noise was sudden, violent and painful. It was difficult to see what was going on beyond the hail of bullets, the smoke and the shower of ejected shells. When the breeze cleared their view, Gierczak and his comrades were able to witness their countrymen dying. Bodies were falling. Heads were exploding in a pink mist. Torsoes were being ripped in two at the waist. Others were shrieking at the sight of the slaughter before the next bullet rendered them also incapable of life. It went on for only a few seconds until none of the men were left standing. To Gierczak, it felt like a lifetime. Sporadic bursts rang out, cancelling breath and movement from any vestige of humanity that showed any lingering sign of life.

Then, as previously requested, there was *Silenz*. The silence that only death can bring.

GIERCZAK'S PLATOON was loaded very quickly into the three waiting trucks. As they pulled away from the carnage, they could see a posse of soldiers busily scavenging from the corpses, salvaging anything of worth, liberating trophies. It was a blessing when the trucks turned onto the road and they were no longer able to witness the gruesome sight. It was gone from their eyes but would stain their minds forever.

All were stunned. The men in Gierczak's truck were

quivering with shock and rage. Others were smashing the sides of the truck with their fists, screaming abuse and revenge on everyone German.

Their destination and their futures were unknown. Nobody knew why they had been spared.

AN HOUR LATER, the trucks trundled laboriously into a large compound. It appeared to be the site of some industrial works. The buildings were smoking shells. Piles of masonry from the broken walls and roofs were being bulldozed to one side of the compound as they were double-marched into a large factory shed. It was the only structure standing which still had a roof.

When they were all assembled and seated, rumours spread around the captured Poles, seat by seat and row by row. They were all going to be tortured; they would be shot; they would be press-ganged into the *Luftwaffe*. None of them made any sense but the overall feeling was of relief that they had survived the savage executions they had all just witnessed.

Some of the whispered gossip was ridiculous. Shot or tortured just did not make sense. They could have done that at the base with the others. Gierczak had his own thoughts on their situation. He was certain that the three trucks had all contained pilots. Just as he was sure that those machine-gunned at Rakowice were either badly-injured beyond further service, or non-combatants – the station's ground-crew, engineers, cooks. Rakowice was simply the first part of the selection process. This was the second. But selected for what?

After what seemed an eternity, by which time many of those assembled had started to doze off, an officer stood and shouted the name of Abramowicz. Gierczak groaned. He surmised that the Germans were doing this in alphabetic order. He could not believe it. Only the Germans would attempt to impose order on what was essentially chaos. And, he noted with sorrow, it was clearly a name with Jewish roots. He was right. The man did not return even after Ambroziak and Antek had been called and came back to reclaim their seats.

By the time he was called, he estimated that roughly about half had been selected. The whispering started again. 'There is only one way to save your life. Just agree. That way, you can live on to fight these bastards and avenge our country'.

So, when he heard his name, he had a fair idea of what faced him.

THE OFFICER DID NOT INTRODUCE himself. He read out all of Gierczak's details from the file open in front of him. That he was married, wife Jagoda, three-year old son, Tomasz, named after himself. They had his address right and also that of his parents in Warszawa.

Then there was silence. He felt himself being examined. The officer told him to stand, walked around him and then told him to sit again.

"You have a good report . . . Gierczak." He pronounced the name badly but the Pole felt it wise not to correct him.

"You look fit. And anyone who has survived in battle against the *Luftwaffe* for three days in the shitty machines you have, has to have some talent, I suppose."

He was right. Tomasz was a good pilot. One of the best in his squadron. He was slight in build, sharp-featured, always attentive and kept himself physically fit. His slimness made cockpits a more comfortable fit.

"Yes."

"Because of that, I am offering you future employment."

The Pole could not imagine what form that would take. The *Luftwaffe* officer did not give him time to ask. He was told in no uncertain terms that he would be allowed to 'disappear'. It was known that escape routes from Krakow to beyond the *Reich* were operating. He would be told how to find them. Ultimately, he was to do whatever he could to join enemy air forces and then pass information back to Germany. He would be told how to pass information back to the *Reich*.

The British RAF, in particular, was an unknown quantity and he was sure that they would welcome pilots with open arms. The officer noticed Gierczak's confusion. He told him with some glee that Britain had now entered the war the previous day. The news made the Pole a lot happier but he did his best not to smile.

The German laughed. "But this is no act of charity. And we are not stupid. We know you would not do this of your own free will. But . . . if you fail to fulfil your part of the bargain, then you will never see . . .", he glanced at the papers, ". . . your wife, Jagoda, or little Tomasz again. Or your parents."

He paused. "I cannot guarantee that they are still alive even now. Let me see . . ."

He turned a page in Gierczak's file and looked at the family address. He closed the file with some force and put it on a pile on the chair next to him.

"I have no idea. But that is a chance that you will have to take."

"And if I refuse?"

The German laughed. "Then you will die, of course. Along with your family. But you won't die alone. I can assure you of that. What better way to march into the hereafter than with your comrades in arms, huh?"

The Pole was mentally numb. He had to cling to the hope that his wife and child were still alive. It was all he had. This man was giving him the chance to see them in the future if they had survived the invasion. He had to take that chance, as ephemeral as it might appear.

He was full of hatred for the Germans but they had him by the balls. He would have to do as he was told. Since he landed, he had heard the chatter from other pilots about the rape and destruction of their country. He knew that Poland was defeated. He would pray every night for his family's safety.

"Come on. Quickly. I have lots to see yet. Make your mind up."

"Yes. I accept."

"Good. Get yourself back in there."

"But . . ."

"No questions. All will be explained. Tell them to send the next one in."

The German was writing. He looked up and shouted.

"*Raus!*"

GIERCZAK WALKED BACK into the assembly area. He nodded to the uniform with the list who grunted and shouted out "Jastrzembski". It took him three tries but nobody was laughing.

As he sat down, he spoken quietly to those who had been doing the whispering. "You were right but this is not the end of the fight. If we stay alive we can teach these smug bastards." He added. "And Britain have entered the war."

There was a real buzz at the news. It spread quickly around the small assembly of men. For the first time that day, he saw smiles on Polish faces.

He turned back to face the front but could still hear the excited chatter behind him. Looking at the blank faces on the soldiers who were guarding them, he guessed that none of them spoke Polish. Somebody at the back started whistling their national anthem. It was quickly stifled by nearby comrades. These German soldiers were not idiots. It was a martial enough tune for them to be able to define it for what it was. And they were trigger happy. What were a few less Polish pilots?

The room fell silent again but Gierczak sensed a new spirit.

CHAPTER 8

Wesley had been training in Hamburg for months now. He and Ziegler had worked hard but the initial fervour had evaporated. Grosskopf had been missing for long periods so they had been left largely to their own devices. Their programme had gone well. So smoothly, in fact, that Wesley was straining at the leash and raring to go. His time with Otto had never failed to be entertaining and productive but he was eager to put his new talents to use. The thespian in him was also keen to strut his stuff on what Grosskopf had called 'a bigger stage'.

Then the *Major* reappeared and called them into his office. He held up a piece of paper. Both men suspected that this was to be a significant meeting. They had made progress reports to the *Major* once a week, or whenever he was there, but he had never before opened a briefing by waving a piece of paper. Wesley thought back to his Chamberlain routine which had started this ball rolling.

Grosskopf spoke. "So, *Leutnant* Wesley. Ziegler has given a glowing report on your wireless skills and is fully confident that your very special communication technique will be . . . *wunderbar*! But . . ."

The officer was wearing a pained expression. The two men looked at each other. Wesley spoke.

"But what, Herr *Major*?"

"We're done with you now, *Leutnant*. Sadly, we have to let you go."

The two men looked at each other again. They shared their bewilderment. Ziegler replied.

"I don't understand. Why?"

Grosskopf held up the paper and laughed. He addressed his reply directly to Wesley.

"These are your orders, *Leutnant*. You are leaving for England. Your overture is playing, my friend."

The Englishman was stunned. He had begun to think that this rehearsal was becoming the main event. He had become comfortable - and possibly too relaxed.

"When?"

"Friday."

Ziegler looked alarmed. Wesley spoke. "But it's Wednesday today."

Grosskopf laughed. "You're very sharp. Well done. Your training has not been in vain."

"But there is so much he does not yet know."

Wesley shot Ziegler a sideways glance. The *Major* smiled. "Oh, his mission you mean?"

"Yes. He already has his kit."

Wesley smiled. Ziegler called it the kit; Wesley preferred the word 'props'. The mainstay was undoubtedly the British National Identity Card and passport, both in the name of John Smith. The name was chosen by Wesley as, according to him, it was the most common male name in Britain.

In addition to that, there was a generous amount of

pounds sterling and petrol coupons, as well as two inge-
nious gizmos that would assist him in acquiring a car. The
first was a simple lock pick, attached to a nondescript
keyring. The second was basically an extendable dipstick
that retracted to a length of only a few inches and was
housed in a slim leather pouch. Once it was extended and
inserted into a vehicle's petrol tank, it would tell him how
full it was - or otherwise. No point in stealing a car if it was
only capable of taking him a few hundred yards. And car it
had to be - Wesley did not intend to use public transport
unless it was absolutely necessary.

Grosskopf nodded. "Have you practised with your car
tools?"

Wesley gestured out of the window. "Yes, we tried them
out on vehicles in the car park."

The *Major*'s jaw dropped. "On *Gestapo* vehicles?"

"Of course. They worked perfectly. And we weren't
detected."

Grosskopf relaxed. "I'm pleased to hear it. That would
have taken some explaining if you had been caught." He
smiled. "Maybe the *Gestapo* are not as vigilant as they think
they are."

Ziegler spoke. "I am sorry, Herr *Major*. You weren't here
to seek permission."

Grosskopf dismissed that with a wave of his hand as he
looked at the notes he had in front of him. "The most
important aspect of your mission, *Leutnant*, is that the
communication between the two of you is as watertight as
possible. So, show me."

He leant back into his chair as if about to watch a performance. Ziegler was the first to speak. "We took heed of
everything you told us, Herr *Major*."

The officer had been adamant that any message passed

between the pair of them should be nothing more than pure gibberish to anyone who intercepted it. Even if the covering code was broken, the words revealed should appear as the work of two lunatics jabbering at each other.

The pair explained that, at Wesley's bidding, they had studied the works of Edward Lear. His nonsense poetry was well-known to any Englishman with a decent education - and it was unique to the English psyche. They chose *The Owl and the Pussy Cat* as their main source. The Englishman had also introduced Lewis Carroll's *Jabberwocky* and *The Walrus and the Carpenter* to run alongside it. They had revelled in reading them both aloud – line by line, speaking them alternately. They had imbued certain words and phrases from the three poems with hidden meanings.

Grosskopf was fascinated and they gave him a demonstration. After a few minutes, they translated it for him. His knitted brow said it all.

"You two are geniuses."

Ziegler responded. "That's not all, we have many references to people we have met on our social outings. Each individual name portrays a message all of its own. Full of concealed intent and . . ."

The *Major* interrupted. "That will confuse anyone listening. This volley of names that means nothing. They will think we have an army of spies at work." He thought that inordinately funny. When he finally stopped laughing, Wesley cut in.

"We have certain alarm messages too. If I should get captured, for instance, and am sending a message while under observation or duress, then one word, disguised simply as a different mode of greeting, will inform Otto of my changed circumstances. And we have committed them all to memory."

Ziegler nodded. Grosskopf sat back in his chair, a wide grin across his face.

"Gentlemen, you astound me. You really do. This is exactly what I wanted – and more!"

"His code name is WIESELIG."

The officer frowned. "What is that?"

The name was Wesley's idea. None of those that his colleague had suggested were quite him, he felt, so he had come up with one of his own. His initials were H O W - Howard Oswald Wesley. 'How' in German is *wie*. The second part of the codename - *selig* - had a few meanings in German, all of which he found appealing – blessed, joyful, overjoyed. It had felt comfortable immediately.

Grosskopf shrugged. "Your choice. It does not matter to me." He took a few moments pause before carrying on. His face was now more serious. "Both of you, unless you have been living on a different planet, will have noticed that the *Reich* has grown in size over the last few months. Denmark and Norway, the Netherlands and Belgium have all fallen. And, gentlemen . . . France!"

He was beaming. Wesley thought he heard a drum roll.

"For that reason, *Leutnant*, we want you back in Blighty. Your presence there is now required. No more waiting in the wings."

There was a positive glee in his voice. He was on a real high. He took some time to explain exactly what Wesley's brief was to be. His purpose. His job description. He was meticulous and clear.

The Nazi regime had started to plant many 'stay behind' agents in Britain long before hostilities became official with Chamberlain's declaration of war in September 1939. Pre-war travel was easy, so gathering information for any future invasion force, held no perils. Even though a state of war now existed between the two nations, there were still a few German companies operating in England. These were now known collectively within Nazi security circles as the *Kriegsnetz*. War network.

One of those was Siemens-Schuckert – an offshoot of the giant Siemens electrical company which had traded in Britain for many years in peacetime. Grosskopf referred to it as part of their *Kriegsnetz* but confessed that nobody in the *Abwehr* could really fathom why Siemens-Schuckert was allowed to continue to exist.

Wesley looked at Ziegler. Both were waiting for some relevance to the current situation.

Grosskopf took pity on their still blank looks. Wesley would be picking up his wireless from their factory in Brentford, west London. "They run agents from there, Wesley. These individuals foster and encourage Fifth Columnist cells. The company sends us information they have discovered from their industrial contacts. They . . ."

Wesley cut in as gently as he was able.

"That sounds wonderful, Herr *Major*. But it does beg the question – why do you need me?"

"Because, without exception, the people we have on the ground there are Germans, or half-German, or Austrians . . . do you see what I mean?"

"Yes, I can see where my Englishness would help me to operate without any suspicion. But that can't be the only reason, surely?"

"That brings me back to what I said earlier. We cannot rely upon the British not shutting this *Kriegsnetz* down and either repatriating or interning its . . . erm, employees. Many think that we are living a charmed life there, Wesley."

There was silence. What he had said was not contentious. It made perfect sense. Grosskopf continued.

"So, your main task after you have been to Brentford to pick up your wireless, will be to head north and seek out those who may have Fifth Columnist tendencies. Malcontents, those who either admire what is going on in the *Reich*, or disapprove of how they feel their government is handling the war - or both."

Wesley spoke up. "North?"

Grosskopf was taken aback. He stared at Wesley.

"Ah, yes. Something I have just learned from Berlin. I tell you this on a strictly 'need to know basis'. Understood?"

They both nodded. Grosskopf continued. "The invasion of Britain is being planned as we speak. The *Führer* is mightily displeased that Churchill has rejected any overtures for a friendly settlement. Britain stands on her own now but the man is still talking of fighting us on the beaches."

The officer laughed. Wesley and Ziegler remained silent.

"All I can say is that the invasion will be widely expected to come on the south coast. However, it is my understanding that it will come on two fronts. A pincer movement."

The pair still said nothing.

"The second front will be to the north and east. You don't need to know any more than that at the moment, *Leutnant*. As things progress, you will be kept informed. The *Führer* is keen on the two-front approach. I would imagine it being a few hefty drops by paratroopers - to seize strategic points with the aim of regrouping and, once established, moving south to assist the main force over a few days."

Wesley nodded.

"So . . . after much deliberation, Wesley, I want you to locate in Hull. I think that is where you will be of most value. We already have agents in the south. They are not of good quality, in my opinion. Some of them do not even speak English, for goodness' sake. Can you imagine how long they will last? You will be able to measure it in hours."

Wesley had been squinting over Grosskopf's shoulder to see if he could spot Hull on the map. He failed. The officer followed his gaze, walked to the wall and pointed at the city. Wesley and Ziegler followed him.

"But don't feel you have to operate exclusively in the Hull area. Move inland too. After all, that is exactly what the invasion troops will be doing." Grosskopf was working his fingers across the paper and pointing at other conurbations - Leeds, Bradford, Sheffield.

He looked at Ziegler as he spoke to Wesley. "You have maps?" Ziegler nodded.

Wesley returned to his seat. The other two followed suit. He summarised. "So, my mission is to find individuals who can facilitate this northern leg of the invasion when it happens and to provide us with information vital to its preparations."

Grosskopf looked pleased. Wesley continued. He was building his part. "And build my own network, in effect?"

"Exactly right. That is, in essence, what you will be paid for. You have seen the cash you are taking with you. In addition, you will be paid a generous retainer plus expenses. What we consider as good results will also be rewarded in relation to the value of the information received or number of firm recruits enlisted . . . as well as the information they may give you . . . inadvertently or otherwise." He laughed. "You will not be disappointed."

Wesley nodded. It was no more than he expected. Grosskopf looked at his watch again and started putting files into his briefcase.

"Now, gentlemen, I need to be elsewhere very soon. Any questions?"

Wesley was hooked. Any thought of asking any more questions had evaporated. This was suddenly looking like the role of a lifetime. And the pay was not bad either – which made a change from the traditional theatre he had been involved in over the last few years. And, he had to admit, he had been paid for doing bugger all for most of the last year. He was in. Also, in a strange way, he was looking forward to visiting the old country, as he had come to think of Britain. Not with any deep feeling for what he had left behind but simply because he loved the gentleness and tranquillity of green rolling hills.

He stood. "Herr *Major,* I am in. You have me to do your bidding."

Grosskopf smiled and leant forward to shake his hand. Still standing, he addressed the other man.

"Ziegler. Please give this man his travel arrangements and see to his safe passage to Britain. Now, I must go. I am due in Berlin tomorrow. Wesley, I am sure we will meet again but I wish you God speed and the best of luck in your endeavours for the *Reich.*"

Wesley made the perfunctory 'I littler' gesture. Even more swiftly, Grosskopf reciprocated and left the room. Seconds later, he re-emerged through the door.

"Oh, *Leutnant* Wesley. Don't forget to change out of your uniform before you leave."

He turned and left. They could hear him laughing as he walked down the corridor.

WESLEY SLOWLY TOOK his seat next to Ziegler. The pair sat in stunned silence. Eventually, the Englishman spoke.

"It looks as if we may have to play everything by ear, Otto, old chum."

Ziegler looked at him blankly. Wesley had to translate the idiom.

"Now, tell me - what are my travel arrangements? Do I have a first-class berth on the next steamer out of Hamburg? I assume you were joking about jumping out of a plane."

Ziegler looked at him and laughed. "God bless the *Major*. I knew he would leave me to deliver the bad news. I am afraid it does involve jumping out of a small aeroplane. But . . ."

Wesley groaned. "But . . . what?"

Ziegler laughed. "You may be able to choose your county. As long as it's Suffolk."

Wesley felt unable to share the merriment. This was going to be tough. A not so grand entrance but, God willing, no audience.

"Suffolk will be fine."

CHAPTER 9

I t had taken another full day of discussions with Maxwell Knight for them to map out what Stokes' *modus operandi* was to be. The full scale of the task was not known. Knight had spent a great deal of his time trying to convince his superiors and political masters that it was vast.

As to Stokes' new identity, it had been put in hand as soon as the man left for home the previous evening. His new English *nom de guerre* was now a simple Geoffrey Salter – a nod to Epsom, which Knight was sure would amuse Stokes.

It was felt unnecessary and almost certainly counter-productive, to create Stokes' German ID as a fictitious German name. His use of the language was probably good enough to fool any British Fifth Columnist but would not bear close scrutiny by a native German speaker. His *Gestapo* pass – his *Durchlassschein* – now in his pocket - bore the name of Geoffrey Salter. It showed him as operating from the fictional but authentically sounding *Gestapo-Einsatzgruppe London*. Issue date March 1939 with no expiry.

Knight gave Stokes' details to the bods who had seen the

genuine article before. They were more than capable of re-creating a perfect copy. The finished paperwork provided the perfect backstory for Geoffrey Salter as 'Hitler's man in London'. Other items such as the awards and medals that they had discussed, would be available before the close of play that day.

"So, Albert. I think we need to get you out there." He slid a slim document folder across the desk.

"Take a look. I think this chap is a prime candidate to cut your teeth on."

Stokes was surprised. "I thought Siemens-Schuckert was the target."

Knight laughed. "It is indeed. Don't worry. I'm sure you'll get in there soon enough. In the meantime, I thought I'd start you off on the nursery slopes. Have a look at the one I've just given you."

Stokes was still puzzled but remained silent. Knight smiled as he opened the file. There was only one item inside - an envelope containing a three-page letter from a Peter Armitage, of Hull. It was handwritten in a tiny scrawl and green ink. It was on headed notepaper with the address of Gladstone Street, Hessle, printed in the top right-hand corner. The address on the envelope was 'The German Embassy, 9 Carlton House Terrace, London'.

He was confused. "But this is dated December 1939. Wasn't the Embassy closed and evacuated on . . . 4th September?"

"The day after Chamberlain's broadcast, yes. Exactly."

"Isn't that a bit strange?"

Knight laughed. "Well, he obviously isn't the full shilling, is he, poor chap? But have you seen the maps?"

"Give me a minute. I haven't read what he has to say yet."

Reading it was not easy. The writing was cramped and copious. So too, it appeared, were this man's thought processes. There was a certain disconnect in his exact philosophy but the overarching theme was his hatred of the Jewish nation - what he referred to as 'this breed' - and its corruptive influence in all spheres of British government and life. He was strongly convinced that a Nazi invasion of Britain would cure all of these expressed ills.

He looked at the other two pages. Each one was a meticulously drawn map. The first showed the Humber estuary with the Hull docks all delineated, shaded in and named. The second was a more detailed depiction of the north bank of the river mouth. Areas were signposted with little boxes containing the initials 'DS'. He slipped the letter back in the envelope, slotted it back into the folder and put it back on the desk.

Knight looked at him. 'Well?"

"He has no love of the Jews. And he can't wait for Hitler to come over and wave his magic wand. He's almost sycophantic."

"Unctuous, I would have said."

Stokes laughed. "Sorry, I went to a grammar school, don't forget. We never got as far as 'unctuous' in our English vocabulary."

The other man smiled. "Don't give me that tommy rot, old chum. What do you think of the maps?"

"What does DS mean? Decoy sites?"

"Yes."

"Genuine?"

"Apparently so. I checked."

"The letter sounds like a first try."

"Judging by the language, I would say so. Yes."

"No mail intercepted since then?"

"Not from him, but . . ." He tapped a second file. "There are others in here. Sent to the German Embassy. It's all similarly illegally disclosed and sensitive information whose purpose is to assist the enemy. Pathetic in a way."

Stokes opened the file and riffled through its contents. He raised his eyebrows. "Are they all Jew-haters like this chap?"

"I have no idea, old boy. Haven't had time to go through them all but be my guest."

"Were they all intercepted after the Germans quit the building?"

"Yes. It started to fizzle out around December. The penny obviously dropped at some point that the Nazis were 'not known at this address'."

"Any of them send Christmas cards?"

Knight laughed. "Not that I'm aware of. Unless the Post Office team filched them and stuck them up in their staff room."

"They could be museum exhibits in a few years."

He gave a short laugh. "Indeed. But as much as we may ridicule this amateurish espionage, we can't dismiss it."

"True - and the danger is that these people have formed themselves into Fifth Columnist cells and . . ."

"And that some of them actually have brains. That, my friend, could be very dangerous."

"You want me to pay a call on this Armitage?"

"Yes – not you, though. I think it's a first job for Geoffrey Salter. Your Nazi alter ego. Find out what Armitage is up to . . . and if he has any like-minded friends."

Knight took Armitage's letter out of its folder and passed it to Stokes. "Here. Take this with you."

Stokes took it from him. "Just one slight problem."

Knight frowned. "What?"

He held up the envelope. "How am I supposed to have got hold of this?"

The other man laughed.

"We hired you for your deviousness and ingenuity, old chap. I'm sure you'll think of something."

By THE TIME Albert Stokes got home that evening, he had devised a plan of action on Armitage. There was a telephone number on the man's letterhead. He would ring it to set the ball rolling. At seven o'clock, he went into the sitting room. His wife was visiting a friend and he knew she would not be back for at least a couple of hours. He dialled the operator and asked for the number, hoping that Armitage would be less fazed by a call from Epsom than the more threatening London.

He heard the number ringing. At the very worst, Armitage would be no more than curious. The man had said in his letter that he posed as a birdwatcher and was able to glean information such as that shown on his maps, without any suspicions being raised, as he was a member of the British Trust for Ornithology.

The call was answered. There was already a question in the man's tone. A certain hesitancy. Stokes introduced himself as the Membership Secretary of the Trust. He sensed a relaxing calm take over in Armitage's response.

Stokes was calling to sound the man out. It was imperative that he met him but just as important that he had a better idea of what he was likely to be facing when the meeting took place. He greeted him as one who was extremely pleased to have tracked him down and was very keen to talk to him.

"Peter. Do you mind if I call you Peter? I'm so glad I've

been able to speak to you at last. I'm not interrupting anything, am I?"

There was a slight pause. "Erm . . . no."

"Good. That's fine. I'll come straight to the point, old man. I'm ringing in response to a letter you wrote to the German Embassy last September. Do you remember it?"

Another silence. This one longer. He would be starting to panic. If sitting, he would now be standing; if standing, he would now be pacing as far as the telephone cord allowed.

"Don't worry, please. I am not with the security services." He laughed. "Well, not the British lot at any rate."

"Oh . . ."

Stokes laughed again. He needed to settle Armitage's nerves as quickly as possible. "I know this is a bolt out of the blue but . . . let me cut to the chase. My name is Geoffrey Salter. The people I work for managed to acquire all of the mail that was received after our London Embassy closed on 4ᵗʰ September."

The closure was presumably news to the man. Or, maybe he had realised, after the event, what he had done and had been expecting a knock on the door. As Stokes knew, though, the letters from Armitage and others of the same persuasion had simply been taking up drawer space in Knight's office for months.

"Do you understand?"

A short laugh from the other end. "I think so, yes."

"You need to appreciate that if I had been with the security services, then you would undoubtedly have been in the Tower of London awaiting His Majesty's pleasure by now. You left your full details old chap. Not clever."

"No . . ."

"But the people I work for are very grateful to you for the

information received. In fact, they would like you to provide more."

"I've got more."

Stokes' heart leapt. "Splendid. That's good to hear. Can we meet up, Peter?"

Armitage seemed mollified now. His fears were assuaged and by the time Stokes rang off, the man sounded positively cock-a-hoop. They arranged to meet a few days later in Hull where Stokes promised to give him more information.

CHAPTER 10

Two days after the conversation with Armitage and informing Maxwell Knight that he was meeting with the first of the Embassy letter senders – or the 'ill-informed' as they had dubbed them – Stokes was on his way to Hull.

It was a large city and stuck out on a limb on the shore of northern England. Not a part of the world that Stokes had ever visited. Kingston upon Hull, to give it its full title, sat on the north bank of the wide, sluggish waterway that was the Humber. To the east was the North Sea; to the north, the Yorkshire Wolds. Flat, rural Lincolnshire sprawled out to the south on the other bank of the river. The city was essentially a large port and home to a thriving deep-sea fishing industry.

It was a bright day. He asked a policeman for directions to the Punch Hotel which Armitage had suggested for their rendezvous. On showing the officer his MoD pass, he was apprised of the fact that, apart from light bombing and a couple of oil tanks being hit, the city had escaped lightly compared with the concerted raids on southern England.

The Punch was exactly where Armitage said it would be - immediately opposite the statue of Queen Victoria, in the city square that bore her name. The hotel's delicate and ornate façade looked as if it might have pre-dated the stern lady herself. Entering the double doors, Stokes looked around. He saw nobody inside except a jolly, bespectacled chap behind the bar. To his side was the usual list of beverages which were 'not available', propped up next to the ubiquitous reminder of blackout times.

"Good morning, sir. What's your tipple?" The barman tapped the board on the bar and laughed. "Subject to availability, of course."

Stokes approached him. "I'm meeting somebody here. Do you mind if I wait until he arrives?"

"Of course not. Why don't you take a seat in the window and give me a wave when you know what you want. I'm not exactly rushed off my feet." He laughed again.

"That's very kind. I will."

He walked across to a small table where he would have a clear view of the square. He put his case down and looked at his watch. He was a few minutes early. With the time available, he brought his case to the table and checked that Armitage's file, together with the letter and attached maps, was inside. He put the file on the table and replaced the case next to his chair. As an afterthought, he took his wallet out of his inside jacket pocket and checked that his new German 'Salter' ID was inside. It would not do to fail at the first hurdle.

His attention was caught by a man cycling across the square. He crossed the road in front of the pub and propped his steed against the wall beneath Stokes' window. He disappeared from sight and walked inside. As Stokes had done earlier, the man looked around. The barman smiled at him and pointed to the table where his only other customer was seated.

The man looked to be in his 40s, with short cropped fair hair and pinched expression. The pencil-like moustache put him in mind of Montgomery. A taut smile flickered across his mouth as he stood and held out a hand.

"Mr Salter?"

Stokes stood. "Yes. And you must be . . ."

"Peter Armitage. Pleased to meet you."

They shook hands and sat down. Stokes leant back to assess the man further. This was the point at which his nerves would start to show, especially if it was his first time out of the woodwork. Stokes allowed a silence to fall between them. Armitage began to fidget. He was nervous. Strange for a man whose activities were putting his very life in serious jeopardy. He was eyeing Stokes' folder with suspicion.

"Peter, I understand you have further information that we may be interested in." The file remained unopened on the table.

"Yes. At least, I have. But how? I mean . . ."

Stokes laughed but it was not intended to put Armitage at ease. "You're wondering how you're not getting a visit from the *Führer* himself. You're wondering how a short, stout Englishman is now talking to you to discuss how you could further assist the *Reich* in its time of need."

Armitage was not sure whether to laugh along with him or to bolt for the door and sprint down the street.

"Let me put your mind at rest." Stokes showed his Salter ID. It bore the crest of the *Abwehr* as well as an image of 'Geoffrey Salter'. Somebody had done their best to make the official signature look undeniably German. He guessed some of the backroom boys were well-versed in the type of script necessary.

He handed it to Armitage. "Examine it. Is that not me?"

The man looked at it closely. He compared the image to Stokes' face and seemed satisfied. He did not understand German but it looked authentic as far as he could tell.

Stokes leant across the table, took the card back and replaced it. He spoke quietly. "I'll get us a drink, shall I? It might look less suspicious." He was revelling in the man's unease. "Not that there'll be much of a choice but any preference?"

The man shook his head. Stokes walked to the bar. The barman had not moved.

"I said I'd come over, sir."

"Very kind but I didn't know what was on offer." He gestured at the board.

"Oh, yes. Well, if it's beer rather than spirits, I've just got some Guinness in. Haven't seen that for a few months."

Stokes looked across at Armitage who was lifting a corner of the folder and peering inside. He did not look like a Guinness drinker.

"Yes. Two pints, please."

The barman started to pull the pints. "Coming up. You up here on business then?"

The question surprised Stokes but he imagined the chap had detected his Southern accent and was just dispensing bonhomie and conviviality. It went with the territory, he supposed.

"I am as a matter of fact. First time I've been to your fair city."

The first dark pint was placed on the bar. Stokes peered back over his shoulder. Armitage was gazing out at the square. He had clearly seen nothing in the file that he had not seen before.

The barman smiled. "Thought you weren't from around here. We've got a couple of rooms if you need somewhere to stay."

The thought had not occurred to Stokes. He was planning on returning that afternoon. Depending on how things went with Armitage though, it was possible he would be returning to Hull in the future. It might be useful to have somewhere to doss down.

"I'll bear that in mind. Maybe the next time."

A second black glass arrived on the bar. "That's one and six. I'm Fred, by the way."

Stokes took a small handful of change out of his trouser pocket, counted out three tanners and dropped them in the man's hand.

"Are you the landlord then?"

"That I am. Fred Wallis." He laughed. "Name above the door at last."

Stokes thanked him, picked up the drinks and walked back to the table. Armitage looked at his glass.

"Guinness. Hope that's alright."

"Erm, yes. I've never had it before but I'm sure it will be fine."

The look on his face said something different. Stokes took a good drink. He was parched from the journey. Armitage took a gentle sip. It was already obvious that he would not be finishing it.

"Now then. To business, Peter. We received your letter and I spoke to you on the telephone. Hence this meeting."

The man was looking suitably reassured.

"As I said, the details you sent us have been examined by

my superiors and found to be very interesting. What you have discovered will be of great value to us."

Armitage was now nodding vigorously - visibly more relaxed.

"You said that you are able to deliver more? If so, then I think we can put this on a formal footing. You will be rewarded, of course."

The man handed over a second envelope. Stokes saw that it was addressed, as the first one had been, to the German Embassy.

"This is the one I didn't send."

Stokes waved it in the air. "So, you realised at some point that the Embassy had been closed?"

"Yes. And I've been worried sick about the first letter, to be honest with you."

The MI5 man laughed. "Don't worry."

"But how . . ."

"How did we get hold of it?"

"Yes." Stokes leant forward. "We – the *Reich*, that is – made representations to the British government that we had not left the premises in good order. We apologised profusely. It was sort of 'we may be at war but we like to observe the proprieties'. It was felt that we might have left some valuable information behind us in our haste to evacuate. The feeling was that Chamberlain would not react as he did to the invasion of Poland. It rather took us by surprise."

"I'm very grateful. And they agreed?"

Stokes shrugged. "Yes. They allowed a diplomatic cleaning team to go in and, well – clean. Safe passage. In and out. I'm sure they would have got around to sifting through everything sooner or later but this war also came as a surprise to many in *this* country. They were also caught ill-prepared."

It was total cock and bull, of course, but the man swallowed it. He needed to. From what Knight had told him though, the 'ill-prepared' bit was quite accurate.

"The team passed letters like yours on to me. Hence the contact."

He thought he had done just enough – not only to soothe the man's sweating brow but also to paint a picture of a clever organisation in London, of which Geoffrey Salter was a leading member. Hitler's man in London, in fact. Armitage seemed very impressed.

Armitage's second letter was much like the first. The same green scrawl with more decoy site. He read it all carefully, taking his time.

"This is excellent, Peter."

He picked his case up and dropped the letter inside. "This will be with my people before you know it. Now, you have already proved yourself to be a friend of the *Reich*. For the reasons that you described in your letters, you have thrown in your lot with your country's enemy . . ."

Stokes let that sink in. He remembered the lunatic reasons cited in Armitage's intercepted letter to the German Embassy in London. His anti-Semitic comments seemed to have been lifted straight from one of Mosley's speeches. He leant forward and spoke more quietly. "And I fully understand your reasons for doing so."

As he had hoped, Armitage was keen to elaborate in what felt like a bid to justify himself. There followed a maniacal rant about the ills that Jewry had brought to the world. Leaders of a financial cabal seeking total domination; wealthy; only out for themselves to the detriment of others; needed to be stopped. And, of course, the inevitable - 'And the *Führer* is the only man who can do that'.

The man's soap-boxing eventually subsided. He sat back

with a look of grim determination on his face. Stokes realised that he had tapped a rich seam. He had nodded throughout the diatribe. The vehemence of Armitage's views made Mosley's seem weak and ineffectual by comparison. His enthusiasm and passion were not matched by his intelligence however. That he and others had continued to send sensitive information to the German Embassy for weeks after it was vacated, was a mark of their stupidity and naivety.

Armitage lifted his chin in a very British sort of way.

Stokes continued to massage the man's ego. "We applaud you." He reached into his pocket and drew out a padded box. The lid bore the name of a Berlin jeweller. Inside was a medal. He watched as the man picked it out and examined it.

"It's beautiful but what is it?"

Stokes took it from him and held it up, much to the man's horror.

"It's a *Kriegsverdienstkreuz*. An award to recognise your service to the *Reich* in time of war. Only Second Class, I'm afraid, but it's a great honour, nevertheless."

He handed it back to Armitage. "I would not recommend that you wear it to your next branch meeting of the Royal Ornithological Society, however."

"Of course not. Although I know of one who would be extremely jealous."

This was news to Stokes. This man really was not alone in his pro-German leanings, it would seem.

Armitage chuckled. Another first, probably. He looked at it more closely. He saw his name engraved on the obverse.

"Keep this on your person, Peter. It will identify you as a person of merit when the invasion comes. And come it will. Guard it well."

The man looked nervously around. The bar was still empty. He replaced the medal into its box and slid it into his jacket pocket.

"Thank you."

"*Bitte sehr.*"

Armitage almost had a heart attack. Even though there was nobody around to hear it, he looked unnerved by the audible use of the German language. Stokes wished he could have stood, lifted his arm and shouted *Sieg Heil*. What fun that would have been.

He was taking great pleasure in making the man feel uncomfortable. From what he had seen so far, he was a petty individual. He wondered how representative Armitage would be of others he would doubtless encounter. All of them would have to be monitored and kept strictly within his ambit. Better the enemy kept close. Stokes saw his role as satisfying their desire to be understood and appreciated. It would be too dangerous to simply assume that they were all total idiots.

Maxwell Knight had referred the first two maps that this man had sent, to the War Department. They confirmed the construction of decoy sites around the Humber estuary. So, Armitage was right – and had been worthy of a visit. These Q-sites, as they were known, were designed to fool *Luftwaffe* crews into bombing the wrong place, causing only harmless damage but thereby protecting an urban population or even a military base. Their locations were not something they wanted the *Luftwaffe* to know about.

He studied Armitage's face. "Are you on your own, Peter?"

The man had a puzzled look on his face. "At home?"

Stokes laughed. "No, I mean . . . do you have friends involved in this undertaking with you?"

Lights went on. "Oh. Yes, I have a friend." He paused. "A friend who thinks the same as I do."

"And does he know you are meeting with me today?"

Armitage was enthused once again. Back in conspiratorial mode and whispering.

"Yes. And he knows of more decoy sites. With lights. Inland." He sat back. Excitement flushed his face. Like a child on Christmas morning.

"That is good. I think the three of us should have a chat, don't you?"

Armitage nodded profusely. Stokes thought he was not going to stop. This was a small beginning but ripples were already coursing across this small murky pond.

"Marvellous news. The more the merrier, Peter."

They shook hands. Armitage even managed a sniggering *Sieg Heil* himself, much to Stokes' silent amusement. He reminded the man, in no uncertain terms, that he was Hitler's man in London and gave him an address to which he could safely send any further information, as well as a phone number where he could be reached. The promise of an unspecified financial reward, and thanks from the *Führer* himself, concluded the business.

They shook hands and left the Punch Hotel together.

"Well, Peter. As Vera Lynn would say, we'll meet again."

Armitage looked blankly at him. Jocularity was not his strong suit.

"Yes."

The strange man retrieved his bicycle. He pedalled off with a quick wave, wobbled past the disapproving Queen and Empress and disappeared from sight.

CHAPTER 11

Howard Wesley, now divested of his still pristine *Luftwaffe Leutnant*'s uniform, was driven by Otto Ziegler to a *Luftwaffe* base just outside Hamburg. The conversation was sparse. They had both completed their training - both on wireless techniques and on the special way of communication that they had developed between them at Grosskopf's insistence and guidance. There was no need for any pre-exam cramming. After Otto helped Wesley to carry his various bits of baggage across to the reception building, there was an almost perfunctory 'good luck', a clap on the back and the Englishman was on his own.

The pilot was waiting for him. He was very business-like but, in Wesley's opinion, unnecessarily brusque. After kitting out his passenger in a black jumpsuit, he explained how to don the parachute pack, how to deploy it by pulling on the D-ring, how to land without breaking a limb and then how to get rid of the chute. An additional chute was provided for his personal luggage. He was told to keep his eye on this one as it descended so that he could find it again.

And then hide the bloody thing, preferably before daybreak. His final instruction was to make a call of nature. The Englishman was going to ask anyway. Nerves were affecting both mind and bladder.

Getting into the plane was fun. It was a two-seater and he would be behind the pilot. The airman told him that when they got over the drop site, he would throw the ancillary chute out of his hatch. Immediately after that, he would pull back the canopy, flip the plane upside down and Wesley would simply fall out. All he had to remember was to pull the D-ring, and keep his eye on the other chute while watching out for the ground rushing up to meet him.

By now, the German was treating the whole situation as some kind of children's party game, like Blind Man's Buff. He could imagine him regaling his mess mates for weeks to come with his story of delivering an Englishman back onto his native soil.

Wesley had been wondering, since he rose that morning, if he had finally bitten off more than he could chew. He was especially worried about the landing itself. It was already dark and he did not imagine there would be an illuminated flight path at the other end.

His last thought as they were hurtling down the runway was that they had not blackened his face. On reflection though, it was probably for the best that he did not look like Paul Robeson in *Sanders of the River* when he encountered his first English citizen.

He could not remember being as nervous as this for any entrance he had ever made. During the time they were in the air, the attendant engine noise made conversation impossible. Wesley simply had to wait until he saw what he now looked upon as his 'wardrobe' chute being jettisoned by the pilot. If he somehow missed that, the turning of the plane upside down and his plummeting headfirst towards an English field would easily serve as an additional clue. That had been another of the pilot's merry jokes.

During the extremely noisy, cramped and bitterly cold flight, he reflected on how let down he felt by Grosskopf. The *Major* had started the relationship well. A rail warrant to Hamburg, sumptuous accommodation whilst there and a Hugo Boss-designed uniform to boot. He now seemed to have been demoted to cattle truck class travel and no drinks trolley. Could it have been something he said?

Despite his fears though, the landing was good. He stood up and walked a few tentative paces as he heard the plane circle and very quickly disappear from sight. He did not seem to have broken anything. He quickly dragged in the chute canopy, bundled it up, hid it under a hedge and covered it with undergrowth. He did all of the dirty work in the jump suit he had been issued with. He did not want to besmirch the natty double-breasted suit that he had bought in Hamburg.

He did not know exactly where he was – other than Suffolk – but the pilot had told him the nearest town should be Ipswich. Should be? He had hoped for something a little more accurate but all he got in reply was a shrug. Once he jumped, he was not the pilot's concern. Package delivered.

WESLEY GATHERED WHAT HE NEEDED, concealed the rest and set off to look for habitation. He felt in his jacket pocket and ensured the dipstick was there. He would need transport soon and there was no point in stealing something that only had enough fuel to get him a hundred yards. Not only would he not get very far but there was also the risk of an enraged owner running up the street to confront him. He did not think the *Abwehr* would be too happy to hear, in his first message, that he was up before the beak at Ipswich Magistrates Court for taking a car without consent.

He found a road quickly enough, chose a direction and came to a crossroads half a mile later. The absence of signposts hampered him but the road crossing was a major one. A pub came out of the gloom ahead of him - the *King's Head*. A large building that looked like an old coaching inn.

Five cars were parked there. He chose a dark blue Morris 10. He bent and unscrewed the fuel cap. Using his stick, he reckoned it had enough fuel in it to get at least twenty miles or so. That should do it. He used the key device he had been given to get into the car and the engine fired up at only the second turn.

He travelled eleven miles, according to the car odometer, and parked in a lay-by. He would wait in the car until daylight arrived. He had his cash. He had his National Identity card and British passport. With his petrol stick and key tools, he had the means to acquire a vehicle. He had all he needed to do the job, apart from accommodation and a wireless. He needed to get to the Siemens-Schuckert factory in Brentford to pick up his set.

He felt proud of himself. His worst fear - the flight and drop into Otto's much-vaunted 'field' - was now behind him. He had a hard job ahead of him but he was looking forward to it immensely.

HE SET off early the next morning and at the first major junction, he saw a heavily-laden 'agricultural supplies' lorry with the owner's address shown as Ipswich, cross his path. He counterintuitively turned in the opposite direction to its travel. It was still early so he reasoned that the lorry was travelling away from the town to deliver to farms in the area. Within ten minutes, he was proved right.

Adopting the persona of a gentleman traveller of independent means, he quickly found digs from an extremely grateful hostess. He carried the bags to his small but comfortable room, washed and slept for several hours. He was ridiculously tired. The stress of the journey and arrival had taken a lot out of him. He slept longer than he had intended so he found a pub that evening, ate moderately well, played a few games of darts with the locals and retired back to his room. Brentford, Ziegler and Grosskopf would have to wait.

EARLY THE FOLLOWING day and thankfully armed with the British maps he had been issued with by the *Abwehr*, he was at the factory just off the Great West Road in Brentford. He had dumped the Morris on the outskirts of Colchester and picked up something with a bit more class and style for the longish trek to the capital. A Riley, left with the keys in the ignition by a careless owner, was easy pickings once he had checked the tank.

The rest of the journey was a joy until, that is, he was stopped at some kind of control point just a hundred yards away from his destination and asked to show his papers. It all seemed rather dilatory though. The bored young gentleman was clearly just stopping vehicles at random. Many passed him by as he was dealing with Wesley.

"Are you checking for German spies?"

The man laughed. "It's just routine, sir."

"Well, you can't be too careful, I suppose."

His papers were returned. When told he was free to go, Wesley was sorely tempted to give him one of his 'littler' arm flicks but guessed it might land him in trouble. Instead, he waved a cheery goodbye and drove the short distance to the factory.

Notwithstanding the fact that this place had been described by Grosskopf as part of the famed Nazi *Kriegsnetz*, Wesley was not impressed. He was hardly expecting the walls of the factory to be draped in the red, white and black Nazi *Fahnen* that were everywhere in Germany these days, but this was distinctly drab and disappointing. It had the air of a prison.

He found room for the Riley in the factory car park and walked around to the rear of the building where he found an entrance. He gave his name to a skinny middle-aged man in grey overalls and asked to see Doktor Nagel. A list was consulted. The man smiled his satisfaction, walked Wesley down a corridor and showed him into a side room.

He looked around. The space was crammed with wireless sets and various bits of related paraphernalia. A man, clearly a technician by his overall, entered. They exchanged handshakes and he introduced himself as Nagel. There was no trace of a 'littler'. He took a list from a drawer and scanned it.

"Ah, yes. We have an SE108/10 for you."

"If you say so."

Wesley had never known the model number. He hoped to God it was the same as the one he had been trained on with Otto. Nagel cleared some room on the table and placed the set upon it. Wesley recognised it instantly. The technician reached under the table and put a few more items next to the set.

"With power pack, receiver and transmitter."

Wesley smiled.

"Have you had much experience with this set?"

The Englishman laughed. "Indeed. I spent months in Hamburg on the same machine so I could use it with my eyes closed."

Nagel smiled. "You may well have to."

The man's accent was strange. Wesley was trying to match it with German regional accents that he had become familiar with. It was not one that he knew. Probably Austrian, he thought, but he was not keen to enter into prolonged conversation with the fellow. He just wanted to leave but was then suddenly struck by an idea. As Nagel started to pack the wireless and its bits and pieces into a suitcase, Wesley asked if he could transmit a short message before he left. He wanted to let Otto know that he had arrived safely.

"Of course. Good luck."

The man smiled and closed the door behind him. Wesley took the wireless, connected it up and tapped out his first message to Otto. It was brief but jocular, and couched in the nonsense terminology they had immersed themselves in for months. A pre-agreed phrase for his safe arrival.

The bottom line was - 'WIESELIG now safe in field'.

CHAPTER 12

Albert Stokes was a busy man. After his meeting with the desperate little birdspotter in Hull, he was starting to feel that he was just scratching the surface of what was regarded in security circles as the enemy within. Knight had once referred to it as 'a cancer on the soul of Britannia'. Unnecessarily poetic, he thought, but that's what a public-school education did for you. He could not argue with the sentiment expressed.

At this point in the war - in its early days and not yet red in tooth and claw - the British public, at least according to the mainstream press, was seeing German spies and British traitors everywhere. They were sharing the space behind every bush. It was said that Hitler's progress had been so rapid because traitors in each of the conquered countries had paved the way for his invading armies. Stokes felt that was a bit of a stretch but much was made of the way that Vidkun Quisling, Norway's former defence minister, had ordered his troops to stand down when the Nazis came knocking. The many thousands of lines of sensationalist print on the Fifth Column issue were having an insidious effect.

He had just returned from Leeds where he had been doing his utmost to infiltrate a suspected Fifth Columnist cell there. It was not an area where he would have expected treachery. Maybe it was his singularly southern viewpoint, but he always imagined doughty Yorkshiremen as owing sole allegiance to the Holy Trinity of God, country and good ale - though not necessarily in that order.

HE CALLED in on Maxwell Knight to report on the Leeds visit, and a few other matters. Knight was struggling to keep an ocean of paper from spilling onto the floor. Eventually, he looked up and spoke.

"Good afternoon, old chap. Good visit?"

Stokes moved a few files from the only available chair, piled them on the floor and sat down. "I've just got back from seeing that man, Windsor in Leeds."

Knight snorted. "I trust that's not our beloved monarch whom you are referring to as 'that man'."

Stokes had to laugh. He thought it quite funny and was annoyed at himself that he had not thought of the association himself. "Not unless he's moved to Leeds and is obsessed with setting fire to factories."

Knight smiled. "So . . . satisfactory conclusion?"

"So far, but his other ex-BUF chums are coming out of the woodwork now to run the rule over me. In case I'm working for MI5, obviously. I'm seeing them again in a few days."

"Good."

He momentarily looked back at his papers and then gave up the effort of renewed concentration.

"Stokes, my dear boy. A word in your shell-like. I have been asked to impress upon you that your job is to contain these miscreants. Do not encourage them in any criminal activity. Do not give them any ideas, old chap. If you do and any of these buggers eventually go to court then we could be deep in the brown stuff."

Stokes' brow furrowed.

"You'd be in court too, old chap. Don't you see? If they name you and we have to admit your true role, then their defence would be that you were an *agent provocateur*. MI5 has its own 'enemies within' too, I'm afraid. They think that what we are doing isn't cricket."

His junior leant in conspiratorially. "And I've heard that Hitler has only got one ball."

Knight laughed. "Oh, very witty. I must remember that one. Seriously though, that's the reality, old bean. Our hands are tied. Battles are raging above our heads as we speak - and I'm not talking *Dorniers*. But getting back to Windsor and his ilk, the danger is, of course, that they are then back out onto the streets again and up to no good."

"And I'd be looking for another job."

"Of course. You'd be blown. I can always give you a good reference though. I hear the Westminster Bank is down one remittance clerk."

They both laughed.

"I think I'm probably *persona non grata* there now. I understand what you're saying though. It could be seen as entrapment, I suppose, if I overstep the mark."

"Precisely. Now, never mind Leeds for the moment. What news on the Rialto?"

Stokes looked at him blankly.

"*Merchant of Venice*. Shakesp . . ."

"Yes, I know who wrote it. What are you talking about?"

"Just my own little codeword for Siemens-Schuckert. Any movement on that?"

He shook his head. He had made no progress at all on that front and he had been dreading the question. "No. But I can quite reasonably plead pressure of work."

Knight smiled and nodded. He spread out his open hands to display the top of his desk. "Welcome to my world, my boy."

Stokes grimaced. "I thought I might pop down there tomorrow just to take a shufty."

"And what about that ferrety little gent from . . . Hull, was it? The one who wrote to the German Embassy."

He had forgotten about Armitage. The man had not got back in touch with him since their meeting in Hull. "Oh, yes. I sense he's on the lunatic fringe but he did tell me he is not alone."

"In what respect 'not alone'?"

"He implied that he has a friend with similar leanings. I need to chase him." He stood to take his leave and pointed at the cluttered desktop. "If you don't mind me asking, why the sudden influx of paper."

"Ha! Pressure has been brought to bear. Been told to get my act in order, files and records wise."

"Oh, well. I'd better let you press on then."

Stokes stood and was halfway through the door when Knight called him back. "Oh, word to the wise. We have a watcher just a few yards from the Rialto gate. He may be able to give you some gen on movements in and out. Could be a good starting point."

THE FOLLOWING DAY, after the first sleep in his own bed for a few nights, Stokes headed off to Brentford to have a look at the Siemens-Schuckert factory. He wanted to see what all the fuss was about. He knew that Knight was very keen to get him in there.

It was a pleasant drive. All seemed well with the world. He actually found himself whistling as he skirted Richmond Park on his left and crossed the Thames by Kew Bridge before turning onto the Great West Road in Brentford.

The factory would not have been hard to find even if he had not noted down the address from the file in the office. Nor was the 'watcher' difficult to spot. He pulled up behind the obvious standard issue staff car, got out of his own and walked to the other vehicle. He tapped on the window. The young driver leant across and wound it down.

Stokes spoke to him. "Excuse me. Are you looking for German spies?" He quickly pushed his MoD ID at the startled face. The watcher laughed and let him in.

"Do you know, that's the second time today that I've been asked that question."

"Really?"

"Yes. Rather strange."

Stokes' interest was piqued. He asked exactly what the watcher's brief was, what hours did he and his shift partner work, whom they stopped.

"It's not all day. Just the factory's business hours, really. I do the mornings and Joe relieves me at lunchtime. Sometimes we swap just to relieve the monotony. And we don't stop obvious business vehicles like vans and lorries. We've been told just to stop private cars . . . and we know staff members' car numbers so we don't bother them either."

"And how many times does anyone ask you if you are looking for German spies?"

"Can't speak for Joe, obviously, but we've been doing this

for months and you're only the second one who's ever asked me."

The man excused himself as he got out of the car to flag down an approaching vehicle. Stokes watched the man at work. He saw him say a few words, examine the driver's Identity Card, look into the interior of the car and the boot, before making notes on his clipboard and waving the car on. He then returned to the staff car.

"Did he ask you that question?"

"No. I've seen him before though. He's a rep for a company somewhere in the Midlands. Nottingham, I think. I'll still have to check him again on the way out." He sighed. "It's quite a boring job, to be honest with you."

Stokes nodded. He had served time on the tedium front when he was with the bank, so he sympathised. "You said it was earlier today that you were asked if you were looking for German spies?"

"Yes, in the last half hour, as it happens. Let me have a look."

He flicked through the sheets on his clipboard. "There it is." He pointed to the entry.

"John Smith. Has he come out yet?"

"No."

Stokes took a pad from his inside pocket and wrote down the car's make and registration number. He looked back at the watcher's clipboard and shook his head.

"John Smith? Really?"

The watcher smiled. "Yes."

"The most common name in Britain, I suspect. Could you describe him to me."

"You'll see him when he comes out. Big bloke, as I recall. Head touching the roof nearly. Quite a pleasant chap, mind you. Most affable."

"Did he have anything with him today. When you looked in the boot I mean?"

The man looked at the clipboard. "Nothing of note. Tools, all that sort of thing."

Stokes made a note of that, put the pad back in his pocket and turned to the man. "I'm going to get back in my own car, drive up the road, turn around and park on the other side of the gate. When he drives away from you after your inspection, I will drive slowly past you. All I want to know is if he has anything else in the car. I will be following him."

He shook the man's hand and told him he had been very helpful. "Oh, by the way. Where is all this ID and vehicle information sent?"

"We send it all to Mr Knight at MI5, sir."

"There must be tons of it."

"Yes, sir. We've been doing this for months."

Stokes remembered the maelstrom of paper and typed words on Knight's desk and the man's admission that he had been urged to bring his paperwork up to date. He groaned.

"Thank you. I may see you again."

He returned to his car, drove to the end of the road, turned, crawled back down and stopped. Within a few minutes, the factory gates were opened from the inside by an unseen individual. Stokes saw the watcher walk across the road, waiting to flag the exiting car down as it pulled into the side of the road past the gates. A green lorry lumbered up the road towards them. As it drew level with the building, it beeped its horn to alert the gateman to leave the entrance open and inched across the road to drive through. It was a tight squeeze and the driver had got the angle completely wrong. It now blocked Stokes' view of the parked Riley.

Stokes tapped his fingers impatiently on the steering wheel. The lorry shuddered backwards and forwards across the road and eventually secured itself a trajectory that would get it through the opening. It disappeared into the factory yard and he saw the Riley now almost at the bottom of the street, its nose pointed for a left turn onto the Great West Road.

The watcher walked to Stokes' car. "He's now got a suitcase in the boot, sir."

"Did he say anything?"

"Nothing. Just smiled and saluted."

He thanked him and drove off. The Riley had now disappeared but at least he knew which direction it had taken. What followed owed more to the *Keystone Cops* than any sensible pursuit of a suspect vehicle. As he grew increasingly frustrated with the snarl-ups in traffic, each of which gave his quarry a further advantage of distance, he finally found himself behind a Riley of the correct model but with a different registration number.

He gave up and headed home. He felt himself getting increasingly frustrated with the whole Siemens-Schuckert business. Pinning his hopes on a probably quite innocent Mr Smith was a sign of his desperation. It was just a hunch. If it had not been for the greeting he had made to the watcher - 'Are you looking for German spies?' - then he would have been back home by now. He pulled over at a phone box and dialled Knight's number.

"Knight."

It was curt. Stokes could imagine the phone crooked under the man's chin while he shuffled paper.

"It's Stokes."

"Oh, thank God. I thought it might be the paper squad demanding their pound of flesh. You been to the Rialto?"

"Indeed, I have."

"And?"

"Interesting."

Stokes could feel the man's exasperation down the wires.

"Come on, man. Spill. Have you cracked it?" He laughed.

"No. It's a bloody fortress. But . . . and this may be absolutely nothing."

"I'll decide that, old chum. That's my field. Apart from filing and minor office duties, obviously. What have you got?"

He told him the whole story of the tall, well-built man with a dangerous line in humour. And how he had left with a suitcase in the boot. He played down how he had lost the car in traffic. "Oh, and his name is John Smith."

There was a pause. "John Smith? Bit of a cliché, isn't it?"

"As I said, it may be absolutely nothing. Very affable chap according to the watcher . . . but aren't they the most credible?"

"Did you get the car registration?" Stokes read out the car details and number.

"OK, leave it with me. I'll get somebody on it, pronto."

Knight rang off. Stokes walked back to his car and drove back home to Epsom.

His wife was answering the phone as he walked through the front door. She held the receiver out to him and whispered. "Mr Knight."

Stokes took it from her. "What a delightful lady your wife sounds, Stokes. Too good for you, I suspect."

"Very funny. Have you news?"

"I do. Our Mr Smith is a person of interest, old chap. The car was stolen yesterday. The actual owner - not called John Smith, obviously - is a retired Army Major living in Colchester. Not happy about the theft. He'd just put petrol in apparently."

Stokes was taking this in.

"So, well done on your hunch, chum. Not sure where it puts us with regard to the Rialto, mind you."

"What intrigues me is what was in the suitcase. Our watcher assumed that he was a rep and the case contained samples."

"Don't be dim, Albert. It will no doubt be a wireless. Anyway, I'll pass that registration onto the police. This Smith might have dumped it now, of course, but it might be interesting to find it and search it. Its location might help too. We need to talk to this man. I'll let you know."

Stokes reminded Knight that he would be contacting Armitage that evening. The outcome of that would probably entail another trip to Hull.

"You certainly know how to live, Albert. Let me know. Toodlepip."

CHAPTER 13

"Sausages at twelve o'clock! Saveloys at one!" Freddie Metcalf bellowed out of the window at the street below. He felt like adding 'Bandits at two o'clock' but decided against it. Not these days. Not in this town. Not, especially, from a German.

Faces peered up at him. One or two passers-by waved and smiled. Several more scowled. He pulled his body back inside, closed the window and slumped back into his worn and faded armchair. He listened with amusement as his brother, Frank, stomped up the stairs, shouting.

"Will you stop doing that! Have you no sense?"

He stood in the doorway, hands on hips. Not happy. Freddie responded like an injured innocent. *"Mein Bruder. Was ist los?"*

"How many times must I tell you? We are English. So, speak it."

Frank was not keen on getting into this argument again. There were many issues on which he and his brother would never agree - not least their shared heritage.

"Ten minutes, you said. That was half an hour ago. The pigs are waiting and I cannot do it on my own. It grieves me to say this but only *you* have the skills I need at this moment."

He turned away and left the room. Freddie shouted after him.

"Apologise to the pigs for me. Tell them Freddie is coming."

He listened to his brother's retreating downward steps, lit a cigarette and walked back to the window. The grimy shop fronts across the road depressed him beyond words. A few souls had ventured beyond their doorsteps to scavenge. That is what shopping had become in North Shields now that the war was well into its second year. People were hunched and hungry. Their clothes were old, threadbare and patched. Where there was anything on offer, they shuffled and they queued.

He heard noises coming from the prep room directly below his sitting room and sighed. He put out his cigarette in the overflowing ashtray and went downstairs. Frank was already wearing the traditional garb of blue and white striped apron and hefting one of four pig carcasses onto a hook bolted into a ceiling beam. He gave one final push to lift the pig aloft.

"I thought you might not turn up. This is the only bit I can manage. You're the Sausage King, not me."

Freddie leant his back against the counter and smiled. "I know."

Wiping his greasy hands on his apron, Frank walked across to his brother. "I do appreciate your help, Freddie, but I wish you would stop shouting that stuff out of the window. They must have heard you all down the street."

"Well, they could do with something to cheer them up. But you know why we argue, don't you? You are English and I am German. You may have seen the newspapers. We are at war. Again!"

"We are *all* English now."

Freddie grunted. "Ha. We all have pieces of paper that tell us so, *mein Bruder*. But one of us has denied his birthright."

His brother walked across to pick up a second carcass. "Freddie. We have this conversation many times. This country has served us well." He continued. "Yes, it was very sad about Lotte's death. But that was a very long time ago. I am worried now that Ernest is living with you, that you will bend him to your will."

His brother laughed. "He just wanted to move out of that mausoleum that you live in, Frank."

Frank was shocked. "Ernest left the company because there is not enough work here for his accountancy skills. You know how much our trade has dropped. And this flat is a lot nearer to his new job at Wilkinson's."

Freddie regretted saying what he did. He had made up the mausoleum comment. Ernest had said nothing of the sort.

"Yes, well. He may not have said you lived in a mausoleum. The boy can make up his own mind though, can't he?"

His brother shook his head. "We don't have time for this. I need sausages as soon as possible. We open at noon."

He turned and walked through to the shop and Freddie busied himself preparing sausages. He would make a few saveloys too just to keep his brother sweet.

. . .

THE FACT that Frank's son, Ernest, was living in the flat with him was proving to be a bone of contention between him and his brother. But it was a very welcome change for Freddie simply to have somebody to talk to. As for bending the boy to his will, why should he not educate him in the failings of what he perceived as a broken nation?

He knew though, that Frank had got his son the job at Wilkinson's. He had not stood in the lad's way. The lemonade factory was run by a Rotary friend of his. Old man Wilkinson's business was multi-faceted. As well as the mineral water side of it, there were a number of off-licences and a portfolio of rental properties. Their company accountant had been a younger man who was now in the services. Wilkinson had jumped at the chance of taking Ernest on as his company accountant. Freddie was looking forward to hearing how his first day went.

He had been surprised at how little his nephew knew of what had happened to his Lotte. She was a young German girl who worked in the business which was run at the time by their late father. In the anti-German riots of 1915, their premises had been violently attacked and she had been killed. The police had done nothing to find her killer, even though it was very likely to have been the result of a fall, as stones and half-bricks rained through the plate glass shop windows.

Freddie's grief at Lotte's death had slowly solidified to a permanent rancour, its focus eventually shifting from the local police to the entire British nation.

Unused to the physical activity of the last few hours, Freddie dropped the last parcel of sausages and saveloys behind the shop counter and trudged back upstairs to his flat. He headed straight for the armchair and fell into it. It was a mistake. He wanted to stay awake for Ernest returning from work but as he picked up the fading photograph of Lotte and settled back into the cushions, sleep took hold very quickly. Lotte slipped to the floor.

CHAPTER 14

Ernest Metcalf was surprised at how readily his father had agreed to his quitting his job in the family business. Not only that, he had been instrumental in procuring this new job at Wilkinson's for him. And, as a bonus, he had not objected to his son moving out of the family home where he had been since birth, into the flat above the shop in Nile Street. That meant sharing with his uncle Freddie, of course, so that move had come with a warning from his father that he must humour the man but not, on any account, get sucked into his anti-British rhetoric.

ON HIS FIRST day in his new job, old man Wilkinson greeted him and took him through to what would be his office. It was not empty. The owner addressed the young woman in front of them.

"Ah, Lizzie . . . Mrs Fenwick, this is Ernest Metcalf. I've taken him on as Arthur's replacement. Would you do all the necessary employee stuff and show him around, please. You probably know what Arthur did better than me."

He turned to Metcalf and shook his hand. "Welcome aboard, Ernest. I'll leave you in Mrs Fenwick's capable hands." He turned to her. "I'll be at home if there's anything desperately urgent. Which I doubt."

With that, he left them standing in the small space and returned to his own office. Lizzie cleared her throat.

"So, do I call you Ernest or Mr Metcalf?"

"I think Ernest is fine. Do I call you Lizzie?"

She giggled. "I think Mrs Fenwick until we're at least into your second month, don't you?"

Ernest laughed as he followed her into her office. "Well, Lizzie. I look forward to working with you."

THE PAPERWORK TOOK LONGER than Ernest thought it would. Forms to sign, personal details, qualifications, allocation of wages number.

She stopped writing at his date of birth. "What, you're . . . forty-two?"

"That's right."

"Really?"

"Do I need my birth certificate too?"

"No . . . I just mean you look younger"

"Thank you. And you. How old are you?"

"Don't you know you should never ask a lady's age?"

"I'm sorry"

"No, I don't mind. Let's just say I'll never see twenty-five again. And I've got a five-year-old daughter, Alice."

He could not disguise his surprise. "But who looks after her when you're at work?"

"Mam does. There's just two war widows and a little lassie in our house."

"Oh . . ."

The light in her eyes had gone out. "Eddie was killed last year. His ship got hit by a torpedo and sank." She put her pen down. "I don't even know what actually happened. The war was only a week old. We couldn't believe it when the telegram came." She sighed. "And then dad died in Swans shipyard when a steel plate fell on him. Just a month after that . . ."

She paused for a few moments and then snapped back into office routine.

"Mr Wilkinson asked me to put Arthur's stuff into a logical order for you before we go through it all."

"That's kind of you."

"But why don't I show you around the place? Then we'll have a cup of tea and go through the wages."

She whisked him out of the office and was almost to the stairs before Ernest caught up with her.

"Hey, wait for me." She turned. "Are you alright, Lizzie?"

He was rewarded with a smile. "Yes, really I am. I'm sorry, I shouldn't have loaded all of my grief onto you. It's your big day." She laughed. "It's not every day you get to meet Mrs Turner. So, come on. Summon up your sinews." With that, she was halfway down the first flight.

"Yes. Mr Wilkinson warned me about her."

She laughed. "Did he? The old man is terrified of her. You wouldn't think it was his shop, would you?"

After four half-flights of stairs, during which Lizzie filled him in on the indomitable Mrs Turner's idiosyncrasies, they came out onto King Street. Lizzie pointed up the road to her left.

"See that big house on the other side? That's Phoenix House where the old man lives."

"Big house"

"Big family. His wife died a few years ago. Not surprised. Probably exhausted. They've got thirteen kids."

"Catholics, are they?"

"Methodist, I think. And he's in the Temperance movement too. Doesn't drink. You churchy?"

"Christmas and weddings." He grinned. "I'm not a devout worshipper."

"Same here. Come on then. Mrs Turner awaits."

SHE LED him the few yards to the broad shop front which sat diagonally across the corner of King Street and George Street. The shop windows were crammed with products, advertisements and signs. Ernest felt it strange that most of the products displayed were alcoholic – Martell's Three Star Brandy, Kirsopp's Lager and all manner and brands of wines and whiskeys, ports and porter.

There were no lights showing in the shop but it was plainly open for business. The resounding 'ding' as Lizzie opened the door was evidence enough. The interior was dark and gloomy. One long counter ran along the left and shelves lined every square inch of the walls. As well as bottle upon bottle covering the whole spectrum of alcoholic beverages, there was every known brand of cigars, cigarettes, humidors, pipes, loose tobacco and walking sticks. Every taste was catered for - across every class of customer. He had to admire the old man.

Mrs Turner made a grand theatrical entrance through the curtains covering the door to the back shop. She was a large lady, dressed completely in black. Lizzie's attempted introduction was interrupted.

"I know who he is, Mrs Fenwick, thank you"

She looked Ernest up and down. "You're that German."

"I'm British . . ."

"German stock then. You can't deny it."

Lizzie tried to intervene but Mrs Turner had not finished. She took a step closer to Ernest.

"You lot killed my Ronald. He took a few lungfuls of your poisoned gas in 1915. He'd only been away a couple of months. Chlorine it was. You any idea what that does to a man, have you? Never breathed proper after that. Took his last just a year after they brought him back."

She moved even closer, looked him squarely in the eye, bent her head forwards and spat on the floor. The globule of spittle landed squarely between his shoes. Lizzie jumped back in shock.

"Think yourself lucky it's not in your face but that's out of respect for Mrs Fenwick. Nowt else. And if Mr Wilkinson chooses to employ you then that's up to him but I'll have no truck with you. You're just a filthy Hun and you're all the same."

She left as dramatically as she had entered. Lizzie dragged him out of the shop. They stopped at the King Street staff door.

"I am so sorry, Ernest. I'll make sure that the old man gets to hear about this, don't you worry."

"No, Lizzie. That wouldn't exactly put me back in her good books, would it?" He looked down. "And she missed my shoes, so no damage done."

"You look a bit shocked though, Ernest. Shall we go and have that cup of tea now?"

"No. No, it's fine. I just didn't realise there was still anti-German feeling around. Like it was in 1915 when the rioters smashed up my father's shop and killed my uncle's fiancée."

She spoke quietly. "Oh, I didn't know that, Ernest. That's terrible."

"Maybe it never went away." He was more shocked than he was showing Lizzie. "Yes, let's go and have that cup of tea."

"Come on, then. I think you need a sit down, at least. Get your breath back."

He followed her again. Up the stairs. This time he watched her.

Back in the office, she boiled the kettle in the small kitchen behind a curtain. She brought two cups back and handed him one.

"No milk, I'm afraid."

Ernest took a sip. Lizzie looked on solicitously. "I don't think we'll be paying a return visit to Mrs Turner any time soon, do you?"

"I can see her point of view, I suppose."

"Really?" She looked at him intently. "It was Germans who killed my Eddie. And I didn't spit at your feet, did I?"

"Don't think that hadn't crossed my mind, Lizzie. Using Mrs Turner's logic, you'd be perfectly entitled to do the same."

Her face changed and she dropped her head. The second mention of her husband's death seemed to have momentarily upset her. She stayed like that for a few seconds before raising her head and looking at Ernest.

"Life's too short, Ernest. War is terrible. It makes people do awful things. The man who fired the torpedo that killed Eddie, didn't know him. He'd never been to the pub with him – or a football match, had he? Her . . ." She pointed down. ". . . her behaviour is just as bad. In my opinion."

They sat and finished their tea in silence. Suddenly she stood. "Come on. Let's go and see the girls."

"The girls?'

"Oh yes, you've heard of a chorus line? Well, this is the bottling line. Come on."

She grabbed his cup and put it back on the desk. Then she took his hand and they were through the door before he could draw breath.

IT WAS STILL ONLY HALF past eight but the bottling line was in full swing. The noise was terrifying - the clanking of glass, the motor drive of the conveyor belt, the wooden thunk of bottle hitting crate. Women of various ages populated the scene. All of them appeared to be gabbling away but Ernest could not interpret a single word over the all-pervading din of the machinery.

Lizzie dropped his hand as they entered the floor. She held her arm aloft and shouted. "Ladies, ladies! Can we switch off for a few minutes, please?"

She mimed the motion in the air. They obeyed the signal and the noise gradually subsided to a low electrical hum. Ernest felt eyes moving to him.

Lizzie smiled her thanks. "This is Ernest Metcalf."

A chorus of 'oohs' rose from the floor. He felt as if he were in a meat market.

"He's doing Arthur's job so he'll be paying you every week from now on."

There was a shout. "Oh aye, what have you done with Arthur? Tired him out, I'll bet!" Then laughter. Another piped up. "He must be bloody knackered!" And more ribald comments.

It was obvious to Ernest that Lizzie and Arthur had history. He smiled, waved and looked across at Lizzie. She looked flustered. She waved too and they left.

"There you are. That wasn't too bad, was it?"

"Erm . . ."

"Shirley's the one you have to watch."

"Which one was that?"

"She's the one who shouted 'bloody knackered' or something. Black hair. Stupid beauty spot on her left cheek."

"I hadn't noticed", he lied.

"She was working her way through every man on the workforce until the war put a stop to it. Now she's starting on the young lads."

"Oh, dear."

She laughed. "I think she carves notches on her bedpost. And she's got a mouth like Tynemouth. Telling her something is the quickest way to get it round the factory. I don't know why the old man bothers with staff memos."

A loud bell rang, only just audible over the renewed din from the bottling line.

"That's the phone." She was sprinting up the stairs. "There's nobody else up there to answer it. Just go into the yard. I'll meet you there in a few minutes."

As she sprinted away, Ernest walked the few paces up King Street to the double gates which the drays used. Trying to avoid the horse droppings, he picked his way into the yard.

"Frightened of getting your fancy shoes mucked up, are yer?"

He looked around but could see nobody. Then a short, squat man revealed himself from the corner of the stables. He did not look as if he wanted a friendly chat. Ernest heard the gates close behind him. He turned to see a scrawny man leaning against them, a sneer on his face.

The first man spoke again. He now had a pole in his

hand. It looked like a piece of broken shaft from one of the drays.

"You're a long way from home, aren't you?"

"What?"

The other joined in, laughing. "Bloody hell, he speaks English".

"I was born in . . ."

Before he could complete the sentence, he felt the massive jolt of the broken shaft as it landed across the centre of his back. The searing pain took the breath from him. A hefty kick in the balls sent him sprawling to the ground. The left side of his head was firmly planted in a pile of horse dung.

As he lay there, groaning and wheezing, he smelt stale beer breath. Spit splashed his ear.

"I don't care where you were fucking born, Fritz! You're still a bloody Jerry bastard." More kicks accompanied the last few words.

"Come on. Leave him where he belongs. In the shit."

He heard them laughing as they walked to the gates which closed behind them. He lay motionless until he was sure they had gone then, slowly and painfully, struggled to his knees. When he got his breath back fully, he hobbled over to the stables and propped himself up against the doors. One of the horses whinnied.

Ernest guessed that his two assailants had nothing to do with the horses. They had left and there was nobody else around. Nor was there any sign of the draymen. He sat there for several minutes, mentally reeling from the verbal and physical onslaughts he had received since he arrived this morning. Being of German descent was proving to be injurious to his health.

.   .   .

LIZZIE ENTERED the yard and knew straightaway that something was wrong. The broken piece of wood on the floor looked out of place and Ernest's leather cap was sitting like a crown, atop a pile of horse muck.

She heard Ernest's groans. The sound drew her eyes to the stable and she saw him, slumped in front of the doors. Lizzie bent down and shook him gently. He came back to his senses and coughed violently.

It took a while to get him upstairs to the office. As they passed the back window of the shop that looked onto the yard, she saw Mrs Turner's impassive face. Her arms were folded across her chest. She appeared unmoved by Ernest's plight.

Despite Lizzie's insistence that he should go to see a doctor, or at least have his wounds tended by a nurse, he refused.

"Well, we've got a first aid kit here somewhere. Let me find it." She walked to the cluttered cupboard and, amongst the stock of paper and envelopes, she found it. Ernest had managed to heave himself onto a chair.

"Now you've got your breath back, who did this?"

"Unknown assailants, I think they say . . ." He winced.

"But who was it?"

"Who were *they!* Plural. Two of them."

"Did they say anything?"

"Oh . . . just something about me being a long way from home and still being a bloody Jerry. Same script as Mrs Turner, basically."

"Well, if it's any consolation, I don't think it's anyone who works here, Ernest."

"What makes you think that?"

"They wouldn't dare, for one thing. The old man wouldn't stand for it."

He suddenly tired of her fussing and pulled his shirt down from where she had been dabbing him with a stinging liquid. He stood and faced her. "Thank you, Lizzie. I'm feeling a bit better now."

"Oh, are you sure?"

"Yes, really. I don't think I've broken anything. Just some bruising." With some effort, he stood and grabbed his jacket from the back of the chair. It was torn.

"What are you doing?"

"I thought I would slip home and get changed. There's a rip in my jacket and horse shit on my shoes and trousers."

He looked around. "Where's my cap?"

"Oh. I saw it on the floor of the yard. I don't think you'll want it back. It's . . . erm, covered in . . . like your trousers. I'll bring it in and clean it up for you, if you like?"

"Don't bother. Funnily enough, though, it was the only part of me that was actually German."

He opened the door and started to leave. "Just throw it in the bin."

She listened as he hobbled down the stairs and heard the street door slam behind him.

CHAPTER 15

Ernest's walk from the factory was long and painful as the blows he had sustained started to make their presence felt. Once he reached the flat, he closed the street door behind him and collapsed in a painful heap on the bottom stairs.

Freddie shouted from the top of the stairs. "Ernst? Is that you?"

"Yes, I've just called in to get changed and . . ."

He stood and started to negotiate the first few steps. There was no hiding his pain and discomfort now. His uncle came down to help him.

"What on earth have you done, boy?"

"Long story, uncle. Let me get upstairs so that I can sit down. I'll tell you then."

With much huffing and puffing, grunting and flinching, the two men eventually got to the sitting room. The younger man slumped into the armchair. While he tried to make himself comfortable, his uncle busied himself in the tiny kitchen, brewing tea.

"Here. Drink. I have put some schnapps in it. You look as

if you need it." He was not willing to leave a gap bigger than that needed for Ernest to take a sip, before he was asking again. "*Also, was ist passiert, Neffe?*"

Ernest took a second sip of the powerful brew. "What happened? I was jumped, uncle."

Freddie looked nonplussed for a few seconds until a mime from Ernest set the matter beyond doubt.

"*Ach! Überfallen!! Aber warum?*"

Ernest explained to his uncle what had happened in the factory yard and what was said. Finally, his uncle fell heavily back into his chair and scowled. He launched into one of his tirades about the British and how they were just very infe-rior Germans. *Untermensch*. A subculture.

He had heard most of it before but Ernest now found himself less disparaging of his uncle's invective. He was not sure that he would have received this sort of sympathy from his father. Frank would have been more anxious that his son was not causing problems for his friend Wilkinson. Almost as if his son getting spat at and then beaten up in the stable yard was no way to repay his friend's kindness.

Ernest had not told his uncle yet about the verbal onslaught from Mrs Turner. When he did, he found that Freddie had known her for years. They were exact polar opposites in terms of national fervour. Ernest recounted exactly what she had said to him.

"Well, I'm not surprised that she was like that with you. She lost her husband, but at least she had some life with him before he went. I was not so lucky, Ernst."

The old man's eyes filled. He stood quickly, delved into a trouser pocket and brought a great sheet of a handkerchief to his face. "These English, Ernst. They are not to be forgiven for what they did to us after the war."

He proceeded to instruct Ernest, yet again, in the iniquities of the Armistice conditions and of the viciousness of the Versailles Treaty. The cruel and savage settlement which heaped hunger and humiliation on the German people for years after the guns fell silent.

"Let me show you something." Freddie stuffed his hand down the side of his armchair cushion and brought out a sheaf of dog-eared newspaper clippings. He laid them on the table and flicked through them. He pulled one from the bulldog clip, put on his spectacles and started to read.

"*Pork Butcher's Shop Window Smashed at North Shields . . .*"

Ernest sighed. "Uncle, I know all about how Lotte died."

"Ha! You think this is about Lotte, huh. You think this is about the last war?" He waved the press clipping in front of his nephew's face. "No, Ernest. This was *last year.*"

Ernest was shocked.

"*Mr H Gruber, owner of a pork butcher shop in Albion Terrace, Tynemouth Road, North . . .*"

"The Grubers? Harry's shop?"

"Let me finish for goodness' sake."

"Sorry."

"*. . . Tynemouth Road, North Shields, had his plate glass smashed during the black-out last night. Mr Gruber, who saw service with the British Army during the Great War, is a son of the late Mr Charles Gruber, a German who had lived in this country for more than sixty years and in whose name the business is still carried on.*"

Ernest was almost at a loss for words. "Why did I not know about this? Which paper is that from?"

"It is the *Shields Daily News* of . . ." He squinted at the date. "Monday 13th May 1940. And as for why you didn't know about it, I think maybe you have been wearing your father's blinkers, Ernst."

His nephew slowly shook his head. Freddie continued. "Basically, Harry ran outside but could not see the
culprits in the dark. The cowards had run away. Oh, and
Harry's brother fought in the first war too - for the
British." Freddie paused and let it all sink in. He wanted his
nephew to get the point of what he was saying without any
further prompting from him. "Here. Take it. Read it for
yourself."

Ernest took the crumpled clipping while his uncle
pulled out another one.

"And this", he held up the second piece of paper, "is
from the same paper but just three days later. I will let you
read it again at your leisure but it's the voice of common
sense. A voice in the wilderness however, I feel."

He held it up. Obviously scanning the introduction, he
started to read.

"*Throwing stones at the plate glass windows of 'German'
pork butchers won't help us to win the war. Indeed, the stones
serve no purpose at all except to shatter the glass which the insur-
ance company - if the butcher has been wise - has to make good.*"

Ernest could see him skimming text again. "And here . . .
'*There are naturalised Germans in North Shields whose forefathers came here a hundred years ago. Many of them fought for
the Allies in the last war*'"

He handed that to Ernest too. "And what has been our
reward, our recognition for that, huh? I congratulate the
man who wrote it but I am afraid he is pissing in the wind,
Ernst. We and the Grubers have been here so long, as he
says, but we are now becoming scapegoats. Anything goes
wrong, blame the pork butcher. I've had enough of it." Now
seated, he leant in to his nephew. "And I have some advice
for you, Ernst."

"What is that, uncle? Don't trust the English?" He

laughed but it was painful, tailing off to a sharp intake of breath. It reminded him that he must change and get back to work. He stood.

"Uncle, I have to get back to the factory. I only came back to make myself look more presentable."

Freddie looked up at him. He was disappointed. After what his nephew had undergone during his first day, and even after reading about the experiences of their fellow Germans, the Grubers, he still could not see the truth. He gave a phlegmy laugh. "Very well. We will speak again though, Ernst."

His nephew made his way through to the bedroom and changed into another pair of trousers and a fresh shirt. The ripped jacket would have to do for now. He could hear his uncle chuntering away to himself even as he re-entered their small sitting room.

"Three words, Ernst. *Rache ist süss*."

His nephew was on his way to the door. He turned. "Which means what, uncle?"

"Revenge is sweet."

Ernest laughed but he was finding himself less able to dismiss what he once saw as his uncle's rantings. Maybe they weren't so foolish after all.

CHAPTER 16

Major Dieter Grosskopf was touring offices that had been set up in the new territories of the Reich. Now that *Operation Sealion* - the invasion of Britain - was at the planning stage, he was keen to ensure that counter-intelligence people in their new commands were playing their part in its facilitation. He had no formal brief to do so, but he was anxious to bring them into his ambit and, as a by-product, promote his own name and career. He had not mentioned his embryonic Wesley 'experiment' at the Berlin meeting. He had been there purely as an invited observer. He had a strong suspicion that his idea would be 'stolen' by more senior officers present. His name as the innovator of the plan would then be quickly forgotten.

Amsterdam was one that he especially wanted to jump start. As he had explained to Wesley before he was delivered to Britain, there would be a second front to the invasion. Holland was in a prime position as one of the launch pads for the second thrust of *Sealion* on to the east coast of mainland Britain. In his view, it was imperative to have a large squad of Nazi sympathisers, activists and facilitators *in situ* to ease the invasion's success.

HE WAS SITTING in a well-appointed ante-room on the first floor of *Gestapo* Headquarters on Euterpestraat in Amsterdam. From some photographs still on the walls, its earlier incarnation seemed to have been the Christian Girls High School before it was commandeered for the service of the *Reich*. A starker contrast in purpose, it would be difficult to imagine. Ahead of him, behind the large mahogany desk and above the fireplace was a hefty gold-framed portrait of *Der Führer* – morose and intense, as always.

A door opened in the far corner of the same wall. Two uniformed officers walked in and approached the table in front of him. Both were smiling. A good start. Mindful of the fact that he was sitting in *Gestapo* HQ, Grosskopf was careful to deliver the text book version of the Hitler salute. They responded in kind.

All three sat. The other two at one side of the large desk, their visitor facing them. One of them spoke. "*Major* Grosskopf. The floor is yours. We are intrigued."

Grosskopf noticed that all three of them were of equal rank. So, there was no need for undue reverence. It was a level playing field. "Gentlemen, I congratulate you on the swiftness of finding this first-class establishment. In true *Blitzkrieg* fashion. The *Führer* would be proud."

The two officers introduced themselves simply as Harster and Lages. They looked at each other and laughed. "We like it, yes. But come on, what do you have for us?"

Grosskopf stood and took the floor as they had suggested. He outlined his mission with not a little flamboyance. Something of Wesley must have rubbed off onto him. They nodded at all the right places when he talked of the imminence of the invasion of Britain; they raised their eyebrows when he described Wesley and his advantages over the current rash of agents; and looked extremely interested when he mentioned the proposed infiltration of the RAF by his two airmen. They were, however, slightly abashed when he enquired about any contacts they had managed to develop in Britain.

Harster spoke. "Sorry, Grosskopf, but we have only just got our feet under the table and have not had time to . . ."

"But it is imperative that we get a foothold in England *before* we get boots on the ground. Do you not see?"

The other officer interrupted before Grosskopf could press his point further. "I think we may have one thing for you."

Harster was staring at his colleague with a bewildered expression. Lages elaborated. "Don't you remember? That little man Visser. Jan Visser."

"Oh, him! Those drawings!" The pair set off laughing again and slapping each other on the shoulder. It was like the final scene from a *Marx Brothers* movie.

"Gentlemen! Share the joke, please."

The two settled. Harster apologised. Lages walked to a cabinet and came back with a folder which he handed to Grosskopf. While their visitor perused the contents of the file, Lages gave him a brief rundown. "Jan Visser is a Dutch Nazi. Member of the NSB. One of our little helper elves now that we are starting to round up the Jews."

Grosskopf stopped scanning the file. "NSB?"

"The *Nationaal-Socialistische Beweging*. They have been really helpful. Paved the way for us in many respects. This man Visser is very . . . keen."

The pair knew better not to laugh again. Grosskopf's

face revealed how irritated he was becoming. Lages took the file from their guest. "I'm sure you haven't got the time to go through all of that in detail. Put simply, Visser has a family member - a distant cousin, I think, on his German mother's side. He lives in . . .", he looked at the file, "North Shields."

Harster butted in. "It's on Tyneside. His cousin's name is Friedrich Metcalf."

"Friedrich? He's German?"

"By birth, yes. They're pork butchers. Emigrated from Germany decades ago."

"And what are all the pretty pictures?"

Lages went on to explain that Friedrich was virulently anti-British. Fiancée killed in 1915 during the anti-German riots following the sinking of the *Lusitania*. The drawings were of naval vessels in various stages of construction at the Swan Hunter shipyard, close to where he lives. Rest of the family are strict Anglophiles - hence the surname change from the original Metzger.

His colleague continued. "His German is still extremely good, as you can see. To be fair, he is a good artist but there is nothing that we don't already know about this activity at Swan Hunter. I am told anyway."

Lages cut in again. "He did mention that there is a younger family member - a nephew - whom he is trying to convert to his own philosophy. They share a flat above the family shop."

Grosskopf was thinking. The shipbuilding pictures might be useless but if this Friedrich could pair up with his nephew, then they could maybe produce more valuable results. "How old is Friedrich?"

There were blank faces at the other side of the desk. "Not sure. Quite old, I would think."

"And where is this Jan fellow now? The Dutchman. I want to speak to him."

The pair looked at each other again and conferred. Harster stood. "I think he is actually working in this building today. I will bring him to you if he is."

He left the room. Lages remained, looking embarrassed. Grosskopf tried to ease his pain.

"It's easier for an outsider looking in, you understand. I just think this could potentially be the germ of a Fifth Column . . . perfect for my fellow Wesley to get his teeth into. And it's almost exactly where we would like it to be."

Lages was sharing the excitement now. He slapped his knee. "Of course. We will help in any way. It would certainly look good for a new office, *ja*?"

Grosskopf smiled but did not have time to respond. Harster had entered the room again with a short, black-clad, middle-aged man in tow. The German sat back in his seat and left the Dutchman standing. He looked terrified. Grosskopf grabbed a chair and placed it next to his own. "Please, sit. Don't be afraid."

Visser sat. His earlier fear had abated. The other pair looked astonished. Grosskopf noticed.

"A little courtesy never goes amiss, gentlemen."

He turned to Visser. "Now, please, tell us about why you are wearing the uniform and then I want to hear of Friedrich."

It was like turning on a tap. The man was clearly more on their side than many Germans he had met. That could not have been easy and probably never would be. Visser told the three of them what Grosskopf had already heard from Harster and Lages, but in considerably finer detail. What Grosskopf was most interested in was the nephew. All three of them listened attentively. Visser was not interrupted but gradually ran out of steam. Grosskopf allowed a silence to fall between them. He smiled throughout. When he spoke, he addressed Visser.

"I am *Major* Dieter Grosskopf from the *Abwehr*. We run a number of informants in enemy territory. I think that these drawings are sufficient of a *Schmecker* – a taster - to warrant further contributions from Friedrich. But *not* . . ." - he held the drawing aloft - ". . . with more of these, as lovely as they are. It would be appreciated by the *Führer*. Of that you can be assured."

"Then . . . how?"

"Neither the drawings nor their delivery by normal postal services from an enemy country, is acceptable. We need everything that Friedrich can give us but . . . by wireless."

"Oh, I'm not sure . . ."

His diffidence was not what Grosskopf wanted. "You will both be rewarded. For your facilitation firstly, by an immediate promotion. Your uncle's remuneration . . . well that may have to wait until we are his occupying power."

The other two officers both laughed. Jan joined them. Then he suddenly remembered the letter he had received that morning from his cousin. He had read it on the tram journey into the office. "Oh, that reminds me. I received one from him this morning."

Harster and Lages visibly slumped in their seats. Their visitor held up his hand. He did not want a repeat of their *Marx Brothers* routine. Jan voiced their thoughts. "I know. I'm sorry, gentlemen. I also hope it is not another drawing." It felt though as if the envelope contained only a letter.

They listened intently and with growing interest as Jan read it aloud, paraphrasing his cousin's more flowery sentences about the continued injustice of his enforced residence in such a pitiful place as North Shields. He gave more emphasis to the meat of the letter – that his cousin's nephew, Ernst, was now 'beginning to see the light'. He was younger, fitter and more mobile And two pairs of eyes were better than one. When he had finished reading, he handed the letter over as proof. Grosskopf read it and handed it back to the man.

"Your cousin's German is excellent. A bit archaic but I suppose that is only to be expected."

"Yes. Friedrich prefers to use his mother tongue . . . but only in these letters."

"Then that will make things much easier. I suggest, Jan Visser, that you do not leave this office until you have written a reply. I will dictate it."

It was a brief missive, passing thanks to Friedrich from the *Führer* himself on his efforts so far and informing him that he would soon be contacted with arrangements to take delivery of a wireless set. Jan was also to write that the letter was being posted from neutral Sweden and that he must send no further letters to what was now an enemy country as it could well be intercepted in transit by the British postal authorities.

When he had finished the letter, Grosskopf took it from him and shook the man's hand. "This will be with Friedrich in a few days. So, thank you - and congratulations on your promotion."

Visser nodded, gave a vigorous Hitler salute and left. Grosskopf returned to his seat. He took an envelope from the desk between them and placed the signed letter within. He placed it in front of them. "Please take a copy of this letter and ensure it is sent as soon as possible by the route I mentioned."

Both appeared nonplussed. Grosskopf sighed. "You have

this Friedrich's address. Put the addressed letter in the next diplomatic bag for onward transmission to either Dublin or Stockholm - preferably the latter."

Neither seemed any the wiser.

"Neutral countries. Do try to keep up, gentlemen."

The pair nodded and exchanged glances. Lages spoke. "Promotion, you say?"

"Yes. I'm sure you can find a permanent job for Visser here - in the office. We don't want any stray Jew caving his head in with a brick while he is so important, do we? Especially after he has given us such a valuable lead."

Groucho and Chico were suddenly speechless.

"Well? I need you to agree to that or I will take it upstairs. I want the man withdrawn from anything that will put him in physical danger."

The pair had forgotten that they were all of equal rank. Suddenly, Grosskopf was acting and sounding like a superior officer. They both came to the realisation, separately and together, that he very soon would be. Lages made one last stand.

"Protecting your asset, huh?"

Grosskopf leant back in his chair and smiled. "Now you get it. Good." He stood. "So, gentlemen, I think our business is concluded. I will drop back from time to time to see how things are progressing but if you have any other connections in Britain that you think are worthy of support, then do not hesitate to contact me."

He turned and left.

IT WAS a few minutes before either of the other two spoke. It was Harster.

"We need to get our act together. He's a go-getter, mark

my words. Better to be hanging on his coat tails than to be swept away in his wake - or worse." He stood. "I had better go and arrange some kind of 'promotion' for the Dutchman."

Lages rose from his torpor. "Yes. You need to inform our new secretary of his duties."

CHAPTER 17

It took Wesley almost two full days to drive from Brentford to Hull. He had made his transmission to Otto Ziegler from there and he now needed to check in again.

Looking from the window of the digs he had found in Gillett Street, Wesley saw a street with an over-abundance of anonymity. Uniform terraced houses, almost identical front doors, net curtains and whitewashed steps. It was perfect.

The room was spartan but suited to his needs. The bed was long enough to accommodate his frame. The wardrobe held his clothes quite nicely. His suitcase - locked and containing the wireless set - fitted neatly under the bed. There was even a domestic wireless which would easily mask the sound of the tapping of the Morse key.

He had a quick wash in the tiny handbasin and stretched out on the bed. He had half an hour before he was due to touch base again with Otto in Hamburg. Just enough time to work out what his persona was to be when he ventured on the street.

It was strange being back in Britain after so many years.

The novelty of hearing English being spoken everywhere had still not worn off and the Hull dialect was not one he had ever heard before. It had a unique feature that he did not recall from any other Northern accent. The 'o' as in 'no', for example, is pronounced 'er'. So, 'no' becomes 'ner', 'snow' sounds like 'sner'. He stood and looked at himself in the mirror above the sink while he practised a phrase he might need if he were still here in winter. *'Er, ner! Look at the sner!'* He smiled after each repetition.

He thought about building his character. The part that would be his for days or weeks or months. His current transport - that he had acquired *en route* from Brentford - was an extremely stern-looking, yet comfortable, Austin 18. He imagined the previous owner being a GP. The car exuded an air of respectability.

So, Wesley was to be a retired country doctor from . . . he struggled to remember exactly where he had picked the car up from, in order that the registration would match his story . . . Grantham. Recently widowed, he had decided to visit university friends from way back. Wesley remembered that there was an attaché case in the boot of the Austin which would provide a splendid prop. Perfect. It would probably not last forever but it was a good one to start with.

He switched on the domestic wireless and waited for the valves to warm up. As the programme leached from the ether, he adjusted the volume. Too soft and it would not shield the sound of his transmission from other ears; too loud and it would attract unwanted attention. When he felt it was just right, he squatted next to the bed, slid the suitcase towards him and extracted his wireless set. He reached across and turned the key in the door.

While he connected the set up, he had half an ear open for what was coming out of the domestic set. It was inane nonsense but he resolved to become a regular listener. In order to blend, he needed to be up to speed with whatever was in the public consciousness. And he must read at least one newspaper every day.

OTTO CAME through right on time. Neither of them had much to say. For Wesley, it was merely to confirm that he now had digs in Hull. For Otto's part, it was simply to impart the fact that Grosskopf was still touring *Gestapo* offices in newly-won parts of the *Reich*. Wesley detected some sarcasm between the lines.

The only nugget of real news was that the Polish airman - STANGE - had already sent information through the cutout. He was to be posted to 92 Squadron at RAF Biggin Hill in Kent. The Pole had supplemented this with brief details of his current location, type of aircraft and number of pilots. It was promising and more than was expected at this stage of the game. Otto instructed him to contact this Pole - Flight Sergeant Tomasz Gierczak - to remind him of his duty to deliver a fighter. Nothing had yet been heard from the Czech pilot, codename MOTORRAD - real name Augustin Preucil, rank and whereabouts unknown. Wesley was to do what he could to chase him.

Wesley groaned at these instructions, especially the last one. A hopeless task. Where would he start? He was just about to sign out when he heard a gentle tapping on his door. He froze. Then the tapping came again. And a male voice.

"Anybody at home?"

The nightmare had arrived. The one where he had neither read the script nor learned his moves. He had always been diligent in committing lines to memory. Intimate knowledge of words and character brought comfort. He had not given this part sufficient thought. He walked to the door and summoned confidence from somewhere deep in his psyche. Wesley called out. "Two minutes."

As swiftly and as smoothly as he was able, he signed out, disassembled the set, stuffed it quickly into its case and slid it out of sight beneath the bed. He opened the door. There stood a small chap, medium build, collar and tie, cheap suit. He was smiling.

"Evening, squire. Just thought I'd give you a knock."

From London by the accent. Or south-east at least.

"I'm staying here for a couple of nights. Commercial traveller. Wondered if you fancied a quick snifter. Fill a bit of time, eh?"

"Er, yes. Why not? Just let me get my jacket."

Wesley withdrew from the door, closing it slightly so as not give the caller too good a view. The man called from the door while Wesley donned his jacket and checked the contents of the pockets.

"Sid Tanner, by the way."

"Oh . . . John Smith."

"As in the brewery, eh?" Sid gave out an annoying laugh.

What was the fellow talking about?

"Yes, but no relation."

The laugh again. "That's a shame. Drinks would have been on you, eh?"

Wesley's initial thoughts were to get this over with as soon as possible. He threw up a silent prayer that the man was only staying one night. On reflection, though, he could learn something from him. And, he hoped, the more he spoke, the less time he would have to laugh in that intensely irritating way. He steeled himself for the experience.

. . .

THEY WALKED down the street toward the river. Sid knew a pub. It was almost as dark and dingy inside as the blackout-shrouded ten-minute walk to reach it had been, but at least it had a surprisingly good selection of beer. It was almost empty. They sat in a corner facing the street door. Wesley mentally compared the pub to the buzzy, thronged, brightly-lit Hamburg joint that he had visited with Otto just a week ago.

He did not have to be the first to broach the subject of the war. Sid was an open book. He was born and bred in the east end of London so he knew everything there was to know about bombing raids. He had lost several family members the previous year. He had stopped laughing but he was now bordering on the maudlin. As soon as he started crying in his beer, Wesley would have to find an excuse to leave.

"Have we seen the worst of it, do you think?"

It was a neutral question. Wesley just wanted to hear the man's broader view of the war.

"Ooof! Not so sure about that, squire. 'Itler might have lost the Battle of Britain but his bombers are still getting through, ain't they? Nowhere's safe, I don't reckon."

Wesley took a sip of his beer. It was actually quite good.

"I mean. It ain't been bad 'ere, far's I can see."

Wesley nodded. He had no clue. "Really?"

"Yeah. Course, you know why?"

"No, why?"

Sid looked around in a kind of low-budget spy movie kind of way. He leant in. "Decoy sites." Each word was enunciated clearly and individually with its own accompanying nod of the head and knowing wink.

Wesley looked at the man. He was still nodding and winking. If he didn't stop him, he got the feeling that Sid would spend the next hour constantly repeating the same two actions in a comic loop.

"Decoy sites?"

That was clearly what Wesley was meant to say and it allowed Sid to expand upon what he obviously saw as a subject in which he was quite the expert. He explained how they worked. An Army chum of his had told him in detail and he should know. That's what he did, see.

"They make pits and fill them with water and some of them have lights. Look like nothing from the ground but from the air . . . from the air, they look like, I don't know, docks or something, or . . . or, an airfield, without the water, obviously."

Wesley's interest had picked up by several degrees. "They didn't work in London, then?"

Sid shook his head sadly. "Not sure they 'ad 'em then. Got the idea after, see."

He was slipping into his slough of despond again.

"And I reckon that's why they ain't 'ad much bombing 'ere, like."

"Haven't they?"

"Well . . . I think they've 'ad bits and bobs but nuffink like the east end."

"So, they've got decoy sites here, then." Wesley thought he was safe asking the question. Sid had given him a flawless flight path running right up to it.

"Oh, gawd yeah." He laughed out loud as if that was the most ridiculous question he had ever heard. Heads turned so he dropped his voice almost to a whisper. "You drive along the north side of the 'Umber estuary, like I did yesterday, and you practically drive into 'em. Can't miss 'em."

He took a swig of his beer and drained the glass. Wesley took the cue and went to the bar to replenish their drinks.

This was like taking candy from a baby. When he got back to his digs, he would get his maps out and plan a little road trip.

He felt that he had got all that he could from Sid. The man had moved on to cataloguing his female conquests while on the road. It was extremely graphic and not a particularly edifying chronicle, in Wesley's opinion, but he sniggered and guffawed at all the appropriate junctures.

The evening came to a natural end when the landlord called time. Wesley looked at his watch. Licensing hours had clearly been reduced. They left the pub and made their way back to the digs. They could hear sirens in the distance and looked upwards at searchlight beams criss-crossing the darkness. Wesley could not resist a comment. "So much for decoy sites, then."

Sid, to his credit, thought this very funny.

Wesley rose early the following morning. He dressed quickly and stared out of the window. Judging by the woman walking quickly down the opposite pavement, it looked chilly. Dark clouds threatened rain. He would need his mackintosh.

When he started his drive towards the northern bank of the Humber estuary, in search of the decoy sites that Sid had mentioned, it became clear that Hull had suffered a bit more than the 'bits and bobs' he had spoken of. The evidence was there. Maybe nothing on the scale of the London blitz but less concentrated and more scattered. As he negotiated the city centre and headed east, there were further signs of bomb damage. Rubble in the street, houses without roofs, broken furniture in gardens and on pavements.

CHAPTER 18

Augustin Preucil had scraped his way through his RAF career so far. He had proved himself not as skilled a pilot as they required. He had not completed his training in time to serve in a front-line squadron, and several prangs and a regular flow of disciplinary incidents had further hampered his progress. He had served 'during' the Battle of Britain rather than 'in' it.

His service in the few months since he arrived in Britain had been with Maintenance Units and storage airfields. Much of that time was spent in the south west of the country at Lyneham, Hullavington and Kemble, all within spitting distance of each other. He knew more about replacing engines than fighting the Hun. A short but pleasurable dalliance with an officer's wife got him transferred to Dumfries – about as far away as the Station Commander could get him.

The wronged wife had been smitten with him. His film star looks were a cross he had to bear. She persuaded her husband not to proceed with disciplinary action. So, he kept his stripes and the pay that came with them.

He was thrilled, at last, to see front-line aircraft at Dumfries. There was a hustle and bustle about the place too. The icing on the cake were the ladies of the ATA (Air Transport Auxiliary) who delivered and collected all the many different types of aircraft. Very often, they were obliged to stay overnight. Preucil saw them as his own touring harem.

His disciplinary record had been appalling, as indeed it had been while he had journeyed across France on the final leg of the ratline from Krakow. One thing he had kept to, though, was the commitment to relay information to the handler allotted to him while there. It had been easy. There was so much going on so he was able to spew forth a steady stream of titbits on all manner of Allied activity. He had no intention of continuing with this diligence once he was eventually ensconced in England.

Once there, he had studiously ignored the instruction to send information to this so-called cutout. He had destroyed the name and address that he had been given. As for the reminder to deliver a fighter plane to the *Reich*, that was simply not going to happen. The consequences of non-compliance were spelled out to him again. To no avail - he did not care what happened to anyone he had left behind.

In the words of his screen hero, Clark Gable - a man with whom he increasingly identified - 'Frankly, my dear, I don't give a damn!'

He had covered his tracks well and considered himself untraceable. His only worry now was that his future hung in the balance. The British had struck a blow against the seemingly invincible *Luftwaffe* in the Battle of Britain and invasion fears had now faded, but the war itself was far from over.

His current posting was at an OTU (Operational

Training Unit) in the north-east of England. He was tasked with teaching new pilots in the finer points of aerial warfare. The fact he had never been involved in such engagements, seemed irrelevant.

And he had a girlfriend. Well, truth be told, it had been more than one, but there was now a special girl with whom he saw himself settling down. They loved each other and were soon to be engaged. Marriage would give him legal roots to stay here after the war, should Britain overcome Hitler. Early days, of course, but as a betting man, he knew that's where the clever money was going.

THE POLE, Flight Sergeant Tomasz Gierczak, was proud of his achievements. He had arrived in Britain just as the Battle of Britain was starting, so the length of his training prevented him making an active contribution. He had nevertheless enjoyed being a small part of the Royal Air Force as they thwarted Göring's *Luftwaffe* over the skies of southern England. He had stood and watched as Spitfires and Hurricanes shot German planes out of the sky. It was the first aerial action he had seen since he was shot down and captured at Rakowice in September 1939.

He thought often about the family that he had left behind. He had already missed two of young Tomasz's birthdays and he wondered how Jagoda was coping under the oppressive Nazi occupation. He now knew just how terrible those first few days of invasion had been on the population. He doubted there had been any improvement.

Thinking about them every day had become his sole reason for existence. He had not been given any information to imply that they were alive and well when he was captured. In his darkest moments, he imagined that they were already dead. His fervent desire for revenge was all-consuming and yet his only chance of being reunited with his family lay in following orders.

His diligence and skill had got him a posting to 92 Squadron, based at RAF Biggin Hill in Kent. Its location, just a few miles south of the capital and very close to the English Channel, made it an integral part of the defence of the south coast.

Since he arrived in Britain, Tomasz had duly passed facts and figures on aircraft, squadron movements and airfield decoys to the cutout's address in Barnsley. He also described 'the mood in the camp' that they had requested. As far as the *Abwehr* knew, there was massive dissent. Losses in the air had been devastating and morale was at its lowest ebb ever. The Battle of Britain had taken an immense toll on men and aircraft. Strikes in the factories had led to heavy disruption in the supply of new planes. It was all totally bogus, of course. He had no intention of giving the Germans any genuine information.

Thinking back, the only item of truth that he had passed to them, was his current location. They now knew where he was. He had been told at the outset that 'the jewel in the crown' of his service to them would be the delivery of a fighter plane. Somehow, it gave him hope. He was sure that very soon they would be contacting him somehow to remind him of that obligation. Especially, of course, after he had been so faithful in delivering vital information.

92 Squadron had just taken delivery of the first of its new Spitfire MkVs. They would replace the now antiquated earlier Spitfire variants. Gierczak had had two sorties in the new type. It would break his heart to hand one over to the Germans but he may soon have no choice.

CHAPTER 19

Ernest Metcalf's walk back to Wilkinson's factory the morning after his beating in the yard was painful. On closer inspection though, his wounds were superficial. A few cuts and bruises, no more. The only real casualties were his pride, his suit and his missing cap. He had replacements for the latter two; the pride would need time to heal.

Lizzie was in the office when he arrived. She looked very pleased to see him. He was pleasantly surprised to realise that he had been looking forward to seeing her too. She came to him. "Ernest. I've been so worried about you. Are you alright?"

He smiled. "Oh, I'll heal, don't fret. I may not be as nimble on my feet as I normally am though."

She laughed. "That's a shame. There's a dance on at the drill hall on Saturday. I thought we could shake a leg."

Ernest laughed. "I think not. Anyway, it might be a bit dodgy getting there and back in the blackout."

Lizzie had a twinkle in her eye. "I know." She paused.

"We could have more fun on the way back than we have at the dance."

They both laughed.

"Anyway, you're in no fit state at the moment. Maybe later though, eh?"

He struggled out of his coat and hung it up. When he turned, she was right behind him. "How are your bruises anyway?" She put both hands on his chest and moved in closer. Their faces gradually met.

The door opened and they were instantly apart. It was old man Wilkinson. He looked instantly embarrassed.

"Oh, I'm sorry. I should have knocked."

Ernest was the first of the pair to speak. "No, please don't apologise. I was just telling Mrs Fenwick about my accident. I fell down the stairs at home."

Lizzie stared at him.

Wilkinson laughed. "Oh, dear. You should take a little more water with your drink perhaps." His brows furrowed. "You're alright, I hope?"

"Yes, just a few bruises. Nothing that won't mend."

"Good. Good."

Lizzie gave Ernest a quizzical smile.

Wilkinson remembered why he was in the room. "Ah, yes. I've come to give you some news." He sat in Ernest's vacant chair and faced them. "We have some visitors. They moved in last night. They'll be sharing this floor with you. The three empty rooms. They will keep themselves to themselves. And ... erm, they don't want to be disturbed."

Lizzie spoke. "Who are they, Mr Wilkinson?"

"Oh, they're ... auditors."

As the new company bookkeeper, Ernest was intrigued. "Auditors?"

"Yes. Just to run over the accounts."

Ernest spoke. "The accounts?"

"Yes. My accounts . . . they want to check my overheads. See if I can reduce my costs." Wilkinson laughed but a nervousness was obvious. "But, as I say, they won't bother you, so please don't bother them."

Lizzie piped up. "But how long will they be here?"

The old man was beginning to look like an actor in a cheap melodrama who cannot remember what part he is playing. "Not sure. Just a few weeks I would think. And they'll be working weekends as well. That won't impinge on your work, obviously."

A few seconds passed. He stood. "Now, I must let you two get on." He stopped as he realised how that could be taken. "With work, I mean. I'm sure you've got things . . . work, to do." He left. A few seconds later, they heard his office door close.

Lizzie whispered. "Be careful what you say. That wall behind you is paper thin. It's just a partition. So, no laughing." They both tried to stifle their amusement. She whispered again. "He'll be gone in a few minutes. I think he probably only came in to give us that news."

Back at their separate desks, they talked in vague terms about invoicing, payroll, takings - anything but what was really on their minds since Wilkinson's visit. Lizzie was right. Within minutes, they heard the old man's door close and receding footsteps. Lizzie spun around in her chair and opened her mouth to speak. Ernest cut her off. "What on earth was all that about? Auditors! Does that make sense to you?"

"No. Arthur - your predecessor - used to draw up the accounts then the old man took them to the accountants. Then a few months later, the old man would ask me to write a cheque to the Inland Revenue. And that's it." She paused. "I don't even know what auditors do. Do you?"

Ernest laughed. "I do. In fact, I'm qualified as an auditor."

"Ooh, you're a dark horse. So . . . go on, what does an auditor do?"

"They look at the accounts after they've been prepared . . . just to see if they're legal. The tax people often use them if they suspect that they're not accurate . . . or dishonest."

Lizzie gasped. "Bloody hell. Do you think the Inland Revenue is looking at Wilkinson's accounts?"

Ernest laughed. "I'd be very surprised. He gave me last year's accounts to look at after my interview and they looked perfectly fine. That was just a cursory glance, mind you. Which makes it all a bit odd."

They returned quietly to the job in hand.

Ernest looked up. "I'll tell you something else that's a bit odd."

Lizzie looked across. "What?"

"I've never known auditors work at weekends."

THE NEXT COUPLE of hours passed with explanations from Lizzie about how they did the payroll. Ernest was about to ask a question when they heard noises coming from one of the rooms along the corridor. They stopped what they were doing and each pressed an ear to the door, facing each other. The noises seemed to be electrical whines, heavy drilling and strange buzzes. They subsided and were replaced by intermittent, low male voices. Then silence.

Neither of them moved for a very long minute. Ernest could have stayed there forever. Their faces were just inches apart and he could feel the warmth of Lizzie's body. He broke away as the noise level dropped.

"That's the trouble with auditors. They're such a noisy rabble."

Lizzie giggled. "Exactly what I was thinking. It sounds like something from outer space."

"I know. Why don't you go to the toilet and have a good listen on your way?"

"Good idea."

Ernest whispered. "But don't get caught listening at the door!"

She stifled a laugh as she left the office and gently closed the door behind her. He heard Lizzie's heels tapping along the corridor and the toilet door opening and closing. After a few seconds, a door opened and he heard two or three heavier steps on the corridor. Had they heard Lizzie walking past on her way to the toilet?

Two minutes later, the toilet door opened and he heard Lizzie's heels again.

A male voice. "Hello. Can I stop you for a minute?"

"Of course."

"Can I ask who you are?"

"I'm Mrs Fenwick. I work here."

A few seconds pause. "Oh, yes. Sorry to have bothered you."

"And you must be the auditors that Mr Wilkinson told us about?"

A pause before the male voice answered. "Auditors . . . yes, that's right." The voice continued. This time cheerier, less officious. "Well, I'd better get on."

"Of course. Me too."

Then a pause as the other door closed and the heels

continued. Lizzie came back into the office. She looked flustered.

"Here, sit down." He took her hand and guided her to a chair. He waited as she got her composure back.

"Well?"

She blew out a long breath and fanned her face with a hand. "That was a bit weird."

"Weird? How?"

"Well, they don't *look* like auditors for a kick off. I'm guessing they don't normally wear overalls."

Ernest laughed. "No. But we never really thought they were auditors, did we?"

"We didn't. You were right about that. So, who are they? And what are they doing here?"

"Good question. Did you see anything?"

"Not much. Just a glimpse as he went back through the door . . ."

"And?"

"Hold your horses!" She sighed. "Not much really. Just a long bench with, like, bits of machinery. Dials. All that sort of thing."

"You seemed to take him by surprise when you asked him if they were auditors."

She laughed. "I know."

"They sound more like scientists to me."

CHAPTER 20

L izzie was in the habit of popping into the corner shop across from the factory every lunchtime. Old man Wilkinson gave her a petty cash account which was to be used for biscuits only. An admission of his sweet tooth which Lizzie shared. Despite the shortages, Mr Shrimplin always managed to keep a packet under the counter for her. He knew how much business he got from the factory lasses. He put a packet on the counter.

"You don't have to ask, Lizzie. I'm running low but I've put a couple back for you."

She fiddled in her purse for the few coppers he needed. "That's very kind. Thank you."

"No problem. Can't be sure I'll always be able to do it, mind. Who knows how long this bloody war is going to last. Sorry. Pardon my French."

He took the pennies from her and leant across. "I see you've got visitors over there." He looked at her expectantly.

"Oh, yes. They're auditors. But how did you know?"

Shrimplin laughed. "Auditors? You're joking aren't you?"

Lizzie was puzzled. Even though she and Ernest were

pretty convinced that the visitors were not auditors, how could he know? She did not know what to say. The shopkeeper dropped his voice and looked around before speaking.

"It's the Royal Navy, pet. We watched them moving in. Loads of equipment. Big lorry. And . . ."

He walked around the counter and walked to the door, beckoning her to follow. He pointed across the road to King Street. "See that car. The navy blue one? That's a navy staff car or I'm a monkey's uncle." He walked back behind the counter as Lizzie stared at the car. "Don't know why I'm being careful about what I'm saying. They were hardly making a secret of it. Oh, and there was a Swan Hunters van. Wouldn't take a genius to work out what's happening, would it?"

In flagrant contravention of the 'Careless Talk Costs Lives' poster on the back of the door, he continued to give Lizzie the composite version of events that had been concocted to explain the arrival and presence of the Royal Navy at Wilkinson's factory.

According to him and every customer with whom he had discussed the issue, these were navy boffins who had been working at Swans. Everybody knew that all of the shipyards on the Tyne were prime targets so they were probably looking for somewhere a bit safer. He reckoned that 'auditors' was their cover story. To be fair though, short of painting the word 'Auditors' in big letters on the side of the vehicles, there was no way their identity could be disguised. He was still laughing at his own joke when the door opened and the man who had spoken to her in the corridor walked in. He smiled and walked past her to the counter.

Shrimplin had stopped laughing.

. . .

WHEN LIZZIE RETURNED to the office, Ernest was at his desk reading the *Daily Mirror.*

"You look flustered, Lizzie. What is it?"

She took off her coat, put the biscuits on her desk while she tried to collect her senses. Ernest looked puzzled. She put both hands on his desk and pointed at the door. "They're not auditors, Ernest."

He laughed. "We know that, don't we?"

"They're . . .". Her voice dropped to a whisper. "They're Royal Navy."

"What?" Ernest put the paper down.

Lizzie sat in her chair, turned it to face him and gave a verbatim account of what had happened in the shop. "And then the bloke who was talking to me in the corridor came in. But Shrimplin had finished his story by then, thank goodness."

Drilling noises had started up again. They both looked at the door and then at each other.

"What do you think, Ernest?"

The man's thoughts were racing. The shopkeeper's tale sounded plausible. The evidence for their visitors being Royal Navy personnel seemed irrefutable. The noises coming from down the corridor certainly pointed to scientific activity of some kind. The Swan Hunters lorry also seemed to indicate where they had come from.

"Well, I think the old man's insistence that they are auditors is dead in the water, for sure."

They both laughed.

"But if they are involved in some kind of secret work, then I think we should just keep mum, don't you?" He paused. "And Shrimplin would have been in big trouble if that chap had walked in a couple of minutes earlier. These are dangerous times, Lizzie."

He remembered that she was a war widow. Her eyes had misted over. He came from behind his desk, bent down and hugged her. "I'm sorry. You know that already."

Lizzie took a handkerchief from her pocket and wiped her eyes. Ernest repeated his apology.

"No, it's alright, really. And thank you for being so sensitive. Not all men are, you know."

The hug was easing but she pulled him back in. He could feel her hot breath in his left ear as she whispered. "Why don't we go for a drink tonight?"

"Yes. I'd like that."

They separated. Lizzie turned her chair back towards her desk and Ernie returned to his. They arranged to meet at the *Crane House* pub that evening. The venue was her idea. This was new territory for Ernest. He was beginning to realise what a sheltered life he had so far led.

BEFORE ERNEST COULD SALLY FORTH on their romantic tryst that evening, he desperately needed to go to the family home. He was still wearing the suit jacket that was torn when he was beaten up in the stable yard on his first day. His uncle had stitched the fabric together, after a fashion, but the garment now more resembled something you would wrap around yourself in a high wind, than something you would be proud to wear. He still had some clothes at Queen Alexandra Road. He would call in, take his mother some flowers and raid his wardrobe.

He and Lizzie, in the absence of old man Wilkinson, decided to leave half an hour early and then meet up later at the pub. She pointed him in the direction of a florists where he could get some freesias. He nipped in to borrow his uncle's bike and pedalled swiftly to his parents' house. He had strapped the flowers precariously to the handlebars and twenty minutes later, he was freewheeling the last few yards to the gate of the family home in Queen Alexandra Road. Miraculously, the floral gift had coped with the trip better than he had. He was drenched in sweat.

He saw his mother peering through the net curtains of the bay window. She rushed to the front door and flung it open. While still buried in her embrace, he bent and extracted the flowers from the bike.

"Oh, Ernst. They are delightful. How thoughtful." She kissed him again and he felt tears on her cheek. "I thought you had forgotten about me. Go and sit down while I put these in water."

He closed the front door behind him and went into the living room while she disappeared into the kitchen. She was back almost before he had sat down. She took a seat in the armchair opposite him.

"Now, how is your new job going? I have missed you, Ernst."

There were tears in her eyes. He was wracked with guilt. He had promised that he would pop back at every opportunity and her obvious pain at his failure to do so was palpable. He started to speak but she was suddenly sobbing. He knelt by her side and cradled her head in his arms, before taking out his handkerchief to quench her tears. As he held it to her, she turned her head away from him. Her weeping had not subsided. She took the handkerchief from him and held it to her brow.

"What is it, *Mutti*?"

She attempted a smile but failed. The handkerchief remained on her brow, above her still streaming eyes.

"It's nothing, really. A scratch."

Ernest reached across and gently prised the cloth from her hands. He saw a three or four-inch wound across her forehead. It had started to scab over but it looked deep. Almost bad enough for stitches, he thought. "How on earth did you do that?"

He allowed his mother a few moments to compose herself. Calmer now, she began to answer his question. "I was attacked."

Ernest could feel sudden anger bubbling to the surface. "Who did this?"

Stumbling in her telling of the tale, his mother recounted how she had been walking to the park for her daily exercise when a man on a bicycle rode alongside her and called her a 'Nazi bitch'. As she turned to look at him, he stopped and swung his metal sandwich box at her.

"I'm rather nervous about stepping across the doorstep now."

Ernest hugged her. "But mother, who was he? Did you recognise him? Have you reported it to the police?"

"No, I don't know who he was. And he was gone in a second."

"The coward."

"And your father doesn't want any fuss."

Ernest's anger was now fully visible. She grabbed his arms. "And please, Ernst, do not mention this to him. He would not be pleased." She paused. "It will soon be healed. And any scar will be hidden by my fringe."

She smiled and flicked at the hair which almost covered the wound. Ernest was lost for words. That his father should not be as outraged as he was by this assault on the woman he loved was unconscionable. He stood his mother up and pulled her to him. Their embrace, he in mental turmoil, she in loving warmth and gratitude at his attention, lasted a full minute. Ernest was the one to withdraw.

"And where is father?"

"You've just missed him. He's at one of his Rotary meetings."

Ernest snorted in disgust. "Rotary!" His respect for his father had plummeted. It was still there – for what he had achieved, for the home he had provided for them all – but what he now saw as toadying to the English, rather than standing up for himself and his wife, was changing his attitude towards him. His uncle was right. This was a miserable nation.

He collected what clothing he needed, reassured his mother that he would not 'cause a fuss' and bade her a loving goodbye. He promised that it would not be long before his next visit. How he would face his father when next they met was something he would have to work on.

THE *CRANE HOUSE* was close to the fish quay. Ernest was worried at first that he would be recognised there, as he had been on his first day at Wilkinson's, as a second-generation German and, therefore, a justifiable target. It did not happen but the earlier meeting with his mother and the shock at hearing that she had been assaulted was still heavy on his mind. He had previously seen his uncle's anti-British invective as the ravings of an embittered old man. Now he was more firmly in Freddie's camp. His father's attitude - of appeasement almost - was making matters worse.

Once he caught sight of Lizzie and as the alcohol started to flow – within the limits of the pub's meagre stock – he felt his mood lifting. Away from the work scenario, she gave him her life story. How an unplanned pregnancy had plunged her headlong into marriage and motherhood; how she became a very early war widow; how her father died in an accident at Swan Hunters just a few months later. He knew some of her story already but she shared the details with him and the emotions behind the facts.

As the conversation turned away from her family, she talked of her good friend Muriel who worked in Joe Wilkinson's lemonade factory in Sunderland. Joe was old man Wilkinson's younger brother. Although his business was smaller than the one in North Shields, the two brothers helped each other out whenever there were personnel or stock and supply issues. As a result, the staff of both factories knew each other well. It had developed into the extended Wilkinson family.

It had become the 'family' custom over recent years to have a joint annual coach outing. The destination – normally a coastal town like Saltburn to the south, or along the Tyne valley to Corbridge or Hexham – was immaterial. It was an excuse for a good knees-up with all food and alcohol provided by the Wilkinson brothers. The practice had been suspended for the duration but she and Muriel had maintained their friendship by letter.

"I actually got one from her this morning. She's invited me across to meet her boyfriend."

"Oh. Where?"

"Near where she lives. Sunderland. Her boyfriend is in the RAF based at Usworth. She doesn't 'arf go on about him. Says he looks like Cary Grant. Brooding looks, you know."

Ernest tried to effect a film star look and failed spectacularly. Lizzie laughed. "Why don't you come with me?"

"Oh, are you sure?"

"Of course. She said I could bring somebody." She paused. "*I* can show off then, can't I?"

It was Ernest's turn to laugh. She punched him on the arm. "Well, can't have her getting all the glory, can I?"

"Hmm. That will be our second date, then." He stroked his chin.

She laughed. "Who knows? It could be our third or fourth by then."

Lizzie took a sip on her drink. Ernest felt he was being swept up in something but he was a willing participant.

"Well, that's fine by me, Mrs Fenwick."

He leant across to kiss her. Lizzie wrapped both arms around his neck and responded in full. After a minute of growing passion, they started to attract an audience. An older woman, rather the worse for wear, shouted across the room. "Howay, pet. Leave him alone. They're on ration, yer knaa?"

That drew everyone's attention to the pair of them and more comments followed, some none too clean. Lizzie stood and pulled Ernest to his feet. As they left, she turned and smiled shyly at the now rapt audience.

They ran up the bank toward the centre of town with the river behind them and the laughter still ringing in their ears. Ernest pulled Lizzie roughly into a dark alleyway and, now alone, they carried on where they had left off.

It was late by the time he found his way back to the Nile Street flat. Despite living in the town all his life, Ernest had never really known his way around it. His sense of direction was not good, especially in the blackout. It was almost eleven o'clock when he finally put his key in the lock, opened the street door and closed it gently behind him. Even from the bottom of the stairs, he could hear snoring.

He moved quietly around the flat. He noticed that his

uncle had not drawn the blackout curtains. He must have dozed off before the official hour. He pulled the black material across the windows and switched on the lamp. It cast a yellow glow across his uncle's face. He grunted, wiped a hand across his eyes and sat upright in the chair.

Freddie cleared his throat. "What time is it?"

"Eleven o'clock. Why don't you get yourself to bed? But I'm glad you're up. I have some news, uncle."

His uncle was wide awake now and excited. "It will not be as exciting as mine!" The old man stood and lifted the armchair cushion. Underneath was a pile of letters. He pulled the top one from the rubber band holding them together. "Read this."

Ernest looked at the envelope. "Who do you know in Sweden, uncle?"

Freddie waved impatiently. "Never mind that. Just read it!"

His nephew withdrew the letter and started to read before handing it back to Freddie. "It's in German, uncle. You know my German is not good."

Freddie read it to him in English. By the time he had finished, Ernest's mouth had dropped open. Silence reigned for a few seconds as Freddie put the letter back in the envelope and replaced it into his stash under the cushion. Triumph was written on his face. "So, what do you think?"

Ernest was confused. He laughed. "Uncle, what have you done. Who is Jan?"

His uncle laughed. "*Ach!* It's a long story, *Neffe*."

Ernest was intrigued. "Then tell me it. Jan has mentioned *me*, for God's sake. I need some sort of explanation."

Freddie took it slowly and his nephew did not interrupt. Jan was some sort of cousin, by the sound of it, living in

Amsterdam and working for the occupying Nazis. The 'pretty pictures' referred to in the letter were his uncle's artistic portrayals of naval ships under construction at the Swan Hunter shipyard, just a couple of miles away from North Shields on the north bank of the Tyne.

He had made himself known to the security people at the yard and ingratiated himself by doing drawings from photographs of their wives, their children and their pets, whilst - illegally - also depicting activity at the yard. The latter were sent to Jan who had passed them on to the *Gestapo*. Jan obviously had an axe to grind - and a desire for promotion up the slippery Nazi pole.

But now things had escalated. Freddie had put his nephew in the frame as 'another pair of friendly eyes' and that had been the tipping point. They were being sent a wireless.

It appeared that he and his uncle had become German spies.

Freddie was smiling. He pointed at his nephew. "This, *mein Neffe*, is how you will get revenge for the appalling treatment you have received over the last few days."

Ernest was attempting to digest everything that was happening. He decided not to tell his uncle about the assault on his mother – and his father's decision not to rock the boat. He knew it would simply light his uncle's fuse. In the position they were now in, it was best to keep a low profile. If Freddie chose to vent his spleen on his brother, Frank, it could jeopardise the new espionage undertaking that they were apparently about to embark upon. It was far too risky.

Instead, he launched into what he had discovered at the factory. He relayed the events of the day, and by the end of the tale about the so-called auditors and what it appeared they now might be, Freddie's eyes had widened and his jaw had dropped.

"You think they are making a secret weapon?"

Ernest laughed. "I don't know, do I? There's only one way to find out."

Freddie looked confused. "How?"

"I'm going to stay late one night. After everyone's gone, I'll take a look."

His uncle clapped his hands with glee. "You would do that?"

"Of course. Everyone finishes very early. And I can't see these boffins being any different."

Ernest started to explain the meaning of boffin but his uncle cut him off tetchily. He clapped his hands joyfully.

"Ernst, I am so pleased you have come round to my way of thinking. And this information will really please Jan and his friends." He stared at his nephew. "And we can pass on what you find out to the *Reich*. By wireless now."

"Ha! Well, we haven't got one yet, have we? But once it arrives, then we have reached the point of no return, uncle. It's not a game any longer."

"I never thought it was. Did you?"

"I suppose not. But we are now talking about a wireless set being delivered to our door by a Nazi spy."

"Is that bad?" His uncle looked worried.

Ernest laughed. "Only if he gets caught and is forced to divulge the recipient of the wireless set." His uncle's mouth fell open again. His nephew continued. "It's starting to look like a one-man operation this, isn't it though? And that one man is me."

"I will do what I can, you know that. I am really good at Morse Code now. Since I got the letter, I have been practising." He paused. "With a pencil. On the table."

Ernest laughed. "Well, there's nothing we can do about any of it at the moment. I'm sure our new agent friend will have advice on all of these matters. I just hope . . ." He paused.

"What?"

"I just hope he doesn't look too . . . well, German."

"Don't be silly, Ernst. He will at least have the sense not to arrive dressed as a nun or something."

His uncle clapped him on the shoulders. "Don't worry. I'm going to bed. Oh, your father asked me to remind you that you haven't been back to see your mother since you moved in with me. And I am somehow getting the blame."

Ernest accepted his uncle's mild rebuke, without revealing that he had already visited his mother, just hours earlier. His father had obviously given Freddie the message before that.

He realised suddenly that a loan of his father's Vauxhall – which had been laid up at the onset of war – might not be a bad idea. It would be useful on two counts – romantic drives into the countryside with Lizzie, and an aid to his and his uncle's new career. Another visit to the family home was on the cards.

CHAPTER 21

Ernest woke the following morning with his mind in turmoil. His first thought was of Lizzie. Their night out had made him realise that he had not been living a full life until now. Despite the setbacks Lizzie had seen, she was so spirited and full of joy and humour. She had expanded his spectrum of experience. Already he was looking forward to seeing her again.

It was not only this new romantic – and now physical – relationship that was causing this exciting disturbance to his equilibrium. Until recently, he had been cloistered in a boring, mundane job with nothing to lighten his days. Now, thanks to living with his uncle and his experiences at the factory, he had seen the error of his ways in denying his German roots.

Although he had never previously thought of himself as anything but British, they had both now become enemy spies. A growing realisation that they were simply not welcome here – the evidence was there in abundance – had convinced him that what he had earlier viewed as the amusing rantings of an embittered old man, were based in truth. What he suspected was going on at the factory would surely help the German war effort and it seemed comparatively low risk.

THE FOLLOWING EVENING, after work, Ernest borrowed his uncle's bike again and made his way to his parents' home. He was hot and sweaty when he arrived. He saw his father's bicycle by the side of the house. Ernest was not looking forward to this encounter.

No sooner had Ernest removed his cycle clips, than his father came out of the front door to greet him. He was not smiling.

"So, Ernest, you visit two days running."

Ernest smiled despite the frosty welcome. "Yes, I have a favour to ask."

"Then you'd better come in."

Father and son walked in and through to the living room. His mother was sitting where she had been a day earlier. She looked tired and there was none of the enthusiasm she had shown on the previous day's visit. Ernest realised that, with his mother present and mindful of the promise he had made to her, he would not be able to confront his father about his unwillingness to make a fuss about the attack on his wife. There was a tension in the air that was palpable.

Ernest bent to hug his mother. She understood what it meant. As he sat down, he saw that his father was looking at his watch.

"I only have a few minutes, Ernest."

His son bit the bullet. "I was hoping I could borrow the car, father."

Frank looked surprised. Ernest pushed on. He told them

both that he was walking out with a young lady. His mother's joy returned. He told them about Lizzie, but carefully omitted that she was a war widow with a small child. He felt that could wait.

His father had his standard look of mere guarded approval at what most people would see as good news. Ernest turned to him and said he would like to take Lizzie out into the countryside now and again, and that he had use of the petrol coupons which Mr Wilkinson had given him. His mother clapped her hands at the thought and looked at her husband. Frank was clearly in a corner.

Ernest was thinking ahead – to a time when they may need to move the wireless set that was now on its way to them, either to operate it in another location or to dispose of it altogether. Sitting on a bus with the set across his knees would, he was sure, raise more than the odd eyebrow.

Frank eventually agreed to the loan of the car but said it would need a bit of work. The battery needed recharging, the wheels replacing and the tank filling. He promised to do that within a couple of days and leave it at the shop when it was ready. "And now, I must go and get changed."

With a perfunctory handshake and nod of the head, his father left the room. As soon as he was gone, his mother stood and wrapped her arms around Ernest. There were tears in her eyes.

"Thank you, Ernst."

"For what?"

"For keeping your promise not to mention my little mishap to your father."

He laughed. "Mishap?"

She put her fingers to his lips and whispered. "No more. It is finished."

Before he could object, she told him how pleased she

was to hear of his young lady and how she hoped it would not be too long before she could meet Lizzie. He assured her it would be soon. He also reflected that his father might also be pleased at the news. Confirmation, almost, that his son was on the right side, with an English girlfriend, after all.

Son and mother said their goodbyes, and Ernest cycled back to the flat in buoyant mood. He felt that he and his uncle were ready for whatever this espionage caper would throw at them. His uncle was right. *Rache* would be *süss*, indeed. It was for his mother now.

CHAPTER 22

Peter Armitage had ridden his battered bicycle all the way from his home in Hessle to the north bank of the Humber estuary. After his exciting chat with Mr Salter at the Punch Hotel the day before, he was keen to impress him with even more information on these decoy sites.

He headed for a spot known as Cherry Cobb Sands, close to the mouth of the estuary. He knew the north bank well. As a keen ornithologist, he often made the trip downstream from the city and out towards Kilnsea and Spurn Point.

On a previous visit to Cherry Cobb, he had witnessed the digging of what looked like massive pits and the building of wooden and canvas structures. There was a network of posts, twenty feet high, from which heavy cables ran overground to brick-built bunkers.

He knew they were decoy sites. The work had been going on for a long time at this and other sites. He had reported his earliest sightings to the German Embassy in London, before realising that it was evacuated as soon as war was declared. A worrying few months elapsed before he was contacted by Geoffrey Salter - Hitler's man in London - at the Punch Hotel and he had been rewarded for his diligence.

He was impressed by the man's credentials. German preparations for the invasion were clearly well advanced. Anything he could do to assist would surely serve him well. For the first time in his life, he would have achieved something.

The ride out was long and uncomfortable, made worse by intermittent rain showers and sudden spells of sunshine which caused steam to rise from his tweed jacket. He stopped to struggle into his oilskin rain-cape but all he achieved was to create a pressure cooker atmosphere. By the time he arrived at the run-down beach café, perspiration had soaked every item of clothing.

He leant his bicycle against a wooden fence, out of sight of those working on the site. He pulled off his cape, draped it over the bike and put his cycle clips into his jacket pocket. He checked the contents of the wicker basket fastened to his handlebars – field glasses, notebook, three pencils – H, HB and F - and a pencil-sharpener, a dog-eared copy of *The Observer's Book of British Birds* and some egg and tomato sandwiches wrapped in greaseproof paper.

This was the third trip he had made to this particular site. He had been seen on his last visit and they had called him over to question him. Satisfied that he was there merely to observe the birds – he showed them his book as proof – they seemed satisfied and walked away, with a gentle warning not to come too close to where they were working. He was now becoming part of the scenery. As integral to the landscape as a clump of dune grass. Hiding in plain sight.

He lay down on his stomach atop a mound of grass.

Making sure he had his notebook and *Observer's* book open, with a pencil ready, he put the field glasses to his eyes and focused on the construction site.

He suddenly heard grunts and scuffling behind him. A large man in a mackintosh slumped down beside him.

"Hello"

Armitage rose to his knees.

"Sorry, I didn't mean to disturb you. I just thought . . ."

Both men got to their feet.

"You thought what?", Armitage said, trying to conceal his rising panic.

"I just wondered what you were doing here?"

Armitage was stunned. Who was this man? His voice sounded out of place for the area. He talked like a toff. "I'm a bird watcher", he managed to reply. "Look". He held up his book like a child defending some sort of discovered misdemeanour.

The other man smiled. "Of course, you are." He lay back down onto the springy tufts. "I've always been interested in birds. What have you seen today?"

Armitage nervously rejoined him on the ground. "Oh . . . sea birds mainly." What a ridiculous thing to say. This man will think he's talking to an idiot and, even worse, not a genuine ornithologist. Not confident he could string two words together any more, he raised his field glasses towards the work site. He could feel, more than hear, his book being picked up and pages flicking.

"That's odd", he heard the stranger say. He put his glasses down and turned his head.

"What is?"

"Well . . . I can't see a single sea bird. Strikes me those chaps are making too much noise for them to settle. There are some circling though, look." He pointed to the sky where three or four birds were constantly patrolling the area. "I reckon they're a bit peeved that their nests are in danger."

"Maybe so", replied Armitage, turning back to his field glasses.

"What are they doing anyway, do you think?"

Armitage was confused. What were *who* doing? The birds or the workmen? He asked the man that very question.

"The men, of course"

"I don't know."

The man rolled over and laid on his back, gazing at the sky.

"I know what they're doing." He turned his head and switched his attention to Armitage. "And I think you do, too. You might fool those red-necked squaddies over there but you don't fool me, old bean."

Armitage found himself totally unable to move, let alone speak. The man in the mackintosh jumped to his feet and wiped himself down. "Come on, old chap. Looks like it's going to rain again and I've got a nice warm car over there with a Thermos flask full of tea."

With that, he walked away and disappeared over the brow of the dunes. Armitage collected his belongings, stuffed them back into the wicker basket and followed him. The car's passenger door was already open. He stowed his baggage into the footwell and got in. The driver stared out of the windscreen. He was tall and made the space behind the steering wheel appear cramped. Armitage stared ahead too. It had indeed started to rain heavily again. He was suddenly grateful for the shelter.

The man turned and smiled at Armitage. "Don't worry,

old son. I'm on your side." He paused for a reaction. "I think I've seen you here before, haven't I?"

Armitage grunted. He was still trying to work out this man's voice. The words were straight out of a gentleman's club. A relaxed upper-class drawl spoken with the lazy confidence of privilege.

"What are you thinking, old chap? That you've been rumbled?"

"Listen, I . . . I'm a bird watcher. I . . ."

The man laughed uncontrollably. "A bird watcher!" He laughed again. "You think that fools anyone? Not even a simple country bobby would be taken in by that."

Armitage held up his book again, hoping that the fierce-looking hen harrier on the front cover would reinforce the point.

The man turned to his passenger. "I watch people like you. Mr . . . erm?"

"Armitage. Peter Armitage. But who are you?"

He laughed. "Why don't you just call me . . . Mr Smith, eh? Cards on the table. You were wondering what the hell those blokes were doing digging pits in the soil, weren't you?" He paused. "Decoy sites, I reckon? Don't you?"

The birdspotter knew he had been sussed. This chap knew more than Armitage about what he had been looking at through his field glasses. They *were* decoy sites. Their intention was to divert German bombers from their targets.

This particular one at the charmingly titled Cherry Cobb Sands involved the excavation of pits to the exact shape and configuration of the docks further along the bank, in Hull. The poles would bear lights which would reflect on the surface of the water. At a few thousand feet up, from the cockpit of a *Heinkel* or *Dornier*, and in the dark, all perspective would be lost.

There was suddenly steel in the other man's voice. "I know what you're up to."

To Armitage's surprise, the man started up the engine and drove slowly away. Nothing more was said. After an offer to drop him in Hull where he could get a bus home, the rest of the journey was passed in silence. As the car pulled into Queen Victoria Square, he spoke again. "This do you?"

Armitage turned to look at him and started to reply. The man was smiling. As if to reassure him, he simply added "Don't panic, old chum. I can assure you we're both on the same side." He paused. "Tell you what, why don't we meet up somewhere a bit less conspicuous than a damned decoy site. Give me your address and I'll stick a time and place through your door. How does that sound?"

The other man nodded meekly. A small notepad was thrust at Armitage. He slid the pencil from the side of the pad, wrote down his address and handed it back.

"Good. Now, this place . . ." He pointed at the Punch Hotel just a few yards in front of where he had parked. "This seems a good place to meet, don't you think? Nice and central. So that's where we'll meet." He looked across at Armitage who seemed stunned by the events of the last half hour. He patted him on the shoulder.

"Don't worry! Now, if you don't mind, I need to be somewhere else."

Armitage gathered up his belongings, desperately wanting to ask the obvious question. *Which* side are we both on? He thought better of it and took refuge in silence. As he mumbled a goodbye and lifted the wicker basket from the car, the other man leant across.

"I'll be in touch. I only live in Gillett Street. Toodlepip."

With that, the door closed and the car moved slowly into

the stream of traffic. Armitage stood transfixed. He was facing the Punch Hotel across the road. He noticed Her Majesty and Empress, Queen Victoria, glistening in the rain. The car was turning right into Carr Lane and slipping from view.

He turned away and felt for his bicycle clips in his jacket pocket. Realising that he had left his bike at the decoy site, he whirled around and ran to the corner of the road. He could still see the car. He ran down the middle of the road past a parked bus and chased after it, waving his hands in the air and hoping that he could attract the man's attention in his rear-view mirror.

"I've left my bike at Cherry Cobb Sands . . ."

The car did not slow down. He stopped shouting. The bus beeped its horn as it pulled away from the stop. People were staring. On the pavement. On the bus. From office windows.

CHAPTER 23

The day after Wesley's meeting with the 'bird watcher' at the Humber estuary decoy site, he received his first mail since he had arrived in Britain. He assumed the landlady must have stuffed it under his door. It was large envelope, postmarked Barnsley, with a printed pink heart in the top left-hand corner of the envelope. He smiled - Frau Viggle's lonely hearts club, as mentioned by Grosskopf as one of the cutouts in play.

Inside the envelope was a smaller one. It contained several sheets of closely-typed names and addresses. British Union of Fascists membership records. He was aware that the organisation no longer existed - so this detail of former members was gold dust.

The last page, however, soon soured his mood. It was a handwritten note from Otto Ziegler, detailing a direct order from *Major* Grosskopf that he must visit the Siemens-Schuckert factory at Brentford again. This time it was to pick up *another* wireless set which was due to be delivered to North Shields. He totted up the mileage and the time needed. What did they take him for? A delivery driver?

As he seethed, he turned on the domestic wireless. He waited for it to warm up so that he could check the volume, then scanned the BUF list for anything local. They were mainly in urban centres. Notably, he saw none listed in Hull. He could not believe there were none in a large city like this. Or, had they sensibly destroyed membership records before they were rounded up for internment the previous year? There could be dozens of them, wandering around rudderless.

He listened at the door and locked it. The wireless was playing away merrily. He bent down, extracted the Siemens set from under the bed and keyed in to contact Otto. He relayed the message that he had heard from Frau Viggle and that he would look at her shopping list. The reply was that it was compliments of Grosskopf and that Leeds was a good starting point.

He passed on the information that he had already made a contact in Hull which he was working on. Finally, he made the point of how much this proposed trip from Hull to Brentford, then North Shields and back to Hull was going to cost him in lost opportunities. He asked Otto to pass on his displeasure in the strongest possible terms.

Wesley returned the set to its appointed place, lay back on the bed and looked at the BUF list more closely, concentrating on Leeds, which he knew was only a couple of hours' drive away. There were a few hundred individuals listed. His eyes were caught by the name 'Windsor, Reginald'. He chuckled to himself. A disgruntled member of the Royal Family, perhaps? A close friend, maybe, of the Duke of Windsor, the title conferred on King Edward VIII after his abdication in 1936. The Duke was notorious for his admiration of the *Führer*.

And 'Reginald', for goodness' sake. If the etymology of

that was not something pertaining to ruler or king, he would eat his hat. Otto and Grosskopf would love that. He would use the word 'crown' as code for this individual and see how quickly they worked it out. He chuckled again. He was starting to enjoy this.

WINDSOR'S ADDRESS was on the list so he decided that he would call on him today. It would be a nice run out. A different car would be needed, though. Maybe something more modest than his current galloping steed. A few less gee-gees under the bonnet as befitting a lower social status. And dress down. Remembering that he had brought several items of headgear with him, he looked in his wardrobe and found a cloth cap - and a sparse wig. They would be ideal. He laughed. He could always hire a whippet on the way.

And voice. He would have to ditch the patrician accent that he had used on Armitage. It would not sit well with the cap. The only northern accent he was familiar with was the Hull one he had come to know since he arrived. He tried it in the mirror, with cap akimbo. It would pass muster. He may not need it, of course, especially as he would, after the foreplay, be presenting as what he actually was - an English German spy. Presenting himself as a common northerner and then switching to his normal voice before showcasing his German would, he was sure, seal the deal identity-wise.

He slipped the sheets back into their envelope and looked around the room for somewhere to hide it. There was a mat that covered most of the floor area. It did not look as if it had had any attention for several long years. The pattern had long since disappeared. He pulled back the edge nearest to the window and placed the envelope under it as far as it would go. He felt it was a safe enough hiding place.

Suddenly remembering his unfinished business with Peter Armitage, that sniffy little twitcher whom he had met at the decoy site, he scribbled a note suggesting the time and date of a meeting at the Punch Hotel a few days hence. He took the other envelope from the bed - the outer one with his address on - and stuffed the note inside. He doctored it so that his address was missing and folded the envelope around it. He looked at the address that the man had written on his pad, and copied it onto what remained of the envelope. He remembered, to his regret, that he had stupidly told the man that he lived in Gillett Street but it would not do to remind him. That was a lesson learned.

The man lived in Hessle. He smiled. That was on his way out. He put on his mackintosh and cloth cap and smiled at himself in the mirror. This Leeds mission had success written all over it.

Once it was over, he would head down to Brentford.

CHAPTER 24

S tokes' first visit to a Reginald Windsor BUF meeting in Leeds had been one of the most uncomfortable he had experienced in his short career as infiltrator. As Secretary of the North Leeds branch of the BUF, Windsor was aggrieved at the outlawing of the organisation. Like many across the country, Stokes guessed, Windsor and his cronies were now doing their amateur 'bit' for the cause of British fascism. So far, that had amounted to a few botched attempts at fire-raising in the hope that their efforts would be seen by German bombers.

What the MI5 man had not figured on was the keenness for Windsor to display Stokes as a prize catch - Hitler's own man in England and the head of *Einsatzgruppe London*. He paraded him at one of his weekly back-shop meetings. A number of his ex-BUF colleagues, had subjected him to intense cross-examination.

Stokes claimed he had been a BUF member. A lot of their questions had therefore centred on officials he could name, which of them had been arrested and which branches they were from. The fact that Stokes was obviously a southerner meant that he could claim ignorance of much that had taken place further north. He majored on names and positions of those closer to the capital. At Knight's insistence and under his tutelage, he had done his homework. Knowledge of the BUF that he had gleaned from him had been his salvation. He was also able to throw in one or two anecdotes about those who had been arrested. A little colour never did any harm.

With his now well-practised bonhomie and pleasant disposition, he had convinced them of his *bona fides*. He had shown them his *Durchlassschein* - the German document which was so expertly forged by MI5 that Stokes was convinced it would have got him anywhere in Nazi Germany, with the possible exception of a private *tête à tête* with the *Führer*. This had reinforced the trust they had in him. There were some individuals present at that meeting who had not been there at the earlier ones. He sensed an openness that had not been there before.

WESLEY KNEW nothing of this when he walked into *his* first back-shop clandestine gathering. Aside from Windsor himself, whose acceptance he had secured in a number of conversations since his first visit, there were stern looks from the outset. He was about to undergo the same baptism of fire that Stokes had managed to survive.

Clearly, as it had been with Stokes, their initial thoughts were that he could be an MI5 infiltrator trying to identify and eradicate the remnants of the pro-Nazi British fascist movement. Wesley's aim was to inform them that he was an agent for the *Abwehr* and to ask for their help in the coming invasion.

It did not start well. He got the distinct feeling that he

was auditioning. The problem was that his chosen piece had already been seen by this set of jaded casting agents and they were acting as if they had seen it before. One of the men listening actually yawned. At one point there was stone cold silence. One of the attendees, a rather hard-faced chubby chap at the back, spoke up.

"You're not German, then?"

"No. I am British by birth but I have spent the last ten years or so in Germany. Believe me, things are going well. The *Führer* . . ."

"'Itler, you mean?"

Christ, this was a tough audience. "Yes. Adolf Hitler. You may have heard of him."

Wesley sensed bristling. He was losing them. Another man spoke.

"The problem we've got, Mr Smith, is that we have no evidence at all that you are who you say you are."

Wesley's mouth opened but no sound came out. Windsor tried to redeem the situation. "Gentlemen. How can we expect Mr Smith to have evidence that he can present to you? As an enemy spy, why would he carry such evidence?"

One or two chuckled. The tone was lightening. Wesley got an idea. He stood and gave a speech in German. It was from *Faust*. It could have been the washing instructions for a pair of trousers for all they knew but the *Faust* appealed more to his dramatic bent. He sat down and allowed it to sink in.

"Gentlemen. That was as German as you get. From a classic German play. What you have to consider is . . . do you know any Englishman who could have done that? I am an actor. I love my adopted country. I love what is happening there. By accident of birth, I was born in Britain. I had no control over that but . . ."

There was the blessèd noise of laughter. He was turning the tide but he still needed to convince them of his *bona fides*.

"But I am not acting now. If you truly think that I am *not* a German spy, then hand me over to the authorities and they will be able to prove you wrong."

More gentle laughter. He knew that they could not hand him in. It was farcical. He imagined the conversation - 'We've got this bloke 'ere who says he's a Nazi spy. And we don't think he is. Arrest him immediately.' In the investigation that would inevitably follow, they would clearly all be pulled in along with him.

There was another scenario, of course. If they could not make their minds up, they could decide to do him serious physical damage and dispose of his remains in separate parcels across Yorkshire. There were at least ten of them.

"The *Abwehr* selected me for my acting ability. And for the fact that, due to the accident of birth I mentioned, I come across a very convincing English gentleman."

There was nodding and sideways glances. There was even smiling. He moved them on by telling them of decoy sites he had detected on the Humber estuary. He knew he was gilding the lily by a few shades but how would they know? That information, he told them, had gone straight back to *Abwehr Luft* in Hamburg.

He stopped short of any mention of handling renegade foreign pilots. That, he felt, was simply not required. He was a big fan of keeping powder dry, cats in bags and cards clamped to chest. (Apart, of course, from giving his address - or most of it - to a man he had only met an hour earlier!)

.   .   .

THE TENSION in the room had significantly diminished. It seemed they believed him but the continuing silence between his words still bothered him. There was clearly something else on their collective mind. Windsor spoke up.

"Do you know Geoffrey Salter?"

"No. Who's he?"

The man who had quibbled over Wesley's use of the word *'Führer'* piped up. He constantly looked as if he had a bad taste in his mouth.

"He says he's 'Itler's man in London, like."

Wesley was flummoxed. He had never heard of this man. He laughed. "Well, I suppose there could be more than one. The *Abwehr* is not the only department putting spies into Britain."

Windsor twisted the knife. "He was due to come to this evening's meeting but he's obviously been held up." Wesley looked at his watch and threw up a silent prayer that this Salter fellow did not show up at all. He wanted to find out from Otto and Grosskopf who this chap was. If he was a genuine German agent - which the present company seemed satisfied with - then they were simply trampling on each other's feet; if he turned out be an MI5 undercover operative, then Wesley was in trouble. The man would track him, catch him, cart him away, lock him up and ask questions later. Probably very many, including a good few that he would not have answers for.

Judging that discretion beats valour hands down, he decided to leave. He looked at his watch again. "Gosh. I hadn't realised it was so late. I've got a long drive ahead of me and you know what it's like in the blackout." He turned to Windsor and laughed. "I take it I passed the audition, Reg?"

That, at least, drew a few smiles and nods. Wesley said

individual goodbyes and shook hands with one or two
before picking up his mackintosh from where he had
stowed it beneath a chair. He put it on and went to open the
door as Windsor swiftly rushed over to switch the light off.
An irate ARP Warden was the last thing they needed.

Wesley turned in the darkened doorway, shook hands
and spoke quietly to the man. "Sorry about this, I'm frankly
worried about your Mr Salter. I need to do some checking. A
confrontation is just what I don't need until I know who he
is. And that is in your interests too, my friend. You
understand?"

He did. Wesley promised that he would be back in
touch. The man returned to the back shop and closed the
door as his visitor slipped into the night.

STOKES WAS LATE, as he had been at several of the previous
Leeds meetings. Driving over the Pennines from
Manchester was the reason this time. At least he did not
have to drive back tonight. He had found a decent enough
hotel in Leeds on one of his first visits. It was run by one of
Windsor's chums so it had his seal of approval.

He knew from Windsor that they were due to have a
special visitor at tonight's meeting. A German agent, he said.
Stokes was shocked but managed to conceal it. He was confident though that he could face this man. He knew he had
garnered a fair bit of support within this small cabal of
former blackshirts. One or two had had suspicions and
considered him an MI5 plant but the answers he had given
at his 'Star Chamber' inquisition had dispelled any
lingering doubts.

As he parked the car in the back lane and walked to
Windsor's door, he could see that a few were already leav-

ing. Reg Windsor himself was saying quiet goodbyes. He spotted Stokes and ushered him through. They were alone.

"Did your special guest turn up?"

"He did, Geoffrey. He was very . . . interesting."

"Really. Tell all."

They both sat in the dimly-lit back room while Windsor recounted the details of Wesley's visit from arrival to departure. Stokes was silent for a while.

"John Smith. Really?"

"Yes. We all had a laugh about that and so did he. Perfect name for a spy, he said."

"So, he's *Abwehr*, you say?"

"Yes. But English bred. Lived in Germany for many years though. An actor."

Stokes thought back to how the watcher at Siemens-Schuckert had described a man of very similar appearance and with the same name.

"Very affable, would you say?"

"Oh, yes! And I don't go t'theatre much but this chap is a wonderful actor." Windsor told him of the dramatic speech the man had suddenly launched into. All in German. It was the first time any of them had heard German spoken, apart from hearing Hitler on the newsreels now and again.

"I think he's the genuine article, Mr Salter. Strange thing though . . ."

"What?"

"Well, I asked this Smith bloke if *he* knows *you*. And he says he doesn't. Then Ken says as how you're 'Itler's man in London."

"And how did he take it?"

Windsor shrugged. "I don't rightly know, if I'm honest. He just laughed and tried to make out there could be a few of them. But he definitely doesn't want to meet you. In the next two minutes he was gone - once he found out you were on your way. He said he were going to check with his people and he'd be back in touch."

Reg started to laugh.

"What?"

"You're like buses, you lot, aren't you?"

"What do you mean?"

"You wait for years for a German spy to come along and then two come at once."

"Oh, yes. Very funny."

Windsor's face was now stern. "Tell you what else is funny."

"What?"

"You're both bloody English!"

Stokes was not sure how to answer that. He pressed on. "Can you give me an exact description of this man?"

Windsor proceeded to do so in detail. Tall, ungainly, likes strutting about and dressing up.

"Dressing up?"

"Well, it were only a cloth cap he were wearing but he started talking what he must've thought were Yorkshire. But then he told us he were an actor which is why they picked him - the *Abwehr*, like. You can't miss him, mind. Bloody big feller. You'd never get past him in a tight ginnel."

"Ginnel?"

"Alleyway."

"What about hair?"

"Come to think of it, he were wearing a wig. Grey, I think. Under his cap. God knows why! He took it off when he took the cap off."

"So . . . he's bald?"

"Oh, aye. As a bloody billiard ball."

Stokes had some checking up to do before he proceeded

any further with the Leeds connection. It was very likely that Smith was exactly who he said he was - a German agent. It was also extremely likely that he was the large 'affable' man of the same name who went through the traffic check at Siemens-Schuckert in Brentford. And Smith had told the meeting that he had discovered decoy sites on the Humber estuary. It did not take a genius to join up the dots. And, Stokes realised, there was Armitage to consider. Decoy sites were his speciality.

Despite the weighty body of evidence, there remained a narrow sliver of possibility that Smith was, like Stokes, working for British intelligence and on the same mission of infiltration. Knight had already told him several times that the British security services were like an octopus - and riven with internecine rivalries. Knight needed to know about this but, regardless of whose side this Smith was on, he needed to be pulled in.

Stokes was also reminded that he needed to get back in touch with Armitage. He bade Windsor goodbye and said he would contact him in a few days. He drove the short distance to the Excelsior Hotel.

HE ASKED the gentleman on reception if he could have a room with a telephone. He might as well have requested a luxury penthouse suite with hot and cold running call girls, the answer would have been the same. On reflection, did he really want one of Windsor's associates earwigging on the call to Knight? He therefore checked into the room he was allotted, dumped his suitcase and took a walk to the nearest police station.

Once he showed his MoD pass, they put him in an interview room and brought a telephone handset which he could plug into a socket on the skirting board. This would be interesting. He asked the operator to get him a London number. It was Knight's home telephone.

The phone was answered promptly. The number was given, rather than name, but Stokes recognised the voice.

"Knight?"

"Yes, who is this?"

Stokes introduced himself, gave him what little there was to tell him on the uneventful trip to Manchester but chapter and verse on the Leeds meeting and the elusive Mr Smith.

"Hmm. John Smith. I think he's taking the piss with the name, quite honestly. Part of me doesn't like that. Shame you couldn't have nabbed him, Albert."

"I missed him by about five minutes. But, in any case, how do you expect me to arrest a suspected German spy, and, in the course of doing so, show him my MoD ID, all in front of ten or so former British Union of Fascists members?" He paused. "All of whom, incidentally, believe me to be Hitler's man in London."

"Oh, yes. Tricky."

Stokes laughed. "Tricky doesn't cut it. No, I am very relieved that I did miss him. It could have blown my cover sky high. But I need him to be taken out, or this kind of situation could happen again."

"This town ain't big enough for the both of you, you mean?"

"In a nutshell, yes."

Knight laughed. "Talking of nuts, your man Armitage has left a message for you. Haven't got it with me, it's in your pigeon hole at the office. He rang the number you must have given him and rattled off a short spiel to the chap who answered it."

"Which was?"

"Can you ring him urgently. He's a man of few words."

"Urgently?"

"That's what he said. Sounds intriguing. Mind you, I think that message was left a couple of days ago."

Stokes groaned.

"Sorry, old chap. That's the way it is at the moment."

"Never mind. What is interesting is that Smith had told the Leeds meeting that he had detected decoy sites on the banks of the Humber."

"I don't see the connection". He paused. "Oh, Armitage, of course! That's his little hobby, isn't it?"

"Indeed."

"Well, I'd ring him pronto if I were you."

There was a pause. Stokes had another question. "I have to ask this. Is there the remotest chance that this Smith fellow is one of ours. Well, not *ours* but . . ."

"Not a chance, old bean. We have exclusive shooting rights on the BUF - and that's where he turned up, isn't it?"

"True, but I don't want him sticking his nose into any other BUF cells. It'll queer my pitch. I'm just wondering how he found Windsor. An ex-BUF member."

"It is rather odd, you're right. But take my word for it. This John Smith is the real McCoy, in my honest opinion. Definitely batting for the other side."

"Very well. I'm ringing Armitage now."

They both ended the call. Stokes had had a long day but he wanted to know the reason for Armitage's urgent call. He trudged back to the police station's front desk. "I need to make another urgent call, sorry."

The sergeant looked over his glasses. "Another one, sir? We'll have to start charging you."

The man had a point. He felt in his pocket and slid half a crown over the counter.

"Oh, I was only joking, sir."

"No. Put it towards the Christmas party or whatever."

The sergeant smiled his thanks, although both men knew that any Christmas party would be a modest affair, if it happened at all. Stokes went back through to the telephone, picked up the receiver and asked for Armitage's number. He only hoped that the man would accept a call from Leeds. He did - at only the second ring.

He recounted his strange and worrying experience - his exact words. Stokes calmed him and asked him to slow down. The tale the man told was of an individual who joined him at Cherry Cobb Sands on the Humber estuary while he was doing some surveillance of a suspected decoy site. He was now ringing Stokes to say that this man had said that he would get back in touch. And he had now done that, by means of a note stuffed through the letterbox.

Stokes had to calm him again. The words were coming out in torrents. He asked Armitage for a description.

"Very tall and broad. Spoke like a toff. Shaven head, I think."

"And did he give you a name."

"No." He paused. "Well . . . I don't think it's his real name."

This was like trying to get blood out of a stone. "What do you mean?"

"He just said something like 'why don't you just call me Mr Smith'. As if it wasn't his real name just a . . ."

"An alias?"

"Yes. As if he wasn't going to give me his real name but if I *wanted* a name then . . . it's Smith."

Stokes laughed. That was exactly why this man had

chosen the name of Smith. And John Smith, to boot. More dots, another line. "Tell me about this note? Handwritten?"

"Yes. I've got it here. It just says. 'Punch Hotel. Thursday 8th May. 10.30am, Much to talk about.'"

"Hmm. Was it in an envelope by any chance?"

"Yes. And it's a good job I don't have a wife, Mr Salter."

One woman spared a miserable fate at least, thought Stokes. "Oh, why's that?"

"Well, it had a pink heart in the top left-hand corner."

Stokes was puzzled. A pink heart? "And he had written your address on it?"

"Let me explain . . ."

Stokes wished that he would. He looked at his watch. Before dawn would be good.

Armitage went on to tell him how Smith had obviously doctored the envelope that he had recycled. The original address had been torn off, Armitage's address had been scribbled on the back, the note inserted and the remnant of the envelope folded around the note. All that was left on the envelope was the pink heart and the postmark.

Stokes was left hanging again. "And?"

"And what?"

"Oh, for God's sake, man. What's the postmark?"

"Oh, sorry. Let me have a look . . . Barnsley. But I can't make out the date, I'm afraid."

That would have been Stokes' next question. The man was learning. He gave him an address where Armitage was to send the whole package - envelope and note - as soon as he could. He needed to tell Knight to look out for it. He felt it was significant. Who was Wesley receiving mail from, and what was it?

He explained to Armitage that this Mr Smith was most certainly not on their side and that he had done the right thing in letting him know. This Smith was definitely working for MI5, seeking out Fifth Columnist activity, and he was only surprised that he had not taken him into custody. Maybe they were hoping that he would lead them to others. It occurred to Stokes halfway through this little speech, that he was outlining his own job description quite accurately.

Armitage was to be congratulated for his acuity in notifying his contact, ie his good self, and there would doubtless be a reward of some kind.

He gently informed him that he, Geoffrey Salter, Hitler's man in London, would attend the Smith meeting in his stead and the miscreant would be taken care of. Stokes actually used the word 'eliminated'. Armitage could make of that what he wanted. He asked the man to repeat the time and date of the proposed meeting at the Punch Hotel and made a note of it. He promised to keep him abreast of events and they would get together once Smith had been 'dealt with'.

The call was ended. Armitage was probably very relieved, happy and proud all at the same time. It was good to spread joy every now and again.

Stokes felt totally drained. He unplugged the phone, returned it to the desk and walked back to the Excelsior. He would ring Knight in the morning.

CHAPTER 25

Ernest Metcalf had chosen the following night for his 'after hours' stay at the factory. If all went well, he would be able to gain access to the three rooms along the corridor to get a closer look at what was going on within. He would spin Lizzie a story that he needed to do some extra work on the annual accounts. It was April, so quite feasible that he would have to do some final fine tuning on the books. She had already told him that Arthur, his predecessor in the job, had often worked late at the same time last year, for that very reason.

Having already established where the master keys were kept, he just had to wait until he heard the navy bods leaving. They had to at some point, surely? And then he would let himself into their rooms and see what he could find.

And then what? Providing nobody came back and caught him, then he would quit the premises as stealthily as he could, and return to the flat. In the unlikely event that he had to stay all night, and face Lizzie on her return to work in the morning, he had crammed a clean shirt into his coat pocket, just in case.

. . .

AFTER LIZZIE LEFT, he gave it half an hour then gathered his coat and briefcase and performed his exit routine. As an afterthought, he removed his shoes before he tiptoed back up the stairs. He unlocked Wilkinson's door, closed it behind him and locked it again. There was the usual continual boffin noise emanating from the three rooms. He took old man Wilkinson's rather comfortable office armchair, set it down next to the door – and waited. He wrapped the overcoat around him and prepared for a long wait.

He started to doze. It was warm inside the coat with his hands stuffed deep into the pockets. He had felt a bit overdressed on his way to work that morning with the sun beating down but he was now grateful for his foresight.

To stop himself dropping off, he went over the events of the last few weeks in his head. He was convinced now that he was right about what he and his uncle were about to do. Spying for a foreign power, when all was said and done.

He had been living in the comfort of complacency. An English cosiness. In reality, he now saw Britain as a miserable nation – petty, parsimonious, miserable, shabby. His father had been seduced into climbing the greasy pole up the class ladder. But he would never be really accepted.

He was, however, a bit worried about this new development – the wireless set. He knew for sure that his uncle would never be able to manage it, despite his protestations that he had been learning Morse Code. And that would put Ernest firmly in the driving seat as far as transmitting messages was concerned. In any case, he thought, he really wanted to protect the old man.

. . .

HE NOTICED with a start that the scientific sounds had ceased. The silence was broken only by a scraping sound – as if something heavy and metal was being dragged across the wooden floor along the corridor. This was followed by metallic clinks and a long, drawn-out whirring and clicking. Then laughter from what sounded like three men.

He heard a door open and footsteps coming towards him, accompanied by happy chatter. They tried all of the doors, including Wilkinson's office. He froze.

"I don't know why you're bothering, chum. This place is like the grave after hours," said one voice.

"Belt and braces. You know the standing orders – good habits make good security."

The other two laughed.

"I won't be sorry to leave this bloody cell block. At least at Swans there was always that pub - the Ship in the Hole. How long do you reckon?"

And then the 'security' voice, probably a senior officer whose arse was on the line. "Just another few days, I think. Then it just needs testing. There's a destroyer offshore just waiting for the test rig."

"Good – well let's hope the Hedgehog behaves itself, then it's job done."

Their conversation started to fade as, he guessed, they were putting on their coats and walking towards the staircase – and onward to their staff car. There was further banter as they descended but nothing discernible.

Hedgehog? What the Hell was that about? And test rig? Destroyer?

Ernest gave them ten minutes just in case they had forgotten something which required a return to their office. He heard the throaty noise of the staff car leaving. He walked to the window and looked at his watch. It was half past eight. Blackout was in fifteen minutes.

Certain now that the boffins were not coming back, he checked that he had not left behind any evidence of his presence in the old man's office, unlocked the door, opened it and re-locked it behind him. He walked on tiptoe along the corridor. Two doors on the left and the door to the biggest of the three rooms, on the right. He went through the keys on the bunch until he found the key for that one and opened it.

Luckily, this room had two large windows which gave him more light than he had in the office. A large tressle table ran the length of the centre of the room with work-benches lining the whole space. Tools lay on the benches, covering almost every square inch. He had no idea what many of them were but the majority were obvious – screw-drivers of all sizes, pliers, wrenches.

Along the edges of the benches were vices and clamps, and scattered around the surfaces were planes, angle grinders, files and hand drills. On the biggest bench was a large metal construction – clearly the focus of their work. A rectangular frame which he estimated was about six to seven feet long and roughly four wide. Bed-shaped. At the base of the frame was a network of square apertures, twenty-four in all, each one with electrical plugs at the bottom, their cables snaking underneath the structure and towards the control panels which sat on the large desk at the end of the room.

Stacked and crated under the central table were neat piles of projectiles, each about five feet long. At one end of each was a small propeller. The projectiles, which had a larger, more business-like propeller at the other end, put him in mind of miniature torpedoes.

He stood back and took stock. This was clearly some kind of naval weapon, and designed to be fired into the water.

So . . . Hedgehog? Why hedgehog? They were spiky creatures. Then he pictured the projectiles fitted into the frame and he saw where the sobriquet came from. The use to which this weapon would be put was not difficult to imagine. They were surely to be directed at submarines and work in the manner of depth charges. Guided depth charges? He knew that German U-boats were wreaking havoc on Atlantic merchant convoys bringing food and supplies to Britain from America. It made sense.

He felt in his coat pocket and fished out the piece of paper and pencil that he had liberated from the office. He walked over to the window where the light was better and made swift notes, roughly describing what he was looking at, with approximate sizes.

Then he retraced his steps, carefully ensuring that he locked each door behind him, and left the building.

By the time Ernest got home, it was almost half past ten. A panic had gripped him at a few points during the circuitous route he had taken back to uncle's flat in Nile Street. He considered what he had just done. Or rather, what he *would* be doing in passing on this information to an enemy power.

He did not care now, in any case, and he knew he had left not one shred of evidence behind him. He took his keys from his coat pocket, let himself in and quickly walked upstairs to the flat door. He saw Freddie dozing in the armchair. He shook him gently awake.

"Uncle. *Wach auf!*"

He grunted and rubbed his eyes open. "*Neffe! Was passiert?*"

Ernest laughed. "Uncle. Speak English, please. Hitler has not arrived yet."

He then realised that he had started it. They must both be more vigilant on that score. The old man sat upright and yawned.

"Now, pay attention. I have something to tell you."

His uncle was fully awake now. Ernest could almost hear the pieces falling into place as he remembered where his nephew had been, and for what purpose.

Ernest gave him the full details of what he had seen in the big room on the third floor – and what he felt was the importance and significance of what was being built just a few feet away from his own desk. It took him ten minutes.

"But what is 'hedgehog', *auf Deutsch*?"

"*Ein Isel*, Onkel."

"*Ach, so . . .!*"

"Uncle Freddie – in the territory we are now in, you absolutely must not speak German. Just one tiny slip is all it takes. Even your '*ach, so*' could start an avalanche of suspicion."

His uncle looked shocked. It quickly turned to contrition. "I'm sorry."

Another thought occurred to Ernest. "And from now on, even the word *Onkel* is also out of bounds . . . and it's Freddie, alright. Not Friedrich. It's forbidden." If they were going to do this, there had to be strict rules.

"Understood."

Ernest felt quite excited about the prospect of actually doing something to help the German war effort. Following all that had happened to him – the verbal haranguing and the physical assault on his first day at work, the violent assault on his mother and his father's subservience to this shabby country – he was feeling a strong connection to Germany now – the land of his forefathers. What he had earlier dismissed as his uncle Freddie's ravings, he now saw as right and proper. He would do anything in his power to support his *Vaterland* in their endeavours.

He felt sure that what he had discovered would be of great interest to them, though probably nothing they could do much about. Knowledge that the British seemed to be developing what looked like an anti-submarine weapon would surely be of some value. He was convinced that it would serve to hamper the Royal Navy in their battle on the Atlantic against the mighty German *Kriegsmarine*.

In the general scheme of war, their contribution was perhaps minor but at least, he felt, with extremely low risk of detection.

CHAPTER 26

Freddie Metcalf received a second letter from his Dutch cousin, Jan, just days after the first one. It contained instructions on the delivery of the wireless. Both he and Ernest had wondered what the logistics of it would be. They were terrified at the prospect of this German agent suddenly turning up, parking outside the shop and lugging the wireless set out of his car.

They need not have worried. It sounded simple. Ernest was to wait in the portico of Newcastle Central Station, wearing a mackintosh and a trilby. He would be meeting Mr Smith.

ON THE DUE DATE, the weather was extremely warm. It forced Ernest to carry the coat over his arm, loosen his tie and push the trilby back on his brow. He was then more likely to attract attention, looking, as he did, more like Sam Spade from *The Maltese Falcon*. This Mr Smith obviously had a leaning to the dramatic.

Ernest was to be at the appointed place by half past ten

in the morning. His train from North Shields arrived some time before that so he bought a newspaper and sat reading it on a bench by the taxi rank. He was trying to calm his nerves but it was not working. He suddenly remembered the incriminating letter in his pocket, detailing the time and place for today's wireless delivery. He quickly crumpled it up, walked to a nearby litter bin and stuffed it out of sight, below the top layer.

He heard a car horn sound and looked across to the roadway that ran through the arches of the station portico. A black Humber was crawling to a halt and the driver, a large chap whose frame completely filled the space behind the wheel, was looking straight at him.

Ernest stood, put his mackintosh back on and pulled the trilby to where it could be seen. His actions must have looked ridiculous to anyone watching. As he walked to the car, the man leant across, rolled the window down and spoke to him.

"Do you know if I can get a train to Glasgow from here?"

He remembered the response. He had been practising it on the train, much to the bemusement of an old lady sitting opposite him.

"No, but you can get one to Edinburgh and change there."

With that, the passenger door was pushed open. "In you pop, old chap." Ernest got in and looked around. It was quite a car. Smith put it into gear and rolled away from the station entrance.

"You admiring the car, eh? Quite a beast, isn't she?"

Ernest could only grunt. He felt out of his depth already.

"Let's go somewhere a bit quieter where there aren't too many prying eyes."

Ernest did not know the centre of Newcastle too well – he could count the number of times he had been there on the fingers of one hand – but he thought heading north towards Jesmond and Gosforth would find them some less public places where they could have a look at the wireless.

"Oh, what idiots we are."

"What?"

"Why don't I just take you and . . . the merchandise", the man laughed, "straight to North Shields? What were we thinking of?"

"We thought it might be too risky."

"Oh, what the hell. Let's live a little."

Metcalf now had to think of how he was to get the wireless out of the boot and upstairs to the flat in Nile Street without his father seeing. There was a lane that ran behind the shops. He knew that the back gate was never locked. Once inside, he could somehow rouse his uncle, and just pray to God that he was not out somewhere on his infernal bicycle. If he was, he could always hide the set in the outside netty until father closed up for the night and went back home.

Ernest had a sudden thought. "Oh."

Smith turned to look. "What?"

"What day is it?"

The driver laughed. "What is this? A test? *Mittwoch*. My German is as good as yours, old chum. Do not doubt it."

"No. Wednesday. That's good. It's early closing day in North Shields."

"Oh, yes – that strange British tradition – the early closing day. Is that relevant?"

"Yes. Father will be closing the shop at half past twelve so it will be better if we don't arrive until about half an hour after that. It will be much easier to get into the flat without being seen if he has already gone home."

"Whatever you say. So, where to?"

Ernest directed him out of the city and eastwards along the northern banks of the Tyne. Their conversation was going well. Smith opened up a little about his background and the years he had spent in Berlin. He was full of praise for the Nazis and what they had achieved. It was amazing how much Smith knew about himself and his uncle. Freddie's letters to his cousin, Jan, had obviously been extremely informative and full of personal detail.

As they drove, Ernest felt obliged to carry on a running commentary about where they were. He chose to take them past Swan Hunters shipyard. They did not slow down so as not to attract any attention from the guards at the gates.

"Ah, the famous Swan Hunters, eh? I half expected to see your uncle sitting at his easel with his pencils."

Ernest laughed. The image of Freddie in smock and beret, trying to sketch a destroyer as it hurtled down the slipway, was a strong one. A few miles further on, they turned north. There were a few spots where he knew that they could park the car without being overlooked. There, they could wait for the appointed time when it would be safe to move on to North Shields. He directed Smith to West Allotment, a small colliery village. They found a narrow track off the minor road that approached the village from the west, and parked. As Smith switched off, he turned to Ernest.

"Right, let's show the dog the rabbit. You get in the back and I'll get the set out of the boot."

Smith placed the wireless in the middle of the expansive back seat while he sat next to it on the other side. They spent a couple of hours familiarising Ernest with the intricacies of the machine. His Morse Code knowledge was nowhere near as good as his uncle's but he managed a few practice transmissions on the key. Once they left the lane and headed the final four miles to North Shields, he felt more than confident that he could share his knowledge with his uncle.

A LITTLE LATER, they arrived in North Shields and drove down Nile Street so that Ernest could see if his father had shut up shop. He had, so Smith guided the Humber gently down the back lane and stopped at the rear gate of the pork butcher's shop. Freddie was waiting for them. They took the wireless, usefully contained in a purpose made shoulder bag, up to the flat.

While uncle made them tea – the schnapps was declined – the other two set up the apparatus. Smith brought uncle into the conversation and Ernest was intrigued to watch Freddie's facial expressions as he listened to the man. He knew that he was going through the same thought processes that he had when Smith picked him up in Newcastle. After a long conversation when the agent opened up about his love of Germany, Berlin especially, Ernest could see his uncle warm to the man.

He was also gratified to see that his uncle had not been joking when he said that he had been practising Morse Code. His practice transmissions passed muster with Smith, whose face lit up with pleasure as he watched.

"You're better than me, *Onkel*!"

Freddie beamed. "So, when do we do it? We know a lot, don't we, *Neffe*?"

Ernest turned to his uncle. "I'm not sure"

Smith cut in. "Well, there's no time like the present. If

they are doing what you think they are doing in this factory of yours, then it needs to be dealt with. And as soon as possible, for the sake of the *Reich*!"

He looked at them both. "Don't you agree, *Kameraden*?"

They all laughed. They were on the same side.

An hour later, Smith had transmitted information to *Abwehr Luft* in Hamburg. It related to Ernest's discoveries on the third floor of Wilkinson's lemonade factory. He explained to the Metcalfs that he had transmitted it under his own codename of WIESELIG, for the sake of speed, accuracy and - most importantly - so that his wireless partner in Hamburg, would recognise his 'fist', his individual key style. Their own future codename, chosen by Smith as a tribute to Freddie's artistic talents, was BLEIS-TIFT – the German for 'pencil'.

They gave everything they knew about what was going on in the factory, as well as its location. The die was cast. While there was daylight left, Smith took his leave of them and headed back to Hull. A place he was beginning to think of as home.

IT WAS VERY LATE when Wesley arrived back at his Gillett Street digs in Hull. It had been over two full days and six hundred miles since he had last been there. He was exhausted. Despite that - stripped down to his vest and crouching below the eiderdown in order to dull the tapping sound in the absence of the good old BBC in the corner - he fired the wireless up and declared 'mission accomplished'. He made sure he complained bitterly to Otto about the inconvenience. He even made the point that he was not the *Abwehr's* messenger boy. He knew that it would get to Grosskopf but he did not care. This was not what he signed up for. It was preventing him from doing what he was assigned to do.

The answer came almost immediately - he got the sense that Grosskopf had anticipated his reaction. He apologised but said it was unavoidable. It would not be repeated.

Wesley had had to spend some of the cash that had been burning a hole in his pocket. Thankfully the petrol coupons they had given him also passed inspection. It saved him from the drudgery of seeking out - and stealing - replacement cars. Over six hundred miles, that would have been a lot of time-consuming switches of vehicle, with all the attendant risk. He asked for more money and his request was granted. A good sign of their guilt at his relegation to delivery man status.

He also reported on his trip to Leeds where he had narrowly avoided an encounter with a certain Geoffrey Salter. The man was heralded by the BUF people as 'Hitler's man in London'. In the event, the man had not turned up but Wesley passed the his name back to Hamburg. He wanted to know Salter's status. Friend or foe? Was he safe to go back to Leeds if the answer was 'foe' ie Salter was in fact working for the British on his *own* mission to infiltrate?

This Salter business was a complication that Wesley had not anticipated. And one that he suspected would also come as a surprise to his masters.

The answer was that he would have to wait. Wesley knew that the *Abwehr* was not the only player in the field when it came to running active agents in Britain. The other was the *SD* - the *Sicherheitsdienst*, the newer of the two organisations. It was headed up by Reinhard Heydrich and more closely allied to the *SS* and Nazi party. Grosskopf had told him that there was minimal communication between these two branches of the security services. Hence the reason for Wesley's enquiry. Hamburg hoped it would not take too long but the advice was to avoid Leeds in the meantime.

He stripped down the wireless and returned it to its place under the bed. He did not bother undressing any further. He laid back, pulled the eiderdown back up and let sleep wash over him.

CHAPTER 27

F rank had been as good as his word as far as delivering his car to Ernest was concerned. The mothballed Vauxhall was returned to roadworthy status. Since then, he and Lizzie had used it to good effect and enjoyed two or three short, pleasure-filled jaunts along the Northumberland coast. Lizzie loved the car and was looking forward to the evening trip to see her friend Muriel and her dashing beau.

The drive to the *Three Horseshoes* at Usworth, on the outskirts of Sunderland, had been easy. The journey had involved driving west along the north bank of the Tyne before crossing the river and heading east again. It was a long time since either of them had ventured this far out of North Shields.

The corrosive evidence of war was everywhere. They saw random bomb sites throughout the journey. Everyone but the children seemed to be in uniform - each with their own specific war duties to perform.

The pub was remarkably close to the airfield. Only a thin chain link fence separated its approach road from the camp. They passed a guard post as they drove the last few yards and security did not exactly seem tight. Ernest knew nothing about what kind of base this was, but he guessed that there were no front-line squadrons behind the fence.

As he parked the car, a plane came noisily and bumpily into land. It was a fighter. Why would they be this far north? He would try to find out more from Muriel's film star.

THE PUB WAS PACKED. The colour of the day was RAF blue. The language not English. The tone was predominantly upbeat and garrulous and the alcohol was flowing. No ops tonight, then.

He could feel Lizzie's tension on his arm. She was smiling and her eyes were scanning the space, looking for Muriel. There was no shortage of females and they all seemed very popular with the airmen. The bar was busy and there were none of the usual blackboards detailing which ales or spirits were unavailable.

A young brunette shouted Lizzie's name from the other side of the room. Ernest had seen her stand up when they entered. She extricated herself from her male partner. From his boyish good looks and black wavy hair, he guessed this was the Czech.

Lizzie made her way through the noisy throng and met Muriel somewhere in the middle, between two groups of loud airmen. The girls shrieked excitedly but nobody seemed to notice. Ernest decided to bypass the histrionics and pushed his way through to the bar. He soon sensed somebody by his side. He turned to see a beaming face. A hand was thrust out to him.

"You must be Ernest. Lizzie's friend?"

This was the chap who had been sitting next to Muriel. He took the proffered hand. "Yes. And you must be . . ."

"Call me Gus. Very pleased to meet you, Ernest. But, please, let me buy these drinks."

Ernest could hardly refuse, especially given that anyone in civilian clothing appeared to be invisible to the bar staff.

"You go and meet Muriel. I will bring the drinks over."

Ernest told him what he and Lizzie would like and he pushed his way across to where the ladies had edged their way into a seated booth. Lizzie clasped his arm and did the introductions.

"Well, you've done alright for yourself, I must say, Muriel.", said Lizzie with a wink.

Muriel giggled. "You too, Lizzie".

More giggling. Ernest smiled and looked over his shoulder. Maybe Gus needed help with the drinks.

The airman was weaving his way expertly through the swaying bodies. He set the drinks down on the table. Ernest moved over so that Gus could sit next to him, with the girls opposite them. Gus took them through a ritual of hand shaking as they all said how pleased they were to meet each other. Ernest felt obliged to contribute to the conversation.

"So, Gus. Is there some sort of celebration in here tonight? Or is it always as busy as this?"

The Czech laughed. "No . . . it's not always this busy. Yes, there is some celebrating. Some of the boys have got their postings. They are off to their new squadrons tomorrow."

Ernest must have looked puzzled. Gus had no hesitation in elaborating. "This is a training unit at Usworth. Once they finish their time here, they move on. So, it's very busy, like . . . erm, some place I can't remember . . ."

"Piccadilly Circus?", Ernest suggested.

"Yes, that is it. Piccadilly Circus. Thank you." He paused. "That is in the middle of London, no?"

Ernest thought he would tease the Czech. "It might be . . . but walls have ears", he said and pointed to the poster.

"Ah, yes", replied Gus, tapping the side of his nose in what Ernest thought was a strangely English gesture.

"But why circus? Are there elephants and tigers there?"

Muriel and Lizzie, who had been listening to the exchange between the men, suddenly burst out laughing at the incongruous picture it painted. After some discussion, the girls decided that they did not know why it was called a 'circus', either. Ernest knew but shrugged his shoulders and laughed with the others. Gus and Muriel were clearly a few drinks ahead of Lizzie and himself.

A COUPLE OF ROUNDS LATER, Gus asked 'respectfully' if he could swap seats with Lizzie. As he explained, "I want to be as close as possible to this beautiful woman every minute of every day."

More giggling. Ernest preferred the new arrangement. He wanted to observe this man and be able to look him in the eye. There was something below the surface that he could not quite work out.

The new seating plan changed the group dynamics. Muriel and Lizzie leant in to each other and started talking shop. The driving force of their discourse seemed to be who was doing what, to whom, and how often - at the respective factories in Sunderland and North Shields.

Ernest bent across to Gus. "So, you're not moving on then?"

"Maybe one day. But I am instructor so end of training

course means that I wait for the next group? To instruct them."

"In what?"

At this point, Ernest would not have been offended if Gus had drawn down the shutters on the conversation, but he did not. He was well in his cups and leaning in very close.

"I train these rookies to fly the Hurricane. Not just to fly it but to . . . fight with it." He made dogfighting gestures with his hands, only narrowly avoiding knocking his pint over.

He explained that these trainees were predominantly Czech, like himself. There were also Poles, Free French and new pilots from Commonwealth countries. He was very disparaging of the Poles and, indeed, his own compatriots. He explained that it was more difficult for those who had flown before in their own countries.

The Czech outlined the differences at great length. The planes they had previously flown were less powerful than the Hurricane, for example. Speed gauges were in kilometres, rather than miles, per hour, and the fuel was measured in litres, not gallons. Two other variations were crucial to both pilot and aircraft integrity – the throttle moved in the opposite direction and their former aircraft did not have retractable undercarriages.

He went on to tell Ernest of all the mishaps that had occurred relating to the last two deficiencies. His laughter was so raucous that one or two of his RAF colleagues overheard and laughed along with him, one of them miming a pancake landing, accompanied by comic gestures of panic.

The girls, who had been dragged from their shop talk by Gus's little stage show, now resumed their own conversation. Gus instantly switched to a further account of his dotage on Muriel, putting his arms around her, kissing her, nuzzling her neck. Lizzie snuggled into Ernest and smiled up at him. Ernest returned the smile, gave her a squeeze but gently withdrew from her embrace.

He went to the bar for another round of drinks. When he returned, the girls were chattering again. Gus seemed genuinely pleased at his return with the booze.

The airman took a sip of his drink and this time seemed a little more circumspect. He looked around the room and leant in to Ernest. The smell of beer was almost overpowering. The man had probably been drinking since the afternoon.

"The Germans wanted me to get one of these for them, you know. A Hurricane."

Ernest raised his eyebrows in surprise.

"Yes. They wanted me to fly away with one."

What on earth was this man telling him? That he had actually had contact with the Nazis? He decided to listen very carefully. What he was about to hear could turn out to be very useful for his, and his uncle's, new venture. He put on his 'extremely interested' face, and exaggerated his awe and wonder.

Gus's voice subsided to whisper level. He clumsily misjudged placing an elbow on the table and had to recover quickly lest both pints were knocked over. He apologised and bent forward again.

"The *Gestapo* caught me. In Prague."

"You're kidding me?"

Gus was enjoying the attention. He was clearly many parts showman but this was something that only required an audience of one. And, in truth, the airman knew nothing about Ernest other than what Muriel may have told him. And *her* knowledge of him was not exactly encyclopaedic.

Satisfied that the girls were well back into chatter mode

and that the noise level in the bar was high enough to prevent any ear-wigging, Gus went on to tell the incredible tale of how he had been captured and tortured by the *Gestapo* as he tried to leave Prague and how he had made his way across Europe with other Czech Air Force airman until he reached France. When France fell, with great difficulty and joined by a lot of Free French pilots, they had managed to get to England, and the RAF.

What followed was then a further – and, Ernest felt, embroidered and glorified – account of his service during the Battle of Britain. His many dogfights over the south coast, the number of kills, and his eventual transfer to this training squadron. Here, he was passing on the skills he had learned, to other foreign airmen who had joined the RAF.

It was an amazing story, alright. Ernest guessed there was a tiny kernel of truth in it somewhere but it all seemed rather fantastical. Gus sat back, seemingly drained by his performance and obviously pleased to see the look of amazement on Ernest's face.

"So . . . what happened?"

"They wanted me to grab them a front-line fighter and fly it over to them." He sat back again, almost begging the next question. The Czech had now said on two occasions that he had been told to steal a fighter. Maybe that bit was the tiny germ of truth. Regardless of its veracity, this was fascinating. Silence reigned – as much, at least, as the barrack-room cacophony allowed. Ernest tried to frame the next question in his mind. It was simple.

"And did you?"

Gus laughed. "No. I am sure they have been looking for me but I have moved around a lot."

Ernest smiled and hoped it looked congratulatory. Gus stood, now needing alcohol following his revelations. He tottered unsteadily to the bar and returned a few minutes with more drinks. The crowd now seemed to be thinning. The girls were still engrossed in their own conversation which now sounded to Ernest as if it were bordering on the sexual.

The Czech took a swig of his beer and whispered across. "But obviously, this is strictly *entre nous*, yes?"

Ernest knew what the French phrase meant but decided to look ignorant.

"Between ourselves". Gus pointed to the 'Careless Talk' sign and laughed.

"Oh, yes. Of course. Say no more." Ernest tapped his nose.

The men laughed. Muriel looked across. "What's amusing you two?"

Gus turned his face to hers and kissed her. "Just a bit of man talk. Yes, Ernest?"

They all laughed. The foursome came back together.

DRIVING BACK to North Shields required every bit of Ernest's waning concentration. A lack of street lighting and a surfeit of alcohol made the drive tortuously slow. Lizzie did not help. A constant barrage of talk about Muriel and Gus filled the air. He had to stop twice for a pee. When he returned after his second visit to the roadside, Lizzie was asleep.

She had told him that, although they were not making it public just yet, Muriel and Gus were intending to get engaged. That did not surprise Ernest, although it did not quite gel with what he had witnessed when Gus was getting a round of drinks in. He had seen him very close to a rather well-endowed blonde, delaying his arrival at the bar. His behaviour went a bit beyond mild flirtation. She did not seem like a passing acquaintance.

He remembered glancing at Muriel to see if she had noticed it too. She had not. Their female chatter had been all-consuming.

This Czech airman was not what he appeared to be. Ernest started to doubt the stability or longevity of the relationship that Muriel thought she had.

He chose not to reveal anything of what Gus had told him about his war service so far. If Muriel did not know about it – although he guessed she did – then he did not want to tell Lizzie something that would certainly be passed on. He was in no position to rock any boats. And, on reflection, the man was very drunk.

CHAPTER 28

Neither Ernest nor his uncle actually heard the bomb hit the factory. Ernest vaguely remembered hearing ambulance bells but they seemed far enough away from them not to be of any real concern, to them anyway. He had gone back to sleep.

The news of the bombing spread across the town like a blast wave. There was barely a street that was not involved in some way with the town's biggest employer. It quickly became apparent that casualty figures would be high. This was no minor nuisance raid of the kind that the town had already suffered.

From dawn, there was a certain buzz outside. Freddie was always the first to rise. Looking out onto Nile Street from his window, he could see knots of people striding purposefully down the road. That was not usual for a Sunday morning. This was no call to Christian worship. The walkers were eerily silent. He was not sure what it meant.

Freddie's sleep had never been disturbed by any of the previous haphazard night raids but he blamed his slight deafness for that. He flung a dressing gown over his pyjamas and shambled down to the street door. While he was waiting for the next group to pass, he heard more ambulance bells. When two middle-aged women entered the street and walked towards him, he asked them what was happening. He was barely able to suppress a shudder when they told him that there had been a direct hit on the factory and that hundreds had been killed.

He was not able to reply. His face reflected the required shock at the obvious tragedy but other thoughts were also crowding his mind. The women walked on, ashen-faced, and Freddie returned to the flat to wake his nephew.

IT WAS NOT the sort of news that Ernest wanted to be greeted with on being shaken abruptly awake by his uncle.

"The factory has been bombed."

"Are you sure?"

"I don't *know* anything, Ernst. I'm just telling you what two women told me. Direct hit and hundreds dead, they said. You'd better get dressed and get down there to see for yourself."

His nephew sprang from his bed and started to throw some clothes on. "This is terrible, uncle." He paused, one leg in his trousers. "Hundreds dead?"

Freddie stared at him in a state of shock. "But how can that possibly be true? Hundreds? There aren't as many as that who work there. Especially not in the middle of the night? Stuff and nonsense."

Ernest grabbed a jacket from the back of the door and then turned to Freddie. "Uncle, there's an air raid shelter in the basement."

Freddie put his hands to his face. His mouth opened but

he struggled to speak for a few seconds. "No. You are joking. I must come with you."

His nephew put his hand up. "No. Definitely not. There may be some older people there who remember you as German. We cannot take the risk. I'll go down and have a look for myself and then we'll talk about it when I get back."

THE FACTORY WAS ONLY a few hundred yards away from Nile Street but it was a zigzag walk. At each street corner, more groups joined him on the way. He could hear crying and sniffling from the women. Men were running, some of them dressed in work overalls and one or two in military uniform, obviously intending to help with what he imagined was now a rescue operation.

As he turned into George Street, fifty yards away from the factory, he was staggered by what he saw. He stopped walking and simply stared. Only one wall of the factory remained – the one that sat on King Street. It looked dangerously insecure with no remaining support from adjoining brickwork, which now formed a mountain of rubble where the rest of the building had stood.

Groups of police officers, ARP Wardens and others in working clothes were scurrying to reduce the rubble and load it into waiting council lorries. A cordon had been placed across the road, behind which stood groups of onlookers, all curiously quiet.

Ambulances were coming and going. Grey dust was everywhere and a gentle breeze was stirring up little whirlpools of lemonade bottle labels. One caught on the toe of his shoe. He bent to pick it up. '*Smila*', it read. He had no intentions of moving any closer. He had seen enough. He turned and walked away. He let the label flutter from his hand.

ON HIS RETURN to the flat, Ernest told his uncle what he had seen. Still in his dressing gown, Freddie was sitting smoking at the table and nursing a cup of tea. He turned to look at his nephew.

Ernest shook his head. "What have we done, uncle?"

Freddie stood. "What? What do you mean?"

"We told the *Luftwaffe* where to bomb."

Freddie was stunned. He put his fag out, replaced his cup on the table and stood. "Don't be stupid. We've had a lot of raids. What makes you think . . ."

His nephew walked the step or two that separated them. He raised his voice. "Uncle! We may as well have painted a target on the roof. And a sign saying 'Bomb here'!" He glared at his uncle. "We sent a wireless message telling them exactly what was going on in the factory and exactly where it is . . . or was, I should say. Remember?"

Ernest was certain that the factory bombing was a direct result of the information they had sent by wireless to Hamburg. He took off his jacket and dropped into a chair.

Freddie was adamant. "But we did not tell them to bomb the factory."

His nephew spoke quietly now. "We did not *tell* them, no. But you heard what Smith said."

"What?"

"He said it needed to be dealt with, uncle. What do you think 'dealt with' means?"

Ernest had only just remembered the exact words used by Smith. He had only just realised their implication. He was starting to panic.

"I knew about the shelter, too. Lizzie told me about it but I had no idea it would be relevant. It never crossed my mind." He paused. "You should see it, uncle. A three-storey building and only one wall left standing."

Freddie's face was expressionless. "How many . . ." His voice tailed off.

"Who knows? I think it's probably too early to tell just yet. They're still pulling them out and God knows how many poor buggers are still in there. But I see the entrance sign to the shelter as I get to work every day. 'Capacity 210', it says."

Freddie lit another cigarette and offered one to Ernest. His nephew lit it, took a long drag and blew the smoke to the ceiling. He paced up and down the room. "What the Hell have we done? And what the *Hell* do we do now?" He sat and took another drag.

His uncle put his hands on his nephew's bent shoulders. "We do nothing. We *can* do nothing. It's done. It's over."

Ernest's head snapped up. "Do you realise the trouble we are in now? Internment won't even be on the menu. It will be the hangman's rope if anyone finds out. Jesus!"

Neither man spoke as the enormity of Ernest's outburst sank in. Ernest stood. "We have to get rid of that thing for a start."

"Well, we can hardly put it in the bin."

"No, but we can send it back from whence it came, can't we?"

"What? To Smith, you mean?"

Ernest spoke sharply. "Well, who else? Of course, Smith." He stubbed his cigarette out roughly. Sparks showered onto the table top. "There's no time like the present. Where is the wireless?"

His uncle pointed at his armchair. "It's in the space under the chair. I cut the fabric away at the base."

Ernest lifted the front of the chair so that his uncle could drag the set out of its hiding place. They took it out of its case, placed it onto the table and looked at it. "Well, uncle. Do you know how to put it together?"

Freddie did not look too sure. Smith had done it the last time. Between them, they managed to figure it out but it took twenty minutes. In another ten, they had followed the transmission instructions which Smith had written down for them, and transmitted a short message under the code-name BLEISTIFT. It stated simply that they wanted the wireless set to be collected at the colliery. Ernest knew that Smith would know the suggested rendezvous to be West Allotment where they had met when he had brought it to them. They gave a date of two days ahead at twelve noon.

That done, they packed the set back up and returned it to the void under Freddie's armchair. Even though the set was still physically present, both of them now felt some relief. The earlier argument then reared its ugly head again. Freddie was trying to instil calm. "But, Ernest, there are raids all the time. It might have nothing at all to do with our wireless message."

His nephew pointed at the window, his anger rising once more to the surface. "Those people don't know what was going on in the factory, do they? But *we* knew. You heard what Smith told us. They were building some kind of weapon. Once the Royal Navy gets wind of this, they are sure to investigate. They're not likely to see it as random act of God, are they? It will be all over town."

Freddie grimly accepted what his nephew told him. But now he was worried that Smith might see their actions as treacherous to the cause of the *Führer* and that there would be consequences. Ernest was unsure about that. They had done their bit. The *Führer* would just have to be bloody grateful. Besides, he had got to know this agent quite well. He seemed a decent chap and would surely understand their wish to put it all behind them due to the dreadful circumstances in which they now found themselves. Smith would also have to consider that they could implicate him too, if it came to that.

The two men were now sitting facing each other across the kitchen table. Their fear and trepidation had abated. Their polar opposite positions had now merged to a consensus. They just had to weather the storm over the next day or so. Both were convinced that, once they got rid of the wireless set, there was nothing that could possibly link them to the disaster. It would be seen, they were sure, as a tragic twist of fate. A random occurrence. Even the Royal Navy may eventually see it as just another nuisance raid - providing they found no evidence to the contrary.

CHAPTER 29

Wesley was unhappy when Otto Ziegler instructed him to collect the wireless set from North Shields. In addition, Hamburg confirmed that this Geoffrey Salter that he had almost met at the BUF meeting in Leeds could not be traced at either *Abwehr* or its competing intelligence operation, the *Sicherheitsdienst*. The man could therefore only be from the British security services. Wesley realised that he had had a narrow escape.

He felt himself starting to sweat as he rapidly keyed in his response to the requested return trip to Tyneside. He had already been told by Otto that his messenger boy status was behind him. And now this. These pork butchers had only had the set for a few days. He was unsure what he would be facing.

His brief was to meet BLEISTIFT at the 'colliery'. A date and time had been arranged. He knew it had to be the spot where he and Ernest had parked up and played with the wireless set for a couple of hours before driving on to North

Shields. He remembered the name of the village. West Allotment.

As he neared the place where they had parked before, he saw a navy Vauxhall in the same spot. He pulled to a halt as soon as he saw it and then drove slowly past the end of the track. He thought it strange. The man had had no transport of his own before. He had picked him up at Newcastle Central station in the Humber. After his experience in Leeds, he was sensing a trap.

He found a turning a hundred yards further on, reversed into it and drove slowly back toward the track. There was a gap in the hedge to his right. He pulled over, opened the door and stood on the sill so that he had a good view of the car. It was Metcalf and he seemed to be alone.

The man would probably be expecting him to arrive in the Humber. He totted up in his head. That was three cars ago. He had since taken ownership of this little beauty, an Armstrong Siddeley 17 saloon. In his view, a step up from the rather staid Humber. He had been forced to leave that one to its own devices in a railway station car park. What this one lacked in size, it made up for in style - and it was not as thirsty.

He drove past the opening, reversed into it and brought the car to rest, boot to boot with the Vauxhall. He opened the door and walked the few paces to the passenger side of the other car. He bent to peer inside. He could see Metcalf looking at him in the wing mirror. He opened the rear passenger door. Unless there was someone lurking in the boot, the car was empty apart from the driver. He got in.

"We meet again. Nice car." He looked around the interior. In his opinion, it was far from nice. He was becoming quite an expert.

"It's my father's. I've borrowed it. I thought it might come in useful."

"One distinct disadvantage though, chum. In our line of business, it pays not to be seen too often in the same car, the same clothes even. People remember." Smith noticed a shadow cross Metcalf's face. "What is it?"

"You said 'in our line of business.'"

Smith was wary. "You mean you're having doubts, old boy? Quite understandable. Is that why I've been summoned here?"

Metcalf looked nervous. "The bombing of the factory was successfully accomplished. Too successful in a way."

He outlined the scale of what was being seen as a disaster in the town and across Tyneside. The fear was that he and his uncle would somehow be found out. Smith listened in silence. He was as shocked as Metcalf but also pleased at the credit he could now attribute to his own efforts when he next contacted Hamburg. He looked at Ernest and saw that the man was close to tears.

"Yes, I heard about the raid.", he lied. "I didn't hear about the aftermath. I don't want to be dismissive but . . . there's a war on. People – innocent people - occasionally die."

"We feel responsible for the deaths."

"You are. Well . . . you and the *Luftwaffe*, obviously." Smith smiled. He was trying to lighten the situation. He failed. Ernest was staring blankly through the windscreen.

Smith tried again. "Listen. Nobody will ever know. And when the invasion happens, your contribution will be recognised, have no fear."

Ernest regained his composure. "I've brought the wireless back. We have no further need of it now and it's a great risk for us to keep it."

"Why are you in such a hurry? You can dodge the flak, can't you? This will be yesterday's news as soon as the next raid happens."

The man looked at him incredulously. "We are German. Everybody knows it. I was spat at and beaten up on my first day at the factory. My mother was attacked. They will be looking for scapegoats." Neither man spoke for a few seconds. Ernest continued. "We can't take the risk of the wireless being found."

Wesley considered this. The man was probably right. Physical evidence was always difficult to counter. "I see. Very well, let's do it now, shall we?" Both men got out, lifted their respective boot lids and swiftly moved the set from the Vauxhall to the Armstrong Siddeley.

"So, Ernest, I guess this is *auf Wiedersehen* until we are both able to speak German with impunity, eh?" He laughed. Ernest, now more relaxed since he no longer had the wireless, joined him. Getting rid of the set was a great relief but he knew that he and his uncle still had problems ahead.

Smith started to leave. Ernest grabbed his arm.

"No, wait. I have some information that I think might be of interest."

Ernest told Smith as much as he could remember about his encounter with the Czech airman at the *Three Horseshoes*. He described the man's relationship with Muriel and how she was connected to his work colleague, Lizzie. He related the tale that Gus had told him that night - about being captured by the *Gestapo*, then allowed to escape and subsequently being instructed to steal a fighter for the *Reich*. He thought he might be a person of significant interest to the agent.

Smith's eyes lit up. He dipped his hand into his inside jacket pocket and withdrew his wallet. "Here! Accept this as a reward on behalf of our beloved *Führer*." He withdrew a pound note and tucked it into Ernest's breast pocket. "I found some cash in one of the vehicles that I . . . borrowed." He laughed. "I see no reason why you shouldn't have it." He paused. "But I know what you're thinking. Blood money, yes? Forget it. It won't bring them back. You'd have got that anyway, my friend. Take it."

Ernest took the note out. A pound was a lot of money and he was, after all, unemployed. He gave Smith a description of the Czech. He told him where he could be found and provided directions.

"I'm grateful to you, old boy. Thank you. He is one of mine but proving very elusive. He has a job to do but, from what you tell me, he seems to have gone native. I think I need to remind him of his responsibilities, don't you?"

ERNEST WAS PLEASED. He had disposed of the wireless from whence it came. He had sweetened the pill with some information that Smith was obviously pleased to receive. And he was a pound better off. He and his uncle would still feel the guilt of what they had done for a long time, but all they had to do was to keep their heads firmly below the parapet.

Smith closed both boot lids and drove slowly down the rutted lane without looking back. A chapter closed. He now needed to confront the Czech and give him a kick up the backside. He needed to be brought back on track.

CHAPTER 30

Albert Stokes stayed in Leeds for the following day after the near miss with Mr Smith at the BUF soirée. He rang Knight from the police station. The man sounded frazzled. He was only mildly congratulatory at what Stokes felt was a bit of a *coup*. He was clearly preoccupied - obviously engaged in more pressing matters.

"Where are you, Albert?"

"I'm still in Leeds but I could make it back tonight if you need me there?"

"I don't. There's been a development overnight. Get yourself to North Shields."

Stokes had never heard of the place. "A development. Where did you say?"

"North Shields. Tyneside somewhere. And find yourself somewhere to stay. You could be a while."

"I can't be too long."

"Oh?"

"No. I've got that meeting with our Mr Smith in Hull in a few days. That's the other reason for my call. You remember the urgent call that Armitage wanted?"

Stokes explained that Smith had contacted Armitage and had given him time and date for a meet-up in Hull at the Punch Hotel. He asked Knight if he had yet received the Barnsley postmarked and pink heart decorated envelope from Armitage.

Knight laughed. "Yes. So, you're involved in that, are you? Explain."

He felt that he already had, but he elaborated on the contact between Smith and Armitage. "Smith shoved a note through Armitage's letterbox with time and place for their meeting in a few days' time. It was wrapped in the remnants of an envelope. We have to assume that its original contents were something that Smith had received."

"That's interesting."

"Does it mean anything?"

Knight laughed again. "I think it might. As soon as I received it, I passed it down the line to those who know about these things . . ."

Stokes was getting impatient. "What *things*?"

"Ah, it looks like this envelope - and its original contents, obviously - were sent to our Mr Smith via what they call a cutout, dear boy." Knight filled the gaps in Stokes' knowledge of cutouts - individuals who act as intermediary for foreign agents. "Spies send information to the cutout who then puts that envelope inside another and forwards it onto its destination. Often the German Embassy in a neutral country - Sweden or Eire. Doubtless Smith has been sent information from *Abwehr* using this method. Probably something a bit too clunky for a wireless message."

"I see. A way of circumventing the scrutiny of our postal services?

"Exactly. You see - you learn something every day, my

boy. It's obviously best suited for information that is not particularly urgent. Or too long and complicated."

Stokes thought for a moment. "Like a list of former BUF members, perhaps?"

"What makes you say that?"

"Well, we know that Smith had contacted the BUF Leeds branch members. We almost collided, you remember? And you said it was a shame as I could have had him arrested. What fun that would have been!"

Knight snorted. "Yes, alright. I wasn't having a good day. Even Homer nods."

"Sorry, you've lost me there."

"Classical reference, dear boy. Horace, I believe. It simply means that even one who is the best in his field can make the odd bloomer."

Stokes laughed. "You and your public school education."

"Indeed. It always helps one feel superior."

They both laughed. Knight spoke. "But that's extremely perspicacious of you, old chap. I'm sure you're right about the membership list. How on earth did the *Abwehr* get hold of that, one wonders."

Stokes ignored that. As they both suspected, MI5 clearly had subversives of its own. "So, Smith simply recycled the envelope in which that list arrived and used it to scribble details of the meeting for Armitage."

"Well, he made a mistake in leaving the postmark and the pink heart on it. My chaps spoke to the GPO in Barnsley. Apparently, the pink heart is the motif used by a lady who runs a lonely hearts agency in the town. A Mrs Ada Wigglesworth. She gets post by the bucket load."

"And is she a cutout?"

"We'll soon know. They are intercepting all deliveries to

her address and one of my chaps is up there now with his sleeves rolled up, ready to wade through it all."

Both men laughed. Knight spoke. "I only hope our man is not easily embarrassed."

"Yes. And you will have seen that Smith lives in Gillett Street."

"That's in Hull, presumably?"

"I am guessing so. I haven't had time to check."

"Well, leave it to me. In the meantime, you can't miss that meeting with Smith. I'll make sure you're back there for that. Just get to North Shields now and I'll give you chapter and verse when you're *in situ*."

Stokes sighed. "What's this all about?"

"Not on this line, old chum. Ring me when you get there. You know the numbers."

"Very well"

"Jolly good. Speak soon."

With that, the call was ended. Stokes replaced the receiver on the cradle, thanked the desk sergeant and headed back to the Excelsior.

THE JOURNEY from Leeds to North Shields was not as bad as he feared it would be. He parked the car in the centre of town and wandered around looking for digs. He listened to the strong Geordie accents all around him. They were certainly talkers but understanding them might require the services of an interpreter. Stokes was from Surrey and spoke English. What he was hearing had little in common with his mother tongue.

A small guest house on Bedford Terrace seemed to fit the bill. A rather wizened old dear with a face like a prune dealt with him perfunctorily. She pointed to the notice on the wall which warned single male tenants against entertaining ladies in their rooms. He smiled at the use of the plural. Even the singular would be a fine thing.

She showed him to his first-floor room. He dumped his suitcase, had a quick wash in the basin and was back out on the streets just minutes later. He still had no idea why he was there.

He asked a bobby for directions to the police station. They were not too happy with him making a long-distance call but Stokes' government pass brooked no argument. They showed him to a small interview room and the call came through several minutes later.

"Ah, you're there. Well done, old lad. Tell me where you're staying."

Stokes gave him the address and Knight shared with him the reason for his urgent visit. It was flimsy and Knight confessed that he knew little other than a request that had come from above and he was getting flak.

"I want you to head to a bombed factory on King Street. Just be eyes and ears at the moment. Get me the scuttlebutt."

"The what?"

"Oh, come on. Scuttlebutt. Haven't you seen *any* American films, my lad? It means gossip!"

"Oh, right. I must broaden my horizons, clearly."

"Yes. And don't go flashing your 'Hitler's man in London' ID. You'll get arrested - if not lynched. I gather it's a bad one."

"A bad one?"

"Still counting the dead, old boy. I'm sure you will be the soul of discretion."

"But what . . ."

"Albert. I know no more than that. Get yourself to King Street."

Stokes did as requested. It was not far from his digs. North Shields was a small town.

THE BOMB SITE was a hive of activity as rescue work was heavily underway. ARP wardens, police, firemen, servicemen on leave and civilians, were gradually removing layer after layer of rubble in the hope of finding survivors. He saw an area of focus around what he assumed was the entrance to a basement.

Two council lorries were slowly being filled with small parts of the large pile. He realised simply by listening to the talk around him, that there was a public shelter beneath the building. Some survivors had been extracted, many with mutilating injuries. Ambulances for the injured and lorries for brickwork, masonry and splintered timber, stood by.

One wall of the building still stood at its full height – the King Street end. Judging from the neighbouring terraced houses, he guessed that the factory had stood three storeys high. A mountain of material sloped down to the ground from halfway up the remaining wall, filled the area where the building had stood, and spilled across the street.

On the road, men worked vigorously shovelling bricks and piles of débris and dust into the council wagons. On the remains of the factory, others had clambered up and were striving to make the pile smaller. Stokes was impressed with the efficiency of the operation. Soldiers, sailors and airmen, presumably home on leave, were being prevented from joining those on the slope. This was dangerous work and some organisation was therefore needed.

Householders were already boarding up shattered

windows in houses close to the site. At Shrimplins – the general dealers on an opposite corner – a man and a woman were sorting goods from the broken glass in the display window. A shredded blackout blind flapped from an upstairs window.

Police were holding back crowds of onlookers in three places. From anguished cries, he guessed that these were family members or friends of those yet to be accounted for. Men were sweeping the road clear. Others were filling bags with letters, invoices, delivery notes. Anything printed, on paper, and deemed to be 'property', was collected.

A shout went up from a gap where the fallen masonry was propped up on jacks. A body, its face covered in dust and grime, was gently laid on a stretcher. Four men took it across to one of the ambulances.

The crowd pressed forward. Somebody shouted "Who is it?" Another screamed "George!" and broke through, only to be restrained by two ARP Wardens. He could see others comforting the woman as she was returned to the crowd to wait.

Stokes began to feel like a ghoul. It was an emotional scene. He spotted a tall gentleman in a smart overcoat and bowler hat, the ubiquitous gas mask case across his shoulder. He looked important. Men were consulting him, then leaving to issue orders to the crews. A bobby stood at his side permanently.

He asked the policeman in front of him who the gentleman was.

"That's the Chief Constable, sir. Mr Blackburn."

Stokes asked if he could be allowed through to have a word. The bobby gestured to the Chief Constable's sidekick, who came running over. He examined the government pass and escorted him across.

Thanking the first officer, he made his way to the senior policeman, his shoes crunching on the scattering of broken glass. Once more he showed his ID. He did not seem that impressed but Stokes put that down to a preoccupation with the scene unfolding in front of them. Blackburn was not looking at him.

"Can I ask what has happened here, sir?"

The man did not turn to face him. His tone was verging on the insolent.

"A bomb hit the factory last night. We're trying to rescue people who were in the shelter."

He had already worked that out for himself but that was all he got. Blackburn was now speaking to his assistant. In the Chief Constable's opinion, the conversation with this Ministry bod was over. Maybe it was time for Stokes to get shirty. He grabbed him by the arm. The look on Blackburn's face was priceless.

"Can I just ask you again, sir? I realise you are very busy but this may well be a security matter." He put the emphasis on the final two words and let it sink in. Blackburn's demeanour changed. He apologised and explained. A single bomb had hit the factory at about midnight. There was a public shelter in the basement holding about two hundred people. The floors were wooden and not reinforced. Heavy machinery had crashed into the shelter and many had been killed, including a lot of children.

The rescue operation was being hampered by the fact that the entrance to the shelter was blocked by fallen brick-work. They had been forced to dig tunnels down into the cavity and extract people when they found them, alive or dead. It was a long job and the splintered wood from the ceiling timbers and shattered bunk beds was not helping their efforts. It was a long job and he feared it was a terrible tragedy.

"I hope that helps but I fail to see why it's a security matter, as you put it."

"To be honest, I'm not sure either yet, but thank you, Chief Constable."

"Now, if you'll excuse me. As you can see, I am rather busy."

"Of course. Just one more question. Do you know where I can contact the owner."

"Yes. Mr Wilkinson lives on King Street. Number 24. Phoenix House. Just around the corner." He pointed in the general direction.

"Thank you again. What did they make in the factory?"

"Lemonade."

JUST A FEW YARDS around the corner, 24 King Street was an imposing building with four stone steps up to an impressive, black painted front door. He had to wind his way through a crowd of onlookers to get there. To the right of the door a blank, rectangular wooden board was screwed into the wall at head height. He gave two short raps on the heavy brass knocker.

The door opened. A matronly middle-aged lady smiled thinly at him. "Yes?"

Stokes introduced himself and showed his pass. She showed him through to a spacious sitting room and invited him to sit.

"Talking to Mr Wilkinson will be a problem, Mr Stokes"

"He is at home, isn't he?"

"Oh, yes. He's at home but I'm afraid he's ill."

"I'm sorry to hear that. If he could spare me five minutes though."

She frowned.

"I won't disturb him for long."

"No. I don't think you understand. Mr Wilkinson had a stroke yesterday. The doctor's just left."

"Oh, I'm sorry."

"He should be in hospital but because of the . . . tragedy", she gestured out of the window, "they don't have any beds. There were so many injured."

"Of course. May I still have just a few words with him. It is of . . . erm, national importance, Mrs . . ?"

"Chapman. I'm afraid you will find that very difficult Mr Stokes. His speech, you see. It's . . . well, he can understand what we say to him but he can't talk. It's just grunts, to be honest. And he gets very frustrated."

Stokes sighed. "I'm very sorry to hear that, Mrs Chapman. But I would like to try at least."

"Very well, but please don't upset him."

"I'll try not to."

"Follow me then."

She led him up a thickly carpeted staircase. They walked across the landing to a bedroom door. She knocked. There was no response. After a second knock, she turned to Stokes. "I'll go in first." She opened the door and walked briskly inside.

He listened. He could not make out what she was saying but the louder male voice sounded scarcely human. He wrote off any hope of getting any useful information from Wilkinson, whose condition was clearly grave.

Mrs Chapman re-emerged from the bedroom. "Oh, dear." She dabbed her eyes with a small lace handkerchief. "I'm sorry. I'm just not used to seeing him like this."

"Please. If he's . . ."

"No, he will see you but, as I said, please don't annoy him. He always did have a very short fuse, if you know what I mean, and this isn't helping."

WILKINSON WAS SITTING up in bed, propped by two pillows. He gave Stokes a twisted smile and a hand gesture of greeting. A low, guttural sound came from barely moving lips. He rolled his eyes in frustration and apology. Stokes briefly introduced himself and asked some very basic questions. The man was only able to reply with a nod or a shake of the head. This went on for about a minute until it seemed that he had given up. He reached across with his left arm – clearly the only one that was functioning - and tried to pick up a small notepad from the nightstand.

Stokes jumped to assist him and gave him the pencil that lay next to it. Wilkinson nodded his thanks. With a struggle to sit himself up again, he wrote on the notepad and offered it up to him. He looked down at the two words on the pad. It was a name. He looked back at Wilkinson. His eyes were closed. He walked across to him and touched his shoulder in thanks.

The man was already asleep.

Stokes explained to Mrs Chapman what had happened. She apologised and told him of the sedative medication that the doctor had prescribed until such time as a bed could be found for him in Preston Infirmary. It was the nearest hospital that could take him but they were, apparently, looking at the possibility of getting him into the Royal Victoria Infirmary in Newcastle. He showed her the name that was written on the pad.

"Do you know who that is?"

"Ernest Metcalf. He's the factory manager. Mr Wilkinson gave up the day to day running of the business a few weeks ago and he employed Mr Metcalf as his accountant and . . . general manager, I think."

"Do you know him?"

"No, sorry. I never go to the factory. My job is here at Phoenix House."

She offered her hand. "I'll show you out, Mr Stokes."

As the door closed behind him, he turned to look at it. The wooden board had obviously been robbed of its 'Phoenix House' name plate. Probably the only damage to the house caused by the bombing. Apart from that, it was unscathed. The factory would not be repaired as easily. Nor would it be rising from the ashes.

On his way back from Phoenix House, Stokes spotted the Chief Constable and nodded to him. It dawned on him that a further chat with the gentleman might help him to find Mr Metcalf.

"Mr Blackburn?"

The policeman turned and nodded. He seemed less tense than he had during their last conversation. "Ah, Mr . . . erm?"

"Stokes."

"Ah, yes. National security."

"Yes. Now, I need your help again, I'm afraid. I've been to see Mr Wilkinson."

"Was he able to help?"

"Sadly not. I'm afraid the old chap has taken a stroke and is currently waiting to go into hospital, but obviously, they're very busy at the moment."

"I'm sorry to hear that. It must have been the shock."

"One would imagine, yes."

"It wasn't entirely a wasted visit though. He is still able to hear and understand what people are saying. To cut a long story short, Chief Constable, I understand that this man is managing the fact . . . sorry, *was* managing the factory, on Mr Wilkinson's behalf."

He handed over the piece of paper on which Wilkinson had scribbled the name of Ernest Metcalf. Blackburn reached into his tunic pocket for his spectacles. The old man's scrawl was difficult to decipher.

"Ernest Metcalf."

"Yes. Do you know of him?"

The policeman returned the paper to him. "I'm afraid I don't, Mr Stokes, but . . ."

A shout rang out. "Sir! Mr Blackburn. I need you over here, sir!"

At that, the policeman made a swift, almost inaudible apology, and ran to the scene of the new discovery.

Stokes walked on, to where he did not yet know. He decided to ask someone who was less distracted by the clearance of the factory's public shelter. He called into the corner shop, Shrimplins, where he had seen them earlier, clearing débris from the window. A heavy-set man, wearing a long calico apron, was nailing board across the now empty and glassless window. Stokes approached, introduced himself and showed his government pass. The gentleman smiled. "How can I help you?"

Stokes explained his predicament. He needed to speak to someone in authority at the factory but, due to Mr Wilkinson's incapacity, all he was able to offer was the name of Ernest Metcalf.

The man, who turned out to be Shrimplin himself, denied any knowledge of Metcalf. The old man's secretary,

Lizzie Fenwick, might be able to help though. She was a regular visitor to the shop for bits and pieces but he was unable to offer an address.

With the factory now out of existence, and all the company's paperwork scattered, literally, to the four winds, Stokes had no means of contacting anyone. He thanked Shrimplin and started to walk away. He was wondering if it was worth revisiting Mrs Chapman at Phoenix House to explain further what he needed and, perhaps, getting another 'chat' with the old man. His thoughts were interrupted by Shrimplin tapping him on the shoulder.

"You could try the navy, like"

"The navy . . . the Royal Navy? What have they got to do with the lemonade factory?"

Shrimplin chortled. "That's what we've all been wondering. Been a staff car parked outside for about a week now. And we saw them taking stuff upstairs late one night."

"Oh"

"Aye, and the car is there all hours of the night. They've really been burning the midnight oil, mind." The shopkeeper was keen to point out that one of the naval bods had been in the shop once or twice but was very tight-lipped.

Stokes thanked him again and walked away.

What the Hell were the Royal Navy doing in a lemonade factory? He headed back to the police station to call Knight. The desk sergeant recognised him.

"Mr Stokes. Unless you have come to report under-age drinking in Northumberland Park or tell me you've found an umbrella on the bus, I'm assuming you need to make another expensive telephone call to London?"

Stokes laughed. "And this may not be the last time, I'm afraid."

The policeman smiled. "So, do you want the interview room again?"

"Yes, please."

Stokes walked through, picked up the receiver and asked for Knight's number. It rang only twice before he picked up.

"Stokes, what news?"

"Up until half an hour ago, I was of the opinion that the factory bombing was just one of the many nuisance raids the town has had in the last few months. It's on the Tyne near the shipyards and docks. It's also a dropping off point for any *Kraut* who's still got bombs in his belly and doesn't want to cart them back over the North Sea."

"So, you said 'up until half an hour ago'. What have you found?"

Stokes told Knight of the abortive meeting with the stricken Wilkinson. "My initial feeling is that there is no Fifth Columnist cell operating here. I have not heard of any thus far . . ."

"Yes, come on, man. Get to the point."

"Well, I know what I am about to tell you will probably mean I have to extend my stay in this forsaken place but . . ."

"For pity's sake!"

"What are Royal Navy scientists doing in a lemonade factory?"

A crackling silence ensued.

"Lemonade?"

"Yes. That's what I thought. I was expecting munitions at least."

"Very odd. It came to me via a call from on high. Not God but pretty close. Just telling me to get somebody up there and you were the closest I had. I had no idea there was a naval connection. I'll certainly find out from the Admiralty bods. Where did you get this from?"

"Oh, they didn't exactly make a secret of it. They were seen moving stuff into the factory overnight quite recently. And, I gather, they parked the staff car right outside during the day. They were there for at least a week."

"Oh, good God Almighty! I'm going to enjoy rubbing their noses in this one. They may as well have lit it up with floodlights and painted a bloody big bullseye on the roof!"

"Exactly what I was thinking, sir."

"Yes. Well done, Albert. You stay there. Find out what else you can. I still think there has to be a cell up there somewhere for them to have reacted so quickly. I don't believe in chance, old fruit."

"I have to leave for Hull tomorrow so no chance of doing any more digging, I'm afraid. I have two names, though, I'll track them down when I get back."

From the tone of Knight's voice, Stokes could almost detect a raising of his eyebrows. "A cell?"

"I don't think so. Don't get too excited. And, as I said, I know of no Fifth Columnist activity around here. It could still have been a random raid."

"Hmm, who are the names then?"

"Just couple of people who worked at the factory who may have a bit of inside knowledge on the naval presence."

"Good. Well, do what you can. I need to know what is energising the Admiralty so much. Speak soon. Oh . . . and be careful in Hull. I don't want this bugger Smith slipping out of our clutches again but no heroics on your part, old lad. I assume you have everything ready for his apprehension."

"Not yet. That's why I need to get there a day ahead."

"Good. Get all your ducks in a row, old boy. I will inform Twenty to expect a visitor in the next couple of days. TTFN."

The phone went dead. Stokes put the receiver back onto

its cradle, left the room and thanked the desk sergeant on his way out. He had already made his mind up that he was going to devote the whole day tomorrow in just getting to Hull. As Knight had said, he needed to get his ducks in a row.

He had almost forgotten that, although Smith's first abode following his capture would be the police station in Hull, his ultimate destination would be Camp Twenty. Stokes knew them only by reputation and from what Knight had told him during his brief induction.

Twenty was the verbal version of the Roman numerals XX, which also conveyed the idea of 'double cross'. The Twenty Committee's role was to convert captured German spies into double agents, who would carry on dealing with their contact in the *Reich*, albeit in a controlled way. The hope was that, in these monitored communications, the British security services would find out what the German intelligence machine was interested in. In return, all that the double agent transmitted to them would either be information of little value - so-called 'chicken feed' - or material that was either downright false or simply misleading.

If these individuals refused, then their lives would be cut short at the end of the hangman's rope. It was 'turn or burn'.

If all went well at the Punch Hotel, that would be the stark choice facing Smith.

CHAPTER 31

Wesley found the *Three Horseshoes* pub at Usworth quite easily. Ernest's directions were flawless. He parked the Armstrong Siddeley well away from the main gate of the RAF base and strolled up to the pub. It was early. He wanted to be there, concealed in a corner, when the Czech arrived. He needed the advantage of surprise.

It was a couple of pints and a sad, curly sandwich later when he spotted Preucil rolling in with two of his brothers in arms. The physical description he had been given was perfect. He could hear the conversation but did not understand it. To his untutored ears, it sounded like Czech.

He watched the airman carefully. There was no impression of a man who was defying the very organisation that had given him his freedom. And no clue at all that he was putting his handler, WIESELIG, to so much trouble. It was the arrogance of the man that Wesley disliked. He needed a short sharp shock. The actor in him had not had to play this role many times in his career but he knew he was up to it. He certainly had the build for a 'heavy'.

He waited until the Czech was most vulnerable and away from his colleagues. The best place for that would be the urinals. He kept himself out of the airman's eyeline and bided his time. It had to happen, of course. Mother Nature will have her way. Half an hour or so after Preucil had started drinking, he swaggered his way to the toilets. Wesley gave it ten seconds and followed him. There were just the two of them in there.

The Czech did not hear him entering. He was whistling a tune that Wesley did not recognise. While his hands were occupied and the sound of pissing at its loudest, Wesley crept up behind him.

"Preucil?"

"Yes."

As short as the response was, it was stifled as Wesley rammed the pilot's face against the white tiles and whispered into his ear. "You have caused me a lot of problems, old chap."

Preucil could not see his assailant's face as he peed down his uniformed legs. Wesley pressed harder. The man was pinned to the wall and unable to draw his hands into play.

"I have been looking for you."

Wesley was not a great fan of violence but this man's behaviour was intensely irritating. There was no soft-glove version of what Wesley had to do, and he had the advantage of height and build. "Meet me behind the pub right now or I will announce to your station commander - whom I have seen at the bar, by the way - whom you are really working for."

He was lying but he surmised that the Czech was not in a position to cross-examine him. He released the airman's head and walked to the door. Preucil turned to look at him. Shock registered on the airman's face, his flies were still open and there was a steaming damp patch down the left leg of his trousers. He was a pitiful sight.

Wesley left the pub by a door that opened onto a small garden area. He sat at a wooden table and waited for Preucil's exit. He did not have to wait long. The Czech emerged, looking nervously around and rubbing his fore-head. He sat opposite Wesley with his back to the door.

The handler spoke first. "What I am about to say will be brief. You cannot see it, but in my left hand I am holding a pistol and it's pointed roughly at your stomach. Quite fitting that it's of Czech manufacture. Now, I haven't had much training in firearms and I have no idea how good my aim is. Let's face it though, how good does it need to be at this distance?"

Wesley laughed loudly. It was pure invention, of course, all of it, but the Czech was not going to take any chances. "Now, I want you to laugh as well. If anyone is watching, they will see nothing but two old chums having a good time. Let me hear you laugh, Gus. I know you can . . ."

Preucil emitted a laugh which, on a one-to-ten scale of sincerity, barely registered a four.

"That will do. Keep doing it please. As you can see, I'm smiling as if to appreciate something you have just said to me." He laughed again. "I will continue. Just listen."

Wesley went on to inform him that his masters were very disappointed in him. Preucil's protestations were brushed aside. It was of no consequence to Wesley that the Czech had been moved from base to base more frequently than seemed to be the norm, due, in no small part, to his abysmal disciplinary record.

The Czech was visibly quaking. Although he knew he probably had the physical power to overcome this man, he sensed that it would not end well. There was a pistol pointed at his guts and only the table between them. He was also sure that WIESELIG would have reported back that they knew where he was by now, anyway. He had been found and somebody else would only arrive on his doorstep to reinforce the point.

Wesley spoke. "I see you have Hurricanes here." The airman nodded. "Good. Then your job is simple. I want you to steal one. As, indeed, you were instructed to in return for allowing you to escape from . . . well, death following a long period of torture, I would imagine."

He laughed. Remembering what he had been told, so too did the Czech. Wesley bent in, remembering to keep his 'gun hand' under the table.

"I would also remind you that, should you try to go into hiding, you will find it exceedingly difficult after the invasion, my friend. Retribution will be swift and lacking in mercy." He paused. "You know how it works, I think?"

Preucil turned to look towards the airfield. He whispered. "But these are not the current marque. That's the Mk II which are only used by front-line squadrons. Training squadrons like this one only have . . . second-hand MkIs. Some of them are not good. We only get the cast-offs here."

Wesley stared at him and smiled. "That's truly unfortunate but what I would suggest is that you pick the best of the bunch from what you have here and just . . . do the business, old chap. I'm sure that would be acceptable."

He mimed putting the pistol back in his coat pocket and stood.

"And don't forget the sort of accidents that might befall your family should you fail to deliver. The camps out east are not for the weak or the squeamish. Looking on the bright side though, you will be extremely well rewarded for your efforts should you succeed. And Dr Göbbels in particular will be a very happy man. Wonderful propaganda. The RAF is a leaky ship etc. Mixing my metaphors there but you get my meaning."

He walked away and then turned. "You have a week. Chocks away and happy landings, old chap. My best wishes to Muriel. Oh . . . and that cut on your forehead, I'd get it seen to. It's going to smart in the morning." He paused. "And I understand that five thousand *Reichsmarks* is the going price for a Hurricane at the moment. Not to be sniffed at. And you'll be famous - a legend in your own lunchtime." He laughed. "But only in the *Reich,* obviously."

In less than a minute, Wesley was back in the car and pulling away.

Preucil was shocked. This was what he had been dreading for a long time. He thought he had succeeded in staying hidden from WIESELIG but the man had surprised him with his ingenuity. He was not bothered about any repercussions involving family and friends but it was the mention of Muriel's name that gave him the biggest shock. How on earth did he know about her?

He pulled himself together and walked back into the bar.

WHILE THE CZECH was wrestling with his conscience and stiffening his sinews for the task ahead of him, Wesley was driving south. It had been an extremely successful day thus far, and he had decided he should also confront the Pole. What better than to be able to report to Hamburg that he had managed to bag a brace? Two fighters landing on *Reich* soil would take on the appearance of a production line. He smiled to himself at the *kudos* that would hurtle his way.

MOTORRAD had always worried him, especially as he

had been told that the man had not communicated at all since he arrived in Britain. It had given Wesley great satisfaction to put a flea in his ear and a kick up his backside. He smiled as he thought of the physical gymnastics that conjured up.

He knew it was a long trek to RAF Biggin Hill. After an hour, he pulled into a roadside petrol station and filled the tank. He wanted to use the cash and coupons he still had and then make the best of the double summer time that was introduced the previous year. That meant he could get maximum benefit from the longer daylight. Besides that, the fact that he had a wireless in his boot made his normal practice of 'car hopping' riskier and more problematic.

As darkness started to envelop the landscape. he pulled over and decided to get a few hours shuteye. He put on his coat and hat, found a pair of gloves and settled in the passenger seat. This car was very comfortable. It had been a good choice.

MORNING FOUND him north of London. He struggled to remember the name of the town he had just driven through and the permanent lack of signposts was becoming a pain in the backside. He remembered - Biggleswade. It reminded him of a book that Grosskopf had given him in case Wesley ever need to get a handle on RAF slang. *Biggles Goes To War*. Jingoistic nonsense, he had called it, but Wesley had found it quite amusing.

As he rounded the metropolis, fear gripped him. This idea of visiting the Pole had been great in concept but now that it was off the drawing board, it had begun to tarnish. What made him think he could simply waltz into a frontline

RAF station and demand to have a word with one of their airmen?

For the next twenty miles or so, an idea began to crystallise in his head. As always, he had his Britishness to fall back on. He had found it invaluable on many occasions already. German spies were seen as shifty, evil-looking characters, forever creeping in and out of the shadows. He did not need to creep. He had what no other German spy had - *panache*. Gallons of it.

The object of the exercise was to get five minutes alone with Gierczak. Threats of violence *à la Three Horseshoes* would be out of the question, naturally, especially as the 'interview' would be conducted on the base itself. This was possibly the most dangerous situation that he had knowingly put himself in. And the fact that he had not clapped eyes on the fellow before made it doubly difficult.

To be fair to the Pole, he had been extremely forthcoming with regular reports via the postal services of Frau Viggle, the cutout in Barnsley, so this reminder of his responsibilities could be a tad gentler than it was with the Czech. More firm reminder than coercion. So diligent had the Pole been that he had actually notified them of his posting to RAF Biggin Hill.

By the time he approached the gates of the base, he had a character and a plan in mind. He had been workshopping it for the last couple of hours. It had holes but nothing that could not be covered with a bit of good-natured British bluster.

HE HAD NO BUSINESS CARD, of course, to show to the guard at the gate. He therefore explained in the simplest possible terms that he was working for the Polish Airmen's Welfare

Association, based in London. He had been touring RAF bases and putting all Polish fliers on their books so that they could be kept in touch with events in their home country. They hoped to produce a newsletter in due course which would be circulated to bases.

The guard listened politely. Wesley ferreted in his pocket for his John Smith ID, which he handed over. He also took out his notebook. "I'm looking for a ... erm, not sure of his rank, sorry. Ah, here we are ... Tomasz Gierczak. We get this information from the Air Ministry but I'm afraid their records are often out of date. I only need him for five minutes."

The armed airman smiled. "I think I know him. Wait there, I need to clear this with the Station Adjutant." The man took Wesley's ID and returned with it five minutes later. He took his visitor to a small ante-room and asked him to wait. Wesley breathed a large sigh of relief. He walked across the narrow space to the window. It was covered in cardboard. He turned to see a wiry young man standing in the doorway. He looked confused.

"Mr Smith?"

"Yes."

They shook hands.

"Shall we sit down?"

They sat facing each other across the small table in the centre of the room.

"Tomasz. I have a confession to make. Please don't be alarmed. And don't make a fuss. I am Mr Smith ... but I am also WIESELIG."

The man's mouth dropped open. Wesley continued. "And you, of course, are STANGE."

"No ..." The man's head slumped. He started to protest.

"I've simply come to inform you that the *Reich* is

extremely grateful for the information you have been supplying. Valuable stuff, I understand."

This did not help Gierczak or make him feel any better. He knew that the information he had given them was false. But this man may not be aware of that. Wesley stretched an arm across the table and laid it on his shoulder. "But, old chap, I am now here to tell you that you must now fulfil the final part of your mission."

The Pole knew what he meant. He had been dreading something like this. A final reckoning. "No . . . I can't." He looked Wesley in the eyes. "Really, I cannot do that."

Wesley smiled. He withdrew his arm. "Of course, you can, old chap."

There was silence for ten seconds.

"What happens to me if I don't?"

"What happens to *you*? Well, probably nothing. But as to what happens to your wife and young child, then I'm not awfully sure . . . but I don't think it would end well."

He thought the man was going to cry. And then he did. "Come on, old chap. A simple flight. A landing. And then you will be reunited with your family."

Gierczak was still very emotional. He spoke quietly as he stared at the table. "I did not even know they were still alive."

Wesley laughed. "Of course, they are. They have been well looked after and are awaiting your return." He doubted that very much but he would tell the man whatever it took to get him in the air.

The Pole now had images of himself, his beloved Jagoda and little Tomasz being reunited. And all he had to do was to fly a Spitfire for less than two hundred miles. Smith was watching Gierczak's eyes glaze over. He knew what he was thinking. He patted his arm.

"And think about it. You have done your bit for your country ... *and* for the RAF ... *and* the *Reich*. There aren't many who can say that, now are there? That's makes you pretty special. Don't you want to just leave this war behind you?"

The Pole looked up at last. He nodded. Wesley smiled at him again. "Good. And ... you will be well rewarded. The last chap will be looking at five thousand *Reichsmarks* at least. That's a good whack. Enough to start again." He paused. "So, what do you say?"

Wesley let him digest it all and walked across to the shrouded window. He tried to peer through gaps in the cardboard. "What have you got here anyway?"

It worked. He knew the man would at least want to talk aeroplanes. "We've just got Spitfire Vs."

"Are they good?"

"Yes, very good. Much better than the previous ones. Faster ..."

Wesley sat back down. He became more earnest than before. "Listen, old man. I put myself at great risk coming here to see you. You could turn me in at any time. You could open that door, shout down the corridor and have me arrested. But you won't ... and shall I tell you why? Because I have incriminating evidence on you too. We have a knife at each other's throat, so to speak." He paused. "And then you will definitely never see your family again."

He paused. Gierczak nodded solemnly. "It will not be until next week. I have seen the rosters."

Wesley smiled as he stood. "That's fine." He looked at his watch. "Now, I think I have had my allotted time. I told the guard I would only need you for five minutes. And that has just expired."

He reached the door and turned. He held out his hand.
The Pole shook it. Wesley viewed that as a contract sealed.

"Good luck."

WESLEY LEFT the base with as much haste as was decent. He
did not want to raise suspicion. He drove gently away and
breathed a long sigh of relief. He could feel sweat drying on
his body.

"That, old boy, was the best performance of your bloody
life. No script. No rehearsals. No anything. *Magna . . . cum . . .
bloody . . . laude!*"

He laughed out loud. He could not wait to tell Otto the
news. And that was without what he might gain from the
meeting tomorrow with the birdspotter, Armitage. The
decoy site chap. He could well prove the catalyst for a Fifth
Columnist cell. That, after all, was the brief Wesley had
been given, in order to facilitate the invasion.

The adrenaline of the day kept him going for most of the
drive back. He eventually gave up as soon as it got dark and
repeated the procedure of the night before. Coat, hat, gloves
and stretch out, as far his frame would allow, on the
passenger seat. He had made it to almost the point where he
would head off to the right and travel east to Hull on the
A63.

He feared sleeping too long and had no alarm clock with
him. He was therefore relieved when he felt the cold seeping
through the bodywork of the car. He woke up shivering.
There was condensation on the windows. He stepped out
and stretched his frozen limbs. After a quick pee at the side
of the car, he got back in behind the steering wheel and
headed off, looking for the Hull turning.

He looked at his watch. There would still be time to

spare for him to call into Gillett Street, drop the North Shields wireless off and have a quick wash and brush up before he headed to the Punch Hotel for his meeting with Armitage. With luck, he would also have time, before that, to dash off a quick message to Otto in Hamburg and inform him of his double *coup*. He smiled to himself. He was very tempted to transmit 'Czech and mate' but was not sure that Otto would get the chess wordplay. Best keep it simple.

He frowned as he approached the city and saw the grey cloud suspended above it. He was driving through an embryonic sunny day so the cloud was a bit of a mystery. He soon realised that it was not meteorological. It was clearly the dust rising from the rubble of a good nocturnal pounding by the *Luftwaffe*. He hoped his digs were still standing. And, come to that, the Punch Hotel too. He had probably got a better night's sleep in the car than he would have done against the background cacophony of an air raid.

Nearing his digs, it looked as if this had indeed been a big raid. The closer he got to the city centre, the more obvious was the evidence of bomb damage. Thankfully, Gillett Street was unscathed.

Back in his room, he slid the North Shields wireless under the bed and extracted his own set. He keyed in as WIESELIG and sent a jubilant, coded message that would encapsulate the line - 'the owl and the pussy cat went to sea' - from Edward Lear's poem. He stressed the lengths he had gone to in tracking down the Czech flier, MOTORRAD, and then priming the Pole, STANGE, into instant response. They should allow a week for delivery.

Hamburg were not to know that the Czech had been virtually dropped into his lap. The whole mission - to confront him, remind him of his duty and issue him with a stern warning - had taken just over an hour, with the minimum of travel and inconvenience. But there was no harm in building his part, he felt.

On the other hand, the visit to STANGE, due to his distance from Wesley's northern base, had been much more problematic. He stressed, once again, that the role of messenger boy was becoming tedious and deflecting him from his original stated mission. That done, and to emphasise the last point, he informed Hamburg that the North Shields set had been retrieved from BLEISTIFT.

Otto came back with congratulations on all that Wesley had told him and, he was pleased to see, a 'job well done' on the factory. That was good. Wesley closed with the information - embellished in perpetuation of his shameless self-promotion - that he had an important meeting that day with another promising Fifth Columnist contact in Hull.

He signed out, shoved the set under the bed and lay back. He looked at his watch. He had a few hours before his rendezvous with Armitage. Time enough to set the alarm clock and grab forty winks before taking the short drive to the Punch Hotel. When he got back later, he would have some serious sleep. He could feel exhaustion draining the life out of him.

Despite his tiredness, he still felt wired with the exhilaration of the past twenty-four hours. All he wished now was a bit less down-time with the constant driving. He enjoyed motoring and the thought of having his pick of vehicles was extremely gratifying, but it was so bloody time-consuming. And exhausting.

After checking again that his alarm clock was correctly set for a time that would allow him to get to the Punch Hotel in time, he flopped back onto his pillow. He was asleep before his head landed. He dreamt of audience adulation and applause.

CHAPTER 32

S tokes now had a full day to get from North Shields to Hull before the planned capture of the mysterious Smith. He was not sorry to leave North Shields but knew that he had to return soon to complete the search for Ernest Metcalf - and the other name he now had, Lizzie Fenwick. He wanted this Armitage sideshow to be settled as swiftly as possible.

He parked as closely as he could to the city centre. Signs of a raid the previous night were all too evident. Hull seemed to have become a popular target for *Luftwaffe* bomber crews. Like Tyneside, it was too easily identifiable both inward and outward - the wide and inviting jaws of the Humber estuary acting almost like a funnel. As well as targeted raids, it had also become an obvious drop site for any aircraft returning with a bomb load that it needed to jettison.

The police station was on Alfred Gelder Street. He showed them his MoD ID, explained the situation and made arrangements for two sturdy, stalwart policemen - in plain clothes - to be outside the Punch Hotel from a quarter

past ten the following morning. A man was to be apprehended on a signal from Stokes. He was then to be taken
back to a cell immediately afterwards, from where he would
be picked up by gentlemen from the security services.

After twenty minutes, Stokes was acquainted with the
two bobbies who would actually be carrying out the arrest
of Smith. He explained the situation once again and
stressed that they must be in plain clothes. He did not want
this fellow to be spooked before he entered the pub. He
stressed the importance of their mission.

DESPITE THE OBVIOUS assault that the city had suffered,
Stokes was pleased to see that the Punch Hotel still stood
intact and proud. It was tea-time before he got there. The
city was closing down for the day. Homeward traffic was
brisk but the many road closures caused by bomb damage
were hampering its progress.

The pub was closed. Stokes had phoned ahead though
so he tapped on the window to announce his arrival. The
friendly, bespectacled face of the landlord, Fred Wallis,
appeared through the stained glass of the bar window. He
smiled and pointed to the door.

Fred was a cheerful soul and ran the pub with his wife,
Kitty. They lived on the premises with their son - also Fred -
and daughter Barbara. "Good evening, Mr Stokes. Wasn't
expecting to see you as soon as this."

"No, it was a surprise to me too, to be honest."

He walked Stokes through to the bar. "Can I get you
something - or is it too early? On the house, of course."

"No, thanks. Maybe later."

"I'll get Kitty to make you a cup of tea. We'll bring it up
for you." He pointed his right hand above his head. "You're

in this room." He laughed. "We've only got two guest rooms. My daughter and son in law are in the other one. Not married long and baby on the way." He turned to Stokes and grinned. "So, I'm going to be a granddad in a few months. They were bombed out last week. Just trying to find themselves a new place."

Stokes laughed. "Congratulations. It can't be easy for them."

"Thanks. No. And not ideal to be born in the middle of this carnage." He pointed out of the window. He laughed. "But Mother Nature had other ideas."

Stokes smiled and shrugged. He explained that he had a meeting the following morning in the bar and needed some time to go through papers in his room. He promised he would see him later.

"That's fine. I'll send one of the kids up with your tea. Bye for now then, Mr Stokes."

The landlord gave him the key. Stokes left him drying glasses and whistling to himself.

AFTER A FRUGAL MEAL and a few drinks in the bar, Stokes turned in just after ten. He was woken a couple of hours later by the sound of sirens and an insistent knocking on the door. It was Wallis.

"Sorry to bother you, Mr Stokes, but no doubt you've heard. We've got another raid - second on the trot." He paused. "Me and the family are going to the shelter."

"Oh . . . where is it?"

"It's under the Prudential building, just on the other side of the square. You can't miss it. Bloody big tower, excuse my language." He laughed. "It's an underground shelter. There'll be a warden on the street door."

Stokes could feel the hairs standing up on the back of his neck. Shelter. Underground. Memories of the basement factory shelter in North Shields were in his mind. "What time is it?"

"Just after midnight."

That was another word that drew shivers. Midnight. No thanks.

"Erm . . . yes, I'll probably join you. Thank you." He knew he would not. He made to close the door.

"We're all going. And . . . I'm taking a friend of mine." He opened his jacket to reveal a bottle of whiskey - Johnnie Walker. He grinned.

Stokes laughed. "Stay safe."

"Oh, by the way - your room key opens the front door as well so you're not locked in."

He closed the door and heard the young couple following Wallis. Then it was Kitty Wallis and the kids clattering down the stairs and the front door being locked.

HE WAS unable to get back to sleep. There was a growing soundscape of thumps, crashes and bangs - some distant, some frighteningly close. The constant drone of bomber engines. Ambulance bells. Shouting. And worse than all that - screaming. He gave up trying to sleep.

His room had a bay window which looked out over the square. The view through the glass was like Dante's Inferno. He craned his neck and tried to look to his left down Carr Lane in the direction of Hull Paragon station, but the angle was too acute.

He heard a mighty, roaring crump. He looked across to where the noise seemed to have come from. He watched in horror as the Prudential building slowly crumpled and fell in upon itself, thrusting a vast, billowing blanket of white smoke out across the street.

Stokes was transfixed. The cloud slowly and relentlessly filled the square. He opened the window. The dust wafted in and gave him a coughing fit. He grabbed his handkerchief and covered his nose. He could see flames at the base of the Prudential building. Within minutes, as the scene settled, the only thing remaining of the Prudential building was its tower at the corner of the square.

He dressed and ran quickly downstairs. His thoughts turned to those who had been trapped in Wilkinson's factory basement in North Shields just a few nights earlier. He felt himself experiencing both raids - the one in his head, the other in full sight. In both cases, being trapped in a dark and claustrophobic underground space was the worst thing he could imagine. He left through the front door and locked it behind him.

The sounds from those who had been injured pierced the steady rumble from above. He knew there must be many dead or dying. Initially glad that he had not followed Wallis to the Prudential shelter, he also reflected that the night was not over. The drone of the overhead bombers was constant.

No building was safe in this sort of scenario. The Punch, too, could be hit. And he could not remain an observer. He spent the next few hours until dawn, helping the injured to an ambulance, or a medic, or simply to a shop doorway where they could wait and be comforted while they sat. A tea van from the WVS miraculously arrived out of nowhere.

STOKES GRAFTED FOR HOURS. He stayed well beyond the 'all clear' and did all he could until exhaustion hit him. He trudged back to the Punch. The door was open. The day's barman had keys. When Stokes told the man that he was a guest, he introduced himself as Tom. Stokes told him that the landlord and his family had gone to the Prudential shelter when the sirens had sounded about midnight. It was a difficult thing to impart to one who clearly knew the Wallis family well. Tom sat on a bar stool, his body hunched. He was close to tears.

"Are you working on your own today?"

The barman looked up and stared straight ahead at the window that looked out onto the chaos in the square. He stood. "No. There's another three staff arriving. Two barmaids and the cook." He started taking chairs off tables and generally preparing for opening.

"You're going to open as normal, then."

"Fred would want it."

Stokes offered to help and between them they laid out the ashtrays, readied the pumps for service, stocked up with bottles and switched on the lights. The dust cloud from the raid was still casting a gloom over everything.

"I'll just go and get cleaned up."

Tom turned. "Yes, of course, Mr Stokes. Thanks for your help. Are you leaving today?"

"Yes, but not until later. I am meeting somebody in here this morning. I'll be back down by then."

He looked at his watch. It was almost nine o'clock. The plain clothes bobbies would be there in just over an hour, with Smith due to arrive at half past ten. Ducks in a row. Knight was liaising with Twenty on the collection of Smith from his police cell and onward transportation to their HQ in London.

With what he had just seen and experienced, he was pleased that his part in all of this was brief and undemanding. He just had to ensure the coppers got the right bloke.

. . .

WITHIN TWENTY MINUTES, Stokes was back downstairs and sitting in the bar. While he was waiting, a group of firemen entered, their faces blackened and streaked with sweat. Tom handed each of them a bottle. From the conversation he could hear, they were coming off shift, having been relieved by another team from across the city.

Stokes walked to the bar and introduced himself. Tom assured the firemen that he was a guest in the Punch who had been on the street himself all night, helping out.

"I was wondering if there was any news of Fred, the landlord and his family. They went over to the shelter just after the sirens sounded. Fred Wallis."

One of the older men grimaced. "We can't get in there. I'm afraid. It's just too hot. We think the heating boiler must have exploded. We can't just flood the place in case there is anyone still alive."

"They'd drown", said another.

"It could be a couple of days", a third man added. The others nodded in agreement.

Tom looked away.

"There was only one survivor as far as we know. We don't know anything else at the moment. Names, numbers - nothing."

Stokes mumbled his thanks and walked back to the table. Memories of just a few hours earlier kept coming to the surface. The heavily pregnant daughter giggling. The children careering down the stairs as if they were going on holiday. The bottle of Johnnie Walker.

He felt almost incapable of facing Smith without wanting to put his hands around his neck and squeezing for a long time, before relinquishing him to the policemen. This was a man who was on the same side as those who had spent a couple of hours raining death and destruction on the city.

He took solace in the knowledge that Smith's days of liberty would soon be over.

EVEN THOUGH SMITH was expecting to meet Armitage this morning, Stokes had told the twitcher that his presence there would not be required. If Armitage were present at this planned meeting - and Stokes was sure that the man would not want to attend anyway - he would witness Stokes using a persona that he did not want him to see. It would blast his 'Hitler's man in London' story out of the water. He promised he would let the man know of the outcome. He had the man's home address in Hessle, so he would call in there on his way out, once everything was done and dusted.

He knew this was going to be tricky. Armitage had reported that the man sounded more British than he did. If Smith really was British, but working for the Nazis – and actually recruiting for them, then that could not be resolved within the confines of the Punch Hotel. In any case, he was not sure he wanted to put the staff through any additional trauma, especially so soon after the Prudential shelter tragedy. This Mr Smith would have to be extricated and taken to another place for interrogation.

AT TEN O'CLOCK, Stokes walked out of the front door. On the other side of the square, he could see a police car. Two heavily-set men were standing, smoking and chatting. He walked over to them, identified himself and confirmed what action was to be taken. They were already in no doubt but Stokes always liked to make sure when third parties were involved. They walked back across to the Punch with him and stood separately, one at each side of the Punch's door, but a short distance from it. Far enough not to look like doormen yet close enough to make a swift entry and apprehension. They were also primed to refuse entry to anyone who tried to enter before Smith himself had turned up. They had been told what he looked like but would await the nod from Stokes.

Armitage had been able to give a much more detailed description of the man. Stokes ascertained from Tom, the barman, that there was no other exit from the pub other than the door which opened onto the square. He had to come clean to the man and assert that it was an issue of national security. He recalled showing his Ministry of Defence ID to the landlord, Fred Wallis, so he surmised that Tom may already have been aware of his real identity and status.

Stokes bought a drink and settled down to read a copy of the *Daily Mirror* that he found lying on the chair. He was watching the door. Restrictions on newsprint had reduced the *Mirror* to a bare four pages but he was not reading it anyway. Smith was now late. Stokes was getting nervous.

It was almost twenty minutes to eleven before a tall well-built man walked in through the door. He fitted the description that Armitage had given him. He looked around. Not seeing the man he was due to meet, he seemed puzzled and walked to the bar. Stokes walked swiftly up behind him.

"Mr Smith, isn't it?"

The man turned quickly. His face stopped moving before his jowls did. He spluttered and continued to look around for Armitage. The man's face shone red and he was sweating. Stokes took out his ID and thrust it into his face. It was just too fast for the man to register the details.

"It's not a difficult question. If you'd like to come with us, we'll try to help you remember your name, at least."

The two policemen had entered the bar from the street. Stokes nodded to them and the pair of them grabbed the now heavily perspiring man and marched him from the bar, much to the bemusement of the barman who was standing behind the bar, waiting for their orders.

"He's decided he's not so thirsty after all. Sorry, Tom."

The young man smiled and Stokes left the Punch Hotel, in time to see Smith being bundled into the back of a police car parked just a few yards away on Carr Lane. He gestured to one of the police officers who walked over to him.

"Sir?"

"Well done. He wasn't too much trouble, was he?"

"No, sir. One of the easiest captures I've ever had." He laughed. "Not the most athletic of chaps."

Stokes laughed. "Just a word to the wise. Do not answer any questions he may have about me. Just put him in a cell and he will be picked up later today."

He made his way to the police station. He ascertained that Smith was under lock and key and out of sight, before phoning Knight. He was pleased with the news that the man had been apprehended. He would inform Twenty that their parcel was awaiting collection at Hull main police station. He would also speak to the Chief Constable there to congratulate him and the two men responsible for the arrest. In his opinion, it never did any harm to oil the wheels of fraternity and co-operation.

Wesley's eventual destination was Richmond, Surrey. Once there, he would be interviewed by the Twenty Committee. Their remit was to interview captured German spies, subject them to a little discomfort and encourage them to assess their future.

Stokes' workload had eased somewhat, although Knight was keen for him to get back to North Shields as soon as possible. Pressure was being brought to bear regarding the Royal Navy's 'setback'.

He would drop in to see Armitage to report on the morning's 'meeting'. Hessle was on the periphery of the Hull conurbation so it was on his way back to Tyneside.

CHAPTER 33

Peter Armitage was riding his bike from his home in Hessle to Queen Victoria Square in Hull. It was roughly five miles and fairly flat all the way as the road hugged the northern banks of the Humber. It was a steady ride and he had time to reflect on why he was making the journey.

He found himself in conflict and afraid that he was being overtaken by events. Since the letter he sent to the German Embassy in London - and the unsent one that he gave to Geoffrey Salter - he seemed to have unleashed a beast that he could not put back into the cage.

He had accepted Salter for what he said he was - Hitler's man in London. The man had pointed out, quite correctly, that he would have been in the Tower of London by now if MI5 had picked up the letter he sent to the German Embassy in London. How could he have been so stupid? The place had been closed for three months when he sent it.

Looking back, so great was the relief at having avoided that fate, that he would probably have believed that Salter was Father Christmas. Like the Yuletide hero, he had also come bearing gifts. Gestures of appreciation for his service to the *Reich*. And the promise of further recognition for what he was doing at the decoy sites. He started to feel appreciated for his actions.

And then this Smith character had turned up at Cherry Cobb Sands. That was a bad day. He left his bike behind and had to walk all the way back from Queen Victoria Square to the decoy site to retrieve it - in the rain. He had not known what to make of the man. He mentioned a couple of times that they were both on the same side. He remembered being too scared to ask the obvious question - which side is that? And the man seemed to know a lot about these Q-sites. Armitage was beginning to think he had imagined the whole thing when Smith got in touch and organised a meeting at the Punch Hotel.

Of the two - Smith and Salter - Armitage felt that the former was more in keeping with his image of a spy - shifty, appearing from nowhere. Salter, although equipped with all the goods, seemed very . . . establishment. Yes, that was the word.

He had, of course, notified Salter who had immediately taken this meeting out of his hands. He was clearly convinced that Smith was not who he made himself out to be and insisted that he attend instead of Armitage. He also recalled Salter's use of the word 'eliminated'. On the face of it, it seemed that Salter was somehow looking after Armitage. Protecting his asset, he supposed.

As the meeting approached, he became obsessed with its portent. On the face of it, there were two apparent Englishman who both professed to be German spies. Salter quite overtly, with all the paperwork and background - and trinkets; Smith not yet out of the woodwork but maybe that

was what he would have been telling Armitage at the Punch.
'Much to talk about' he had written in the note.

The odds were that one of them was, in fact, working for
MI5. If that were true, why had Armitage not yet been
apprehended by one of them? What was frightening him
now was that the winner in this tussle for his favours - and it
had to be the MI5 man - would eventually turn up at his
door. And his next place of residence could indeed be the
Tower.

There seemed to be numerous permutations and only a
few of them would produce a favourable outcome. He
wanted to be within sight of the Punch Hotel while this
meeting was going on. He needed a bit of notice for what
was to come, rather than simply sitting and waiting for the
knock on the door.

ARMITAGE WAS SHOCKED at the sight of so many ruined
buildings on his brief journey into Hull city centre. He had
heard the constant rumble of the bombers over the last two
nights but it had not prepared him for the carnage he was to
witness on his ride in. The weather was warm but the
clouds, caused, he realised, by the bombing, were obliter-
ating any sign of the sun.

Negotiating the various bomb sites was difficult. He was
glad he was not trying to drive in by car. Many times he was
forced to pick his cycle up and walk around obstacles in his
path. It was like the end of the world. He thought of the
decoy sites being built so quickly and assiduously along the
banks of the Humber and felt strangely troubled. He had
been passing information about these sites to Salter and
onwards, he had assumed, to Berlin. Clearly, the *Luftwaffe*
were now aware of the subterfuge and ignoring the trickery,

enabling them to wreak death and destruction on the city. His city, he suddenly realised.

He studiously avoided the Carr Lane route to the square where the Punch Hotel stood. It would bring him too close to the venue for the meeting. Instead, he decided to negotiate his way up Paragon Street which ran parallel to Carr Lane and brought him out onto Queen Victoria Square, a little further from the Punch.

The top of Paragon Street proved problematic, however. Many bombs had struck premises on the thoroughfare and all that was left of the Prudential building on the corner, was its tower. A large cordon had been thrown around the site and what was left of the structure looked none too stable. By now, he was carrying his bike on his shoulder. He sweated and panted his way into the square, cursing his thick trench coat which he had worn as a form of disguise. He crossed to sit on the steps of the Maritime Museum and put his bike behind him. It was a perfect vantage point. From there, he could see that the Punch Hotel, along with the statue of Queen Victoria, were both unscathed. So, the meeting would still take place.

He looked at his watch. Ten to ten. Just right. Forty minutes to go before the meeting took place in the Punch. He settled back into his coat and shrunk himself into the collar, which he pulled up far enough to conceal his hair. He put on his spectacles and was now satisfied that neither Salter nor Smith would recognise him. He was probably a hundred yards or so from the Punch and there was a fair bit of pedestrian traffic. There were a lot of spectators, gawping at all the work that was going on around the square. He was invisible.

He felt in his pocket for his field glasses and, as casually as he could, trained them on the entrance to the Punch.

Perfect. He reminded himself not to make a habit of it though. The last thing he wanted was to be arrested as a spy. That would require some explanation -

"I was looking for two German spies. They're both English and I'm not exactly sure which one - if any - is actually a spy. In fact, they may both be MI5 . . . Why the binoculars? Oh, I'm a bird watcher . . ."

That thought took him full circle back to his first foray to the decoy sites. He was getting that troubled feeling again and trying to rid himself of the near conviction that the information he had passed on was partly responsible for the chaos he could see around him.

The Punch seemed to be open. He could see lights on in the bar. Through the window, he could see a chap at the bar, obviously getting ready for opening. He was just about to put the field glasses away when he saw movement - three or four firemen exiting, blackened faces, exhausted looking. He swiftly removed the glasses from his face, dropped them back into one of the trench coat's cavernous pockets and looked in the other direction, to the other side of the square from the Punch.

A police car had now appeared there. Two large gents wearing what looked like regulation 'plain clothes' - trilby and mackintosh. There was another man behind the wheel. As he watched them chatting and smoking, another man approached them. This one in nondescript suit. As the three engaged in conversation, the third man turned to point across the square.

It was Salter. The one whom he knew as Hitler's man in London then crossed the square and went into the Punch. The other two followed him at a discreet interval and positioned themselves at the door, but each a good six feet away from it and trying to look totally disinterested in everything.

Armitage was enthralled. He checked his watch again. Twenty past ten. Still ten minutes to go. He did not dare use his field glasses again. Although the Punch was his sole focus, his eyes swept the square from time to time. He watched as the police car circumnavigated the square and parked just twenty yards or so from the door. Neither the two plain-clothes men nor the driver looked at each other. He had to admit it - these men were good at their job.

As his watch slowly ticked past ten thirty, then ten thirty-five and then approached twenty to eleven, he could almost feel the tension in the air. The two plain-clothes men were looking at their watches. So, too was the driver. He guessed by now that Salter was inside, probably sitting at the table in the window that they had occupied at their own meeting some weeks earlier. Reading a paper and watching the clock on the wall.

Then everything happened so quickly. Smith made his entrance - not from Paragon Street, as he had done, but from the opposite end of Carr Lane that branches off Alfred Gelder Street. So, he made his appearance from behind the Maritime Museum. If Smith had looked to his right, he would have been looking straight at Armitage - the very man he was expecting to meet. A shiver ran down his spine.

Smith did not look to his right. He walked directly to the Punch and went inside. The two watchers appeared to recognise him. They looked through the window into the bar and then their bodies seemed to tense. They exchanged glances. Seconds later, they both rushed through the door and re-emerged with a stumbling Smith between them. His face was a mask of shock. Eyes wide, mouth gaping. The police car moved to where the men were valiantly trying to subdue a stuttering, struggling Smith. The driver got out and helped them to apply handcuffs, then bundled him into the back of the car.

Salter followed them out of the Punch, chatted briefly to one of the policemen, laughed and shook his hand, before going back into the pub.

Armitage was transfixed. Once the pavement congratulations were done, the car - now sitting heavily on its back axle with most of the combined weight on the rear seat - trundled away, he imagined, to a place of incarceration.

He pulled himself together. No time to assimilate what he had just witnessed. He needed to quit the scene. He stood up, grabbed his bicycle from where he had stowed it on the steps behind him and pedalled away as quickly as his bloodless legs could now carry him.

The post-mortem would come on the ride back home. And then he would decide what to do.

As SOON AS he left the centre of Hull on his ride back to Hessle, Peter Armitage had to stop. He was in severe mental torment because of what he had just witnessed, but what was exercising his mind more than anything was the weight of his trench coat and the way it hampered efficient pedalling. He pulled onto some waste ground, took it off, bundled it up and threw it away - as far as he could. Then he remembered the field glasses in one of the pockets and had to sprint back to it. He put the glasses around his neck and pedalled on.

Before he was halfway home, he had managed to interpret what he had just seen. Two main conclusions - firstly, Salter was working for MI5 so - by definition - was *not* Hitler's man in London, nor anywhere else for that matter;

secondly, Smith *was* a German spy. Furthermore, both were intent on getting as much out of him as they could.

The evidence for his conclusion about Salter was incontrovertible. He had watched the man greet the police - that in itself a firm indicator that he was working for the British authorities. He had seen him ensnare Smith and arrange the man's capture. His persona as Hitler's man in London was a thinly veiled attempt to find people such as himself - whether acting alone or as part of a Fifth Columnist cell - and then sending what information they had garnered straight to ... well, certainly not Berlin, and more likely MI5. It was a containment exercise. He could see that now.

It was very professionally done though, he had to confess. The Nazi ID - the *Durchlassschein* - that he was shown was, to his eyes at least, impeccable. The cleverly wrought award also expertly done, subtly appealing to an individual's self-esteem, thus guaranteeing a willingness to provide further information, to go that extra mile. He recalled Salter being very interested when Armitage told him that he had a 'like-minded' friend.

He suddenly remembered Salter saying that the British authorities had allowed them to re-enter the German Embassy in London after its personnel had left, to 'clean up'. That was how they had found his first letter. The whole idea was absolutely preposterous, and yet he had believed it.

SMITH WAS a different kettle of fish. When they met at Cherry Cobb Sands, he had been quite reticent but had left Armitage with the distinct impression that he was doing it all wrong and they needed to talk further. He probably did Armitage a favour by discouraging his 'bird watching' activities, and - the deciding factor - he had told him that they were on the same side. Would anyone else but a German spy tell him that? He would doubtless have told him more at their planned meeting at the Punch. He would now never know.

The man's success as a German spy, if he had seen any, was the fact that he was just so English. Upper-class English at that. Everyone believed what they said. Aristocratic Englishmen had this certain aura of infallibility and invincibility. It would have been interesting to hear what he had to offer Armitage.

HE WANTED to rid his life of both Salter and Smith. He would clearly never see the latter again but Salter, on the other hand, could be knocking on his door in the next half hour. Armitage smiled. The man would doubtless be telling him that Smith was an MI5 agent, that he had indeed 'eliminated' him and that they could carry on with business as usual. Oh, and who is this like-minded friend that you mentioned?

Armitage needed to get to Hessle before Salter. This is where his bike had the advantage. He had a head start on the man and he knew that leaving the city in its current bombed-out state through its rubble-strewn streets would be tricky in a car.

He flicked the Sturmey-Archer gears up to third and increased his speed. He had come to a decision.

CHAPTER 34

Armitage sat in his armchair, looking out of the front window of his home in Hessle. He needed to get his breath back. The cycle ride back from Hull had been frantic. He had never ridden so quickly before.

The MI5 agent that he now knew Salter to be, knew so much about his activities that he could see real danger ahead. He wanted nothing more to do with him. What if Salter tired of what small titbits he supplied and tired of *him*. What then? Or perhaps these concentrated raids on Hull proved that his information had caused too much damage? If indeed any of that information had ever got to the Germans. He was confused. The complicated world of espionage baffled him. There was no firm ground anywhere and he was not willing to take any chances. It was all too much. He had to flee.

Once his breathing settled, he rose from his seat. A flight plan had formed. He spent the next few minutes frantically throwing basic clothing into a suitcase. He took his bank book and what cash he had, and stuffed it into his jacket pockets. He had enough to survive on for a good few days before he needed to access his bank account. He would head for Cornwall from where his father's family hailed. There, he could pursue his passion of bird watching without the attendant task of monitoring decoy sites. That was behind him now. The journey would take him a few days but he would stop each evening and seek out a small country inn, off the beaten track. He felt liberated. He would miss Hull though. He was sorry for the damage he had wrought upon the city.

Within five minutes he was pedalling away from his home, with the grey of the bomb clouds slowly receding behind him.

BY THE TIME Stokes pulled up outside Armitage's house in Gladstone Street, the man himself was almost ten miles away and heading west. He knocked on the door. He was looking forward to advising the man that he now had no need to fear the mysterious Smith who had accosted him at Cherry Cobb Sands. He had been taken care of.

It was odd that there was no answer. Peter knew when the meeting was, so he had expected him to be eagerly awaiting his report. He knocked again. Still no response. He looked through the front window. Nothing to see through the net curtains. He bent and shouted Armitage's name through the letterbox. He put his ear to the opening and listened intently for twenty seconds. Nothing.

After a few minutes of repeating this procedure, Stokes decided that he could not hang around any longer. He had to get back to North Shields. It was a long drive and he did not want to be doing any of it in darkness.

He wrote a note asking the fellow to give him a call, and

stuffed it through the letterbox. He got back into his car and drove away.

Stokes got the sense that his workload had eased even further. Smith and Armitage were both suddenly sidelined. The whole Hull chapter seemed to have closed.

CHAPTER 35

Flight Sergeant Augustin Preucil was sitting on a bench opposite the opening to Bainbridge Avenue in Sunderland. Muriel lived just a few doors up on the left, and it had been their home for the last few weeks. Living with her parents had been cramped but, he had to admit, fun.

Since his fraught encounter with his handler, WIESELIG, at the *Three Horseshoes*, he had been forced to do a lot of thinking. It was not something he did a lot but he knew it was decision time and neither of his two options were good. The big man had insisted that he 'honour his obligations' to his German masters, to whom, he said, he owed his liberty. By that he meant Preucil was to steal a Hurricane and deliver it anywhere within the expanding *Reich*.

On the one hand, he could ignore the threats and hang the consequences. He had told Muriel many times that he loved her. She had said it first but he had never really known what the word meant before her. He knew she adored him and he could now not imagine a life without her. Before that, love had only a physical dimension. It was a gratifying performance. A quest for pleasure. Muriel was different. She brought an emotional dimension to the concept of love, and he had begun to see a life together - a future.

They were to be engaged on her birthday and were now simply waiting for the 'permission to marry' to come through from the Czechoslovak military authorities exiled in London. This would then be endorsed by the Royal Air Force.

He knew his past behaviour had been appalling and he bitterly regretted that. He was, even now, trying to extricate himself from a young lady working at the base. He had enjoyed her company in the carnal sense but had since been trying to cool her ardour. She was pre-Muriel but was not taking his new cold shoulder well.

Muriel offered him a life that would have been impossible just a couple of years ago. He had met her family and had immediately felt part of it. It was a life that he wanted, regardless of the outcome of the war. But events were now dragging him back into the conflict - and away from Muriel. From what he had seen, Britain was now more likely than before to prevail and he was looking forward to settling here, with a British wife.

But, WIESELIG knew where he was now. He also remembered the man's veiled threat to Muriel. If he went on the run, there was always the chance that the RAF would find him and he would be shot as a deserter.

His only other option was to do as instructed and steal a plane. He would fly away into the sunset in one of the Hurricanes on base and land it in Belgium. That would be tricky but not that difficult. He would leave no note. If he planned it right, his disappearance would be seen as a training accident over the North Sea. He already knew of at least four previous such occurrences. He would rather Muriel thought of him as a hero. A force for good.

As he walked away, he saw Muriel's father returning from work and wheeling his bike through the gate, just a few yards from where he sat. As he disappeared from view, Preucil turned away and retraced his steps toward the base.

He would do it tomorrow.

RAF USWORTH, close to the town of Sunderland on the north-east coast, was home to 55 Operational Training Unit (55 OTU). Its role by mid-1941 was to train fighter pilots for Fighter Command. Specifically, at Usworth, the training centred on aerial combat – and particularly dogfights. Although the Battle of Britain had reduced the threat of imminent invasion, there was still a need for experienced fighter pilots. Many had been lost in the skies over Britain in the summer of 1940. The attrition rate had been high.

The urgent need for pilots had caused training periods to be drastically shortened. The influx of young airmen from Nazi-occupied territories helped the replenishment process. Free French, Polish and Czech pilots, as well those from Commonwealth countries, soon emerged through training and got their wings.

Flight Sergeant Augustin Preucil was an instructor there. He was due to be giving instruction in dog-fighting techniques today to one of the new entrants. He looked at the roster on the wall. Flight Sergeant Miloslaw Kadziolka. A Pole.

He groaned. Some of these Polaks had difficulty mastering even the basics of the Hurricane. The language difference was a problem and he constantly had to drum it into the few pilots he had trained, that British aircraft had a retractable undercarriage. There had been instances where a Polish pilot would remember to retract it on taking off, then forget to drop it again before landing. Some of them had paid for that mistake with the loss of both life and aircraft.

AFTER SPENDING half an hour in the map room and planning his route, Preucil kitted himself out in the warmest gear he could find. As an afterthought he stuffed one or two of the maps inside his tunic. He fastened it up again and walked out to the apron.

Preucil was not aware that he had ever come across this chap, Kadziolka, before. Given that he was a fellow sergeant, he guessed that he was an early arrival in Britain so would at least be able to fly the aircraft without him needing to be given the 'idiot lecture'.

The Czech walked out onto the dispersal apron. A young airman stood by a Hurricane, chatting to a member of the ground crew. He approached them.

"Kadziolka?"

The airman turned toward him. "Yes. Sergeant Preucil?"

"Jolly good." Preucil was always keen to sound more English than he was. And, importantly, more than they were. After they shook hands, the conversation that followed made it obvious that this one had been here for a while. His language skills were good, albeit delivered with a thick accent.

It turned out he had been flying Blenheims for a squadron that was converting to Hurricanes. Some of his colleagues were with him at Usworth. He had only very few flying hours in the Hurricane itself and had no dogfight experience at all. Preucil now had over 170 hours under his belt and it was judged that he was capable of instructing these pilots who were new to the aircraft.

He informed the pilot what they would be doing - a 45-minute sortie where the object of the exercise was for Kadziolka to stick on his tail while Preucil would be doing everything he could to shake him off.

He also explained that, since the Pole had little flying experience in Hurricanes, he would be going easy on him. Just familiarise himself with the movements necessary to keep a Hun in his sights and/or off his tail – the latter more important, but that was not for Lesson One.

He looked around for an aircraft for himself and shouted across to the Corporal.

"Is there one for me, Corporal?"

The man turned. "The only one that's fuelled up and ready is A-PA. But it's the Station Commander's kite."

Preucil knew whose it was. The old man was proud of it. It stood there, the CO's pennant showing proudly below the canopy. The Czech believed the plane had come from 43 Squadron - a Hurricane squadron based at RAF Acklington in Northumberland. It was obviously surplus to requirements or deemed too unreliable for front-line work. That was par for the course but for the CO to nab it, probably meant that it had been thoroughly overhauled by the ground crew.

"No matter. I'm not proud. Strap me in, will you? I need to get out on to the field and show this Polak how to fly."

The Corporal laughed. "The boss won't like it, Sergeant!"

As far as Preucil was concerned, that was of no importance at all. He would not be coming back to face the music.

PREUCIL TAXIED SLOWLY from the dispersal area to the end of the runway and turned. They were heading for the North Sea. The rules did not allow dogfight training over land. With the casualty rates he had seen just in the few months he had been at Usworth, he understood why.

This crate was in better nick than most of the Hurricanes he had flown. As the Station Commander's steed, it obviously received preferential treatment. The British class society in action. He might be grateful for that later in the day.

He rolled forward slowly to accommodate Kadziolka behind him in the second Hurricane, and double-checked his fuel - the two wing tanks and the reserve under the fuselage. He had checked with the ground crew Corporal that it was fully fuelled before he took it. He was going to need every drop.

The needles were satisfyingly at the top of their gauges. He switched the transfer buttons to and fro to see that they were working. His temperature gauges were warming up nicely. He pushed the throttle forward a touch to bring the revs up. He did visual checks on his control surfaces – the ailerons and elevator. He waggled the rudder. Easy movements on all. He was ready to roll.

With a wave to indicate that he was starting take-off, he closed the canopy and pushed the throttle further forward. He had told the Pole to wait until his wheels had lifted off before starting his own run-up. He had seen a few take-off mishaps when rookies tried it tandem for the first time.

THE CO's Hurricane reached take-off speed reassuringly quickly and he was airborne. As he climbed above 200 feet, he brought the cart up and looked around. Visibility was not especially good, with patches of dark grey cloud. He banked to the right and looked over his shoulder. Kadziolka was with him and climbing in line. Preucil had no particular flight plan. The whole purpose of the sortie was tight manoeuvre, diving, banking and, primarily, chase.

That last bit worried him too. The OTU had lost pilots and aircraft all too frequently in the last few months. Neither came cheap and the loss rate was appalling. Chase could become collision in a matter of seconds, especially in dogfight runs. It was all too easy to freeze on the stick.

With his experience, Kadziolka should be well-skilled but he was an unknown quantity. These blokes kept themselves to themselves and did not mix. He knew that this one would be off to one of the RAF's Polish fighter squadrons once he got through this – 303, probably.

The Czech had no intention of letting this one get too close. He had picked a good Hurricane. Probably the best on the station. She was smooth and responsive. Luck appeared to be on his side.

He had told Kadziolka he would be gentle but he fully intended to up the ante after about ten minutes. He was watching the cloud base. As Preucil piled on the airspeed, he noticed that the Pole was not responding as quickly as he thought he would. If he were to point his nose up and poke up into the clouds, he might actually lose him – but he played it nice and smooth.

There had been cases on this sort of mission when the dog had lost the tail completely. It was then that the mission became more of a test of the student's navigational skills than his prowess at aerial combat. Twice before, he had arrived back at Usworth and was sitting reading the *Sunderland Echo* in the mess before the hapless, exhausted trainee trudged in. He had been ticked off about it by the Station Commander himself.

HE WAS TIRING of this now. Kadziolka was proving sluggish in his reactions. It might be the aircraft, of course. The one *he* had chosen though - the CO's plane - was the cream of the dubious crop. He took the Pole down almost to sea level. The dull grey of the ocean skimmed beneath them and, as he could see when he carried out the simplest of manoeuvres, the lack of height was scaring the other airman. Kadziolka was at least 100 feet above him. He smiled. From a purely dogfight point of view, that was actually a good tactic. It was just not what was required today.

Preucil laughed. "Against the rules, old chum", he spoke into his dead intercom. With that, he climbed more steeply into the cloud, until he was in clear blue sky and looking down on it. Kadziolka was nowhere to be seen. He continued the climb until he was vertical. He could feel his heart pounding. The Merlin engine stalled and the Hurricane started to fall. The engine coughed and spluttered back to life and he levelled the plane out. He was back in the clouds now and, he hoped, well behind the Pole who was presumably throttling up to catch the disappearing A-PA.

While the Pole was still flying like a Blenheim, Preucil was safe. He banked to the right, slid gently down to 200 feet and headed south. He prayed he had enough fuel and daylight in equal measure.

He looked out of the cockpit to his right at the north east coast. He thought of Muriel at work and shuddered to think of the shock she was going to get when he was reported missing - and never returned. He prayed he would somehow get back to Britain after the war. It was not beyond the realms of possibility. He blew a kiss through the perspex. He would miss her.

CHAPTER 36

As Ernest Metcalf drove back from West Allotment, his initial relief at having returned the wireless set to Smith had begun to turn into a growing disquiet. The enormity of what he and his uncle had done had not diminished. It now looked as if the death toll of the bombing of the factory was going to reach a hundred. One hundred people who would still be alive had he and his uncle, aided and abetted by Smith, not sent that wireless message.

This was turning into a nightmare. By the time he got back to the flat in Nile Street, he had convinced himself that the only way forward was to divorce himself and his uncle Freddie from the grief, anguish and communal wringing of hands that would soon sweep North Shields. He wanted to avoid that at all costs, while they were still dragging the dead and injured from the shelter. Once that ceased and the funerals were over, the anger and the bitterness would begin. Then they would remember that the Metcalfs were German. Or from 'German stock' as Mrs Turner had put it on his first day at work, just before she spat at his feet. And his ribs were still aching from the beating he received minutes later - for the same reason.

Although he had got rid of the only physical evidence that existed - the wireless - people would hold them personally responsible for the tragedy. Exactly as they had done in 1915 when the *Lusitania* was sunk. There had been no sign of that after any of the minor raids the town had so far suffered, but the factory was on a different scale.

He pulled into the side of the road. He wanted to delay his arrival until he knew his father had closed the shop and gone home. He could not face him yet. Not until he had spoken to uncle Freddie. He looked around. A hundred yards ahead was the roundabout where he would turn right to North Shields. Straight ahead would take him to Whitley Bay. Maybe he and his uncle would benefit from a few days away, up the coast. He seemed to remember that Freddie had told him of the fond memories of such a trip that he and Lotte had taken when they were courting.

Ernest would suggest that to him. After all, he had his father's car as well as the pound note which Smith had given him. It was blood money, of course, so best to spend it as soon as possible. That would not be difficult. And, with the factory gone, he was now out of work. He concluded that it would not appear too strange that they had decided to go away for a few days. He would leave his father a note explaining the circumstances and the reasons for his decision.

He waited until it was almost blackout time before he completed the last few miles to Nile Street.

FREDDIE WAS WATCHING out of the back window. He had been there for a while, waiting for his nephew to return. He had expected him back sooner and was growing increasingly anxious. He walked down to the back door to let him in.

"Ernest. Where have you been?

His nephew sighed. "Uncle, you know where I've been."

"I was worried about you."

"Yes, I'm sorry. I needed to think."

The two men went upstairs to the flat. Freddie broke out the schnapps. They sat opposite each other in the two armchairs. Ernest stared at him. He looked all in. "Uncle. I think we should go away for a few days. I think North Shields could be a bit uncomfortable for a while."

He looked shocked. "But how can we do that? It will look as if we are hiding, won't it?

Ernest explained his plan. Just a few days break. It was no admission of guilt. And there was now no actual link with the event. The wireless - the instrument of their betrayal - had now gone.

"And in any case, uncle, despite what Smith told us about the matter needing to be dealt with . . . we *still* do not know for sure that it was *not* a random raid, do we? I think you were right about that. It's we who are making the connection between the wireless transmission and the bombing. Ask yourself - who can lay the blame at our door? And did either of us ever imagine that they would bomb the factory simply because of the information we sent them?"

Freddie looked doubtful. His nephew continued. "But if we stay here and you are constantly looking like the cat that swallowed the canary, then we are more at risk. I will leave father a note to say that we have gone. Just for a few days. I have no job now and . . ."

"Oh, my God. I had forgotten that. But won't your father smell a rat?"

Ernest was getting exasperated. "Why should he? He knows nothing at all about what we did."

"He knows how I feel about the British."

"That's a bit of a stretch though, isn't it? You don't like the British so you arrange to bomb a factory and kill one hundred people."

Freddie nodded sadly. All of his anti-British fervour suddenly seemed to have evaporated. He nodded again. "Yes, so ... when do we go?"

"Tonight. Now. Once I have written the note. I will put it on the shop counter. Go and throw some stuff into a bag."

Freddie stood and shuffled through to his bedroom.

"Oh ... and don't forget the schnapps."

He heard his uncle laugh. It was a welcome sound.

Ernest wrote a hasty message to his father. It was brief, explaining what they were doing. He made mention of the Northumberland coast, of which Freddie had many happy memories. His father would know exactly what that meant - and would possibly be grateful that Ernest was sharing what was almost a burden of care as far as his brother was concerned.

He also wrote that he did not want Freddie to witness any reprisals or vandalism if their property were to suffer, as had occurred in 1915. Early days yet but so cataclysmic was the factory tragedy that it was a distinct possibility. He had not shared that with his uncle but he felt it was another valid reason for their disappearance which, again, his father would understand.

Ernest thought of writing a note for Lizzie too. They had not seen each other since the raid on the factory. The horrible thought struck him that she might actually have been in the shelter that night. He tried to put that out of his mind. On balance, he thought it best not to write her a note.

She might remember the Royal Navy's presence in the factory and the discussions they had about boffins and inventions. He would leave that conversation until he got back.

He stuffed the note into an envelope, ran downstairs to the shop and placed it on the counter where he knew his father would see it as soon as he came into the shop the next day.

TEN MINUTES LATER, uncle and nephew had locked up, stowed their meagre belongings into the car and were crawling up the back lane. Ernest turned at the top of the lane, onto Nile Street and away from the shop.

"Ernest! Stop the car!"

His nephew brought the car to a halt. "What?'

"Two men. One of them has just thrown a brick through the shop window. We have to stop them."

Freddie already had his door open.

Ernest shouted. "No, uncle. Close the bloody door!"

"But . . ."

"It has happened. And we aren't here!"

Satisfied that the passenger door was shut, Ernest moved the car forward to the top of the street and turned towards the coast. He hoped that things would have quietened down when they returned. He was beginning to think it might be an 'if' rather than a 'when' but that was a decision he did not need to make now.

CHAPTER 37

After ten minutes or so of staying low and in visible contact with the coastline, Preucil felt he could relax. But this was the easy part. The aircraft at 55 OTU were fitted with an IFF (Identification Friend or Foe) box so he knew he would not be shot out of the sky by some itchy-fingered anti-aircraft gunner while he was in friendly airspace, but he would have to be vigilant once he crossed the enemy coast.

And, for obvious reasons, as this was a training mission, A-PA was unarmed.

The range of the Hurricane MkI was 500 miles at least. That gave him some leeway and he knew that the tanks were full. He checked again.

Flying with the coast in sight on his right, it should be a piece of cake. He had not left anything to chance and had planned his route. He passed the Humber estuary and was crossing the Wash a few minutes later. It was still light, which helped. Double summer time had been introduced a few months ago, thus increasing the daylight now available to him.

Banking left to find his next landmark of Norwich, he was soon over the city. The Cathedral was unmistakable. He pressed on to his sea crossing, aiming to touch the European coast just east of Ostend, somewhere between the Belgian port and Flushing on the Dutch coast.

That passed without incident but he knew he needed to put this kite down before he was shot down. Since the Nazi occupation of Belgium and Holland, the place was crawling with *Luftwaffe* fighter nests. He was simply searching for somewhere quiet to land the plane and then hand himself - and the Hurricane - over to the nearest member of the German occupying forces in the morning.

All he needed now was for darkness to fall so that he could lay her down gently and invisibly, without being detected. Almost before he was aware of it, he was approaching the Ardennes – a thickly forested region with peaks of over 2000 feet. He lifted the plane as he flew toward them. A gloom was slowly starting to descend.

He idly wondered if Kadziolka had made it back. He would be in a blue funk, to be sure. After the Pole's flight report, Flight Sergeant Preucil would then be on the 'missing' list. They would search for signs of A-PA's wreckage. They would not find any. The Hurricane was still in good fettle and performing well.

The forest below was thinning. He scoured the horizon for a clearing and prayed that he found one before night fell. He reduced height and was just skimming the treetops. All he needed was a couple of fields, preferably without cattle or sheep, in which to bring her to rest as gently as possible.

The trees were starting to slope down. He banked right and left to get a better view of what was directly ahead. Straining his eyes through the incoming gloom and moving his head from side to side, he spotted a lighter shade of green.

He eased back on the throttle and applied flaps. He was losing height rapidly now. Cart down or a belly flop? The terrain looked smooth but a single pothole could catch a wheel if he dropped the undercarriage. The whole crate would flip over as a consequence. He opted for caution. Belly flop it was. The irony of constantly reminding his students to remember to put the cart down before landing did not escape him.

The green patch was larger than he had thought. It sloped down to what he assumed were farm buildings but there were no signs of animals or other obstructions.

The field rushed up to meet the Hurricane. Dropping revs and speed now, he pulled the nose up seconds before she thumped onto the grass. Although it was a stable craft, it always paid to land in a semi-stall position. He knew he would probably rip the tail-wheel off but that was a small price to pay if it avoided the usual bounce from the wheels of a dropped undercarriage. On a downward slope like this, he did not want to cartwheel - especially as his gauges still showed sufficient fuel left to cause a fireball on impact.

The landing was heavier than he thought it would be. The prop bit into the earth and threw up great clods of soil. A spray of stones clattered against the canopy. Even above the noise of the engine, he heard the windscreen Perspex crack. He felt one of his harness straps give way. His body slewed to one side and his head met the top of the instrument panel.

The Merlin engine stalled. Smoke poured from the exhausts. In its death throes, the stuttering prop slewed the whole craft around and it finally came to rest. Preucil found himself facing the trees. His track from impact to resting position was clearly visible.

He needed to get out as quickly as possible. There was still a danger that any unspent fuel would go up and he did not want to be around when it did. He unclipped what was left of the harness and looked over each wing. The port wing was chewed up badly where the tip had dug in. The starboard one was intact. The downward slope had helped to limit the damage. Not too shabby, that.

All the same though, as the Corporal had said "The boss will not be happy".

He reached across and tried to yank back the canopy. It would not budge. It was almost off its runners, twisted in the impact of the landing. He tried again and it gave, just half-way, but enough to enable his exit. He twisted his torso through the gap and stepped out onto the wing. He now only had to step to the ground. It felt strange exiting from a plane that was not sitting on its wheels.

He was still panting with the exertion of landing. He leant against the fuselage to get his breath back. He sensed a warmth on his face and touched the spot. Blood. He felt for the wound. He was not bleeding profusely but he noticed that it had run down his tunic. It was also flowing into his left eye.

His legs were stiff from the inactivity of the flight but he ran as quickly as he could for a hundred yards or so. He turned to look at the plane. There was no sign of flames. The descent of darkness was now complete. He peered up the bank ahead of the twisted prop. There was no sign of movement from the tree line.

Making his way down the slope to the tailplane, however, he saw activity. In the window of one of the farm buildings, there was a dim, flickering light. He guessed it was a candle. A door opened and a thin shaft of pale light fell across the yard. As the light widened, he saw two men and a smaller shape to their side. A dog. They started to walk up the gradient toward him.

Preucil held his hands above his head and walked down. He was not taking any chances. As their outlines and features became clearer, he could see that they were a young man and an older one. The dog was growling. If he could see them more clearly, then they could also see him and would know that he was RAF. Would they hand him over to the local *Gestapo*?

The group stopped. One of the men shouted.

"M'sieur. Vous êtes anglais?"

Preucil felt some relief. "*Non, j'suis tchèque, monsieur.*"

"RAF?"

He pointed to the plane which was now just a black shape. He pointed to the wings on his tunic. *"Oui, oui!"*

"Alors, viens! Vite, vite!"

The two men took him by the arm and ran him down the slight hill. The dog, now satisfied that he was not a threat, ran ahead of them.

THE BELGIANS WATCHED as he ate their bread and goat's cheese and drank their wine. The now extremely friendly dog, Jules, sat at his knee and waited for scraps.

"Alors. Vous êtes tchèque, m'sieur. Comment?"

It was a fair question. The airman was immediately grateful for the French he had learned during his training in France. It would make things a lot easier. Preucil explained how a Czech came to be wearing an RAF uniform. They were pleased to hear it – especially when he mentioned the Free French in his squadron and - he went to invention - a few Belgians. He was sure there must be some. Their base was like the League of Nations.

The Belgian farmer explained to him that he could not stay at the house. It would be too dangerous for all of them. After satisfying themselves that he would be warm enough, they told him that they would take him to the woods where he could hide for the night and they would return for him in the morning. They suggested that he strip down to his shirt and trousers, with a smock and breeches over the top. They gave him clogs to replace his boots. His knowledge of French would be good, they agreed, if he was found overnight. Although all were of the opinion that it would not stand close inspection. How they laughed.

They took him a hundred yards inside the periphery of the forest and bade him *bonne chance*. He mumbled his thanks and looked for a spot to settle. The ground was soft and dry. He made himself as comfortable as he could and pulled off a few low branches to cover himself with. It was pitch black now. The stars were hidden by the forest canopy. He was exhausted from the concentrated effort of the last few hours but sleep eluded him.

This was ridiculous. The whole point of this mission was to deliver a Hurricane to the Germans. He had done that but he was not expecting to be thwarted in that endeavour by a family of Belgian farmers and a dog. He mulled over what he should do in the morning. Sleep overtook him before he arrived at a decision.

HE WOKE AT DAWN. A noise stirred him. He could hear voices. German voices. He crept to the borderline of trees and field. Keeping low, he could see five soldiers crawling, literally crawling, over the Hurricane.

This was it. He did not have to go looking for them. They
were here. He stripped off the smock, breeches and clogs
and hobbled into their field of vision. RAF blue shirt, tie
and black socks - one of which, he noticed, had a hole
which revealed a big toe. He edged forward with his hands
on his head. Any sudden movement could be fatal. It was
only a few seconds before one of the Germans spotted him
and levelled his rifle.

"*Halt! Hände hoch!*"

The Czech put his *Hände* as *hoch* as he could get them
and stood stock still. The Germans advanced on him. Each
with a rifle pointed at him. One of them told him to get on
the ground. Preucil did as asked but feared he was about to
die.

There was an interminable conversation which was
alternately German and English, the Czech explaining that
he was the pilot of the Hurricane, that he wanted to give it to
them, that *Kriminalinspektor* Oskar Fleischer in Prague and
Abwehr in Hamburg knew all about it. He was dragged to his
feet and put in the back seat of their *Kubelwagen*. He was
driven into the village where they had a small office in the
back of the local *estaminet*.

He sat and waited. After an hour, a *Gestapo* man arrived.
He spoke English. This made the explanation of Preucil's
presence a lot easier. He nodded in all the right places, took
notes, instructed the local squad to look after him and
promised he would return within the hour.

The Czech was given something to eat. About halfway
through his meal, there was a sudden hubbub outside. He
saw the Belgian farmer, his wife, son and another youth
being dragged out of a half-track. Preucil was aghast. As he
was watching, one of the escorting soldiers came in through

the door and threw his RAF flying kit, helmet and boots at him.

They must have assumed that the farmers had taken him in and therefore paid them a visit. He was horrified. He stood and walked to the window. The older man caught his gaze, held it for a few seconds and then spat on the ground.

The soldier pushed the small group roughly down the street and into the church. One of them raised his rifle and took aim at a dog who was scratching at the closed door. A single shot was all he needed. The animal fell and the men cheered while its blood coursed slowly down the pavement.

Preucil was starting to regret the decision he had made.

CHAPTER 38

Lizzie was taking her daughter, Alice, for a day out. Ever since she had told her about it, the girl had been so excited and had woken her mother up shortly after six o'clock. She thought Christmas had come early.

She had received a letter from her friend Muriel and they had arranged to meet up. She was also feeling guilty that, even though she now had no job since the factory was bombed, she had been moping around the house and continued to let her mother look after Alice. And Ernest had not been in touch since the bombing.

His dad had been lovely when she visited the shop a few days earlier. He told her that both Ernest and his uncle Freddie had gone off to Northumberland in his car for a few days. He had not heard from them but was sure that they would not be away much longer. He had put her mind at rest that Ernest had not fallen out with her for any reason and promised to let her know when they came back.

Muriel was in a state. Her fiancé, the dashing Czech RAF Flight Sergeant, had been lost in a training accident over the

North Sea and she was distraught. Lizzie did not know any more than that but desperately wanted to comfort her.

They had agreed to meet in South Shields, roughly halfway between North Shields and Sunderland. That meant taking a ferry across the Tyne which, she knew, was the bit that Alice was looking forward to. She had never been on the ferry before.

It was only a short trip but Alice savoured every second. It made Lizzie feel even more guilty. Her lovely daughter had missed out on so much of her childhood. To salve her own conscience, Lizzie reflected that the war had caused all of this – the death of Alice's father and her own, the disappearance of Muriel's fiancé, the loss of her own job and the lives of one hundred poor souls who had died in the factory shelter. Bloody war!

She pulled herself together and found herself enjoying the ferry crossing as much as Alice obviously was. It helped to see it through her child's eyes. That joy soon evaporated when she spotted Muriel waiting, as arranged, in the market place. She was a pitiful sight, dabbing her eyes with a handkerchief. Alice piped up as they walked toward Muriel.

"Are we going to meet your friend now, mammy?"

"Yes, Alice."

"What's her name?"

"Mu."

Alice giggled. "Moo? Like a cow?"

Lizzie smiled. Trust Alice to cheer her up. She hoped it would work with Muriel. She would love the 'cow' bit.

"No, Alice. It's short for Muriel."

She stopped and faced away from Mu who had not seen her yet. She bent down to Alice. "Listen, Mu is a bit sad today, so . . ."

"Why?"

"Well, because . . . because her boyfriend has had to go away."

"Where's he gone?"

Lizzie had to be careful what she told the child. She did not want to sanitise it too much but she was only five years old. She would simply not understand the truth. Alice had stopped asking about her daddy a while ago and had been barely aware of her granddad's death. She wondered how much she had heard at school about the factory bombing. And she did not want her repeating anything of this to Mu.

"We don't know."

"Will he come back?"

"I hope so, pet." She kissed her daughter and straightened her cardigan, then stood and turned round. Mu was waving at them. She looked more cheerful, obviously putting on a face in front of Alice. They walked across.

Muriel stood and spoke to the little girl first. "You must be Alice", she said, shaking her hand.

Alice looked up at her mother and giggled again. "Yes. And you're Moo."

That broke the ice. All three of them were laughing now. Muriel hugged the little girl. "I've got you a little present, Alice."

The child looked up at her mother, smiling broadly, her eyes wide with excitement. Muriel drew a bar of chocolate from her handbag and gave it to her. She squealed with delight.

"Chocolate, mammy!"

"Yes. That was nice of Moo, wasn't it?"

That set them off laughing again.

"What do you say, Alice?"

The child looked at Muriel, curtseyed and said "Thank you."

Lizzie hugged her daughter again. She was pleased she had brought her.

THEY FOUND a small café on the main street that led off the market place. The waitress made a great fuss of the little girl and they were very soon sitting in front of two cups of tea and a milk-shake. As Alice occupied herself with her drink and eating the chocolate that Muriel had given her, the women settled into grown-up talk.

Muriel told her all that she knew of Gus's fate. The Chaplain of RAF Usworth had visited her and explained that it was a training accident over the North Sea. Two of them were flying but only the other pilot, a Pole, had returned. There was little hope, he had said. They had searched for wreckage but none had been found. It was not an isolated incident.

"Huh! I think the last bit was supposed to make me feel better."

Lizzie leant across and took her hand. "I'm so sorry, Mu." She could see her friend's eyes welling up with tears.

"We were going to get married, Lizzie."

"I know. You told me when we came over that night."

"Oh, yes, sorry. I'm not thinking straight at the moment." Muriel pulled herself together, keenly sensing that Alice was now staring at her. "But what about you, Lizzie? How's Ernest?"

Lizzie told her that she had not heard from him at all since the factory was bombed and their jobs no longer existed. She was missing him. She shrugged and gave a thin smile of resignation. She told her friend that she had visited his dad at the family shop.

"What did his dad say?"

"Just that they've gone away for a few days . . . but it's been over a week now."

"They?"

"Yes, him and his uncle Freddie."

"Oh."

"I know. His uncle's fiancée was killed in the first war when the shop was vandalised." Lizzie realised she had omitted an important fact. "The family's German, you see, Mu."

Her friend put both hands to her face.

"Oh, not German German, if you know what I mean. Ernest told me they came here about seventy or eighty years ago. In the last century, for goodness' sake! They're pork butchers, see. Most of them are German. Hadn't you noticed? But they're British citizens now."

Muriel put her arms around her friend's shoulders. Lizzie could feel tears stinging her eyes. "It's his uncle that I'm worried about."

"Why?"

"Oh, just things Ernest has told me about him."

Muriel looked puzzled. Lizzie dropped her voice. "Ernest told me his uncle would welcome Hitler with open arms. We used to laugh about it." She could have bitten her tongue off. She knew Muriel would want to know more. Lizzie certainly would have done in the same situation.

"You're joking?"

"No. Oh . . . it's a long story, Mu. I'll write." As she finished saying that, she looked at Alice so that Muriel would know it was not something to discuss in front of a child.

She got the message. "Oh . . . oh, yes. Write to me."

They left the café and walked down towards Ocean

Road which led to the beach. Muriel put her arm in Lizzie's. "Gus told me that Hitler will never invade this country. Not while the RAF are protecting us."

Lizzie did not want to get into the uncle Freddie business again. She changed the direction of the conversation. "Gus must have had a bad time escaping from Czechoslovakia, I'll bet."

"He had to go all across Poland and France and everything. The *Gestapo* caught him once, you know."

"The *Gestapo*?"

"Aye. They told him they wanted him to nick a plane and fly it back to them. Told them he would and then he just ignored them after that. Once he was over here, like."

"Bloody hell."

Alice looked up. "Mammy. No swearing. I'll tell gran."

"No, you won't, you little tell-tale." She chased a shrieking Alice up the pavement before scooping the girl up in her arms.

Muriel pinched the girl's cheek. "Is she a little tittle-tattle, mammy?"

"She is, auntie Moo."

"Then there's no chocolate the next time. Tittle-tattles don't get treats."

Alice stuck her bottom lip out. "I'm NOT a tittle-tattle."

"Good, then I'll see what I can find for you the next time."

Despite being in her mother's arms, Alice somehow managed to swivel across and clasp her arms around Muriel's neck. "Thank you, auntie Moooooo!"

Alice leant back into her mam, laid her head on her shoulder and closed her eyes. Muriel looked at Lizzie as they walked back into the market place. "We're a right pair, you and me."

"You're right about that. It's been a lovely day, Mu."

Alice, half-asleep now, whispered a quiet 'Moooo . . .'

The two women parted with a promise to get together again soon. Alice was getting too heavy to carry to the ferry landing. Lizzie woke her gently and put her down. She was crotchety at being disturbed. Lizzie quickly told her they were going on the ferry again and her face brightened.

She wondered if she had told her friend too much about Ernie and his uncle Freddie. She was worried about the conclusion Muriel might arrive at. There was the niggling fear that her friend might be right.

CHAPTER 39

When Stokes got back to North Shields from his engineered apprehension of the worrisome Mr Smith at the Punch Hotel and the strange non-appearance of his twitcher-cum-traitor, Peter Armitage, he was feeling more than a little jaded. The first event was choreographed; the second was unexpected and was beginning to worry him.

He put both men to the back of his mind for the time being. He now needed to get to the bottom of this factory bombing situation. He had two names from his previous visit - Ernest Metcalf and Lizzie Fenwick. Both had been employees at the lemonade factory which now lay in ruins at the corner of King Street and George Street.

He made straight for the police station and was greeted cheerily by the desk sergeant. "Oh, Mr Stokes. We thought you must have gone back to London."

"No, not London, but I did have business elsewhere which curtailed my stay in your wonderful town, I'm afraid."

"Well, it's good to see you again. What can we do for you?"

Stokes slid a pad on the desk towards him and wrote down the two names. The desk sergeant asked if he would like tea. He nodded and moved the pad back across to the sergeant, who looked at the names and smiled. He gestured towards a bobby and mimed 'cuppa' to him. The young man smiled and receded down the corridor.

The older policeman leant across the counter. "Lizzie Fenwick. I know the family. She's a war widow already, bless her. Husband caught it when his ship was torpedoed. Her mam's a recent widow as well. They're not having a lot of luck. Here, I'll write the address down for you."

He did so, ripped the page off and handed it to Stokes. The sergeant gave him directions.

"Ernest Metcalf. I know of a few Metcalfs but not sure about this Ernest."

The tea arrived. Hot and very dark. Stokes guessed milk was at a premium, especially for guests. The sergeant thanked the constable, who gave the cup to Stokes and looked at the two names.

"I know who Ernest is. He's Frank's son . . ." He looked at the sergeant. "You know. The pork butchers. Nile Street."

"Nile Street?"

"Aye, but the son doesn't work there now. He works . . . sorry, *worked* at the factory. I think he was the manager. Not sure about that, like."

Stokes spoke up. "Yes, Mr Wilkinson gave me his name."

The PC addressed Stokes directly. "They're Germans, you know!"

"Really?"

"Aye. When you go down there, have a look at the name above the shop. They haven't always been Metcalf."

He lowered his voice even further, as if he were

divulging some kind of state secret. "If you look carefully, you can just see the old German name. I tell yer."

Pleased with himself, he looked at them both and, stepping back, put both hands in the air as if depicting how the sign would look. With that, he gave a sniff of satisfaction and walked back down the corridor.

Stokes looked at the sergeant. "He's a bright spark."

"Aye. That's wor Billy. PC Atkinson. He'll go far that one."

"Thank him for me, will you. Now . . . I'm afraid I need to make another telephone call to London."

Stokes took his tea into the room he had used before. The phone was already ringing.

"Albert. What's new?"

"Give me a chance. I only just rolled up from Hull last night. I was hoping *you* had something to tell *me* about this infernal factory business."

"Well, I had a very enjoyable five minutes rubbing the Admiralty's nose in it *vis à vis* the laxness of their security. It seems there was some pretty secret and important work being done on the top floor of the factory. An anti-submarine weapon, I gather. He said I had to keep that to myself. That made me chuckle. I told him the bloody Germans obviously knew about it so he had little to fear from my loose lips."

Stokes laughed. "And how did he take that?"

"Oh, all I got was one of those military harrumphs that I've heard before from his type. I think he got the message."

Knight continued. "They had moved their operations from one of the local shipyards because - and get this - they feared it was too much of a target. This has to have been an inside job, old son."

He gave Knight the information he had just received

from the young policeman - that one of the names he was pursuing, Ernest Metcalf, was member of a German pork butcher family in the town. And he was working at the factory as some kind of manager.

"Oh, my word. You're telling me this man is of German heritage and worked at the factory, which has just been bombed – by the Germans. I don't believe in coincidence. Find him, Albert. You're still handy for Leeds if you need to be there. You have swiftly become my man in the North."

"It looks that way, doesn't it? But have no fear. I am about to go into bloodhound mode. I think I'll buy my lunch at the local pork butcher's."

MINUTES LATER. Stokes was standing on Nile Street. It was a simple ribbon of small shops on each side of a narrow thoroughfare. There was a Post Office, two or three general dealers, a barber's, a pub and . . . there it was, the pork butcher's. He was on the opposite pavement, staring at the sign above the shop front.

It read 'M E T C A L F'. The last four letters, though, were obviously newer. He walked slowly across to the shop, focussing all the time on those last few letters. There was a shadow beneath the last four. Under the C A L F, he could just make out the shapes of Z, G, E and R.

M E T Z G E R.

Metzger! A German surname and also, he knew, a noun meaning butcher. It was clearly an occupational name, like the English Baker, Cooper or Fletcher.

The family had obviously Anglicised their surname. He could not blame them for that. The riots in 1915 had been short-lived but vicious and undoubtedly unfair to those Germans who had been in England for generations. Even the Royal family had done it, moving from Saxe-Coburg-Gotha to Windsor at the sweep of a pen. It was not for him to judge.

The green tiled shop entrance to the left of the window was shiny and clean, as were the panes themselves. Very little was on display but that was in common with the other shops. What he could not fail to miss were the boards across one pane of the double shop window.

He entered the shop and was immediately struck by the cold. The weather outside was quite mild but the inside of the pork butcher's shop was chilly by comparison. There was nobody to be seen. A price list hung from the wall opposite the counter, between prints of farmyard scenes. As he was studying them, an older man walked in from the back shop, wiping his hands on his apron.

"Good morning. Can I help you?"

Stokes dug his security pass from his top pocket and held it out. The other man introduced himself as Frank Metcalf, the proprietor. He finished wiping his hands, fished out a pair of wire-rimmed specs and placed them in position. He took the card from his visitor and his eyebrows rose.

The MI5 man continued. "I am looking for a Mr Ernest Metcalf. Is that a relation of yours, by any chance?"

"Yes, Ernest is my son. Is he in trouble?" The man looked anxious but not suspiciously so. Stokes could tell the difference.

"I'm not sure. Can you tell me where he is right at this moment?"

"Not exactly. But he did leave me this note." He felt under the counter, took out the note his son had left and handed it across. Stokes read it. "Who is this Freddie?"

"That's my brother. They share the flat upstairs."

Stokes handed the letter back to Metcalf. "So, your brother and your son are somewhere in Northumberland? In your car? And you don't know when they will be back?"

Frank shrugged. "That is correct. But they will be back very soon, I think."

Stokes frowned. "Are you sure they will return? I need to speak to Ernest urgently."

Frank looked shocked. Stokes now sensed fear. He pushed on. "I saw Mr Wilkinson a few days ago . . ."

"William is a good friend of mine. We are both Rotary members."

"You know that he has had a stroke?"

Frank's mouth dropped. "I didn't. Oh, my word."

"I think it was a result of the shock after the factory tragedy. I spoke to his housekeeper and she said they were trying to get him into hospital. Sadly, though, because of casualties from the factory, they have no beds free at the moment."

Stokes was laying it on thick. He had no idea that Metcalf and Wilkinson were friends so that much was a gift. He let it all sink in. He watched as the man walked around the counter to the shop door and locked it. He turned the sign to 'closed'.

There was silence. Metcalf removed his glasses and rubbed his face. Stokes took the questioning forward.

"I couldn't help notice that you have a broken window."

He left that hanging in the air. The man looked at the boards then back at Stokes.

"Yes. Somebody kindly smashed it a few days ago. I have not been able to get it reglazed just yet."

"Vandalism?"

"I fear so. It happened before . . . during the last war."

Stokes frowned his disapproval.

"We are of German heritage, you see. And I'm afraid that . . ."

"Was this after the factory bombing?"

"Yes. Oh, I'm not saying that whoever did it actually blames us for the . . . what happened at the factory, but we have once again become an easy way to vent anger against the Germans."

"Understandable, I suppose."

"Ha. Yes, indeed. But what can we do?"

Stokes smiled in sympathy and waited for Metcalf to continue.

"As you will see from Ernest's note, he feared that this would happen." He pointed to the boards. "And he was right."

Stokes sensed that there was more to come. He allowed the man a moment to reflect. Frank sighed and told the full story of the vandalism in 1915, culminating in the death of his brother's fiancée, Lotte.

"And the sinking of the *Lusitania* which prompted many such acts of revenge against Germans and their property was, although tragic, nevertheless far removed from North Shields."

"But the factory bombing isn't."

"Precisely." He paused. "My brother would have been extremely upset if he had been here when this happened. It would have brought it all back, you see." He shrugged his shoulders and sighed again. "My brother is an extremely bitter man, Mr Stokes. He tells me often that his life effectively ended on the day that Lotte died. And I'm afraid he has held it against the English ever since."

Stokes was puzzled. Just a few short minutes ago, Ernest Metcalf was the sole person of interest. Now, it was beginning to look as if the uncle was joining him. "Mr

Metcalf. How did your brother's bitterness manifest itself?"

"Oh, sharing his rants with me on an extremely regular basis. Believe me, I could mouth every word once he gets started."

"And it didn't go any further than that?"

Metcalf looked puzzled. "And both of them live in the flat upstairs?"

"Yes. Ernest moved in with my brother a few weeks ago."

Alarm bells were ringing in Stokes' head. He decided not to question the man any further.

"Frank, you have been very helpful. I am grateful for your time and I will leave you in peace now. Can I just ask that you inform me, via the police station, as soon as Ernest and Freddie return?"

Metcalf raised his eyebrows. It was clear that he was expecting more. "Of course. Yes."

"Oh. Just one more thing. Would you mind if I borrowed the note that Ernest left?"

The man hesitated for a second or two. "Of course not."

He took it from his pocket and handed it to Stokes.

"You will get it back, of course."

Stokes had no real need of it, other than to read it verbatim to Knight. He simply wanted to sew further seeds of anxiety for Metcalf. He felt the man knew more than he was telling but Stokes always held to the belief that a voluntary statement was worth a thousand forced admissions. The man was torn but he needed to resolve that internal conflict soon.

CHAPTER 40

A fter he left the Metcalfs' shop, Stokes took a swift walk back to the police station. He needed to apprise Knight of developments. The desk sergeant spotted him as he entered, smiled and pointed to his phone. Stokes nodded and walked through to the interview room. He picked up the receiver and heard Knight being put through.

"Albert. You can't have cracked the case already, surely? You are in North Shields, I take it?"

"Yes." Stokes outlined his visit to Frank Metcalf. He brought him up to speed with the Freddie angle. He was also planning to visit Lizzie Fenwick very soon.

"Progress then. Well done. You think these two - Ernest and Freddie - could have something to do with the factory bombing?"

"It's looking distinctly possible. Now what I need is a search warrant for the flat they share. And then arrest warrants, in due course. Is that a 'can do'?"

"Hmm. On what charge, old boy? Being a bit German?

Having a liking for pork? They are all British citizens now, I assume?"

"Yes, but there are many in internment camps with the same qualification."

"That's true but we can't arrest anybody until we know a bit more."

"That's academic. They are both somewhere in the wilds of Northumberland so there's no question of putting out search parties. No, it's the search warrant for the flat I need - and pronto."

"Oh, just sort that out with your favourite Geordie bobbies, old son. Do they know who you work for by the way?"

"More or less. My pass says Ministry of Defence. Will that cut it, do you think?"

"You're being too timid, old chap. Just bang your fist on the desk once or twice. It's only a piece of paper you're after. Gild the lily a bit. Rules are made to be bent, old boy. Speak soon."

Stokes knew what the last two words meant. Sure enough, the line went dead.

HE RETURNED to the desk where the sergeant was in the middle of paperwork. Stokes leant across the counter and explained what he wanted, as succinctly as he could. The fewer people who knew about it though, he stressed, the better it would be.

The policeman was of the same mind as Knight, it transpired. Whatever it took to get the job done. He completed the form and slid it across the counter. He whispered. "I hope you don't mind me asking but is this to do with the factory?"

Stokes nodded. As an afterthought, and enhancing their complicity, he tapped his nose.

"Mum's the word then, Mr Stokes."

"Indeed, she is, sergeant."

They both laughed at the jokey response. Stokes folded the search warrant and put it in his inside pocket. The sergeant spoke to him in a near-whisper.

"You'll see I've left a couple of sections blank. We can fill them in later if we need to. As for the arrest warrants, let's see what we find first, shall we?"

"Oh, are you willing to accompany me?"

"I would deem it a privilege. Something to tell the grandkids . . . when I get some, that is. When do you want to do it?"

"As soon as you like."

"Hang on, I'll get somebody to cover the desk."

PC Billy Atkinson was pleased to take over. Within five minutes, Stokes was back at the shop with the sergeant in tow. The sign was still turned to 'closed' and the door itself was locked.

The sergeant - Harris, Stokes found out during the walk - knocked on the shop door. Frank Metcalf arrived after a second try. He looked surprised to see him back so soon.

Stokes explained as gently as he could that he needed to search the flat above the shop. He was non-specific as to the reason. He muttered words like 'routine enquiries' and briefly showed him the warrant. Frank asked no questions. He had no qualms in allowing them upstairs to search the flat but declined the invitation to accompany them. He gave them the key and pointed to the staircase door.

. . .

IF STOKES THOUGHT his own digs on Bedford Terrace were cramped, then he had seen nothing. He found it difficult to imagine that two of them lived there. It reeked of cigarette smoke.

"So, Mr Stokes. What are we after?"

"Anything written. Letters, that sort of thing. Anything that looks out of place in a flat shared by two respectable gentlemen. Basically, you are also here to verify that we don't remove anything that was not here in the first place, if you get my meaning."

Harris laughed. "Let's get started then."

They started with the kitchen, examining the cupboards, the interiors of any boxes or bottles. Of the latter, there were many, all empty. Nothing was found. The small bathroom and both of the tiny bedrooms similarly yielded nothing. It was hot work stripping the beds, looking in any cavities and lifting them so that they could see underneath. By the time they ended up in the living space, they were both grateful for the chance to sit down and get their breath back.

Stokes sat in the better of the two armchairs. "Just the cupboards in here now. And the loft, of course."

Harris sat opposite him in the other chair. He stood straight up again.

"What's the matter?"

"Something lumpy under my posterior."

He stood and lifted the cushion. Stokes came across to look. There was a quantity of letters held together by a rubber band. He took them, put them on the floor and returned to the chair. There were drawings of some quality, down both sides of where the cushion had rested, and a bulldog clip holding a sheaf of press cuttings.

Stokes' armchair held no such joys. Nor did the cupboards. Harris volunteered to clamber up on the back of the armchair to peer into the void of the loft, while Stokes held the chair steady. The sergeant relayed to Stokes what he could see. It amounted to winter clothing, bedding, ornaments - all of fairly obvious German origin - and piles of old newspapers and magazines.

Harris shook his head. "It's a wonder the ceiling hasn't collapsed."

Stokes agreed. He looked at the letters and drawings on the floor. "So, let's get this lot back to the station to see what we've got, shall we?"

Before they left, they dragged the well-worn carpet back as far as it would go - from one wall first, and then the other. Their efforts revealed only bare floor boards. The two men closed the flat door behind them and trooped back downstairs. They knocked on the shop door and handed the flat key back to Frank Metcalf.

"Did you . . . erm, find anything?"

He looked as if he really did not want to hear the answer but it was plain that he had already spotted the bundle of letters and drawings clamped tightly under Stokes' left arm.

"Just some correspondence. Don't worry. It's probably quite innocent stuff. We're just looking to eliminate people from our enquiries at the moment, you understand."

"Enquiries? Into what?"

Harris answered that one. "We're not at liberty to say, Mr Metcalf. But like Mr Stokes just said, it's just normal routine in any investigation."

Thankyous and goodbyes were exchanged. MI5 man and sergeant walked back to the station. Stokes could not resist sliding the odd letter out of the sheaf and scanning it as he walked. Occasionally, Harris could hear him saying 'bloody hell' or 'struth'. Eventually, after narrowly avoiding walking into a lamppost, he gave up. None of what he had seen was proof of anything apart from sedition, possibly, but he could not wait to get back to the station to pore over it in depth.

Even before they reached the police station, Stokes was convinced that Freddie was as guilty as hell. It was a waiting game now. He just hoped that poor, guilt-ridden Frank would see sense and let them know the instant Ernest and Freddie returned.

In the meantime, he would see what Lizzie Fenwick had to offer. The shopkeeper, Shrimplin, had described her as 'the old man's secretary'. He assumed the old man to be the sadly afflicted factory owner, Wilkinson. If this Lizzie was his secretary, then she would possibly have worked with Ernest Metcalf.

Part of him yearned to be dealing with ex-BUF members like Reginald Windsor and his tribe. You knew where you stood with them. Trying to pin down the Metcalfs was like herding cats.

CHAPTER 41

H oward Wesley's journey south after his apprehension at the Punch Hotel in Hull, was a nightmare. It was five hours long and virtually non-stop. Two hundred miles in the back of a police Wolseley, packed tightly between two silent men on the rear seat while facing the heads of two equally uncommunicative individuals in the front, had - almost literally - crushed him.

During a brief conversation while he was waiting at the police station for his guardians to arrive, he was told that he was being taken to Latchmere House - with an ominous raising of eyebrows. That meant nothing to either himself or the police constable who brought him a cup of tea. 'Somewhere in London, I think', was the bobby's educated guess. The portents were not good.

There was no conversation during the trip. It was excruciatingly tedious, punctuated only by a few stops to collectively relieve themselves by the roadside. The single highlight had been knocking some chap off his bike at some point. It was very dark by this time and Wesley had not seen the incident. He was merely aware of a sharp swerve and a volley of curses from the front of the vehicle. A short debate brought the conclusions that 'somebody will find him' and 'we haven't got time to stop'. The drive continued and he fell back into his fitful sleep.

On arrival, he was unceremoniously searched and all his personal possessions taken from him. He was given grey shirt and trousers and pushed into a room that was no more than a cell. He should have known that this would be no seaside guest house. The sight of barbed wire as he was driven between the Gothic entrance pillars, was a strong clue.

It was late. All he wanted to do was sleep but the room was cold, the light was on and there was no switch on the inside. The door was locked. Within a few minutes, he was brought a meal. Before he had finished eating, the light went out. Whatever light the morning might bring would have to be filtered through a small window at almost ceiling height, where a wall of glass bricks took the place of a regular pane.

He was nervous and afraid. As he suspected, he was not able to sleep. The light was switched on and off at regular intervals for what he supposed was two or three hours, and then remained on.

HIS ESPIONAGE MISSION had obviously been detected and he had a lot of thinking to do before the inevitable interrogation took place the following morning. He had been so careful. Somehow – although he could hardly believe it as the man had seemed so ineffectual – Armitage must be the key to all of this. After all, this was the man he was expecting to meet at the Punch Hotel before he was roughly and unceremoniously apprehended.

What, though, did they have on him? He thought about whom he had met.

He thought again about Armitage. He did not recall leaving the man with any certainty that he was trying to recruit him or to help him in any way with his amateurish efforts to gather information on decoy sites. Maybe the man had just assumed it was to be the subject of their Punch Hotel meeting. Or, perhaps, he *was* a genuine bird-spotter, simply doing his best to analyse the effects of decoy-site construction on the nesting habits of the local sea bird population. An innocent, upstanding citizen whom he had frightened so much that he had reported their meeting to the authorities. It was a possibility that had only just occurred to him.

The Metcalfs? They were as deep in the shit as he was. Guilty as sin and German too. He discounted them immediately. No.

The Czech. He was certain that he would by now have committed the perfect heist. Wesley could not have done more to secure the man's departure unless he had personally strapped him into a Hurricane cockpit and pointed it toward the *Reich*. He recalled his threat to the Czech to 'pick the best of the bunch and do the business'. No.

He struggled to think of any other people he had met and spoken to, and who could be seen as complicit. None came to mind. There had been various landlords and landladies and, of course, the dirty-minded little cockney, Sid Tanner, with whom he had shared a drink on his first night at the Gillett Street digs. The odd petrol pump attendant when he was unable to find a car with sufficient fuel for a certain journey.

How about places? Had he been seen somewhere that would put him under suspicion? Certainly not in the Suffolk field where he had landed. Unless there were MI5 people disguised as Friesian cows, and he thought he could discount that. He also recalled the courting couple doing the beast with two backs, spread-eagled across the rear bench seat of a Hillman Minx, in his search for a vehicle that night. He felt sure he could rule them out as well.

Ipswich, Hull, North Shields and . . . Brentford. He had visited the Siemens-Schuckert factory there twice. On the first occasion to pick up his own wireless; on the second, to collect a set for the Metcalfs. It had to be Brentford. He had been stopped both times, a few hundred yards from the factory, and asked to show his Identity Card. It had not worried him at the time as he had already been asked to show his ID on several other occasions beforehand, and therefore thought little of it after that. It was a fact of wartime life.

His current accommodation in Hull. He knew they must have discovered his digs by now. He remembered telling Armitage that he lived in Gillett Street. Why the Hell had he done that? He recalled needing to impress upon the birdspotter that he was local, for some reason. If the man had passed on that information, then the security services must have had to go door-to-door in a search for his room. There must be twenty or thirty houses on Gillett Street, of which, he guessed, many had been subdivided into individual rooms. Both wireless sets were there, under the bed. It would not take much of a search to find them.

In short, there was certainly more than enough evidence to incriminate him. Whether innocent or guilty, Armitage was top of the list, with Brentford a close second.

.   .   .

HIS THOUGHTS then turned to Hamburg. Whether he ever spoke to Ziegler or Grosskopf, or even saw the place again, was in the lap of the Gods. He was at a crisis point and he knew it.

CHAPTER 42

Latchmere House was a sprawling Victorian edifice on Ham Common in south London. It was owned by HM Prison Service and, as such, surrounded by entanglements of barbed wire. The dozen cells were no more than functional - and permanently under surveillance by hidden microphones.

This was now the home of Camp Twenty. Its purpose was to interrogate captured enemy agents. The aim was to show them the error of their ways and convert them into double agents. If they agreed, then they would continue - under supervision - in both roles; if they refused, then they were, quite simply, taken out of circulation. The man in charge was Lieutenant-Colonel Robin 'Tin Eye' Stephens He had bestowed upon himself the title of Commandant of Camp Twenty - despite the fact that the rank was normally reserved for the Colonel in charge of regiment.

Notwithstanding the fact that Hollywood movies had already set the template of 'spy interrogator' as a bully boy who used violence in order to extract information, Tin Eye had vehemently eschewed such tactics. They were taboo. In his view, they would merely generate answers designed to please, or simply elicit low-grade information. His counter philosophy had proved, he felt, more effective than any *Gestapo* techniques where the major features were pain, blood and periods of unconsciousness.

He was a great advocate of what he called 'sensory deprivation'. Subjects were more likely to confess their sins if they had been without any human contact or external stimuli for a few days. Feed them - of course. Provide them with the basic human needs like toileting, washing facilities, bed – definitely. Then, once forced by solitude and sleep deprivation into the deepest recesses of their own minds, better results would follow. He viewed violence as an act of cowardice. It was not an intelligent approach to the task of extracting valuable information. Stephens' philosophy had so far proved most efficacious.

IT HAD NOW BEEN three days since Smith's arrival. Stephens judged that to be a suitable period for the man to have been softened up. Enough, anyway, for him to have considered his future with trepidation and, hopefully, to have developed a desire to talk.

Since he had last spoken to Maxwell Knight at MI5, when the immediate request to incarcerate this Smith chap had been made, Stephens had been furnished with a wealth of information on his subject. He now knew a fair deal of his provenance and the reason for MI5's urgent desire to get him off the street. Peter Armitage, the chap whom Smith was due to meet at the Punch Hotel was already an incipient case for their agent, Albert Stokes. Smith's intervention had not only rocked the boat; it had threatened to ditch Stokes' mission altogether.

Armitage had started to panic about that meeting and had alerted Stokes. The MI5 man had been instrumental in Smith's apprehension. Armitage had provided them with a partial address for the man. It turned out to be the street name only but half an hour of door-knocking was all they had needed to find Smith's digs – as well as two German wireless sets under the bed. Lying beneath the mat upon which the bed stood, they uncovered a long list of ex-BUF Leeds members. All had been removed and the landlady informed that her tenant would not be returning.

Knight had been delighted to hear about the list of BUF Leeds members. It turned out Smith had also been careering around on that piece of MI5 turf too. The man was a bull in a china shop. Since the BUF had been outlawed, there was great concern about underground groups cropping up and acting as Fifth Columnist cells. That was Stokes' brief and the two men had almost met. The encounter would have blown his cover and spelt the death of his 'persona' as Hitler's Man in London.

Stephens had been industrious himself. He wanted to build a strong case against Smith so he had not relied solely on the incoming material - found and gleaned by others. He had spoken to Oliver Strachey at Bletchley Park, the previous afternoon. They had a network of external wireless listening posts – simply called Y-stations – which were able to pick up transmissions to the enemy from locations within Britain. There were a few of them dotted up and down the east coast. Strachey had given him details of a few messages from the Hull area. All from the same location.

He rubbed his hands, picked up the phone and requested one of his corporals to bring Smith to him.

· · ·

WHEN HIS INTERVIEWEE shuffled into the room and stood in front of the desk, he looked distinctly haggard. His sleeping pattern had been disturbed. He let the man stand while he opened a file and read for a few minutes. Finally, he stood with hand outstretched.

"I am Lieutenant-Colonel Stephens. You will be incarcerated here until I obtain information from you. The house rules here are that you will stand every time that I or one of my officers enter the room. You will not speak unless you are spoken to. Do you understand?"

Wesley shook his hand and nodded. They both sat. He looked at the officer. The most remarkable feature of his appearance was the heavy monocle he wore in his right eye. That either spoke of pure, almost theatrical, affectation and therefore an inflated ego - of which Wesley himself was occasionally guilty - or a touch of real class and non-conformity.

Stephens took a good look at him. "Oh, good God. You look rather grim, old chap. Trouble sleeping? A guilty conscience will do that for you."

Wesley glared at him. There was venom in his eyes. When he did speak, it was a lengthy and spiteful diatribe about the open unlidded toilet, no shaving gear, light being switched on and off, *ad nauseam*.

Eventually, Stephens put his hand up to curtail his rant. "I can rectify all of that and you can look upon it as a reward for your full co-operation from henceforward. Now, just shut up and bloody listen."

Silence reigned for a few seconds. Stephens looked at the list of topics in front of him, wondering which to hit Smith with first. He folded his arms and looked intently at his subject.

"You were brought here at the behest of MI5. They think you're a spy, Mr Smith. Are you?"

After a few seconds, his subject replied. Coolly and calmly. He was clearly intending to brazen it out.

"If you think I'm a spy, why don't you just have me shot?"

He hoped he sounded more confident than he felt. Stephens stared at him.

"Oh, believe me John, that is still on the table. No, to be more accurate, we don't use the firing squad very often in this country – not for treason anyway. It's only a method of execution if you are in the military and found guilty of cowardice or desertion at a court martial."

He paused and sat back, locking his hands in front of him on the table.

"No, you would be introduced to Mr Pierrepoint. The meeting would be brief. What I gather from those who have witnessed both methods, is that the firing squad is preferable. For the recipient, anyway."

Wesley did not know who Pierrepoint was. Stephens read his face.

"He's the public hangman. Very good at his job too. But then he's had a lot of practice just lately. The problem with those who aren't as skilled as him is that they tend to miscalculate the length of the rope. You can dangle there for half an hour, slowly suffocating. It's a long, lingering death."

He fell silent for a few seconds, leant forward and dropped his voice.

"I have heard tell that they often go for a tea break while they're waiting. So, you had better hope that our Albert isn't too busy that day."

Wesley felt uneasy. He could not conjure up a response that would gain him any ground. Stephens pushed on.

"We found your digs in Hull. Gillett Street."

No reaction. His inquisitor leant across, sporting a rictus grin.

"Guess what we found?"

"My shaving gear hopefully."

Stephens sensed the man was coming out of his corner. He had heard the bell for the first round.

"Afraid not, old man. Never mind, you might suit that beard once it achieves full status. Anyway, that's what spies do, isn't it? Try to change their appearance."

He settled back into his chair and started to read from his list.

"We found two wirelesses. Two, mark you, not just one. Identical machines. The SE108/10, comprising power pack, receiver and transmitter. Standard *Abwehr* issue – so that answers another question, doesn't it?"

Wesley shrugged. He knew they would have found the digs and the wireless sets.

"A person answering your description and bearing this Identity Card . . ." He held up the Smith ID. ". . . visited the Siemens-Schuckert factory in Brentford on two dates, using a different vehicle each time. A Morris Eight on the first occasion and then a Humber Super Snipe." He smiled. This man was testing his patience. "You pushed the boat out on that one."

Wesley assumed a perplexed expression.

"What really intrigues me, old chap, is why you needed two sets. Are German manufactured wirelesses so unreliable that you need to carry a spare?"

"You tell me."

"We keep a very close eye on the factory. And I have the registration numbers of both cars - previously reported as stolen."

Wesley remained silent. So, it was Brentford. He had

thought nothing of those two ID checks. He took them for granted. He even remembered joking with the checker, asking him if he was looking for German spies. He hoped the man got a promotion for his diligence.

Stephens reached into the drawer and took out an envelope. He withdrew several sheets of closely typed names and addresses. Wesley could not mask the fact that he recognised what they were. He had forgotten that he had put the sheets under the threadbare mat in his room. And then modified the envelope in which they had arrived, to house a note to that fellow Armitage about the meeting at the Punch.

Wesley's discomfiture was obvious. At last, the insouciance was showing cracks. Stephens continued.

"I have reason to believe - and I have checked, trust me - that these sheets are membership details of the now-defunct British Union of Fascists." He paused. "Sorry, they dropped the 'Fascists' part of their monicker." He looked at Wesley. "Clever, eh? They ended up as just 'British Union'." He laughed. "Anyway, Leeds branch, by the look of it." He waved them in the air. "Friends of yours?"

Wesley spluttered. "Believe me, I have never seen them before. Probably left there by a previous tenant, I would imagine."

"As were the two German wireless sets, I suppose?"

Stephens laughed and then became suddenly serious. "You're now insulting my intelligence." He stood and bent towards Wesley. He glared at him. "That . . . is a big mistake."

Wesley watched as he gathered up his papers and walked around to his side of the desk. Stephens turned to speak.

"You are deluded if you imagine you can proceed in this

manner. If you think this is a game, then be aware that I hold all of the cards." He patted the file under his arm. "It will go better for you if you give me your real identity and purpose voluntarily, rather than having it dragged out of you. There are two ways this can go. Only one of them grants you good health and, indeed, survival."

He smiled and walked to the door. Wesley swivelled on the stool to face him. Stephens spoke again. "Somebody will come for you and take you back to your room. How long you stay there is up to you. Let me know when you are ready to talk again. And when we do, I want full and frank disclosure."

Stephens looked at his watch, the message being that he had bigger fish to fry. He left the room. Wesley heard the key turning.

WESLEY WAS RETURNED to his stale, stinking cell. He collapsed on his bunk. He was desperate to sleep but he had to make do with dozing spasmodically.

Suddenly, Wesley was sitting up and Stephens was beckoning him. He had no idea how long he had been back in his cell.

"Room 5, if you please. You know the way."

Wesley splashed water on his face and shook his head several times. He dried his face on the now grubby towel and trudged down the corridor. The door to Room 5 was open. The desk and stool were in opposite places. He sat down. Stephens was smiling.

"I need to speed things up a little. Now, collect your thoughts. There's a cup of tea on the way."

As he said that, the door opened. A man entered with a tray bearing a teapot, two cups, a milk jug and bowl of sugar.

He laid it on the table and left as suddenly as he had arrived. Stephens stood.

"I'll be mother, shall I? Milk and sugar?"

Wesley nodded and observed Stephens as he performed the minor domestic ritual that he had not witnessed since childhood. This felty like a dream. He took a sip and watched Stephens place a now larger file on the desk between them.

"Now. Let's recap, shall we?"

Wesley put the cup back on the tray and listened. Stephens smiled.

"Good. You would be wise to listen very carefully."

Wesley nodded.

"I am going to lay my cards on the table, old chum. And remember, I have all of them. I will tell you what I know as truth and, from time to time, I will ask you to fill in the gaps." He paused. "Does that sound sensible?"

Wesley nodded again.

"Good." He opened the first of what now appeared to be two files.

"We know that you are an *Abwehr* agent. We know that your codename is WIESELIG and that you communicate with Hamburg. What is your real name?"

"Howard Oswald Wesley."

"Good. Are you British? You don't sound like any German spy that I have ever come across."

"Yes. And thank you."

"Tell me more."

Wesley proceeded to recount his upbringing in Coventry. Only child. Domineering English father. Loving, attentive German mother. Her death and Wesley's desire to meet her family in Berlin. His liking of the place. His recruitment.

He suddenly stopped short and stared at Stephens who was scribbling furiously.

"What have you done to me?"

Stephens did not look up. "Don't worry about that, old chap. Just a little enhancement to your desire to be honest and truthful." He looked up and smiled. "The tea will help."

He continued. "Given that your codename is WIESELIG, we have detected several wireless messages that you have been sending - from Hull, unsurprisingly. In a few, you have mentioned what we assume is another agent. Who is MOTORRAD?"

Wesley needed time to think.

"What will become of me?"

Stephens put his pen down and looked him straight in the eyes.

"The last time we spoke, Howard, I mentioned that there were two ways this could go. Mr Pierrepoint is one way. I believe I described his talents extremely graphically. I apologise for that but it's important that you know what your choices are. The second option is that you mend your ways, leave the crooked path and work for us. I did not describe that in any detail. That will come, I promise. Now, we need to move on. Who is MOTORRAD?"

Wesley's mind was starting to clear. He suspected that he had already revealed more than he intended to, but reckoned he was so far down the line now that he had to continue. If he became what he assumed would be a double agent - if that was what Stephens was alluding to - then he knew that he could work both sides against the middle.

He guessed that Stephens' desire to rush through this script that he seemed to be using, was mostly a desire to glean as much information as he could before the effects of what he was now sure he had been dosed with, wore off. He surmised that there was something in the tea to aid his general coherence and articulation. This would be a struggle. He needed to appear more under the thrall of the medication than he actually was. He could already feel the fog lifting.

Stephens repeated the question. "Who is MOTORRAD?"

"He is - or possibly, was, who knows? - a Czech RAF airman who was supposed to be in touch with me. It never happened. I never had any contact. And please don't ask me his name."

The questions were coming faster now. Stephens was nodding. "And what was his mission?"

"Oh, I don't know. To deliver information about squadron strengths, locations, movements, technical stuff. Anything that would be of interest. I'm sure you know what I mean."

"Through yourself?"

Wesley had to think now. He could ditch this on the cutout. That woman in Barnsley. The one they had christened Frau Viggle. He would appear to be reluctant. Stephens had to appear to be breaking him. And it would give him more credit for whatever lay ahead.

"Not all of it. There was a cutout. In Barnsley."

"Name?"

"Ada Wigglesworth."

He could go further here. He did.

"That's where the BUF Leeds membership list came from."

Stephens raised his eyebrows and moved his pen even faster. He was now on his second sheet of paper. Wesley sneaked out a smile when he knew the man would not see it. He was pleased with himself but he knew it was not over yet. He sensed there were more questions. He was right - the man had stopped writing and was now staring at him.

"I'd like to go back to the reason for the second wireless. We've tested them. They both work perfectly."

Wesley was flummoxed. This was the one area that he really did not want to visit but he felt that it would do no harm to divulge part of the story. He would use his response to suggest that he was more than a little pissed off by the way he had been treated by *Abwehr*. That would please Stephens and hopefully put him in a better light as a candidate for the double agent vacancy. There was a large element of truth in that, too.

"Oh, I was asked to pick it up from Brentford and deliver it to Tyneside. North Shields."

That meant very little to Stephens.

"So, why was it in your possession when we searched your digs?"

"I was subsequently asked to pick it up again but I was damned if I was going to return it to bloody Brentford. It's a bit of a hike from Hull. To be honest, I was a bit aggrieved by the fact that Hamburg was using me as some sort of courier service."

Stephens laughed. "Indeed. And how long was it in North Shields?"

Wesley looked at the ceiling. "Erm . . . not sure. A week, ten days maybe. I don't keep a diary, for obvious reasons."

Stephens ignored the sarcasm.

"Didn't that strike you as odd?"

"A little. But you learn very quickly not to ask questions, although I did complain bitterly about the waste of my valuable time. In any case, I was not that keen on knowing the answer."

Stephens smiled. "In case you were ever closely questioned about your activities?"

"Precisely."

"And what have you actually been doing since you arrived on these shores?"

"Oh . . . trying to infiltrate Fifth Columnist cells. Or initiate them. And generally sniffing around. Decoy sites was proving to be quite remunerative. The *Luftwaffe* are very interested in them, for obvious reasons."

Wesley knew he was downplaying his own role. In reality, he felt that Hamburg had already done that to some degree. All this running up and down the country, delivering wirelesses and booting two pilots up the backside had done that. All of which he was loath to mention to his interrogator.

"Which explains your Mr Armitage, no doubt."

Wesley simply nodded. He would like an hour alone with that man.

Stephens scrawled a few more lines. It was making sense so far but he needed to speak to Strachey again to check his Y-stations for any traffic emanating from North Shields. He decided to conclude the interview.

"I think that's enough for now. Thank you for your co-operation. I will arrange for some shaving gear to be brought to you."

A besuited gentleman entered the room and returned him to his cell. A few moments later, the same man came back and, without speaking, deposited a bag inside the door. It contained a razor, soap and shaving brush inside the door.

WESLEY SETTLED ON HIS BUNK. His head was pounding but, on balance, he was feeling quite good about his performance before this audience of one - Lieutenant-Colonel Stephens. His future was not fully assured but things were now looking distinctly rosier. He deserved some decent sleep and he was confident that he would achieve it this time. Not the sleep of the righteous, perhaps - nor even the sleep of the just. The sleep of the bloody exhausted would do for now.

CHAPTER 43

Stephens was moderately pleased with his interrogation of John Smith – now revealed to be Howard Oswald Wesley and operating for *Abwehr* under the codename of WIESELIG. He was on the point of converting him to what he called 'the one true faith', by installing him as one of their double agents but there were a couple of questions to answer before he did.

He was on the telephone, waiting for Oliver Strachey at Bletchley to take the call. He had promised Knight that he would trawl through whatever their outlying Y-stations had picked up on WIESELIG traffic. Thus far it had just been from the Hull area. Given that that was where they had picked him up from, and that they were already aware of his decoy site activities, that was now old news.

"Strachey."

"Ah, Oliver. Robin Stephens."

"Yes, I've been meaning to give you a call. I do apologise. How's it going with your Mr Smith."

"Well, he's opened up to being WIESELIG and we have

his real name now. Howard Oswald Wesley. Everything he has told us so far checks out splendidly but . . ."

"What?"

"One of the two wirelesses that we found in his digs was, he says, delivered to North Shields at the request of his masters . . . and then collected just a matter of days later. Not sure that he knows anything other than that and he's whinging about the constant driving up and down the land to carry out such menial duties. Oh . . . and point of origin for both sets was Brentford. We've verified that."

"I see. And North Shields is where?"

"Tyneside. About 130 miles or so north of Hull. And factoring in the trip to Brentford to collect it, can't say I blame him for complaining. I think he has a point."

Strachey laughed. "It would have been quicker to just drop it off at the nearest railway station and have it delivered by train."

Both men laughed. Strachey spoke.

"It would never have got there. Anyway, I assume you would like me to look for any Y-station traffic close to North Shields?"

"If you wouldn't mind, Oliver."

"Consider it done. There is one thing I was meaning to mention to you about the Hull traffic that we found for WIESELIG."

"Which is?"

"It's unfathomable. Never seen anything like it."

"What do you mean?"

"It doesn't make any sense. In fact, it's the exact opposite – nonsense! I've shown it to the experts. Enigma is nothing on this chap's chatter. It's almost as if they are speaking in some kind of language or code that is known only to the two participants. So, it's . . ."

Stephens groaned. "Unbreakable?"

"Yes, unless you can get any more out of WIESELIG. These two – WIESELIG and his buddy on the other end – are talking in riddles. I've had our literary chaps look at it too. They just held their hands up." He paused. "The only thing we can get for sure is when one or the other mentions a codename. They are immutable. WIESELIG, for instance. And I mentioned MOTORRAD to you, I seem to remember?"

"You did. And we now know who he is, or was. More or less. He's claiming no contact but we'll see."

"OK. Let me look at any mention of North Shields on Y-station stuff and I'll come back to you, old man."

The call was ended.

STEPHENS DIALLED another number and was put through to Maxwell Knight at MI5.

"Knight."

"Robin Stephens, here. Just to bring you up to speed with your Mr Smith."

"Ah, yes. How is he?"

"We've put him through the wringer a couple of times. Interesting."

"How so?"

Stephens looked at his notes and read out the salient passages.

"Whoa! Steady the Buffs! Did you say North Shields?"

"Yes, why?"

"We have a bit of a flap on there at the moment. I say 'we' . . . it's more of a personal thing for the Navy. Stokes is trying to get to the bottom of it as we speak."

Knight told him all that he knew of the factory raid, the

work that had been going on there, the Navy's lax security and the fact that Stokes' progress was severely hampered by the disappearance of two key individuals. They were possibly Fifth Column involvement, given their German ancestry.

Stephens thought about it. "I see. Curiouser and curiouser. If it wasn't for the fact that North Shields is so specific both to the raid *and* the delivery of a wireless, then I would probably not think anything of it. But our man may just have been the delivery boy." He paused. "But I've already got Oliver Strachey on looking at any WIESELIG traffic closer to North Shields. So, watch this space, old chap."

"It's one hell of a coincidence, you must admit."

"Indeed. And don't think I won't question our chap further about that. In the absence of any further information though, I am inclined to turn him."

"Really?"

"Yes. He has already been off the key for too long. I need Hamburg to think he is still in play, as it were."

"Point taken. I'll let you know if Stokes makes any further progress in North Shields. He's in limbo at the moment with these two persons of interest on the missing list."

"I understand. Do keep in touch."

The call was ended. Stephens stepped out of his office and asked a corporal to bring Wesley to Room 5. The man had some questions to answer. His replies could mean life or death.

CHAPTER 44

Wesley arrived in Room 5 before Stephens. He was dutifully seated on the 'interrogation stool' and looking rather pleased with himself. He was clean-shaven and, although still clothed in his prisoner regulation grey, he was looking much more presentable.

Stephens sat and looked at him. "Well, what a difference a shave makes."

Wesley stroked his chin. "Yes. Thank you." He watched as Stephens opened the ubiquitous manila folder. It did not look any thicker, which he supposed was good news.

"Now then, Howard. You mentioned delivering a wireless to North Shields. When I mentioned that to my colleague at MI5, he got rather agitated. Do you know why it might have had that effect?"

Wesley felt a chill go through his body. He suppressed it and placed a 'very puzzled' look upon his face. This was impro. He had always been good at that.

"You know nothing about why he should feel that way?"

"No idea, old chum."

That was a mistake. Stephens' face was an angry mask.

"I am *not* your chum. If you hadn't already noticed, you are *still* under interrogation. Kindly remember that." He stared at Wesley. The man looked suitably contrite. He moved on.

"I cannot tell you about what has happened in North Shields. Suffice to say that we suspect Fifth Column involvement in a serious incident. One that is of national importance. A wireless, such as the one you say you delivered, would have been of great assistance to the perpetrators. Tell me about the delivery, if you please."

Stephens sat back. He looked relaxed but Wesley was no longer fooled. He felt that chill again.

"I never actually visited North Shields. I was told to meet a chap at Newcastle Central station with the wireless that I had picked up at Brentford. There was an exchange of code phrases. He got into the car. He directed me out of the city. We parked up somewhere. I don't know the name of the place. Somewhere out in the sticks. A colliery village, I think."

"And what then? Did he simply put it over his shoulder and walk to North Shields?"

Wesley was tempted to laugh but Stephens was not even smiling.

"No. He had a car there. It went from boot to boot. No names. No pack drill."

Stephens had duly scribbled it all down. Wesley had purposely spoken quickly. It amused him to watch the other man trying to keep up. His pen was almost a blur.

"And that was it?"

"Yes. I just wanted to get back to Hull as soon as I could."

"I understand. And when you collected it?"

"Same thing in reverse, I seem to remember."

"How did you get your instructions to collect it?"

"I was told by Hamburg. The instructions were to pick it up at the point of delivery."

Stephens raised his eyebrows. "And you remembered where this . . . colliery village was?"

"Yes."

"I'm amazed. I know a little about Tyneside, Howard. I should imagine there are dozens of these pit villages dotted around the landscape."

"Ah, I went to Newcastle Central station to start with and remembered the route from there. I have a good memory. It's a good prerequisite for anyone engaged in espionage."

Stephens grunted. This man was too clever by half. Wesley was pleased. He remembered Grosskopf's instruction on how to face interrogation – to keep it simple and include as much truth as possible in your responses.

"And nothing was said?"

"No. No need of the silly code phrase that time, obviously. It was the same chap. If it had not been, I would have driven straight past and left him to his own devices."

"You didn't ask why the set was being returned?"

Wesley felt it acceptable to laugh at this point. "Absolutely not. I told you before. I've got into the habit of not asking questions. I simply did not want to know."

Stephens had a thought.

"One thing puzzles me. Why, if you never actually went to North Shields at any point in this process – either delivery or collection – did you tell me that the second wireless was . . . delivered to North Shields? Why did you not simply say 'Tyneside' or 'Newcastle'."

Wesley was stumped. The man was right. His mind was

racing. It was not enough to just shrug as he had done a few times before.

"I . . . I think it was because I complained that I did not know exactly where North Shields was . . . and could they not make it somewhere more central. Like . . . Newcastle Central." He smiled. "They agreed and changed it but I always came to think of it as 'the North Shields wireless'."

He smiled again but with no hint of triumph.

Stephens was impressed. It made some sort of sense. He would probably never know if this man was telling the truth but there was no doubt in his own mind that he would be an asset as a double agent. There was still, however, the question of his mode of communication with his chum in Hamburg – as highlighted by Oliver Strachey. He would report to Knight what the man had just told him but he was satisfied for the moment. He put his pen down and sat back, hands on head.

Wesley was pleased with his performance and was having difficulty in concealing his self-satisfaction. He waited. Was that it? New career as a double agent about to be offered?

Stephens leant forward again but did not pick up his pen.

"Just one thing. Something I don't understand. In fact, it's something that even my more experienced colleagues do not understand."

Wesley was puzzled. His face showed it.

"As I think you are aware, we have picked up one or two of your outgoing wireless messages . . . which is obviously how we know that your codename is WIESELIG."

"Yes."

"Sadly, that one word 'WIESELIG' was the only one that made any sense. The meat of the message was sadly . . . well, gibberish. In what I have seen from the handful of messages we have detected, your style is . . . odd, to say the least."

He nodded again but it seemed the man wanted more. His gaze had not wavered. He continued talking.

"Describe it to me, if you'd be so kind."

Wesley was now fully alert. He could feel all his grey matter suddenly sparking into life, his synapses making all the necessary connections. He was onstage, alone and with only one cursory glance at the script. He explained that he and his opposite number in Hamburg had developed a real rapport.

Stephens raised an eyebrow. Wesley noticed.

"No, nothing like that. We just came to a shared appreciation of the absurd, the ridiculous. There is plenty of it around in Germany at the moment, I can assure you."

Stephens actually laughed at that point. "As many of our music hall comedians have noticed."

"Yes, indeed. But that sort of piss-taking in Germany would not be tolerated, believe me." He thought back to his own portrayal of Göring which could have finished his own career before it started. And, he mused, also got him to where he was sitting right now.

He went on to tell Stephens that he had introduced his opposite number to the works of Lewis Carroll and Edward Lear, especially *Jabberwocky* and *The Owl and the Pussy Cat*. Some words or phrases often appeared in their messages.

"It's in shorthand, I assure you. It saves time which, when you are transmitting in a tight spot, can be very valuable."

What Wesley had been at pains not to tell him was that a single word could carry a message all of its own. That word would appear entirely innocent. Its intent was covert communication in its purest form. A simple and efficient compression of information. They had a whole lexicon of them.

Stephens was not totally convinced that this private code might not also contain hidden meaning but he let that go. Vigilance would have to be the key with this man. He was as slippery as an eel. He leant forward.

"What I do *not* want you to do, however, is to change that. Not by one iota. In fact, any variation from your normal key behaviour would register as false by your friend in Hamburg."

"Indeed. Point taken."

"Oh, by the way, your codename with us is METHODIST."

Wesley laughed. "I like that. Very drole. So . . . I am now a double agent?"

"Yes. And I'm glad you like your new handle. A bit simpler than your *Abwehr* tag of WIESELIG. But which you will continue to use, of course."

"Of course. Wouldn't that cause confusion? If I started transmitting as METHODIST, I mean. Both security services would shudder to a halt in the confusion that would ensue."

Both men laughed.

"And then we'd both be out of a job."

Stephens stood. "So, let me take you to your new accommodation. I think you'll find it much more comfortable."

Wesley stood too. "Oh, dear. I shall miss the old place."

"Sarcasm is the lowest form of wit, Wesley. Come with me."

He walked to the door and then turned. His tone was harsher.

"Never forget, Wesley, that I am watching every move

you make. Keep your nose clean and we will both be happy men."

Wesley was starting to worry already about what he was to tell Otto, and in what form. And with somebody leaning over his shoulder and breathing down his neck.

CHAPTER 45

W hen Stokes and Sergeant Harris returned to the police station following their search of the Metcalfs' flat, the MI5 man went straight to the interview room that he normally used.

He placed the pile of material that they had found in front of him on the desk. The drawings were on the top. They were obviously done by somebody with talent. There were portrayals of cats, dogs and children; street views obviously sketched from the flat's front window; landscape scenes of what Stokes took to be the River Tyne. Nothing that broke any laws.

Finally, he came across a half dozen images of ships under construction. Even to his untutored eye, they looked like naval vessels. As far as he knew, they certainly contravened current secrecy laws. They were almost draughtsman-like in their execution and as good as photographs.

The letters were quite a different proposition. They were from somebody who signed himself as 'Jan' in Amsterdam. They were in German. Stokes had not used the language in years and it was difficult to decipher some of the handwriting, but he knew enough to get the gist of the content.

Jan boasted about his ascendancy up the ranks of the Dutch National Socialist party. Later letters told of his meetings with German Nazis post-invasion. He detailed his work rounding up Jews on behalf of the *Gestapo*. Some of the letters thanked Freddie for his drawings of Swan Hunters shipyard.

The most recent letter, although in the same handwriting, was different in style from all of the others. Almost as if Jan had copied it, or perhaps had the words dictated to him. For one thing, the quality of the paper was better and it was postmarked Sweden. A neutral country. The plot was thickening.

It took him an hour to assess it all. It was a veritable treasure trove. He picked up the phone and asked Harris to get him the usual number. Knight had to know about this. It reinforced his belief that arrest warrants should be issued for both Freddie and his nephew, Ernest. The pair would be apprehended when they reappeared. He was starting to get worried.

Knight answered after a couple of rings. "Ah, Albert, I'm glad you rang. I've just had some news that may interest you . . . about your man, Armitage."

"I've had no contact with him. I called in on my way back from that Smith business in Hull just to keep him in the know but he wasn't at home. Left him a note but he hasn't responded. Has he left me a message?"

"No - and he's not going to, dear boy."

"Meaning?"

"Stone dead, I'm afraid."

Stokes was shocked. "What?"

"Home Guard found him in a ditch near Selby. With his bike wrapped around him. Inseparable, I gather. Looks like he was hit by a vehicle going at speed. Bike had no lights on."

"What the Hell was he doing there?"

Knight laughed. "You tell me, sport. They took him into their church hall, or whatever. Identity card in pocket. Address in Gladstone Street."

"That's him."

"They searched the suitcase strapped to the back of the bike. Just normal stuff - clothing etcetera. Then they came across something which prompted them to shove the whole thing upstairs. Landed on my desk this morning."

"What?"

"It was a *Kriegsverdienstkreuz* . . . some sort of German award for good service, is it?"

"Yes . . . oh, bugger!"

"Indeed. Was that your doing, Albert?"

"Yes. I gave it to him when we met." He paused. "Oh, my Lord . . ."

"What?"

"Has this been suppressed?"

"Oh God, yes! I've had a D-notice slammed on all mention of it. His unfortunate accidental demise may be reported but nothing more. Just half an inch, buried deep in the local rag, I shouldn't wonder."

Stokes was still taking it in. "I wonder what made him fly the coop?"

"We'll never know. Naturally, I thanked the local boys in blue for their diligence. End of story as we are concerned though. Sad though it may seem, the man never existed -

within our records, anyway." Knight laughed. "I'll just put this thing back in stock, shall I?"

"Don't bother."

"Why not?"

"Armitage's name is engraved on the back." Stokes paused. "I just wonder why he took it with him."

Knight laughed. "Oh, yes. I see his name now. I guess he was hedging his bets. If the Germans invade, he just whips it out and gets preferential treatment."

"I suppose so. It also confirms he had not intended coming back. He wouldn't have wanted the next occupant of his house to find it, would he?"

"Indeed. And they also sent me his field glasses. They may come in useful."

Stokes laughed. "On a serious note, you'd better get a team into his house. You never know what else they may find."

"Fair point, my lad." He paused. "Well, that's my news. What have *you* got for *me*?"

Knight listened intently while Stokes summarised the cache of documents that they had found in the Metcalf flat. Stokes stressed that they needed to be examined by someone whose knowledge of German was better than his. He would send them down by the fastest means possible and would mark the parcel for Knight's personal attention. That should get around the bottle-neck that often delayed the arrival of mail onto Knight's desk.

He left the best until last. He told a shocked Knight of the final letter, sent from Sweden, stating that a wireless set was being delivered to the Metcalfs. He told Knight that he was going to hang on to the Swedish letter for later use when he interviewed the missing Metcalfs.

There was a stunned silence. Eventually Knight spoke. "And that letter is dated before the factory bombing?"

"By about a week, yes."

"This is dynamite, old son. Very well done."

"So, I assume it's arrest warrants all round?"

"It certainly is. Get on it. What is exercising my mind is the mysterious 'gentleman' who delivered the wireless and instructed the Metcalfs in its use. If they aren't a Fifth Columnist cell, my boy, then I'm Hitler's dentist. This is right up your *Strasse*." He paused. "There's no second letter containing delivery instructions, then?"

"Strangely not. Maybe they destroyed it."

"Ha. Shame they hadn't had that foresight with the rest of the gubbins."

Stokes laughed. Knight continued. "And what about the other name you had? Lizzie somebody, was it?"

"Fenwick. I'm seeing her soon. I've got her address. She was the owner's secretary at the factory so, presumably, was in close contact with Ernest Metcalf. Oh . . . family name Metzger, by the way."

"Ah, they Anglicised it then."

"I got the potted family history from Frank Metcalf."

"Who he?"

"Ernest's father. Freddie's brother. He may know more, but now we've found the letters, I'm not sure he'll be able to add much. Freddie is clearly rabidly anti-British. Fiancée killed in the 1915 riots."

"The archetypal bitter and twisted old man, eh?"

"Looks that way. And he seems to have brought his nephew into his thrall. They share the flat above the shop."

"It's all falling into place, Albert. Well done."

"Speak soon?"

Knight laughed.

"Exactly. I can't wait for the next instalment, old chum."
The line went dead.

STOKES GATHERED UP ALL of the paperwork into as neat a
bundle as he could manage and walked back through to the
desk. He dropped them in front of Sergeant Harris.

"I wonder if you could do me a favour, Sergeant? I would
like you to put all this into a sturdy parcel and send it to this
address."

He slid Harris's pad across and wrote down Knight's
name and address. He carefully added the words 'For the
immediate attention of Maxwell Knight Esq.'.

The sergeant put it under the counter. "I will make sure
it goes off today, Mr Stokes."

"Oh, and if you could arrange two arrest warrants now,
that would be kind. I think we have reasonable cause now,
don't you?"

Harris laughed. "Cast-iron case, I would say. I'll see to
that, don't worry."

The sergeant reminded him of Lizzie Fenwick's address
and directions. It was getting late but still daylight. In
Ernest's continuing absence, he wanted to know more about
the naval presence at the factory.

CHAPTER 46

Stokes found Linskill Terrace quite easily. The door was answered by a plump middle-aged woman. She was holding hands with a little girl.

"Mrs Fenwick?" He knew it was not Lizzie but he felt it was the easiest, least clumsy way of saying whom he wanted to talk to.

"I'm not but me daughter is. She lives with us." She turned and shouted up the stairs. "Lizzie. There's a gentleman here to see you."

There followed two minutes of Lizzie asking who it was, her mother taking and reading aloud the card which Stokes gave her. Eventually, Lizzie appeared at the top of the stairs and walked down. Woman and child disappeared upstairs. Stokes was still on the doorstep.

She invited him in and took him through to the front parlour, inviting him to sit opposite her in one of the two armchairs. She looked as if she had been crying but she was smiling, at least. She raised her eyebrows.

"What's this all about, Mr Stokes?"

"I'll come straight to the point, Mrs Fenwick ? You worked at the lemonade factory, I believe?"

"Call me Lizzie. Aye, I did. It's terrible what's happened."

"Indeed. I'd also like to ask you about Ernest Metcalf? You worked with him, I think?"

"Yes. I was the old man's secretary and . . ."

"You mean Mr Wilkinson? The owner."

"Yes. I was his secretary and Ernest was his accountant. We worked in the same office, right next to the old man's. I say 'office'. It was more of a cupboard really."

"Oh . . . I thought Ernest was the manager?"

"Well . . . more or less, I suppose. There was nobody else, really. All of the management from the third floor had gone, you see. Joined up."

Stokes broke the news to her about the old man's condition - the stroke he had suffered and, hence, the reason he was not able to ask him about Metcalf.

Lizzie was shocked. "Oh, that's terrible. I thought it was funny that nobody had been in touch. I must go and see him. Is he at home?"

"I'm not sure. When I saw him the day after the factory was hit, his housekeeper said he was due to go to hospital but the local ones were a bit short of beds."

"Oh, of course." She frowned.

"You could always go and knock on the door."

She smiled. "Aye, I think I will."

"I'm sure he would be pleased to see you."

He let her enjoy that thought before he spoke again. "The news of his affliction came as a shock to Mr Metcalf too. Mr Frank Metcalf, I mean."

"Ernest's dad? You've talked to him?"

"Yes, I'm anxious to speak to Ernest and that seemed the obvious place to start. I gather that Ernest and his uncle Freddie have gone off to Northumberland for a few days."

"Aye, he told me that too." She frowned. "What's he done anyway?"

"We're not sure at the moment. Can I ask you what you know about navy personnel working at the factory?"

It was like opening the floodgates. Lizzie told him the story of the navy scientists moving in, of Wilkinson's insistence that they were auditors and must not be disturbed, and how she and Ernest had very quickly come to the conclusion that they were scientists.

"What made you both think that?"

"Well, it wasn't difficult." She described all the strange noises they had heard coming from the main room occupied by the so-called auditors, and the brief glimpse into their room that she had got on her way back from the toilet.

"And . . . there was a Royal Navy staff car parked close to the factory all the time they were there. Not just during the daytime, neither."

"How do you know that? You can't see the factory from here."

"No. The Shrimplins told me. They've got the little shop on the opposite corner. Everybody was talking about it. It was no secret." Then she added. "They came from Swans, I think."

Stokes knew about the Navy's less than veiled presence, of course, from what Knight and the shopkeeper had both told him.

"Swan Hunters?"

"Aye. The shipyard."

He paused and smiled. Stokes would never cease to be

amazed at how just a few words spoken in Geordie could sound like the first line of a music hall song. He was as sure as he could be that Lizzie Fenwick was not in any way involved in what now plainly seemed a deliberate raid on the factory, but he made copious notes of everything she told him. He wanted to hear more of her take on Ernest.

"I don't wish to ask you any personal questions, Mrs Fenwick, but what was your relationship with Ernest Metcalf? Colleagues, friends or . . . something more, perhaps?"

She looked at him with something approaching amusement. "I know what you're implying, like. Aye, there was a . . . relationship." She leant forward, her face suddenly sad. "In fact, I miss him like Hell, Mr Stokes."

She seemed relieved to get that off her chest and slowly withdrew a handkerchief from the sleeve of her cardigan. He felt sorry for her. Lizzie told him how she had been attracted to him as soon as she saw him. She had felt very sorry for him, too, after what he had experienced on his first day. They seemed to get closer after that, especially when they both felt as if they were secret agents, spying on the scientists. She broke off at that point.

"I don't mean we were *really* spying or anything like that. It was just with the old man insisting they were auditors when they obviously weren't . . ."

"Because of the noises and the staff car?"

"Aye. And Ernest – he's qualified as an auditor too, you know – he told me he had never known an auditor work after five o'clock or at the weekend. We had a good laugh about it, to be honest."

"And that brought you closer together?"

"It did, aye."

She paused and looked up, as if reflecting. There was still some digging for Stokes to do. He looked at his notes.

"You mentioned something earlier. You talked about 'what he had experienced on his first day'. Can you explain that to me?"

She thought about it, clearly reluctant to put it into words, especially as this man was writing it all down.

"Are you afraid you will get him into trouble?"

"No – just the opposite, in fact."

Stokes was surprised. Metcalf's guilty behaviour and recent disappearance was painting him even blacker. Was he about to hear mitigating circumstances from Lizzie?

"He was attacked verbally by Mrs Turner and then ..."

Lizzie explained who Mrs Turner was and what had happened in the Wilkinson off-licence which she managed. She had to point out where the shop had been, forgetting that Stokes had only ever seen the ruins of the building. She also described the beating that Ernest had received at the hands of two unknown assailants in the stable yard.

"He tried to hide it but I think he was quite badly hurt."

"Did he report it to the police?"

"No."

"Why not?"

"He didn't want to get anyone in trouble."

"Really?"

"And he thought the police wouldn't take much notice of it."

"I'm surprised to hear that."

"I asked him to, mind. I also said he should tell Mr Wilkinson about what Mrs Turner did."

"Oh, yes. Tell me about that."

"It was just a bit of a tongue-lashing, that's all. About

how her late husband had died from poisonous gas in the first war, you know. Oh . . . and she spat at him. Well, between his feet. Not in his face, like, though I think she wanted to."

Stokes laughed. "And what had the fellow done to deserve that?"

She paused again and looked away for a few seconds before seeming to carefully select the words for what she was about to say.

"Well . . . it wasn't what he'd done. It was what he was . . . is, I mean."

"Do you think Mr Metcalf did not want to make a fuss about this in case it alerted anyone who didn't know he's German . . . to the fact that he is?"

She was shocked. "Oh, you know? But how . . .?"

"I've talked to his father, don't forget."

"Oh, of course. But he isn't. A German, I mean. He's a British subject."

"I stand corrected but he is certainly of German heritage. A couple of generations ago."

"His dad lent us his car. Ernest said he wanted to take me out. Not just to the pub – although we did go to the pub and . . . no, he wanted us to, you know, spend a day or two together and he said he was going to borrow his dad's car."

"And did he?"

"What?"

"Take you out in the car?"

"A couple of times, aye."

"Where did you go? Into the countryside?"

"Yes. Up into Northumberland." She paused. "And we went over to Usworth to see me friend, Muriel."

"Usworth?" He had never heard of the place.

"Yes. Sunderland way."

Lizzie explained that she and Muriel both worked at a Wilkinson lemonade factory. She at North Shields and her friend at Sunderland. She went on to say how the two Wilkinson brothers often exchanged staff and that was how she and her friend had met.

"Muriel had just got herself a new boyfriend. Really handsome."

"And he worked at her factory?"

"No, he was in the RAF. There's a base at Usworth. He's Czech."

"Ah, a dashing young pilot, eh?"

The handkerchief came back up and she was suddenly in floods of tears. Stokes was not sure why. She told him of their double date at the *Three Horseshoes*, the pub right next to the base.

"We spent the night with me and Mu chattering away in one corner, and Ernest and . . . Gus, that was it, talking and drinking in the other corner. The pub was packed and really noisy. Me and Ernest never spoke to each other till the drive back home, I don't think."

Stokes remained silent, waiting for her to compose herself. He was stunned. For all his experience, he did not often witness real grief at such close quarters.

"They were going to get married, Mr Stokes. They looked so happy together. And now he's been killed in a training accident. Over the North Sea. The Chaplain from the base came to see her and he told her these accidents happen all the time. He was out in his plane with one other but only that one came back."

"That's tragic."

She blew her nose again. Her tone changed.

"Mind you, it might be a blessing in disguise. I know Muriel worshipped him but I'm not convinced it was . . .

mutual, if you know what I mean? Sorry, that's a terrible thing to say about someone who's probably just died. I would've said something to Muriel but . . . I can hardly do that now, can I?"

Stokes smiled. "No, it would be kinder not to say anything."

He paused. This Czech fellow was starting to intrigue him.

"What made you think it wasn't . . . mutual?"

Lizzie immediately slipped into over-the-garden-fence gossip mode. She leant closer to Stokes.

"Well, I was watching him. He was very flirty with some of the women in the bar. Muriel had her back to him when she was chatting to me but I could see what was going on over her shoulder. I wouldn't trust him. The women were lapping it up, mind." She frowned.

Stokes was not sure how to respond but in the event he did not need to. Lizzie had not finished with her character demolition of the Czech.

"And some of the stories he's told her. I think he's stretching the truth. Laying it on a bit thick, like."

"In what way?"

"Just about what he's done in the war. You know, fought in the Battle of Britain, shot down God knows how many German bombers. Mind you, *she* told me this, not Gus. I hardly spoke to him at all, as it happens."

"Well, it's possible, I suppose?"

She looked doubtful. "So, what's he doing in a tuppence ha'penny training squadron up here, then? If he's that good, why isn't he still with a fighting squadron down south some-where? The war's still on, isn't it? According to the papers it is anyway. And . . . and, they bombed the bloody factory, didn't they?" Lizzie's sadness had turned to anger. "I'm really sorry."

He gave her a few moments. He was beginning to feel intrusive. She blew her nose again. And she still had not finished with the Czech. "And he told Mu some weird story about him being captured by the *Gestapo* in Prague."

Stokes was now seeing the story of this Czech as particularly significant. A man who had started out as some kind of Ronald Colman was now slowly turning into a deluded fantasist. If only half of what he was claiming were true, then it was certainly worthy of further investigation. He made notes for further reference.

"Really?"

"Aye. He told Mu that they wanted him to nick a plane for them. I'm not even sure *she* believed that bit." She laughed. "All the same she's devastated, as you can imagine. What with her loss . . . and me missing Ernest and the factory being bombed and all those people dying, there's not much to feel happy about is there?"

"You've got Alice."

She smiled and seemed instantly brighter. "You're right. Yes."

Stokes got himself back on track. "Did Ernest ever talk to you again about the abuse he suffered on that first morning?"

"No, not directly. But I blame his uncle."

"His uncle?"

"His uncle Freddie. Ernest told me a couple of times, on his first day, about his uncle. He moved in with him, you see, in the flat above the shop."

"And what did he say about him?"

"Oh, just that he couldn't wait until Hitler invaded. Stupid stuff. He called it the ramblings of a bitter old man.

And then Ernest stopped talking about it. Never mentioned him again."

"Yes, Frank told me a little of his brother's background. I gather there is good reason for his bitterness."

Lizzie nodded. She obviously knew the dead fiancée story too. Stokes decided to call it a day. He needed to talk to Frank again at some point, unless Ernest and Freddie turned up in the meantime.

"War is just so bloody sad, Mr Stokes." The handkerchief was raised in readiness. "Mu and I met up in South Shields a few days ago. Alice loved the trip on the ferry, bless her. But even in the Market Place there, there's now a bloody big underground shelter. You just can't get away from the bloody war, can you? It's everywhere."

She paused for a while. The tears had abated. "Pardon my French, Mr Stokes."

He smiled. "Mrs Fenwick, you have been extremely helpful. I have taken too much of your time."

They both stood. She showed him to the door. He wrote the police station telephone number on the card he had given her. After asking her to let him know if she heard from Ernest, he wished her a good evening and walked away.

STOKES FELT he had learned a lot from Lizzie. Not only the background on Ernest and Freddie but also the strange tale of the Czech pilot. The conversation also confirmed to him that the Metcalf pair needed to be brought in. He had to find them. If they were part of a Fifth Columnist cell, then he might have his work cut out, especially as he was now well known in North Shields as a member of the British security services. His other incarnation as Geoffrey Salter, Hitler's man in London, would simply not pass muster.

He looked at his watch. It was too late to ring Knight but he needed to tell him about this Czech pilot as soon as possible. There may be absolutely nothing in it but the man's reported contact with the *Gestapo* was impossible to dismiss.

CHAPTER 47

Before Wesley was evicted from his obligatory short residence at Latchmere House, Stephens had constantly battered him with threat after verbal threat. He warned him in headmasterly fashion as to his future conduct, even after formally enrolling him as a 'double agent' in the name of METHODIST.

The spectre of the hangman was put firmly back into its box, and he was moved – lock, stock and wireless - to more salubrious accommodation. A safe house, he was informed. Safe for whom, and from what, Wesley wondered.

Stephens' final remarks as Wesley left Latchmere were not along the lines of thanking him for his company and saying how much he would be missed. Far from it.

"I am still not convinced that you have been completely open with us."

Wesley turned and smiled. "Really. Why do you say that?"

"If I knew, then you wouldn't be leaving us now. You would be back in your exclusive bijou accommodation and contemplating your navel."

Wesley was becoming more adept at acting the innocent martyr, the aggrieved victim - but it was best not to overplay his part.

"You have nothing to worry about, old boy. I won't let you down. I will be one of your most successful graduates."

Stephens grunted. "Now . . . be off with you. Don't forget - you're being monitored." With that, he turned tail and walked back into the building.

Wesley was bundled into the back of a scruffy police van and driven away from the prison of Twenty to what he hoped would be a horn of plenty. Not that the small semi-detached house on Woodside Road, just a hop and skip away in the neighbouring borough of Kingston upon Thames, was exactly utopian, but a bathroom, hopefully better meals, and a window looking out onto a garden, were certainly steps in the right direction.

It FELT good to be living in a real house once again, rather than the crumbling stately pile at Latchmere House with its suite of prisoner accommodation in the basement. Woodside Road was the polar opposite. A perfectly nondescript, tree-lined suburban street within spitting distance of the Thames. And not a barred window in sight. Better even than his cramped digs in Gillett Street in Hull.

What he felt extremely pleasing was the fact that they had given him his own clothing back. Gone were the grey shirt and trousers. He had grown mightily fed up with wearing what he regarded as prison garb, and the Latch-mere House laundry arrangements were distinctly below-par. Most of his personal belongings were there too, along with his wallet, albeit somewhat slimmer. A solitary ten bob note remained. Still, at least he was saving on rent and he was being fed and watered.

This was to be his home, he assumed, for the length of time he was a double agent and, by definition, under two masters. From now on, all of his outgoing transmissions would be monitored. The British would require him to transmit information that would appear valuable to the *Abwehr* but would, in fact, be what they described as 'chicken feed' - material that was either of little value, intentionally misleading or downright lies.

MI5's purpose was to elicit information from *Abwehr* as to what *they* were interested in, what tasks they wanted WIESELIG to perform, where they wanted him to stick his nose . . . in order to provide an insight into Nazi plans.

Wesley was sure that they would give him snippets from the subject area where he told Stephens that he was particularly active - decoy sites and infiltration of Fifth Columnist groups. They would try to mimic his movements and activity in that respect. That would make sense but, in fact, he had exaggerated his involvement in both.

An inordinate percentage of his time had actually been spent delivering and collecting the Metcalfs' wireless, thus ensuring the eradication of a secret anti-submarine weapon. And, latterly, to coerce the Czech and Pole into fulfilling their respective missions to deliver a brace of fighter planes. He had been successful in both of these ventures and was rather pleased with himself.

The only missions he had actually carried out that fell into the categories mentioned to Stephens, were the meeting with Hull decoy site twitcher, Armitage, and the visits to the BUF clique in Leeds. The latter had proved dangerous and the former was responsible for his current quasi-incarceration. On reflection, the delivery boy duties that he had complained about so much to Hamburg, had proved to be far safer and much more productive.

His opposite number in Hamburg, Otto Ziegler, would already be on his guard. It was almost a week since Wesley had sent his last message. He could not recall missing more than a day before. *Abwehr* would figure that he had either been 'burned' ie taken out of play in one way or another, or 'turned' into service for the enemy. They knew that the latter was more of a possibility and would therefore scrutinise his next message, when it came, very closely. They would want to know his exact status.

Wesley could put their minds at rest by letting them know in no uncertain terms, and in just a word or two, that the content of any message from him now on, was absolute bollocks and not to be heeded. This is where their unique mode of communication would come into its own.

He had come to consider Otto a personal friend. They had their own lexicon of 'in' jokes and witticisms, with reference to shared experiences on their many outings around Hamburg. Despite what he was sure would be strict surveillance by his wireless minder at this safe house, he had no reason to suppose that this honed and multi-level means of conveying information could not be continued. He had no doubt that Otto would be instantly aware of the true weight and import of every message and be able to separate fact from fiction.

The Englishman was not, by nature, an evil genius. He was, though, a game player with a sharp intellect. He loved the thrust and parry of words, the musicality, the pleasing lilt of a certain phrasing or coupling. Within this seemingly child-like medium, he could wrap whatever information he needed to impart. He was confident that he could still communicate with *Abwehr Luft* in Hamburg, albeit at a more basic level.

From Wesley's last message before he was apprehended, Otto would already know of the likelihood that both a Hurricane and a Spitfire would soon be landing somewhere within the *Reich*, thanks to his own sterling efforts of detection and persuasion. At least one of them - the Czech's Hurricane - could be there already, following the tongue-lashing and overt threats that he had given MOTORRAD at the *Three Horseshoes*. As for the Pole, his departure would depend on rosters, he had said. Wesley was nevertheless more than hopeful that the deed would be done within a few days.

The *Luftwaffe* would likely be more pleased with the Spitfire V that the Pole, STANGE, would deliver. It was a front-line working fighter. It was a far superior craft in many respects to its older sisters and it had just come into service. Not like the comparatively antiquated Hurricane I training craft that the Czech will have presented to them. But even German beggars could not be choosers.

His main worry now was that he would have to continue with the nonsense verse stuff when, at times, he had nothing to disguise, no covert material. The need for constant subterfuge was gone. But Stephens had told him in no uncertain terms not to change his behaviour on the keys 'by one iota', so Otto would have to make his own judgement. But at least Hamburg would immediately know that its agent was 'under surveillance' and being monitored.

DESPITE BEING one who lived in the moment, Wesley had been giving some thought to the future - beyond his current occupation and, should he live long enough, beyond the war when life resumed some vestige of normality.

His fate would ultimately depend on the outcome of the conflict. If Hitler ruled supreme and the invasion of Britain was successful, what would the British do with him? Would he be summarily 'taken care of' before he could be found? There may be no time for Mr Pierrepoint - it could be a simple two shots to the back of his head and the unceremonious consignment of his corpse to the Thames. He would be of no further use to the British security services.

And if the Allies should win? What then? They might want to 'retrain' him and resume his British citizenship. If it did not get that far, but nevertheless got to the stage where an Allied success was more likely, they may even wish to put him in the field if they felt he could be trusted. France or Holland, maybe?

It was all up in the air. He just prayed that Grosskopf and Ziegler would remember the details of *Unternehmen Blauer Tiger* (Operation Blue Tiger), the escape plan that had been devised. The *Major* thought it amusing to name it after the Berlin nightclub where he had first discovered Wesley. It had been a rather jocular session. There had been talk of concealing a pair of water wings and a compass about his person. He laughed along with them but he was starting to lose the humorous memories that the meeting once held. There *was* a plan though and it was considered achievable. If, and only if, *Abwehr* maintained their faith and did not just cast him adrift.

Wesley was an optimist. He always anticipated a positive outcome to everything. He was not a betting man - never had been - but if he were, then he would put his money on finishing the war as a hero of one side or the other. At that point, he would not be bothered which - as long as the medals were not awarded posthumously.

THE BACK BEDROOM of the house in Woodside Road faced south. On a warm day, it was a small, stuffy space that was made no more comfortable when occupied by two sweaty men. Dudley Richardson, Wesley's appointed wireless monitor, placed a file of papers on the bed.

"This is not on. They give us the tiniest, hottest room in the bloody house. I'll bet the *Abwehr's* wireless room is better than this."

"It is."

Richardson chuckled. "Oh, yes. You would know, I suppose."

"It's no palace but at least it's fit for purpose. Unlike this oven. Have a word, why don't you?"

"I shall. Have no fear."

Richardson continued to grumble as he stomped downstairs to get himself a chair. While he was gone, Wesley flicked the file open. There was nothing he could understand in the time allotted so he closed it and moved back across to the table when he heard Richardson clattering back upstairs.

Man and chair came crashing back into the room. "Sorry about that but I can't be expected to sit on the bed while you're tapping away."

"Exactly – don't want you nodding off just as we get to the exciting bit!"

Richardson chortled as he put the chair into position at the side of the table. "You mean there's an exciting bit? I can't wait."

"I can't guarantee it, obviously. It largely depends on how well I can deliver what looks quite a lacklustre script."

"Do your best, old chap. And no funny business."

Dudley's faux gravitas was actually quite amusing. He seemed a decent cove, cheerful enough to be sure, but he was still not yet certain whether or not this geniality was a sham. This transmission was a test of that, as well as how bright the man was. From what he had already seen, he was certainly a superb technician, extremely skilled on the set and comfortable with all its whistles and bells. Wesley reminded himself that his new companion was an officer in the Intelligence Corps. He surmised that this probably required more than a morsel of the old grey matter.

Richardson reached across and opened the bottom half of the sash window. A pleasing gust of air entered the room. He took his jacket off and sat back down. "That's better."

Wesley was seated facing the window with Richardson at his left-hand side, from where he had a perfect view of the telegraph key. Wesley had a written digest of the chicken feed that he was to send. He was expected to top, tail and punctuate it with what would be expected by Otto at the other end - and Stephens at this. He knew there would be a debrief following the session, with Wesley being asked to explain any extracts that were not part of the script.

He had been given the opportunity to read the content over a few times so that he was familiar with the text. He was told to take care that the message was no longer than his previous transmissions. Any working spy would, by definition, need to be brief. Wesley had no need of brevity now as he had already been captured but obviously - as Stephens pointed out - the *Abwehr* would be suspicious because of his short absence and consequently watching his output very closely.

They would be well aware of his new situation in the next few minutes, thought Wesley. His mere out of sequence use of English - they would normally toggle between the two languages - would immediately alert Otto. The delay in his transmissions while he was with Twenty, will have confirmed this new phase. The possibility also existed that he could have been 'burned' and was currently residing in some place of incarceration, awaiting trial for his crimes.

Once he resumed and Otto recognised his unique 'fist' they would know he had at least survived. Then the doubts would start as to his true standing and he was anxious to dispel any misgivings the *Abwehr* may have. After his normal salutation, Wesley inserted a reference, a single word signpost to verse seven of Lewis Carroll's *The Walrus and the Carpenter*. It contained the couplet, *'The eldest Oyster winked his eye, And shook his heavy head'* - a clear hint, he knew, to his current status. If Otto looked at the whole verse, he would see that the following line *'Meaning to say he did not choose . . .'* reinforced the point.

This was all achieved in just four characters. He had an alternative, innocent version of its meaning should it be challenged on the debrief to this, his first message in captivity.

He explained to Richardson that the four-character block was simply a reference to Lewis Carroll's poem which was a favourite of Wesley's, and in which he had educated Otto. He had also been at pains to point out that this means of communication was simply a way of conveying information without spelling it out in plain speak. A time-saver. He reminded Stephens that time was at a premium for any agent in the field when he was transmitting by wireless.

Stephens had grudgingly agreed but he was clearly still

not happy. "Are you seriously telling me that you and this Otto are using nonsense rhymes simply to save time?", Stephens had said.

"I am. Check the traffic that you've so obviously dug up."

They had checked the traffic. Bletchley had checked the traffic – what little there was of it. Wesley had been consistent. Stephens had thought it no more than a 'damned stupid affectation'.

Clearly unable to fathom it all, he had simply said, "Simple question, Wesley. Why?"

"Because it's amusing. It relieves the boredom." He paused and feigned surprise. "Oh, I see what you're thinking. That I could be hiding specific messages from detection. The pearl within the silly oyster, as it were."

Wesley felt that confirming what they already suspected was probably a good move. Yes, he could well use this camouflage of childishness to his advantage now that he was in captivity. But why would he want to? He had nothing to impart to Hamburg apart from what was contained in these British scripts. He was turned and happily turned and, guess what, actually getting paid by both sides.

Stephens really had no answer to that. But, Wesley argued, they change it at their peril. Game over. Hamburg would know he was turned if he were to vary from his usual practices. As an afterthought, he mused that, in those circumstances, they would then have no further need of him. They might yet arrange an appointment with Mr P.

WESLEY BUSIED himself tapping in from Richardson's 'chicken feed' sheet. By this time, the man had found and lit a cigarette. He flicked the spent match out of the open window.

He continued with the detail of the British content. It was troop movement details and a couple of decoy site locations. Just dross, he guessed - smoke and mirrors. He couched a lot of it in his accustomed shorthand. Apart from the early - and important - message as to his new status, he had been careful to insert some other small cryptic blocks to disguise it. He did not want it standing alone, as it were, when the inevitable inspection of his transmission took place. He finished with his usual personal sign-off and sat back.

"Done."

Richardson looked across. "Good. Your speed does not seem to have suffered from being out of action. I'll listen to the recording and get it transcribed. Cup of tea?"

A hefty new *Telecord* machine sat next to the table, its bulk rendering the room even smaller. Richardson had cleverly linked it to the wireless set so that transmissions could be recorded.

Wesley mumbled his thanks and hoped his companion had not noticed that he was bathed in sweat. He was suddenly grateful for the warm weather and Richardson's earlier voiced complaints about the temperature.

"Yes, that would be splendid."

"I just hope to Hell the milk hasn't gone off."

Richardson closed the wireless down, picked up his jacket and set off downstairs to the kitchen. Wesley followed, throwing up a silent prayer that Otto had received and understood, and would couch any news about the arrival or otherwise of the two RAF fighters as delicately as possible. He was confident that Otto knew better than that, especially as he was now completely *au fait* with Wesley's new situation.

STEPHENS HAD the transcript of Wesley's first supervised transmission as well as the almost immediate reply. It was in English, thank God, so no need to exercise his knowledge of the German language.

It still stuck in his craw that Wesley insisted on this charade of nonsense that he and his opposite number, Otto Ziegler, indulged in. He had pulled Wesley in as soon as the response came through. The explanations were perfectly satisfactory on the surface but he was still sure the bugger was trying to pull the wool over their eyes.

Wesley had explained the obvious shorthand greetings and sign-off. The rest, Stephens was convinced, was pure fiction. And Wesley was one smug bastard. He knew that they just had to accept all this 'nonsense' drivel for what he said it was. In fact, he remembered telling Wesley not to vary his approach 'by one iota' so he was on a pretty sticky wicket. There was still a rabbit off somewhere.

He picked up the phone and asked for a call to Oliver Strachey at Station X, Bletchley Park. It was answered almost immediately.

"Oliver. Stephens here. At Twenty. I need you to do a bit of digging for me, if you would be so kind. You've got the latest METHODIST traffic, I hope? Or, I should say, WIESELIG."

"Of course. Yes, we have. It's . . . interesting."

"Well, that's one word for it. There are others. My immediate reaction is that he's taking the piss."

Strachey laughed. "It's neither a code nor a cypher so almost beyond even our remit. As I said before, these are rather like private messages between two individuals. Almost incomprehensible to bystanders. Imagine eye contact at a dinner party between husband and wife. Just a glance and a facial clue can literally speak volumes."

Stephens sighed. "Hmm, I suspected as much."

"And, of course, Wesley can have a perfectly innocent explanation for each one of them. Humorous . . . a joke. So, he won't be worried."

"That explains why he's so bloody cocky."

"I imagine so, yes."

Stephens thought for a moment. "You found no transmissions emanating from North Shields yet?"

"Not so far. It's like looking for a needle in a haystack, though."

"Well, keep looking if you would but can we try another tack."

"Of course. What other tack?"

"How convinced are you that your Y-stations have picked up all of WIESELIG's previous traffic?"

Strachey paused. "I'll be honest, old man. We're not. We never know if we ever have the full story. What are you after?"

"Well, according to him, he landed here in August last year. Somewhere in Suffolk. I wonder if you could look at the timings of his contacts, the locations, the peaks and troughs."

"Only with what we've got. No guarantee that some haven't slipped between the floorboards. Trouble is, we also never know how many pieces are missing from the jigsaw. It's not a just a case of looking at the picture on the lid of the box."

Stephens laughed. "Of course, I understand that."

"It's far from an exact science. Are you looking for something in particular?"

"I'm not sure. Clutching at straws, probably."

"That's not to be dismissed. Straws can often yield quite surprising results."

"Well, let's start with 'surprising' and work from there."

"We'll do what we can, old chap."

The call was ended. Stephens picked up Wesley's transcripts once again, sighed and threw them back on his desk.

CHAPTER 48

When Stokes next appeared in the North Shields police station, the morning after his fascinating meeting with Lizzie, he was immediately accosted by PC Billy Atkinson.

"Oh, Mr Stokes. There was a call for you from your Mr Knight. If you want to go through to the interview room, I'll get him on the line."

"My office, you mean?"

"Aye, if you're here much longer, we'll put your name on the door!"

Stokes laughed. "That would be extremely kind, thank you."

What on earth did Knight want? Was he that anxious to know about his meeting with Lizzie Fenwick the previous evening? The phone was ringing as he entered the room. He picked up the receiver.

"Ah, there you are, Albert. Any news on this factory business? I'm getting pressure from above, exerted, I suspect, by the Royal Navy."

Stokes sighed. "Well, no sign of the Metcalfs yet but I

have both Frank Metcalf and Lizzie Fenwick primed to let me know if they hear from them. And, of course, the police are keeping a watching brief on the shop and flat."

"Hmm." Knight was sounding impatient with the lack of progress. "Well, do your best, old man."

"I do have some interesting information from Lizzie Fenwick though. She turns out to be Ernest's girlfriend as well as a work colleague."

"Whatever. The reason I rang you is that I have just received some very interesting news, Albert."

"Which is?"

"I've had sight of a signal just sent to the War Office. Here's the gist. RAF Hurricane lands in Belgium. Not forced down - seems to come down voluntarily. Pilot taken in by local farmers. Hands himself - and the plane - over to the Germans the next morning. Shops the family who took him in and is seen being very chummy with Jerry in the local greasy spoon. Cool as you like."

Stokes was stunned. He was already joining the dots.

"Report came from the Belgian *Clarence* resistance group. And guess what, Albert, old son. They got the squadron code and the aircraft number."

There was silence. Knight broke it.

"You still there?"

"Yes. Don't tell me any more. Was the squadron based at RAF Usworth by any chance?"

It was Knight's turn to be silent for a few seconds. "How the Hell did you know that?"

"I was just about to tell you about what else this Lizzie character told me but you cut me short. Frank - that's Ernest Metcalf's father - lent his car to his son so that he and Lizzie could go out for romantic trips into the countryside. They also had a trip out one evening - to RAF Usworth."

"You're pulling my leg!"

"Well, it wasn't the base. The pub next door. Can't remember the name offhand but I'd guess there's only one."

Stokes paused for dramatic effect. Knight spoke. "Come on, I'm hanging on your every word."

"Oh, it gets better, believe me."

He related the reason for the visit of Ernest and Lizzie to Usworth. A double date, effectively. He told of the friendship between Lizzie and Muriel and of her friend's dashing Czech RAF airman. And then - the *coup de grâce* - his recent disappearance. Reported as a training accident. Over the North Sea. An experienced pilot.

"Good God! The airman's name is Flight Sergeant Augustin Preucil. That was in the signal too, along with details of the Hurricane."

"This all fits, sir. Muriel told Lizzie that this Gus had boasted of the fact that he was captured by the *Gestapo* and ordered to steal a fighter. He told them to bugger off, according to him. Her Gus equals the RAF's Flight Sergeant Augustin Preucil, presumably."

"What about dates?"

"Not entirely sure but can you get me clearance to visit the CO at Usworth? I need chapter and verse on when he disappeared over the North Sea and never came back. Everything."

"Absolutely. I'll get clearance for you as soon as I ring off, old chap. I'll telephone it straight through to Usworth. I'll just make another quick call first so that you know what and who you're facing when you get there. I'll ring you back."

The call back from Knight arrived after a few minutes.

"Albert. As you probably already know, Usworth is not a front-line station. It's an OTU - Operational Training Unit - where newly qualified pilots are trained in the finer points of flying fighters. In their case it's Hurricanes. Then they're drafted to front-line squadrons. It's part of 81 (Training) Group within Fighter Command. Station Commander is one Air Commodore Marcus Barnes DFC. A career officer who served in the first lot over France. So, mind your p's and q's, my boy. Oh . . . and I got your security clearance from the chap I spoke to. He's phoning it through to the base now."

"Thank you. One more thing before you ring off though. I've been thinking."

"Always dangerous, old boy. What is it?"

"If, as the Belgian *Clarence* people seem to suggest, this Czech was in league with the Germans, then was this a voluntary act? Did he jump, or was he pushed? Was somebody pulling his strings? This man was engaged to be married, by the way. Not the sort of thing you'd do if you're about to bugger off with an RAF fighter."

"I suppose not. A handler, you think? And somebody known to have been operating in the north of England, perhaps?"

"That would certainly fit the bill."

"I'll have a word with Twenty. I haven't heard how they're getting on with this Mr Smith of yours yet, anyway. They're due a call."

"In that case, speak soon."

Stokes quickly put the receiver down and smiled. He got directions to RAF Usworth from the desk sergeant and walked out towards his car. This would be interesting.

CHAPTER 49

The base at RAF Usworth was just as he imagined it. On his walk to the gate, he saw Hurricanes dotted around on the hard standing. He had seen the sense of urgency that pervaded the few RAF bases that he had visited in counties to the south – Lincoln, Kent, Sussex – and this felt like a backwater by comparison.

He showed his pass at the gatehouse and was escorted to the CO's office. The airman knocked, saluted and announced him. The CO greeted him warmly and offered him a seat. Stokes did not intend to reveal what they had just heard about Flight Sergeant Preucil from the Belgians. He simply wanted to know more about this man.

"You've got me mystified, Stokes. Not least because of the speed you got this arranged, so I'm surmising this is important?"

"Well, we think it is. Sorry to be vague but I really can't tell you much, to be honest."

The officer smiled and tapped his nose. "Top secret, eh? I understand. How can I help you?"

Stokes took out the notebook in which he had scribbled

the gist of Lizzie Fenwick's conversation with her friend, Muriel. He had also jotted down the information from Belgium about Preucil's landing. That, though, was not for the CO's ears. He wanted to hear what this man knew of the 'training accident'.

"I am interested in a Czech airman. A Flight Sergeant with the Christian name of Gus. I believe he was one of your instructors here."

"Only chap who matches that description would be Flight Sergeant Augustin Preucil. If you're wanting to see him though, I'm afraid you're out of luck."

"Oh?"

"Yes. Missing presumed dead. Just a few days ago, as a matter of fact."

"Can you elaborate, Air Commodore?"

"Marcus, please. Yes. He went out with one of our Polish pilots on a training exercise over the North Sea." He paused to think. "Kadziolka, yes. That was him. Came back in a bit of a tizz. Very excitable lot, these Poles. Reported that Preucil just disappeared. Assumed he'd gone down in the drink."

The officer stood and walked to a filing cabinet in the corner. He opened the middle drawer, extracted a file and sat back down.

"Got the report here. Here, I know you've got top clearance. Read it for yourself."

He took out the incident report and slipped it across the desk to Stokes. He did not understand some of the numbers and acronyms but the text itself was easy to understand. It showed Preucil's full name, rank, service number and nationality. Stokes made notes of anything he did not already know. He also wrote down the date written at the foot of the page.

Duty: Dog fighting with a Polish Sgt
Place: At sea between Sunderland and W Hartlepool
Aircraft: Hurricane I W9147
Engine: Merlin III

In a comments box at the bottom of the form, headed with a single word *WIRELESS* in block capitals and doubly underlined, was the following report.

EF presumably. Lost sight of by other pilot after flames seen coming from radiator. Have written to Fighter Command HQ proposing that all Poles are sent to 58 OTU & other bases elsewhere – diff. to get Poles to use R/T correctly, especially when excited.

"EF?"

"Engine failure. Covers a multitude of sins."

"How is this being viewed? As an accident?" Stokes read aloud from the incident report, "*Flames seen coming from radiator?*"

"That's the bit I don't understand. It was my kite that Preucil took. Best on the station. CO's privilege and all that." He laughed. "And because of that, I know that she was in tip-top nick. The groundcrew are mystified."

"What are you saying?"

"I think the Pole is covering his backside, to be honest. One of the other instructors has said that this one, Kadziolka, is particularly slow on the uptake and will never make a fighter pilot in a million bloody years. He lost Preucil. Simple as that. And he's making a get-out for himself."

Stokes was keen to challenge what seemed to be a cosy acceptance of the official report. At the moment, the CO seemed to be ascribing more blame to the hapless Pole. He was sensing a smokescreen.

"So, if there weren't any . . . *flames coming from radiator -*

as the Pole reported - but the Czech nevertheless did not return, what do you think we can infer from that?"

The CO looked at him blankly. "I'm not sure what you mean."

Stokes got the distinct impression the man was over-looking the only other option – that Preucil had done a runner with his own Hurricane.

"Well . . . could he have stolen it, possibly?"

The officer stared. Stokes could almost hear the cogs turning. Or was he ignoring the possibility because of how it might reflect on the base and his command?

Barnes laughed. "I doubt that very much. Be difficult to get it very far anywhere. He'd be shot down in an instant as soon as he crossed the enemy coast. And the guns on these trainers are empty."

Stokes decided not to pursue it. "Was there a search for any wreckage?"

"Of a kind. The next few training missions that went out over the North Sea were instructed to keep their eyes peeled. Nothing seen."

"Hmmm."

Stokes' apparent scepticism irked the CO. "Look here, Stokes. Do you know how many training accidents we have from this base? Sometimes more losses in a month than some of the front-line stations."

"I'm sorry to hear that."

"We lose planes and men, sometimes by dint of the fact that they forget to drop the bloody cart or . . . or shove the throttle in the wrong direction. It's like Fred Karno's Circus here some days."

It was a short angry outburst. "So, if there's nothing else." The officer stood, presumably to show him the door. Stokes remained in his seat.

"Marcus . . . how well did you know this man?"

A blank look from the CO. Almost as if Stokes had just asked a shepherd how well he knew his sheep. He sat back down.

"Well, erm . . ."

"I mean the students – if I can call them that – are only here for a short spell. They come and go, obviously. But from what I understand, this Preucil was an instructor, so has been here for . . . how long?"

"We opened up here in March and Preucil was one of the first instructors transferred in."

"A few months, then? Do you have his service record?"

"It will be in the file. Just a minute."

This was like pulling teeth. The CO chose the page and started to read it – to himself. With the raising of eyebrows on at least three occasions, it appeared he was reading it for the first time.

"Not good?"

"No. Hardly exemplary."

"Can you be a bit more specific?"

"Discipline not good. Been all over the shop. Most COs seem glad to have got shot of him." He raised his eyebrows. "One apparent affair with a Station Commander's wife."

"Have you ever had to question him yourself about any . . . misdemeanours, shall we say?"

"There have been one or two disputes with fellow airmen. Both instructors and trainees. Gambling, fighting, complaint from the landlord of the local pub – the *Three Horseshoes* – over violent behaviour. Incitement, more or less, against one or two Polish chaps. I had him in here. Read him the riot act. He seemed to have settled down." He paused. "Oh, and there's a recent entry here. He is . . . was, I should say, up for a charge of air indiscipline."

"Which is?"

He looked at the file again. "In this case it was low flying. It goes back to before his arrival here. Buzzing the base probably. Or frightening some old biddy while she was feeding the cat, who knows?"

Stokes laughed but it was really not funny. This man clearly had no finger anywhere near a pulse. No wonder he was CO of a far-flung training unit and not a front-line base. The nation should be grateful. Stokes considered this. Given Preucil's abysmal record, as just outlined, the prospect of yet another disciplinary hearing would surely not faze him that much? Not enough to judge that his only way out was to steal a fighter and deliver it to the Germans.

"Just one more thing, Marcus. You've been very kind but . . . were you aware that this Czech bod was engaged to be married to a local girl."

Barnes' earlier animosity dissolved as quickly as it had erupted but Stokes had obviously disturbed his equilibrium. Or maybe it was torpor. He flicked through the file.

"Yes. Here we are . . . there's a note here to say that they are engaged to be married. Her father's permission has been granted as she is under-21. For reasons that are beyond me slightly, he has now applied to the Czechoslovakian Air Force for *their* permission."

"May I ask the lady's name?"

"Yes. It's Muriel Kirby. Bainbridge Avenue, Sunderland. Oh . . . and apparently, the base Chaplain has been out to see her. Condolences, all that sort of thing."

"Of course."

Stokes made a note of the exact address, stood and proffered his hand. "Marcus, you have been extremely helpful. My thanks."

They shook hands. The officer smiled and called an

airman through to escort Stokes back to his car and off the base. Stokes was now certain that Preucil was a *Gestapo* agent. A sleeper, whose purpose was to do exactly what he had just done - deliver a fighter to the *Reich*.

Everything matched with what he had gleaned from Lizzie Fenwick and the *Clarence* report. Name, date, aircraft, even the name of his fiancée, Muriel. The only grey area was the possibility - though Stokes would put it as more of a probability - that the Czech had a handler.

CHAPTER 50

Stokes returned from his chat with the Station Commander at RAF Usworth and got straight on the phone to Knight.

"Albert. How was Usworth?"

Stokes referred to his notes and proceeded to give Knight a verbatim account of his conversation with the Usworth CO. He stopped and allowed Knight to sum up.

"So, this ties in pretty well with what this Lizzie whatshername told you. Her friend Muriel, whom she *and* Ernest Metcalf met, tells her that this RAF Czech Lothario of hers has been lost in a training accident over the North Sea. In a Hurricane . . . which we now know that he landed in Belgium."

"Indeed. I didn't tell the Usworth chap any of this, of course."

"Good. Carry on. I have something to tell you that is linked to all of this."

"Ah. I'm nearly done. Muriel tells Lizzie that the Chaplain had been to the house expressing condolences. And that's in the CO's file. As well as the engaged to be married thing. It all fits."

"Word of warning though, old boy."

"Oh?"

"Yes. This is what *I* have to tell *you*. I rang RAF Fighter Command in case they hadn't had the news of this signal from Belgium. They have and they're covering the Hurricane heist up, old bean."

"Seriously?"

"Absolutely. They're killing the story. Bad for morale all round. And especially for the relationship between our boys and the Czechs. I get that."

"Understandable, I suppose, but I don't think the Usworth CO has got the memo yet."

"Could be a question of timing. Maybe they haven't got word to every station yet. Or . . . maybe the CO felt that you were not on the 'need to know' list."

They both laughed. Knight continued. "I think this Czech pilot must have had a handler? I will make sure Twenty are apprised of all this."

There was a pause, with both men mentally assessing the implications. Knight spoke first.

"The RAF are afraid that there could be more. In fact, possibly that this is not the first and, heaven forbid, may not be the last. They are examining their records for all instances of aircraft that have gone missing in similar circumstances. With the benefit of 20:20 hindsight, they feel - and I agree with them - that any pilot who has arrived on these shores from a nation that had already been conquered by the Nazis may well be suspect." He paused. "Sadly."

Stokes considered this. "Captured, allowed to escape with the aim of getting to the RAF but family under threat if they don't perform as bidden. Under the thumb of the *Gestapo*. It makes grim sense."

"Indeed. And I think the RAF have been pretty sharp. They want to root it out and keep it under wraps in the meantime."

"Every barrel has a rotten apple, I suppose."

"That's very poetic, Albert. Now, off you toddle. I need to ring Tin Eye . . ."

"Tin Eye?"

Knight laughed. "Lieutenant-Colonel Robin Stephens to you. Twenty Committee at Richmond. The 'Tin Eye' moniker comes from the monocle he wears. He's the one sitting in front of your Mr Smith at the moment."

"Ah."

"And I need to pass everything relevant on to him. And *vice versa*, of course. It's two-way traffic."

"And so it should be."

"Toodlepip."

The call ended. Stokes replaced the handset and walked back through to the desk. Sergeant Harris was on the phone. He spotted Stokes, put his hand over the mouthpiece and whispered.

"It's Frank Metcalf. The boys are back in town."

CHAPTER 51

E rnest and Freddie had arrived back at the flat above the shop in Nile Street.

"Good to be back, uncle?"

Freddie walked to the window. He took one look up and down the street and then drew the curtains. "Not really. Amble was safer."

Ernest sniffed the air. "It still stinks of your bloody fags." He looked across at Freddie who had not budged. "Uncle. How many times have we been through this? We couldn't have stayed away for much longer. You've got to think of what it would look like."

Freddie grunted. Ernest felt a resurgence of the anger that had overtaken him on a number of occasions over the last few days.

"Look at you, for pity's sake. You're acting as guilty as sin. I know we've been vandalised again but it's definitely *not* because we had anything to do with the bombing of the factory. How could it be? It's because our family is German. That doesn't make us guilty of any crime, uncle." He paused. "In fact, come to think of it, it actually makes us victims."

He knew that was a bit of a stretch but anything to drag his uncle away from the darkest end of the guilt spectrum. "Now, pull yourself together and sit down. You're even making me nervous now, for goodness' sake. I'll put the kettle on."

Ernest disappeared into the kitchen to make them both a cup of tea. Freddie continued gazing out of the window for a few more minutes before turning and walking into the room. The inactivity outside was far from the baying mob that he was expecting. He started to relax.

His nephew walked out of the kitchen with two cups. "No milk, obviously." He put the teas on the table between the two armchairs. They both sat. Freddie immediately stood up again and looked at his seat.

"What's the matter?"

Freddie lifted the cushion. "They've gone!"

Ernest stood. "What have?"

"Jan's letters, Ernst. And my drawings."

His nephew stared at the empty space under the cushion. "But that means . . . oh, my Lord, uncle! All the effort I made to get rid of the most incriminating piece of evidence - the bloody wireless! - and you've still got your heavy stash of letters . . . with your name, quite literally, written all over them, under your flaming cushion. How could you have been so stupid?"

Freddie was not going to take all of the blame for this. "Me? You knew they were there!"

"Yes, I did, but . . ."

"But who has taken them, Ernst?"

They both trawled through the possibilities in their heads. Ernest spoke. "Well, somebody with a key, obviously, but . . ."

"Frank?"

"That, uncle, would be by far the best result. Believe me."

"So, what do we do now?"

"Nothing. Absolutely nothing. What do *you* think we should do? Walk around asking all and sundry if they happen to have seen your . . . secret papers?"

Ernest was still waiting for the answer to that question when there was a loud knock on the front door. Freddie jumped. His nephew pushed him back into the armchair.

"Drink your tea. And, remember, we know nothing. Deny everything. It's probably just your brother."

ERNEST OPENED THE FRONT DOOR. It was not Frank Metcalf standing there. It was a police sergeant with another man he did not recognise. The sergeant spoke. "Ernest Metcalf?"

"Yes."

"Can we come in?"

"Of course."

Ernest opened the door wider. The two men entered and he led them upstairs to the flat. Freddie was still in the armchair in a catatonic state. The sergeant spoke to him.

"Are you Frederick Metcalf?"

"Yes."

"In that case, we have you both together. This is . . ." He gestured to Stokes who introduced himself and showed both of them his MoD pass. Freddie looked as if he were about to vomit. Harris spoke again.

"I'm sorry to tell you that you are both under arrest. I'll read the charges when we get to the station. I'd like you to accompany us. Mr Stokes has some questions for you."

Ernest had not made any reply. He got his now shaking uncle out of the chair. They went downstairs behind Harris and Stokes and locked the street door behind them. Less than ten minutes later they had been formally arrested and were in separate cells.

Stokes decided to interview Ernest first. Having just met them both for the first time and noting Freddie's reaction to their presence, he felt that the younger man would be more *compos mentis.* His uncle could be left to stew.

Ernest was sitting with his arms folded. It was a gesture of defence, verging on defiance. Stokes smiled. He spoke quietly.

"Ernest Metcalf. I have been looking for you since the day after Wilkinson's factory was bombed. You have been very elusive."

"I did not know that. I'm sorry."

"Initially, of course, I was just looking for anyone who was an employee of Wilkinson's. Mr Wilkinson wrote your name on a piece of paper."

Metcalf looked confused. Stokes explained the old man's state of health.

"I'm sorry to hear that."

"Yes. I think we can write him in as another casualty of the bombing, to be honest with you. There seems no doubt that the shock brought on his stroke."

Ernest was visibly shaken. He had a soft spot for the old man, who had taken him on with the minimum of formality and a great deal of trust. It was a few seconds before he spoke again.

"Oh, dear."

"Indeed. That's on top of the one hundred or so who have so far died, of course. And the dozens of others who are so badly injured that their lives have been irrevocably changed." He stared at Ernest.

"At first, I was of the opinion that the raid on the factory was quite random."

Stokes was trying to provoke a reaction. Eventually, the man rose to the bait.

"We've had quite a few of those, Mr Stokes."

"So I understand. However, my mind was changed."

"Oh?"

"Yes. I was told that there was top secret work being carried out on the top floor of the factory by the Royal Navy. Work that was extremely important to the war effort, I understand." He paused. "Where was your office, incidentally?"

Metcalf smiled. Stokes took umbrage at the smile. It was as if they were playing a game of chess. Stokes had just moved him into check but his opponent thought he had a move out. This man thought he was being clever.

"On the top floor."

"Ah! Then you will have seen the team, then?" Ernest smiled again. "At least, that's what Mrs Fenwick told me."

The confidence was starting to drain from the man's face. "Oh, you've spoken to her?"

"Yes, she was the only other name I had of somebody who worked at the factory." He paused. "It seems you worked quite closely together."

Stokes knew what Metcalf was thinking and, all of a sudden, he became less tight-lipped.

"Yes. In the same office on the same floor, as it happens. When the Royal Navy men moved in, Mr Wilkinson told us they were auditors."

"And what made you think they weren't?"

Metcalf told him of the noises - the bangs, the whirrs and the like. He was suddenly much more voluble.

"They just weren't the sounds that you expect to come from auditors. Oh, and another big clue was the Royal Navy staff car parked almost permanently outside."

Stokes gave a small laugh. "Yes, that was a bit of a give-away, wasn't it? But weren't you curious as to what they were doing there?"

Metcalf shrugged. "Not especially. I assumed it couldn't have been that important if they were doing whatever they were doing in full view of anyone who cared to look."

Sadly, Stokes thought, the man was right. He pushed on.

"And did you?"

"Did I what?"

"Care to look?"

"What do you mean?"

"Well. You weren't tempted to have a sneaky peek when they clocked off?"

Ernest feigned indignance. Maybe a bit too much.

"Of course not."

"Mrs Fenwick was honest enough to admit that she had a quick glance into the room on her way to the lavatory."

"I believe she did, yes. But she was just being nosey. There was no evil intent."

"Evil intent?"

"Well . . . yes, I mean she wasn't spying, obviously."

"Let me ask you this. If she *had* been a spy like Mata Hari, say, do you think from what she told you she saw, that there was anything worthy of telling an enemy power about?"

He paused. "I really don't know."

Stokes let a long pause form and hang in the air above them. He slowly and deliberately took the Swedish letter from his inside pocket. It was the one from Jan, advising Freddie that they were being sent a wireless set and that 'the gentleman delivering it' would instruct him in its use and 'give any further assistance'. He watched Ernest's face while he did it. Recognition flickered in his eyes. He clearly knew what it was and what it said. His shoulders slumped.

He did not extract the letter from the envelope. It looked as if he had no need to do that. Ernest had resigned - check and mate.

"So, Ernest. Describe the man to me. The one who delivered it. Did you get a name? What did he look like?"

Ernest was staring at the table top. His mind was racing but he was very quickly discovering that there was now no way out other than a full confession. Stokes could read his thoughts. He had trodden this path before.

"The next few minutes could be the most important of your life. I would advise a full and frank confession."

He held up the letter.

"Anyone who reads this will be in no doubt as to the guilt of yourself and your uncle. You may wish to search your mind for any possible mitigating circumstances. Giving me as much information as you can now, can only help your case."

He placed the letter on the table between them.

"I must stress that we obtained this and other documents, in an authorised search of your uncle's flat. The warrant was shown to your father, Mr Frank Metcalf. He let us in."

Ernest nodded. He was in no position to argue the legalities of the situation.

"Now. Come along. Tell me about the gentleman who delivered the wireless. I want everything. Spill every bean, old chap."

Metcalf did not hold back. He could not see the point. This man, Stokes, held all the cards. Over the next ten minutes he told the MI5 man all that he knew about Mr Smith - what he looked like, how the set was delivered, what information was transmitted.

Stokes made notes. There were only one or two occasions where he needed to stem the torrent of words.

"How did you discover the information that comprised the message?"

Ernest was taken aback. "What?"

"Well, from what you and Lizzie told me, she got a quick peep through the door on her way back from the toilet. That can hardly have been of any quality . . . or quantity."

It took Metcalf a few seconds to answer. "Erm . . . I stayed overnight one night, waited till the men had gone. I had keys to their rooms, you see. It wasn't difficult."

"How long were you in there?"

"Best part of an hour, I would think. Probably."

Stokes was shocked. He made more notes.

"An hour? You had a bit more than a peek then, didn't you?"

He asked Metcalf what he had seen. The reply itself took over ten minutes. The thought struck Stokes that it was no wonder the Germans wanted to wipe the factory off the face of the earth. What Ernest had described sounded exactly like what it was - work on a secret anti-submarine weapon that had the potential to change the course of the war. To tilt the balance in the Battle of the Atlantic, at least.

He had to curb his increasing anger as he listened to the man gradually ramping up the scale of the treachery that he and his uncle had perpetrated. It was a deed of such magnitude that the MI5 man could hardly believe it had been carried out by a pair of amateurs.

Ernest went on to tell him how this Mr Smith had met him at Newcastle Central station. They had broken the journey at a pit village on the way to the flat in North Shields and Smith had then transmitted the message himself.

"And that set was then reclaimed, I believe."

The statement was a way of telling Metcalf that MI5 had apprehended Smith. It also served to inform him that they knew more about what had gone on than he might imagine.

"Yes."

"And how was that arranged, may I ask?"

Stokes was being ultra-polite. He wanted it to appear to Metcalf as if the investigation was now a *fait accompli* and that he was merely collecting final details. Stokes knew it was a bit more than that. It was more akin to the icing on the cake. Ernest slumped by another few degrees.

"We transmitted only one message, asking them to arrange for the set to be collected."

"Had you remembered Smith's call sign? His code name?"

"Erm . . . no. He gave us one of our own. I think he imagined that we might find more information to . . . pass on, as it were."

Stokes felt his subdued anger trying to erupt. He laughed. "As if what you had already done was not enough? You couldn't possibly top that!"

He let that lie between them. Metcalf had no response.

"And what was the code name he gave you to use?"

"BLEISTIFT."

Stokes was puzzled for a second or two. "Ahh . . . pencil, is that? A nod, perhaps, to your uncle's artistic talents? I have seen his drawings."

Metcalf's confidence imploded even further. Gone was the self-assured, cocky individual of a few minutes earlier.

"So, Smith came back to the flat?"

"No. I asked him to meet up at the pit village, the colliery where we had stopped when he delivered the thing. West Allotment."

This was more new information for Stokes. He wrote it down. "And how did that go? Was he annoyed at having to come back to collect it? Any sense that he was peeved at your desire to desert the *Reich* in its hour of need?"

Ernest sighed. "No. He seemed quite understanding of the plight we were in."

"Plight?"

"Of course." He sighed again. "We are Germans in the eyes of a lot of people. Easy targets". Metcalf gave a hollow laugh. "In fact, yes, I *was* worried about how he would react."

Stokes could hear the man's brain ticking away. There was more to come.

"But then I gave him some information that I thought would . . . sweeten the pill. I didn't want him suddenly pulling out a gun and putting a bullet through my head."

"And what information was that?"

Ernest related the story that Lizzie had already told Stokes. How they had met with her friend Muriel and her Czech airman boyfriend at the pub next to the RAF Usworth base.

"Yes, Mrs Fenwick mentioned the Czech chap."

"Ah, but he told me a little more on the QT when he was sure the girls weren't listening. He'd had a bit to drink and a lot of his so-called service on the front line was embroidery, I'm sure, but then it took a surprising twist."

"Oh, really?"

"Yes. According to him, he was captured by the *Gestapo* in Prague, allowed to escape to Poland, then France . . . until he arrived in the RAF."

"There are a lot of Czechs and Poles . . . and other nationalities in the RAF these days. And doing a grand job, I understand."

"But this one - Gus they called him - was working for the *Gestapo* in return for his . . . escape. He was told to steal a fighter."

Stokes knew this to be Preucil, whose records he had recently seen at RAF Usworth. So sure were the RAF that he had stolen a Hurricane and delivered it to Belgium, that they had buried all evidence of the incident for the sake of morale. What Metcalf was telling him was just confirmation of all that.

Ernest continued. He seemed keen to mark this man's card.

"He told me that he was sure 'they' had been looking for him but that he had 'moved around a lot'. He seemed to be gloating."

Stokes was putting two and two together. So far, he had got to three and a half.

"And you told all of this to Smith?"

"Yes. Why?"

The MI5 man did not admit to Metcalf that Preucil had actually carried out the task allotted him by the *Gestapo*. He looked at the mental calendar in his head. He would have to check the dates but it seemed that the renegade Czech had flown the coop just days after Ernest had given Smith chapter and verse on his *Gestapo* story - and where the pilot could be found. Smith must have thought all his Christmasses had come at once.

"Interesting."

"Smith seemed to think so."

Stokes sensed that he had got all of the firm facts from the younger Metcalf. He could not resist one further question.

"Why did you do it, Ernest?"

Metcalf wiped his face with his hands. No answer was forthcoming for a while. It was almost as if he was not sure. Stokes helped him out.

"I mean. I can almost understand your uncle hating the British after what happened to his fiancée but *you* . . .?"

Ernest realised that Stokes knew more about the family than he had imagined.

"You don't know how relentless he was. What happened to him ruined his life. And he showed me some press cuttings that made me realise that other Germans in North Shields, other pork butchers, had also been tyrannised."

"Ah, yes. The Grubers."

"You know about that too?"

"Yes, but do carry on."

"He made me realise that we will always be the enemy in this country, Mr Stokes. And that we should not lie down and take it like we did before. Then, after I suffered verbally and physically on my first day at the factory, I started to come round to his point of view." He paused. "But I think what put the tin hat on it was when mother was attacked."

This was news to Stokes. "Really?"

"Yes. Some thug called her a Nazi bitch and whacked her on the head with his bait box. Nasty deep cut on her forehead."

"I didn't know. I'm sorry to hear that."

"Well, you wouldn't have found out through father, that's for sure. He did not report it and told her not to make a fuss."

His face was full of loathing.

"Not all English people are like that, Ernest."

Metcalf laughed. "Most of the ones I have come across in the last few weeks have been. And now the shop has been vandalised again."

Stokes was unsure what to say next. Metcalf continued. "And it did not feel as if what we had done in passing information to the Nazis would have any damaging effect here. If either of us had thought . . ."

"That your actions would kill one hundred people?"

"Yes. Altering the course of the war just one iota would have been enough for us. The war in the Atlantic is so distant."

"As distant as the sinking of the *Lusitania* was, you mean?"

"Yes, exactly like that. And, as my uncle would tell me over and over - *Rache ist süss.*"

"Revenge is sweet?"

"Yes, what we did was intended just to be a bit of revenge for the bad treatment meted out to ourselves and other German families. Despite the fact that we are all British citizens, Mr Stokes. In fact, some of the Grubers served . . . *fought* for Britain in the first war."

Stokes had read the press cuttings in the pile of Freddie's stuff that they had liberated from beneath the cushion in the flat.

Silence reigned for a few seconds. Ernest put his heads in his hands and groaned. "I wish we could turn the clock back."

"Yes, I'll bet you do."

The MI5 man had no further questions. He had finished with the grilling but he now had a deeper understanding of Ernest's motives.

Metcalf spoke up again. "So, what happens to us now?"

Stokes closed his notebook. "It's out of my hands. My opinion, for what it's worth, is that you are both as guilty as hell - of treason alone. And the wilful murder of over one hundred innocent people. Believe me, you do not want to be seen in this town ever again - though I suspect that is not on the cards."

He looked at Ernest. The man's head was still down. He finally looked up and spoke slowly and quietly.

"We honestly had no idea they would bomb the factory."

Stokes laughed. "Come now. You gave them the information. What did you expect them to do with it? Send over a crack squad of commandos to break in and destroy the invention? How far do you think they would have got? Did you know, by the way, that there was an air raid shelter in the factory basement?"

Metcalf nodded. "Does my father know all of this?"

"He will soon." He stood. "Thank you for your co-operation. Now, I must go."

Stokes left the room. Metcalf slumped back into the chair. He wanted more than anything else to talk to Lizzie. He imagined though that she would not want to see him.

It was late. The interview with Ernest Metcalf had taken longer than Stokes thought, and he doubted that he would get any new information from Freddie. He suspected that the nephew knew more than the uncle. He was tired and he was not sure he would be able to contain his anger in front of Freddie - the prime catalyst to this terrible human tragedy at the factory.

He could not help feeling some sympathy for the situation that all three Metcalfs now found themselves in, but it was the bitterness of the old man, Freddie, that had tainted them all. He could not foresee a good outcome for either uncle or nephew. He walked to the desk where Sergeant Harris was still on duty.

"I'm going to call it a night, sergeant. I have interviewed Ernest but have neither the time nor the stomach to face Freddie. Can you arrange to give them both a little something to eat and a cuppa."

"Of course."

"And I think in the morning that they should both be taken to Durham Prison. We need that distance. If it gets out why they have been detained, this place could be under siege. They'd be lynched. We need to keep it quiet to a certain extent - if only for Frank's benefit, don't you agree?"

"I understand. We'll keep it under wraps, Mr Stokes."

Time was getting on but he felt it essential that he passed on this broader, more vivid picture that they now had of Smith, as soon as possible. He fished Knight's home number from his wallet.

"I just need to make another call, I'm afraid. Once Metcalf junior is back in his cell." He passed the number across. "It's Mr Knight again but a different number."

Sergeant Harris walked through to find out if Ernest had been reincarcerated. He was back within a minute. "He's gone. I'll get you Mr Knight now if you want to go through, Mr Stokes."

"Thank you."

DESPITE HIS NEAR sympathy for the Metcalfs, he had no such warm feelings for Smith. Once Stokes passed all of Ernest's information on to Knight and thence to Twenty, the man's goose would be well and truly cooked.

Before Stokes left the police station, he gave Knight the salient points from his interview with Ernest Metcalf, paying special attention to the fact that Smith had been much more than just a delivery boy. He had actually transmitted what must have been a long and involved message about the factory and what was going on inside its walls. The icing on the cake was the fact that Metcalf had also told Smith where he could find the errant Czech airman.

Knight thanked him and said he would pass on all the new information about Smith to Stephens the following day.

CHAPTER 52

Tin Eye Stephens was getting increasingly irritated at his most recently turned agent, Howard Wesley, known now as WIESELIG to the *Abwehr* and METHODIST in his new role within British counter-espionage.

The man had been sending regular monitored transmissions to his opposite number in Hamburg. On the face of it, he had been more than efficient in delivering the material that he had been given. Stephens knew that. He had seen the transcripts. But there was always something between the lines, for which the man always had an innocent explanation. He was quite dismissive about it, with the constant reminder that he had been instructed not to vary 'one iota' from his previous practice and style.

With what Stephens had found out overnight from Knight, a showdown was imminent. He felt there was an underlying risk that Wesley was playing them. He had come over to Woodside Road to confront him, but he needed to run this past Maxwell Knight first. He picked up the phone and called MI5. It was put through to Knight within a minute.

"Robin. How the devil are you?"

"I'm about to burn WIESELIG. He's stringing us along, I'm sure of it."

Knight laughed. "Well, he is a spy, after all. Deception goes with the territory."

"I agree. And compared to some of the dross I've come across, he's good, Maxwell."

"Dross?"

"Yes. The biggest collection of misfits, liars, womanisers, drunkards, gamblers and murderers that it has ever been my misfortune to work with. Some of them would not recognise the truth if it smacked them in the jaw."

"That doesn't give Wesley much competition."

"No, that's true but he's a different breed, almost. He's not an action addict. He's got a brain and he has such a keen rapport with his wireless contact at the other end. So much so, that we really haven't got a clue what he's actually transmitting."

"So, you're taking him off the programme?"

"Yes. If he has somehow managed to communicate to his bosom buddy over the water that he has been turned and, let's face it, given the claptrap he couches these messages in . . . and what almost amounts to telepathy, that could already have been done with the tap of a single key. Then, of course, the whole exercise becomes pointless."

"Are they talking to him?"

Stephens paused. "You mean - are we getting anything in return for the gems we are sending them?" He laughed. "Yes. Or at least he is telling us they have asked for more decoy site information in the Midlands. Nottingham area."

"A ruse?"

"To make us glean from the question that they are planning raids in a certain neck of the woods? Probably."

"So, they are matching chicken feed with chicken feed just to keep METHODIST, or WIESELIG as they know him, in the loop. Why? If they know he is turned, as you suspect, then why don't they just drop him like a hot brick? What's in it for them?" He paused and continued. "Robin, do you think he still has something else in play? Something that has been started but not yet completed? Which is why they want to keep tabs on him."

"Almost certainly. I think this Czech fellow, MOTOR-RAD, was a sleeper. Probably under the thumb of the *Gestapo*. Threatened with the direst of consequences if he didn't get them a Hurricane and promised the earth if he did. He's a chancer."

"So where are you going with this?"

"I think there's another sleeper. Oliver Strachey has been having another look at the wireless traffic that they had already discovered. There is mention of a STANGE which we now believe to be a codename."

It was quiet for a few moments. Stephens continued.

"Working on the evidence that MOTORRAD filched a fighter from under the RAF's noses, I think STANGE could be one of a pair." He paused. "I looked STANGE up in my *Wörterbuch*. It has a number of meanings - stick, rod, staff, perch etc. But it has several other synonyms too - would you like to hear them?"

"I suspect I have no choice."

"Correct. I've written a few down. STANGE can also mean bar, beam and ... pole."

"Good God."

"It's pole with a small 'p' obviously but nevertheless ... and it's not as oblique as WIESELIG, I'll grant you but ..."

"You may well have something there, old chum. I think you should definitely explore the possibility at least."

"Absolutely. I'll dangle it in front of Wesley. And watch his reaction."

Stephens was not finished. "My conclusion is that *Abwehr Luft* know he's been turned but he has somehow convinced them that his other sleeper . . ."

"The Pole."

"Yes. Wesley has convinced them that STANGE is about to come good. And for all we know . . ."

"He may already have done so."

"It's also my firm belief that Wesley wants to keep the *Abwehr* hanging on. If they think STANGE is dead in the water, then . . ."

"They could pull the plug on him. And that would put him in a very vulnerable position. He would go from valuable triple agent to a waste of space overnight. Maybe that's why he has been so busy building up a portfolio of other interests - to diversify, as it were."

"His recruitment activities?"

"Exactly. Well, good luck, old chap. Speak soon."

The call was ended.

WESLEY WAS SITTING at the wireless desk in his room when Stephens entered. He and Richardson had finished their daily transmission to Hamburg and were doing *The Times* crossword. Stephens surveyed the scene for a second before ushering Richardson out of the room. He sat down on the vacated chair and put his folder on the table. He extracted a single sheet.

"Do you remember me telling you that I would be watching you, Howard?"

Wesley smiled but it barely masked his anxiety. What had he done? "Yes. Several times."

"I think you have been rather economical with the truth. To put it bluntly, you have told me lies."

Wesley was spoilt for choice as to what the man might be alluding to. "Oh?"

"Yes. We now know that you did actually deliver the second wireless set to North Shields. Not only that, you instructed the recipients in its use. Furthermore, you transmitted a message from the premises under your own codename of WIESELIG. In addition to that, you gave them their own codename of BLEISTIFT for further use." He paused. "Above and beyond the call of duty, wouldn't you say?"

Wesley's mind was scrabbling around to find some damage limitation but was unable to before Stephens spoke again.

"So, you weren't just a delivery boy for the *Abwehr*, as you claimed. Were you?"

Wesley sighed. "I was supposed to be but I felt sorry for the chap that I met at Newcastle Central and . . ."

"Ernest Metcalf?"

The name told Wesley that Stephens knew the whole picture. He wondered why he had bothered trying to cloud the issue. He had been trying to protect the Metcalfs but it sounded as if they were beyond redemption now. He spent the next ten minutes confessing exactly what he did, right down to sending the message for the Metcalfs.

"And they used the BLEISTIFT codename that I gave them, to request the collection of the wireless a few days later. If I had known that would eventually involve me in another trip north, then I wouldn't have bothered going to the lengths I did. It was a pain in the backside, to be honest. I had no idea they would take fright."

Wesley reflected that it was during the collection of the wireless that he had got to know of MOTORRAD's location, at the quite reasonable cost of one pound sterling stuffed into Metcalf's top pocket.

Stephens listened throughout, his gaze dropping from time to time to the notes that he had made from his conversation with Stokes earlier that morning. The MI5 man had interviewed Ernest Metcalf the previous evening. When he felt that the other man had finished, he smiled and spoke quietly.

"You know what happened in North Shields, then?"

Wesley shook his head slowly. "Yes. Terrible business. That's why they wanted to get rid of the wireless. The Metcalfs are German, you see. Frightened of reprisals." He paused. "Bit off more than they could chew, if you ask me."

Stephens was satisfied. It made sense that he had been covering for the Metcalfs. Although the denizens of North Shields would doubtless feel differently about it, Wesley had merely facilitated what happened. He had not instigated it.

He put the Metcalf interview notes back in his folder and withdrew another sheet. He stared at Wesley.

"Tell me more about MOTORRAD."

Wesley smiled. Oh, shit. This could be nasty.

"Nothing to tell that I haven't already told you. Czech airman. No contact. And, as I said, I'm not even sure if I was told his name. If I was, I can't remember it now."

He thought he should put a bit more colour into the picture.

"I remember, from what *Abwehr* told me, that he had been very communicative on his journey to England. And then, when he arrived here . . . nothing."

Stephens withdrew a copy of the Czech's RAF Usworth accident report.

"I think I can help you with the name. Flight-Sergeant Augustin Preucil, late of RAF Usworth." He paused. "Which is not that far from North Shields, I understand."

Wesley would have to bluff this out. He looked puzzled. He *was* puzzled – where they had got all of this from? Ernest Metcalf? Almost certainly! Had the Czech made it through? It was sounding possible but he was definitely not going to seek any further information. He had had no confirmation from Hamburg.

"I'm mystified."

"Strange though."

"What is?"

"Oh, I know you made some excuse about it when we spoke at Latchmere, but you did mention MOTORRAD quite a lot in your transmissions to Hamburg. Let me see . . ."

Stephens paused to dig further into the folder and pull out what were obviously transcripts of his initial interrogations. He read from a sheet of paper, quoting what Wesley had said about MOTORRAD.

Wesley made the same response that he recalled making before – that Hamburg were constantly on his back to track the Czech down. Nevertheless, he felt that he was on the ropes.

"I speak German, Howard. I know what MOTORRAD means. Motorbike. I'm sure your German is much better than mine so, tell me . . . what does STANGE mean?"

Wesley had to make a superhuman effort to stop his jaw dropping. Stephens was not finished.

"You see, you mention both MOTORRAD *and* STANGE in what we assume, looking at the dates, were

your last few transmissions before we lifted you in Hull."
He smiled. "Almost as if the two were flying side by side, in
fact."

For once, Wesley was speechless. The man for whom
words were his main currency, was lost. Stephens was on a
roll. The officer looked straight at him for a few seconds
before speaking. Wesley could see his own sweating face
reflected in the monocle.

"So . . ." Stephens consulted the file again. "According to
you, MOTORRAD just disappeared off the face of the earth.
He just vanished."

"Yes. As I said, he had been very communicative on his
epic journey from Prague to Britain, especially in France, I
gather, and then . . ." Wesley made a magician's 'thin air'
gesture. ". . . poof! I never met the man. He never mate-
rialised."

Stephens smiled. "Really. For a man who, you claim,
virtually never existed, you seem to have spent an inordinate amount of time talking about him."

Wesley shrugged. "Well, that is because Hamburg kept
asking if I had traced him. I told you."

"Let's move on. Who is STANGE?"

Wesley feigned deep thought. He had got over the initial
shock on hearing the Pole's codename but he was still
shaken. "I believe that was the codename of another pilot,
thought to have made his way to the RAF . . . like MOTOR-
RAD. But I really don't remember."

Stephens laughed. "And I suppose he did not make an
appearance either?"

Wesley felt himself involuntarily squirming. "Funnily
enough, no . . ."

Tin Eye suddenly stood and walked around the small
room – desk to door and back to desk, slowly circumnavi-

gating the space. Wesley was getting a crick in his neck trying to keep his head facing in the right direction.

"We have discovered some further messages that you sent under your German codename of WIESELIG. Very recently in fact. Judging by the date, I would imagine the final one was sent immediately before we lifted you from the Punch Hotel in Hull."

It had taken Stephens almost four circuits of the room to get those three sentences out. Wesley was getting dizzy which did not help him to concentrate on an answer that would satisfy the man who was now standing with his hands on the table and facing him. Stephens spoke again.

"The names of both MOTORRAD and STANGE are both mentioned in that last message. The rest of it is pure indecipherable drivel, of course. As is your wont."

Wesley did not have a suitable response. Stephens gave him a few seconds and then continued walking, this time in the opposite direction.

"You speak German very well, Howard. What does the word STANGE mean? MOTORRAD was an easy one. We had trouble with STANGE, I must confess."

Wesley spoke. "It just means stick, I think. Oh . . . and I believe it's a slang term for erect penis." He laughed. He needed to introduce some levity. "I seem to remember a phrase that was in circulation at the time when I was living in Berlin. *'Nichts ist langer als deine Stange'*

Stephens lifted a querulous eyebrow. "Which means?"

"Roughly – there's nothing longer than your . . . erection." It was a desperate attempt at diversion but Stephens was having none of it. He grunted as he looked back at his notes. He spoke without looking at Wesley.

"Very droll, I'm sure. However, I don't think even the Germans would stoop to such smutty names for their agents. You will be aware that the noun *Stange* can also mean rod, perch . . . and even pole." He paused. "And it's so easy to imagine it as Pole - with a capital P. Wouldn't you say?"

Stephens sat down again, facing Wesley. "I seem to be doing all the work here. Well . . . was it Pole? A Polish airman?"

Wesley looked out of the window as if dredging his memory. "Yes, I believe he might have been."

"Good. Now that your memory seems to be returning. What was his name?"

Wesley laughed. "I only vaguely remembered the Czech's name when you mentioned it. But have you seen Polish names? They're like anagrams – and all consonants, with just the odd vowel tossed in for good luck."

Stephens paused before he spoke again. This time, he leant across the table, his face close to Wesley's. "I am starting to get angry now, Howard. Let me tell you this. It is no exaggeration to say that your life may well depend on this conversation." He sat back in the chair.

"Here's something that may encourage you. You are officially off the key now at any rate so you will not be able to pass on what I am about to tell you."

Stephens leant across, disconnected the Morse key and threw it across the floor. The violence with which it struck the door felt like a threat. Wesley's stomach took another churn. He could feel sweat trickling down the back of his shirt. And the man went back on the attack.

"The Czech airman, Flight Sergeant Augustin Preucil, your MOTORRAD, flew a Hawker Hurricane MkI, from RAF Usworth to the village of Ortho in Belgium. He was then seen surrendering himself *and* the plane, to the Germans. So, I am surmising that your final WIESELIG message was to inform Hamburg that this was due to happen. I think you also know the name of this Polish airman. This . . . STANGE . . ."

Wesley could not stop his jaw dropping this time. He felt it go. The sweat was now flowing in torrents. Stephens noticed and flung himself closer to Wesley. The man rocked back in his seat.

"This Pole is on a similar mission, isn't he?" He was shouting now. "What. Is. His. Name?"

Wesley was done in. One tiny part of him was pleased to hear the Czech had accomplished his mission. He was slightly miffed that he had not found out through Otto. That was odd. The vast remainder of him was terrified. He had to give this man something credible before he exploded. He struggled to maintain anything approaching a sense of composure when he finally spoke.

"I honestly do not remember the chap's surname. It's unpronounceable, for goodness' sake. But I think his Christian name was Tomasz - as in Thomas or Tommy. I remember it because that was what they used to call British soldiers. But I have no idea what he was tasked to do."

He looked down and realised that his hands were clasped as if in supplication. That would smack of desperation. He slowly unfurled them, sat back and tried to regain some equilibrium.

Stephens stared at him. "So . . . Tomasz Unpronounceable"

"Yes, that's the best I can do, I'm afraid."

"And nothing about which squadron he is in?"

Wesley shook his head. This was not the best day he had ever had. He was suddenly unsure about his future. He wondered if the Pole's flight rosters had enabled him to make his flight to the *Reich* yet.

"They were always asking me to track people down. They thought I was some kind of bloodhound. I know nothing about these two chaps and . . ."

He tailed off. He could feel the tone of his voice rising, like some child begging for a sweet, or pleading not to be punished. Stephens had stopped listening, in favour of scribbling furiously in the file. He closed it and stood. He looked at Wesley, who stared up at him.

"So, what happens now?"

Stephens' reply chilled his blood. "You'll find out soon enough. In the meantime, I wouldn't take out any magazine subscriptions if I were you."

Wesley heard the key turning as his interrogator left the room.

STEPHENS WENT DOWNSTAIRS to phone Maxwell Knight. His sense of urgency was immediately apparent to the MI5 man.

"You need to pass this on, Maxwell. Fighter Command have to ground all Polish pilots with the Christian name of Tomasz."

There was a long pause. "Oh. No surname?"

"No. But the first name is a start. Get every Tomasz and you won't need a surname."

"Could be quite a task. If Tomasz is as popular a name as Tommy, then there could be scores of them.'

Stephens sighed. "That's all we have, Maxwell."

"Any idea where they should start?"

"No, and that's all we are going to get, believe me. Our man is burned, Maxwell."

"Oh."

"But . . . if you need some more meat on the bone, it is

my considered opinion that this Pole will be looking at the new Spitfire."

"Which is?"

"For goodness' sake, Maxwell. Finger on the pulse? It's the new Spit V."

"Wesley has been in talkative mood, then?"

"I squeezed it out of him."

"And he's definitely burned?"

"Yes, I'm just figuring out what to do with him. Watch this space but you can definitely take him off your Christmas card list."

Stephens rang off and put in a call to Scotland Yard.

CHAPTER 53

The frenzy of the Battle of Britain in summer and autumn 1940 was a distant memory for the Royal Air Force. They were still very much on a war footing but the previously dire shortages of crew and machines were improving dramatically. Fighter Command HQ at Bentley Priory now had time to be more proactive, to take the war to the Germans rather than always being on the back foot.

So, Air Marshall Sir William Sholto Douglas, Air Officer CIC of Fighter Command, was more than a little put out to be dealing with trouble in his own camp. They had recently been informed that a Czech pilot had done a bunk in a Hurricane from a training squadron, and then delivered it to the Germans.

He had decided to cover the incident up. It was bad form but, as the machine in question was a MkI Hurricane at the end of its useful life, he thought that putting it under wraps was the best way to proceed. The political side of things was also a factor. It could cause friction for the rest of the Czechs who were doing a sterling job.

Sholto Douglas had, however, alerted front-line squadron chiefs to keep a watching brief on all aircrew who had come to the RAF from countries conquered by the Nazis. It was strongly suspected that this renegade Czech was in cahoots with the *Gestapo*. There could well be others.

It now appeared that he was right. They had another situation. A Pole this time. It seemed the Czech incident was not an isolated one. All they had to go on, though, was that this new quarry was called Tomasz. It did not take a genius to guess that it was a pretty common name.

HE WAS SEATED behind a large desk in his first-floor office, its balcony overlooking what had once been a beautifully landscaped vista. Through the open windows, he now looked out at row upon furrowed row of vegetables of all descriptions. Plots and allotments had replaced the immaculate lawns.

A file containing lists of RAF Squadron personnel was open in front of him. A warm breeze fluttered the pages.

Unlike the first incident where the information had come directly from a Belgian resistance group which had virtually witnessed the whole thing, this second one had been uncovered by MI5. Their strong suspicion was that there was a rogue Polish pilot who may be in the process of stealing a Spitfire. Its point of delivery was unknown. With the Nazis having conquered great swathes of the European mainland in the previous twelve months, the pilot would be spoiled for choice of landing place.

Much against his better judgment, he had telephoned this new information through to the War Cabinet in Westminster, for onward transmission to the PM. It was a sensitive situation. Churchill needed to know. Whatever the result, the flak would fly. He told the official all that they knew, what they were planning and the worst possible outcome. He was told that he would be informed of the PM's response.

He walked to the door and flung it open. He bellowed down the staircase for his Adjutant. Group Captain Nigel Heseltine appeared and followed him into his office.

"Sit. Where are we on this Pole?"

"Well . . . erm."

"Come on, man."

"Yes, sorry sir. There are . . . and we haven't actually counted them but literally hundreds of Polish pilots on the books. And all we have is the Christian name of . . ."

"Tomasz. Yes, I know."

"Indeed. We're going through the dedicated Polish squadrons first obviously and I have another team going through the ones that are scattered across dozens of other . . . erm, British squadrons, if I can put it that way."

"Do Uxbridge know about this?"

If it was looking like a Spitfire - and a Mark V, at that - was to be the object of the theft, then RAF 11 Group, which incorporated front-line squadrons in the south east, ought to be kept up to speed.

"They know everything that we do, sir. Clearly though, it's like looking for a needle in a haystack. We can't actually do anything until we know which haystack."

Sholto Douglas grunted. "It may not be 11 Group, of course. Could be 12 at a push. Let's not put the cart before the horse."

"Safer not to, I think, sir."

"What do you suggest. How do we tackle this?"

"We've been discussing this downstairs. I have chaps collating lists of all Polish pilots named Tomasz as soon as they are gleaned from the staffing lists. They're then contacting the Squadron in question and ordering that these chaps are placed under close guard until such time as we authorise their release."

"It's a rum do. What are we giving them as a reason for their incarceration?"

"Nothing, sir."

"Good. Hopefully this will be solved one way or another in a few hours."

"We do have a bit of a situation at Duxford, sir. 302 Squadron are based there. One of the Polish squadrons. They already have three chaps called Tomasz locked up together in the guardroom. They haven't been told anything, as I said, but they will cotton on pretty soon that they all have the same name."

Sholto Douglas laughed. "Well, tell them it's against King's Regs to have more than two with the same name in a Squadron. That'll fox them for a while."

Heseltine laughed too but with less gusto. There was a paper-storm developing downstairs and he needed to manage the situation.

"Sir, do you mind if I . . ."

"Of course, dear boy. You get on. Keep me in touch."

Heseltine stood, saluted and turned to leave.

"Oh . . . and don't rule out the bomber boys. They're not all fighter pilots, these Polaks."

The adjutant stopped and turned. "Very true, sir. But I don't believe any of the bomber squadrons fly Spitfires." He wanted to laugh out loud but knew he would have to settle for spreading it around later. He might tell the bomber boys.

Sholto Douglas never wavered. "Good point. Well, you'd better get on."

"Indeed, sir."

Heseltine repeated the salute and started to walk away again.

"Oh . . . and some of these boys may be in the air. Had you thought of that?"

He had thought of that. This was the old man trying to redeem himself.

"Yes, sir." He turned and left the room.

Sholto Douglas shouted after him. His Adjutant was by then at the foot of the stairs and turning.

"And don't forget the OTUs and OCUs. There are Spits all over the shop on the way through . . . and pilots."

Heseltine shouted back. "Yes, sir. Good idea."

It *was* a good idea and one that he had thought of ten minutes earlier. The training, storage and conversion units had already been checked but front-line squadrons were the priority.

CHAPTER 54

Howard Wesley was on high alert. He had not wasted a second since he heard the key turning in the lock. He was alone in the room. His wireless minder, Dudley Richardson, was not due to return until the following morning. By then, he would be gone.

The portents were not good. Stephens' parting comments left him no hope. Some things were left unsaid but he got the gist. He could not be trusted. He was burned. He was no longer of any use as METHODIST.

The worst scenario was that he would soon be transported to a cell in Pentonville Prison or - should his crimes be felt to warrant it - the Tower of London. A meeting with Pierrepoint would follow. It would be strictly professional - but brief.

As good as his improvisation skills were, he knew they would not get him out of this particular fix. He had to leave it by physical means. His presence needed to be absent - and untraceable.

This safe house was a massive improvement on the imposing prison at Latchmere House and his dank, unsanitary cell - certainly from a comfort point of the view. For one thing, it lacked its barred windows but the whole property fell a long way short of its description as 'safe'. In fact, he felt it 'safe' to assume that he could be out of here in less than two minutes.

The door of his room was locked but that would not be his means of exit. He knew the layout of the property. Immediately below him was a small dining room which he knew was unoccupied.

The windows of both looked out onto the back garden. The rear of the property faced south and, as he knew from his experience when he made his first transmission, it could get very steamy unless the windows were opened. He had noticed that the ground floor dining room curtains were kept closed to keep the temperature down.

On the ground floor and looking out upon the front garden, was the living room. Stephens used it as his office when he visited. He could hear the man's voice now. Nobody else speaking, so he was on the phone. The subject of the conversation was almost certainly Wesley. What to do with him. Where to have him taken.

He had no need to go to the door and earwig. He had been preparing for this scenario, just in case he needed to flee. He took his overcoat and trilby out of the wardrobe. He quickly put the coat on and stuffed the hat into its pocket. That was all he would need.

The next stage was the one he had not been able to practise. He opened the bottom half of the sash window as Dudley had done on that first day, and eased his body onto the table. He lay on his front and extended his legs out of the open space. He slowly squirmed around and let them both dangle outside, lowering his body against the brickwork until he was completely suspended in the open air.

He knew that the closer his feet were to the ground before he let go, the less likely he was to injure himself. His height helped in that respect too. His brief pre-flight training before his parachute jump into that Suffolk field came back to him. He let himself drop and rolled on impact.

It proved much easier than he had imagined. No limbs broken. He looked quickly around him. The dining room curtains were indeed closed. He took the hat out of the pocket and angled it jauntily on his head.

The gate leading to the back lane which ran between Woodside Road and the adjoining street, was unlocked. He stepped quickly through it and walked briskly to the end of the lane. He knew where he was headed. It was good of his hosts to situate him so close to his destination. He could walk to where he was going in two or three hours.

It was a pleasant day. Summer had almost arrived and Wesley was beginning to feel rather overdressed in his overcoat and hat. The last thing he wanted to do, however, was to divest himself of either. He felt that they offered him some vestige of protective anonymity. In any event, he reflected, there were plenty of other people wearing more layers than he was. That was one of the weird things about the British. Always overdressed. They never trusted the weather.

His walk from Woodside Road took him north out of Kingston upon Thames, keeping the river to his left. It was not difficult to find it. At some point, he would need to cross to the north bank, turn right and continue walking until he came to Brentford.

On one of his trips to the Siemens-Schuckert factory, he had reconnoitred the area and he was confident that he could find the Great West Road. From there it would be easy. Even if he was unsure at any point, he looked and sounded British enough not to arouse anyone's suspicions when asking directions.

He remembered the watchers at the gate of the factory, checking ID. He had no such document now. It was probably lying in Stephens' file, stuffed inside his desk drawer. So, approaching on foot was probably a much safer option.

Once he crossed the river and was sure he was heading in the right direction, he sat on a park bench, leant back with his hat over his face and had a snooze. He would wait until late afternoon when he imagined the factory would be closed for normal business - at which point the watcher would also have headed home.

His intention was to get into the factory and introduce himself as WIESELIG. He was thankful that he had already been there twice. He was sure that he would be remembered. Then he would send an immediate message to Hamburg, asking them to implement his rescue plan, *Unternehmen Blauer Tiger,* with immediate effect.

The few weeks he had been back in Blighty had been entertaining, if nothing else. He knew that he had achieved a lot and that Grosskopf and Ziegler would be pleased. They would welcome him back for sure.

CHAPTER 55

Gierczak settled himself into the cockpit of his Spitfire Vb. He took time doing his pre-flight checks and switched the fuel gauges on, off and on again two or three times. He was not sure how much fuel he would need and he did not want to fall short of the European mainland.

He felt beneath his tunic for his crucifix and held it for a few seconds. It was warm to the touch. He thought, as ever, about Jagoda and little Tomasz. He had not seen them for almost two years. He had not lost count of the days. It was six hundred and eighteen since he had kissed them both goodbye. He made a silent prayer that the flight he was about to undertake would bring an end to that tally.

Tomasz had written to his wife many times. The letters would have been censored, of course, but he was not interested in telling Jagoda where he was, or what he was doing. Nothing sensitive. His only purpose was to let her know that he loved them both and was looking forward to being reunited with them. Apart from that, he simply informed her that he was safe.

He received no replies which was not surprising. He was not even sure if his letters would be delivered to what was now an occupied country and part of the *Reich*, but the simple act of writing their names and expressing his feelings, gave him comfort.

What had prompted him to carry out the theft of this Spitfire was what WIESELIG had told him. The man could have been telling him lies, of course. He realised that, but it gave him hope. A hope that he and his family would be back together. A hope that had been rekindled.

HE HEARD the Merlin engines of the other two Spits cough two or three times and then roar into life, belching clouds of blue smoke which were swept away instantly by the wash from the prop. He started his own engine.

Motioning for ground crew to pull the chocks away, he eased open the throttle. The craft inched forward. To his left, the first Spit had started to roll and bump gently across the grass to the hard runway. The second followed. He moved forward, gently tapping the rudder to bring the small flight into a three in line take-off. He closed the canopy and checked his gauges one last time.

The new Spitfire V was a vastly different bird from any of its older sisters. Its more powerful Merlin 45 engine made it superior in speed, climb rate and ceiling. Its two 20mm cannons and four machine guns made its armament even better the current *Me109*. It was also very responsive. The Squadron could now outpace, outclimb and outgun the opposing *Luftwaffe* fighters. Superior weaponry too, but he hoped not be needing it on this flight. The plane was a joy to fly. He was loath to part with it. He regretted already that this might be his last flight in a Spit. But there was a bigger picture now. One which eclipsed all of his admiration for this new plane.

THIS MISSION WAS a *Rhubarb* on Dunkirk. Hit hard and get out. He knew what Dunkirk meant to the English and the other two pilots were keen to do this one. The port was symbolic of their low point in the war and he understood that. Photo reconnaissance had revealed that the town was already in a bad way. The land battle that had accompanied the mass exodus of British forces a year ago had left deep scars.

The purpose of these sorties – along with others in the *Operation Rhubarb* portfolio – was to keep the *Luftwaffe* on their toes and to inflict damage wherever and whenever they could. They were 'B' Flight today. 'A' Flight had just returned from a similar run over St Omer that morning. They had reported nothing to worry about either by way of flak or enemy aircraft.

Patchy cumulus was visible at 5000 feet out over the Channel. These great, fluffy ice cream cones of white cloud were perfect for *Rhubarb* – climb into them, follow a heading and then drop down and out of them when closer to the target. It was great cover and a flat base made it easy to enter again quickly, if needed. That was the plan today and their mission was to strafe ships, port buildings and installations of any size. In, hit hard and back.

Gierczak's flight plan was subtly different. He would not be coming back.

CHAPTER 56

Sholto Douglas was in a spot. They had traced all airmen by the name of Tomasz. The personnel lists had not been quite up to date. Three had died since they were last revised; five were in hospital; another three had been located and dragged, protesting, from a leave pass; two were inbound and due to land. No less than seventeen were in coolers at camps and bases across the British Isles.

Which left one.

Churchill had been informed about the Polish pilot and - it was felt prudent to do so - he had also been apprised of the Czech pilot's earlier theft of a Hurricane. The PM now knew that Flight Sergeant Tomasz Gierczak was in the air and outbound. The brief exchange between Churchill and Sholto Douglas was bad-tempered. It was immediately apparent within a few seconds that the PM knew about both renegade pilots. Czech and Pole.

"For pity's sake, how many of our aircraft do they want? They'll be teaming up to get a Wellington if we're not careful. What's this Pole flying?"

"A Spitfire, sir."

"I know that, you dunderhead. What marque?"

"A Vb"

"Oh, for Christ's sake. The engine will be barely run in."

"It took us a while to . . ."

"I don't want excuses. Bring him back. Shoot the bugger down if you have to."

And there the call had ended.

GIERCZAK WAS with 92 Squadron at Biggin Hill. It was one of II Group's stations. Sholto Douglas needed to speak to Air Vice-Marshall Trafford Leigh Mallory who headed up the Group. He knew the man well. He was often at Bentley Priory.

II Group was as front-line as it went. Responsible for the defence, safety and protection of London and the South East, it had borne the brunt of the Battle of Britain. It now found itself busily occupied with all the sideshows that had succeeded it. *Circus*, *Rhubarb* and a few hybrids of the two.

Leigh Mallory was not going to like this. Sholto Douglas stood from his desk, threw the balcony windows open to let some air in, and walked out of the office to the top of the staircase.

"Adjutant", he shouted.

Heseltine appeared below. "Sir?"

"Where's Leigh-Mallory?"

"Not here, I'm afraid."

"Well, try Uxbridge. I need to speak to him pronto. If not sooner."

"Sir."

Heseltine disappeared to make the call. The phone on Sholto Douglas's desk was ringing before he sat down. He grabbed the receiver as he slumped into his seat.

"The Air Vice-Marshall for you, sir."

There was a click as the call was put through. "Trafford?"

"Yes. You've got a flap on, I gather."

"It's your flap now, old boy."

Sholto Douglas quickly gave him chapter and verse on the errant Pole as well as a verbatim account of his conversation with the PM.

"Shoot him down?"

"If he won't respond. His very words."

"Bloody hell."

"Exactly. But I would respectfully suggest that you do not use 92 Squadron to get him down. Using his own squadron at Biggin Hill to do it, goes against the grain somehow."

"That won't be easy."

"Nothing is these days, old chum. Hadn't you noticed?"

Leigh Mallory made the short walk to the underground bunker that housed 11 Group Operations Room. It had been completed in a few short months and just days before war was declared. The writing had been on the wall in the year preceding the declaration and it was felt a priority to bury this operational hub underground, out of sight and safe from German bombs.

He took the seventy-six steps downstairs and entered the space. There was always a stale smell down there. A heady mix of sweat, spent tobacco and, occasionally, fear. He called two of his most senior officers, took them to one side and briefly outlined the situation.

"Shoot him down?", one of them said, his voice falling in volume as he realised that sharing his own panic with the rest of the assembled company was probably not a good idea.

Leigh Mallory sensed what he was feeling. He lowered his own voice. "Oh, don't worry. The whole bloody room will have to be told. Now, what's the plan? Speed is of the essence."

The second officer pointed to the situation board, sitting high on the wall at one end of the room. It gave them an overview of everything that moved in 11 Group.

Compared with last summer, it was quiet. When Churchill had visited them at the height of the Battle of Britain, the great map on the operations table was littered with coloured and numbered blocks, each denoting the movement of planes, both friend and foe, all tracked and moved by the WAAF plotters on receipt of information from a number of external sources.

The three of them walked forward to get a better view. 92 Squadron's *Rhubarb* mission to Dunkirk was on the map for all to see. A three-ship formation, including the Spitfire piloted by Gierczak. Leigh Mallory asked one of the WAAFs to give them its exact position, height and speed.

She gave him the details. The flight had just taken off and was still barely at 2000 feet. It was due to turn right over the Channel at Margate. He thanked her and took the two officers aside again.

"Right. I want the closest Spit V Squadron to its projected flight path. Nothing else will catch him if he makes a bolt for it."

As the pair walked over to examine the ops board in closer detail, Leigh Mallory walked up to the gallery to address the room. He explained the situation. He saw their fearful expressions. He pointed out that it may not come to anything. If this pilot responded and landed as requested, then panic averted. If he did not, then the worst scenario was that they would, quite literally, have to plot the shooting down of one of their own aircraft.

But, he stressed, if the pilot ignored requests to land, then he should rightfully be treated as *not* one of their own and that they must not, therefore, feel any tinge of sympathy nor shed any tears.

By now, the two officers had returned. Leigh Mallory told the assembled teams that he would issue further news when he had it and asked them to resume their duties. The room was silent.

He turned to the two men.

"Well?"

The pair looked at each other. One of them spoke.

"We've been on to Biggin Hill, sir. The flight was still within R/T range. They've been told to return to base."

"And?"

"The Flight Leader has responded. He and one other have turned. Look."

He pointed at the plotting table. The two returning Spitfires were now shown on a new block, separated from the other plane in the flight. Leigh Mallory pointed at the single Spitfire. Let me get this straight. This third one is Gierczak's, correct."

"Yes, sir."

"Heading?"

"He's turned away from them and it looks as if he's aiming to head back for the French coast."

"Oh, bugger!" Leigh Mallory had a thought. He turned to the two officers. "I want all Observer Corps posts in this Sector to be given this Spit's squadron code. What is it?"

"QJ-P, sir."

"Good. Inform them as forcibly as you can, that this is of

vital importance. If they see it, I want them to record height, direction of flight, approximate speed - everything. They're all we've got. Chain Home can't help us while he's still over-land. It's pointing the wrong way."

The two men ran to the phones.

lbert Stokes parked his car in Hood Square, Pimlico and walked the twenty yards or so to Maxwell Knight's office. He had driven down from North Shields the evening before and had slept in his own bed for the first time in weeks. He felt refreshed.

The situation with the miscreant Metcalfs had been resolved. He had no doubt at all that their wireless transmission, courtesy of WIESELIG, had been responsible for the bombing of the lemonade factory, the destruction of the Royal Navy's new anti-submarine weapon and the loss of one hundred or so lives. Both uncle and nephew were now awaiting His Majesty's pleasure in Durham Prison. They were no longer his problem.

He had informed Knight of all that had transpired and the man had agreed that he could now wash his hands of the whole affair and return to London for a debrief. There was news, Knight had said, and he asked Stokes to come into the office.

"Albert. Long time, no see. Do sit."

They shook hands and Stokes sat. Knight's desk did not

look any tidier than it had on his last visit. It was still not possible to see its surface.

"Well done on North Shields, old chum. You have the Royal Navy's thanks, by the way. I also asked them to review their security procedures."

Both men laughed. Stokes spoke. "If it had not been for WIESELIG's appearance, it would never have happened."

"I'm sure. And talking of that man. Here's the news I told you about. He's flown the nest."

Stokes was puzzled. "Meaning what exactly?"

"He's gone, vanished, disappeared in a puff of smoke, old bean."

Knight could see that Stokes needed more. He recounted his conversations with Tin Eye Stephens. How the Camp Twenty man had been on the phone so long, talking to Knight then trying to organise Wesley's arrest and removal, while the man himself had simply jumped out of the window.

"I don't believe it. And there was no-one to guard him?"

"Nope. He's feeling very embarrassed about the escape. Trouble with these safe houses is . . ."

"That they aren't", Stokes interjected.

Knight laughed. "Sadly, no. They are just conventional suburban, semi-detached dwellings, requisitioned into government service. Only meant to house those with double-agent status and whom they feel can be trusted. Low risk in other words."

"And Wesley betrayed that trust."

"In spades, old chum. He could be halfway to the *Reich* by now."

"It seems the Royal Navy isn't the only leaky ship around, then?"

Knight looked perplexed for a second or two. He laughed. "Oh, very good, Albert. You should be in variety."

"Hmmm! About our friend Wesley, also known as Smith, we both know where he will have headed though, don't we? From his semi-detached window on the world."

"Brentford?"

Stokes nodded. Knight continued. "I thought that too. And, before you say it, I did ask if we could storm the place but got the thumbs-down."

"But surely . . ."

Knight could see that Stokes was getting agitated. The Anglo-German spy had occupied most of his agent's time for the last few weeks. Their paths had crossed - not only in North Shields but also in Hull in the case of the now-deceased Peter Armitage. In addition to that, he had narrowly missed Wesley at the cell of former BUF members in Leeds where they had both been vying for its attentions. And, of course, Stokes had been instrumental in Wesley's arrest in Hull. The man had a right to seek closure but he sensed that Stokes was starting to take it too personally.

"You remember the discussion we had on your first full day. The powers to be are looking at the big picture on this. They feel that more will be gained in the long term by infiltration and killing the whole beast rather than going at it piecemeal - one body part at a time."

Stokes frowned. He was not convinced. "I'm not sure I agree."

"Not certain that I do either, my lad, but ours is not to reason why. I gave you the Siemens-Schuckert file that same day but since then you have not had a chance to get your teeth into it."

"Thanks to North Shields."

"Precisely." He paused. "In any case, Stephens felt that

he had wrung the man dry. They were not getting any return on the chicken feed which he was sending to Hamburg - who were obviously aware of the fact that he was turned. The only open question was this Polish pilot business which we now know the answer to. And which turned out to be the tipping point for him. Which is why he was locked in his room, pending arrest."

Knight realised that Stokes knew little or nothing about the ongoing Polish pilot situation which was exercising RAF Fighter Command's mind at that very moment. He brought him up to speed.

"Good God. So, Wesley had more than one pilot on the go?"

"It would seem so. Let's hope it was only the two of them."

Silence prevailed for a few seconds. Knight was the first to speak again.

"Oh ... and this may interest you. Do you remember the cutout through which Wesley received that list of former BU members in Leeds."

Stokes smiled. "The lonely hearts club?"

Knight laughed. "That's it. Run by one Mrs Ada Wigglesworth. She is currently helping Barnsley police with their inquiries."

"What did they find?"

"Oh, lots of incriminating stuff. All in sealed envelopes for onward transmission to a neutral destination. Sweden or the Republic of Ireland. She was definitely a cutout. Probably a lot of stuff there from Fifth Columnists and *pukka* spies. I'll show you the relevant stuff when I get it."

Stokes laughed. "Once they've separated it from genuine letters written by husbands whose wives don't understand them, you mean?"

Knight sniggered. "Yes - let's hope their good ladies don't answer the door when the rubber heels come a-calling."

The laughter slowly subsided. Stokes wondered if their meeting was at an end. Knight cleared his throat. He clearly had not finished. He picked up a file from the floor and put it on the desk between them.

Stokes recognised it. "Siemens-Schuckert? Despite all we've just said about the matter?"

"No. *Because* of what we have just discussed, not in spite of it. As you're at a bit of a loose end now, I want you to completely immerse yourself in it. Take it home and don't leave the house until you can dictate it back to me from memory, my boy."

The other man raised his eyebrows. "That's a bit of an ask."

Knight laughed. "Do what you can, old chap. You'll see that I've also put the latest info in there from the gate watchers. There'll be some stuff you can chase up, I'm sure. We have to get in there, old chum, but not through the front door with a battering ram and a fistful of arrest warrants."

Stokes peeked inside the file. It was considerably thicker than the first time he clapped eyes on it and, sure enough, the watchers' sheets were at the top of the pile of paper within. He stood and stuffed its girth under his arm.

"I'll pop down on my way home and have a look-see anyway. Reacquaint myself with the place." He paused and, remembering Knight's fondness for American films, said, "I'll stake the place out."

He could feel Knight bristle. His reply was instant. "No, Albert. I do not want every German spy who calls that place home, to see your scowling face every time he enters or leaves. It would seriously hinder your efforts to infiltrate." He paused. "Don't you think?"

Stokes knew he was right. "Hmm. It would be good to know if Wesley was in there though." He paused. "Don't you think?" He realised immediately that those last few words were close to insubordination but Knight just laughed.

"Galling, I know, old chap. But orders is orders, as they say. Let . . . him . . . go, Albert." He pointed at the file. "See what you make of that."

Knight had another idea. "I will, however, have a word with the chap in charge of these watchers. See if we can't add a shift. And find out if anyone has been round the back of the place. I have the name of the chappie who was with you when you almost nabbed him, too. Shame we haven't got a photograph."

"But we do, don't we? I thought he had a British passport when he was pulled in by Twenty."

Knight's eyes lit up. "By George, you're right. I'll get it copied and issued to all of our 'gate guardians'." He paused. "Mind you, passport photographs are notoriously shoddy."

"Better than nothing. It's a start."

"Let's not confuse the sprat with the mackerel though, old son."

"Or the pest with the nest!"

Knight laughed. "Indeed."

Stokes was disappointed but becoming conscious of the fact that he was taking the loss of Wesley personally. It was clouding his judgment. Having been responsible for the man's apprehension, he was peeved that Twenty had let him jump out of the bloody window when their backs were turned.

He turned to leave. Knight spoke again. "And don't forget. We don't know for sure that he *is* there, do we? It could simply be a product of your fevered imagination, old son."

Stokes sighed. "True."

"Now, go and mop up some Fifth Columnists, Albert. At least Wesley is *hors de combat*!" He looked up and saw Stokes' puzzled expression. "French, Albert. Out of action - as most of them are."

They both laughed. Stokes waved and left the office.

CHAPTER 58

Major Dieter Grosskopf was back in his Hamburg office. Much of his job now required him to visit other sub-offices of the *Abwehr* with the result that his appearances in Hamburg were spasmodic and usually unannounced.

Otto Ziegler had been trying to find out where the officer was. He needed to discuss the situation regarding WIESELIG. So, it was fortunate that Grosskopf had returned just at the time when a decision had to be made. The two men were facing each other across the *Major's* desk.

"So, Ziegler. You look panic-stricken. What is bothering you?"

"I'm not sure how many of my messages you have seen. About WIESELIG, I mean."

"Assume none. At least, I don't recall seeing any. What's happening?"

It took a few minutes for Ziegler to explain all that had taken place. He knew that their agent, Howard Wesley, had been turned. There had been a few days silence immediately after he had reported on his successful contact with both of their pilots, the Czech and the Pole - known as MOTORRAD and STANGE respectively. The former had since fulfilled his promise of delivering an RAF fighter; the latter had not.

Then, WIESELIG resurfaced but Ziegler had known from a covert word in the first message that he was turned as a double agent. By definition, everything he transmitted from thenceforward should be treated as *Quatsch* - rubbish. Ziegler had referred this to another officer, in Grosskopf's absence, and they had matched chicken feed with similarly flimsy requests for British information.

The agent's last message to Hamburg had come under a different codename - VOGEL. Ziegler recognised his 'fist' and the nonsense mode of communication. It was inimitable. The content was brief - it stated where he was and that *Unternehmen Blauer Tiger* should be put into play.

Ziegler guessed that Wesley had been unwilling to use his usual WIESELIG codename for fear of interception. He guessed that VOGEL, meaning 'bird', was an indicator that he had flown the nest. In flight, presumably.

He was not willing to implement the rescue operation. He did not know the exact details and nor did he have the authority. None of Grosskopf's fellow officers wished to intervene. He waited for the *Major* to respond.

"So . . . where is he?"

"At Siemens-Schuckert. That factory in London where he picked up the two wirelesses. Part of the *Kriegsnetz* that you described to him, Herr *Major.*"

"Ah, yes. Of course."

The officer was now pacing the room. He turned to face the wireless operator. "Tell me, Ziegler . . . this *Unternehmen Blauer Tiger* escape plan? Does it exist?"

Ziegler was shocked. He had a vivid memory of their

final meeting with Wesley before his departure. The *Major* himself had mentioned the rescue plan, which he had named after the Berlin nightclub in which he had first encountered the Englishman. Wesley had been very relieved to hear of it.

"I don't know. It was you who first mentioned it, Herr *Major.*"

There was a silence. Ziegler had nothing more to say. The officer paced a bit more, paused to look out of the window and then returned to his seat.

"I think I made it up, Ziegler. There is no such plan." He paused. "I could tell he was nervous about his imminent parachute jump. I thought it would make him feel better if he knew there was a Plan B."

Ziegler gasped. "So . . . do we just leave him there?"

"I think for the time being, we do. Yes. He's good on the wireless. I'm sure the people at Siemens will find him very useful. Besides, once the heat dies down, we can bring him out to play again, can't we?" He paused. "With a different codename, of course. I never liked his previous one - WIESELIG, or whatever."

"What do I tell him, Herr *Major*?"

"Just tell him to sit tight. I'll speak to Siemens and tell them to look after him for us."

Ziegler nodded and stood to leave.

"Wait. Please sit down, Ziegler."

After the man took his seat once again, Grosskopf began to talk in more guarded tones. "This is for your ears only at the moment. The landscape of the war is changing. All eyes are turning to the east. You may be aware of the rumours by now, I suppose. Because of that, I think the prospect of an invasion of Britain is now dead in the water, if you'll excuse the pun. There are, of course, still acts of aggression against such a stubborn enemy but . . . what I am trying to say is that Wesley's brief is not as important as it originally was."

Ziegler's forehead wrinkled. "You're not thinking of pulling the plug on him, are you, Herr *Major*?"

Grosskopf did not look as affronted as Ziegler hoped that he would.

"No, of course not. He is a very talented man and I'm sure he will continue to deliver when we put him back into the field again. In the meantime, I do not see any urgency in getting him out of Britain . . . only to drop him back in there when we *do* need him." He paused, sensing that he should have used a little more tact.

"Don't worry, Ziegler. I have no doubt at all that Wesley will feature in future plans." He lifted his eyebrows and smiled.

There was a long silence. Grosskopf hoped that Ziegler understood what he was unwilling to spell out.

"He will hate it, Herr *Major*."

"Of that I have no doubt. But, in any case, there is no *Unternehmen Blauer Tiger*, Ziegler." He paused. "Just do as I have asked you to do. Sit tight is the message. But, I do not want you to give him the false impression that he is to be incarcerated in Siemens forever. Got that?"

Ziegler was dismissed. The officer was verging on the tetchy and the wireless operator did not want to push his luck. He walked back to his desk where his set was already connected up.

It took him ten minutes to draft a message to his friend, Wesley, before he dared commit it to the key. He understood all that Grosskopf had told him and, in the changing scenario of the war, it made sense. That did not make what he was about to tell the fledgling VOGEL any easier.

CHAPTER 59

Gierczak heard the order from his Flight Leader to abort the mission and return to base. He was sitting 100 yards to port of the Flight Leader's Spit. The third plane was about the same distance beyond that.

His mind was made up. He would not be returning. He put his thumbs up as they started to turn back to base and then banked left as if in compliance. He started to ease off on the throttle as he dropped back from the other two Spits and put clear sky between them. Gierczak wanted to stay in their rough formation long enough for them to register his presence before he slipped quickly and quietly away. They would assume he was scouting for business.

He side-slipped into the scant cloud cover over his left shoulder. It would not obscure him completely, but it would do for the length of time it took for the other two to fade into the distance. He kept the plane in a long, gradual turn, losing height in the process, until he felt that he was back on an outward tack and on course again to hit the coast at Margate.

As evasion tactics went, it was not complicated. He was fairly sure that the reason their mission was aborted was that they wanted him back. That, somehow, they had got wind of his own very private sortie. He was feeling now, in his bones, that every inch he flew away from England was an inch closer to his beloved family. He brought up his right hand and switched off the headset.

IN THE UXBRIDGE BUNKER, Leigh Mallory was in a heated discussion with his two colleagues. Gierczak was still in the air and starting to put clear blue sky between himself and Biggin Hill. The other pilots were almost back. It was time for action.

To the two officers, the obvious solution would be to turn the other two 92 Squadron Spits right around, to give chase. That was problematic on a number of counts. The obvious objection was that it would now be like looking for a needle in a haystack. At this time of the day, with similar *Rhubarb* missions returning to the many II Group stations in the sector, there could be many lone fighters in the air. And, although Gierczak was not responding, there was still the chance that he would be listening into the radio chat of anyone in pursuit.

None of these, Leigh Mallory thought, were compelling reasons but Sholto Douglas had been emphatic in his instructions not to use anyone from 92 Squadron on such a delicate mission. The worst scenario would be friendly fire, so better another squadron. He voiced these thoughts to them. The Sholto Douglas factor was the clincher. Nobody was willing to countermand a direct order from CIC Fighter Command.

They looked down at the map table. Leigh Mallory was

right. There were a considerable number of small flights of fighters either returning from, or heading to, the sort of raid that 92 Squadron 'B' Flight had been about to engage in.

He peered across at the long-range situation board on the far wall. He was looking for stations that had recently received the new Spitfire V. Geographically, Manston would have been ideal but he knew from his recent visit that they were still using Hurricane MkIIs. Compared with this new breed of Spit, the Hurricane was a plodder - 30mph slower and a comparatively pedestrian rate of climb.

Gierczak would not need to be the best of pilots to leave them standing if he spotted them. The Spitfire Mk V was being rolled out across front-line fighter stations. Gierczak's 92 Squadron at Biggin Hill had been one of the first to receive them.

"The Observer Corps have been notified, sir."

"How did they take it?"

The officer laughed. "The controller insisted on calling me back. I think he thought it was some kind of prank."

Leigh Mallory sighed. "I only wish it was. He's putting the word out though, I assume?"

"Yes, sir. Across the whole of 11 Group, but I told him to concentrate on the Kent Channel coast . . . and the Thames estuary."

"Good. So, we have eyes on the ground. Now we need some in the air."

The second officer joined them. He was breathless.

"91 Squadron at Hawkinge took delivery of the Spit V two weeks ago, sir."

Leigh Mallory smiled. He looked at the map table below. It was deceptively quiet but he could feel the tension in the room. Hawkinge was bang on the coast, just a couple of miles north of Folkestone. If he could scramble a small flight of Spits from there, they could almost intercept Gierczak, providing the Pole kept to his original flight plan and headed for the turn at Margate.

He picked up the phone and asked the switchboard to get him the Squadron Leader Paddy Green at Hawkinge. He did not know him that well but thought that he must have met him on several occasions. He was not sure how much this chap would know about the current situation but he was about to be pulled into the thick of it. Leigh Mallory had no time for pleasantries. He would make amends the next time they met.

"Paddy."

"Commander. I trust you're well?"

"Yes, indeed. No time for chat though. Sorry, old chap - we have a bit of a flap and I need your help. I need you to scramble three Spits. You've got the Mark Vb, am I right?"

"Certainly have. What's the op?"

"Just bare bones at the moment, I'm afraid. And please bear in mind that this comes right from the top, old chum."

Leigh Mallory gave the Station Commander only as many details as were needed to get three Spits in the air. The mission was quite simple. Locate Spitfire QJ-P. Order it to land. Shoot it down if necessary. He gave him the fighter's approximate current location, flight plan and height before promising him regular updates.

"That's 92 Squadron!"

"Consider it an enemy aircraft, Paddy. I cannot emphasise that enough. Keep me in touch. I'm in the II Group bunker. And, I stress, this order has come from the top - the War Cabinet no less."

"Oh, my Lord."

"And I should tell you that the pilot is a Pole so best not

send one of his compatriots up there to shoot him down, if you can avoid it."

PADDY GREEN WAS SHOCKED. He went straight to the roster room and selected three bemused pilots. They were no keener than he was to shoot a Spitfire out of the sky, especially one from neighbouring 92 Squadron, based only a few miles away.

He had no choice but to select one of the two Polish pilots on the squadron as a member of this 'seek and destroy' mission. Fabisiewicz was a superb flier with a number of kills already marked on his fuselage.

His mitigation would be that he had selected the best three pilots from what was available to him at the time. Fab *was* the best of the bunch - always the first to attack and ferocious in his approach. He gave no quarter. If they wanted this plane down, then he was the man.

DESPITE THE PILOTS' qualms, they were in the air within three minutes. They had barely passed the base perimeter when control gave them a heading which would take them at ninety degrees to Gierczak's probable flight path to Margate. They were aiming at a point ahead of his route.

Green had told them everything they needed to know to get the job done, including the fact that their target was a Polish airman. He felt that Fabisiewicz had a right to know and he *was* the best airman in the squadron.

CHAPTER 60

For the three 91 Squadron pilots taking off from Hawkinge that afternoon, it was throttle open all the way. They revelled in the speed and guts of this new Spitfire V variant. Not to be flying it over enemy territory - where it might get bent - was a bonus.

The green and pleasant land of Kent scudded beneath them as they headed north over the Downs. Their flight plan took them to Canterbury. Their quarry, Spitfire QJ-P, should be approaching them from the west. The assumption was that he would be conserving fuel to make the crossing to mainland Europe. He would not be flying at speed.

It was decided on their way north that they would split. Flight Sergeant Ron Davidson would peel off before the cathedral city, and maintain a presence to the south. The Canadian Flight Leader, Pilot Officer Bob Hughes, would circle the city while the third Spit, piloted by Flight Sergeant Lech Fabisiewicz, would patrol the area to the north, between Canterbury and Whitstable on the coast. Clouds were scant and visibility was good.

Once it was spotted, the plan was to close in on the renegade plane. Hughes would run alongside, with a gesture for
the pilot to land. If that were declined or ignored, then he
would bank away and allow the other two to come in.
Davidson was to attack from his rear. Fabisiewicz, sitting
higher, would stand off to counter any attempt to flee.
Hughes' plan was totally dependent on exactly where the
Pole made his appearance.

The danger was that the pilot they were hunting might
take fright immediately and throttle it. He would know, as
soon as he saw what they were flying, that any speed or
climb could be matched - and it was three against one.

LEIGH MALLORY HEARD from the Observer Corps at Sheer-
ness that QJ-P had been spotted. It was at 1000 feet, heading
almost due east and following the coastline. Approximate
speed 150 mph. He now had to use the information pronto if
they were to catch the escaping pilot. He knew the 91
Squadron chasers were now well out of R/T range from the
bunker. He looked at the map on the table below.

"Get me the Station Commander at Manston."

RAF Manston was on high ground and very close to 91's
three-man 'posse'. The switchboard put him through to the
senior ranking officer. The Air Vice-Marshall explained the
situation as succinctly as he could.

Manston would contact the 91 Squadron flight, give
them Gierczak's co-ordinates and act as liaison between the
pilots and Uxbridge. That was done within seconds as Leigh
Mallory listened in.

He closed the call. This way forward was clumsy but it
would work, as long as Gierczak did not bolt for it and take
them all out of R/T range. If he crossed the coast, then it

would be down to the Chain Home radar outposts to find him but, even if they did, it would be tricky.

The chasing Flight Leader passed the information to the other two immediately. It seemed Fab was the closest, flying north of the city and in the six-mile gap between Canterbury and Whitstable.

As HE CIRCLED, Fabisiewicz was troubled. He knew the Spit they were hunting was 92 Squadron and the pilot was a fellow Pole. Most of those from his initial flight training had been Poles but they were now scattered at fighter and bomber squadrons all over the country. He knew of only one who had ended up at 92 Squadron but there could be more there, from other intakes.

He remembered the name - Tomasz Gierczak. Although he had never been one to join in the carousing, he was likeable enough, albeit a bit intense. None of the others in their draft had family ties as close as his.

This pilot may not be Gierczak, of course, but if he was, then he must have a really good reason to be doing a bunk with a Spitfire. He could only imagine that he must be under some form of coercion.

Fabisiewicz knew from experience how cataclysmic the German invasion of their country had been in September 1939. He had also heard from other Polish pilots who had been captured that some had been coerced. Most had managed to escape despite the threats to bend their will to the Nazi cause. Gierczak never referred to his experiences but he did talk often of his family. Whether Gierczak or not, he would do all he could to get the pilot to return.

He suddenly spotted a Spit a few hundred feet below him and starting to edge out over the sea. It could be other traffic, of course, but he was coming from the direction they expected. Fab started a shallow dive, increased his speed and approached the other plane from below. It was QJ-P.

The other Spit's course did not waver, so Fabisiewicz knew he had not been spotted. He gradually tucked himself twenty feet below the starboard tailplane. There was no reaction. He was in the pilot's blind spot. He gently climbed to pull alongside.

Once he knew he was visible, he matched QJ-P's speed and looked across from cockpit to cockpit. There was no change in speed or direction.

GIERCZAK HAD NOTICED the other fighter above him and thought nothing of it as it proceeded to lose height and disappear from view in the opposite direction. He was following the coastline which he knew would lead him eventually to Margate. This was the easy bit. He was not anticipating any problems over the Channel. The worry would be the flak stations along the enemy coast. There was also the possibility of encountering *Luftwaffe* aircraft. He would deal with that by evasive action but he was not looking for a fight.

As he started to concentrate his attentions on what lay ahead, the bulk of another Spit filled his vision on the right side of his cockpit. He looked across. The pilot was staring at him. He recognised him as Lech Fabisiewicz with whom he had trained a few months earlier. He had not seen him since but the unmistakable black moustache and toothy smile were undeniably his. He was pointing backwards and down. He was calling him back.

· · ·

FAB RECOGNISED TOMASZ IMMEDIATELY. They exchanged glances and smiled. Fab pointed down and behind. Gierczak slowly shook his head. He took his right hand from the control column and placed it slowly and carefully across his heart. Twice.

Fab nodded. He understood. He made the pointing manoeuvre again. The smile had gone but there was a plea written on his face. He switched off his R/T. He wanted their meeting to be private.

Tomasz was now looking ahead. He waved once, and dropped his hand back to the control column. He closed his eyes briefly before thrusting the throttle forward and lifting the nose.

Fab thought about trying for a third time but his compatriot was already picking up speed and starting to climb away.

GIERCZAK FELT a strange sense of calm as Fab's Spit disappeared behind him. Light cloud now lay between them which gave him a cloak of invisibility. He continued to gain height and weave upwards with the throttle open as far as he could push it.

This was it, then. He was now into the well-practised art of the dogfight. He knew that Fab would be on his tail. He knew that, despite their common origins and comradeship, his fellow Pole would give no quarter. Any chance of meeting up again with Jagoda and Tomasz junior depended on the next few minutes.

FLIGHT LEADER BOB HUGHES and Flight Sergeant Ron Davidson were still searching for Fabisiewicz and were unable to contact him. He was somewhere ahead of them, north of Canterbury, but intermittent cloud was obscuring their vision at this height. Hughes had called him on the R/T but had received no response.

He tried again but still no reply. He told Davidson that they were to head north of Canterbury and to keep their eyes peeled for both the runaway QJ-P and Fab's Spit.

FABISIEWICZ SOON CAUGHT a brief glimpse of Gierczak powering upwards through a gap in the clouds. He could see the plane was being hammered. He guessed the airframe was suffering. He came at him and managed to get within range, even though his own Spit was starting to complain. He fired two short bursts as a final warning.

GIERCZAK KEPT the throttles open and clasped his crucifix in his right hand. He silently prayed to all that he held precious, and imagined the faces of his wife and son in happier times.

Before the thought melted away, he felt his Spitfire jolt. He heard and saw cannon shells smashing into the fuselage. Then, a second burst hit him forward of that. He saw sparks coming from the engine cowling and a black stream of oil starting to crawl up the screen. He looked out to both sides. Down to the right, he saw the other plane climbing to his rear. Fab was getting height to come at him again.

In an instant, Gierczak knew the plane was dead. He was not going to make it. All hopes of meeting his family again had vanished. He closed his eyes and intoned the names of his wife and son before crying out . . . "I love you".

He kept the pressure on the Merlin, knowing the plane

would go into a death-dive. Thick black smoke was pouring from the exhausts. The engine was misfiring. He hoped Fabisiewicz would see that he had done the honourable thing. He had not resisted. He had made it easy for him.

FAB COULD SEE the problems that QJ-P was having. Although his shots were only intended as a warning, they had actually hit Tomasz's Spit on the engine block. The smoke told him he had caused a lot of damage. He watched Gierczak climb swiftly and then gradually falter. Tomasz was putting too much pressure on a Merlin that was already dying.

He watched, transfixed, as QJ-P fell below his own height and showed no signs of recovery. The prop was not turning and the Spit had started to spin. He decided to put Tomasz out of his misery. He would want the same if the positions were reversed.

Fab banked and dove toward the stricken aircraft. By now, it was only two hundred feet below him. He came in fast. He hit the Spit again and watched the canopy explode in a shower of perspex fragments.

GIERCZAK'S second declaration of love was not completed. A .303 machine gun bullet traversed his skull. He died before QJ-P entered the water. Fab watched as the smoke and flames from the plane were suddenly extinguished. A great white plume of water followed its disappearance.

· · ·

FLIGHT LEADER BOB HUGHES saw the splash on his approach. He knew it must be one of two Spitfires. Fab had still not responded to calls on R/T. He tried again.

"Fab, speak to me."

His voice finally came through, strangely calm and with none of the usual jubilation that accompanied the shooting down of a plane.

"Spitfire down."

Hughes now saw him below - circling the crash site. He noticed Davidson out of the corner of his eye. He was pulling alongside - smiling and waving.

Hughes replied to Fab. "Did he refuse to turn back?"

Fab was conflicted. He knew Gierczak and was sure of what he was trying to do. And why he was doing it. He felt his pain and wanted to protect his memory.

"He was coming back. I fired warning shots." He paused for a few seconds. "But they hit him on the turn and he went down. Couldn't get out of it."

Save for the usual crackle, the R/T was momentarily silent before Hughes interrupted it.

"Bad luck, Fab. I'm sorry" And then. "Let's get back. Fab - line astern, you're number three. Ron, lead the way. But keep an eye out. We're still on a war footing and we now have one less Spitfire."

Nobody laughed.

LEIGH MALLORY BROUGHT the assembled personnel at the Uxbridge control bunker together. The job had been done but nobody was showing pleasure in it. This was no victory. They had lost what sounded like a very able pilot, albeit with a perverted view on life - he was not going to judge - and a damned fine aeroplane.

"Thank you everyone for your efforts this afternoon. I want to restore some calm and put what you have just witnessed into context. First of all, this must not – repeat, not – leave these walls. Is that fully understood?"

There was silence. He looked at them, trying to catch the gaze of as many of them as possible. There was a chorus of 'yesses' which rose to a crescendo before he calmed them down once more.

"Thank you. The three young airmen who solved the problem facing us would, in normal circumstances, be rewarded for their efforts. Sadly, because of the special nature of what they did, that will not be possible. Please believe me though when I tell you that they have done this country a great service."

Sad nods from one or two.

"Once again, thank you. And may I say how proud I am to serve with you all."

Applause broke out as he left the room to tread the few steps to his office. He had phone calls to make.

THE FIRST CALL was to head of Fighter Command, Sholto Douglas, asking him to pass the news up the line to the War Cabinet and the man himself. He was grateful and agreed with the need for blanket secrecy. There had been a friendly fire incident the previous year over Barking Creek where they lost two pilots. That had been smothered. This one would take a bit of work.

Then to Paddy Green, CO of 91 Squadron. His boys were just landing but the Flight Leader had already given him a blow-by-blow account of what had transpired, as soon as they were within range.

He asked Green to thank them personally for a job well

done. Leigh Mallory added that he was very pleased that they had not had to use a Polish pilot in any part of the operation.

"Sorry, sir. I had no choice in the end."

There was silence before Leigh Mallory spoke again. "Hell and damnation! I trust you can fix it, Paddy?"

"I'm sure of it, sir. He's a good man."

When the call ended, Green walked across the apron to greet his three pilots. He headed straight for Fabisiewicz.

THE FINAL CALL was to Squadron Leader Johnny Kent at 92 Squadron. He broke the news almost apologetically. He need not have bothered.

"Sir, with all due respect, I take it as no slight that this rotten apple was in bloody barrel. I do trust though that it will be kept under wraps."

"Yes. Let's hope we can put this to bed now. It leaves a nasty taste in the mouth though, I have to say. But it has not diminished by a single jot, the faith I have always had in these Polish pilots."

"Quite right." Kent continued. "Oh, and I've got the RAF Police here - waiting for Gierczak to reappear."

"They don't know?"

"No. I thought I'd let them stew."

Leigh Mallory laughed. "You have my full permission to put a flea in their ear. Just a small one, though. They're only doing their job."

"Roger."

The call was ended.

.   .   .

TWO RAF POLICE officers had been waiting at RAF Biggin Hill for hours. They were told that Flight Sergeant Tomasz Gierczak had not returned from the aborted *Rhuburb* mission to Dunkirk. Just on tea-time, when it looked as if it was not going to happen, they asked to see the CO.

Johnny Kent was not a fan of the RAF Police. He considered them a necessary evil, but an evil nonetheless. By the time he admitted the pair to his office, he knew the full story about young Tomasz Gierczak. The circumstances of his demise, at least.

He explained to them that the pilot they sought was at the bottom of the Thames estuary. One of the officers spoke.

"Sorry, sir. Are you telling us that he's dead?"

"Yes. Within the hour, so please cross him off your list. I've just come off the phone from Air Vice-Marshall Leigh Mallory. He asked me to inform you that the case is closed. Good day, gentlemen."

The two policemen thanked the Squadron Leader for his time and left the office.

CHAPTER 61

Albert Stokes had decided to put Howard Oswald Wesley, the *Abwehr* agent and handler otherwise known as WIESELIG, to the back of his mind. Knight was right - the man was clouding his judgment. He needed to move on. He recalled that he had left things somewhat up in the air with Reginald Windsor, the leader of the cell of former BUF members in Leeds.

Even that memory was tinged with the near miss that he had had there with Wesley. He was finding it difficult to escape the man's spectre. That was the night when the Leeds cell had two visitors - Wesley and Stokes - within minutes of each other. Each man purported to be a German agent. If they had encountered each other in front of that audience of underground British Fascists, it could have been highly dangerous for both of them. Now that Wesley was off the street - or at least no longer plying his trade - then Stokes felt it safe to return.

. . .

WINDSOR LOCKED the shop door and turned the sign to 'closed'. While the man made tea, Stokes put his German *Durchlassschein* on the table, to reassure him and reinforce his identity as Hitler's man in London. It seemed like an age since he had last been in front of Windsor.

He told Windsor the story of the man that they had both known as John Smith. He listened intently how Smith had, as suspected, been working for the British security services to infiltrate Fifth Columnist cells and gradually round them up.

In describing Smith's modus operandi, Stokes used his own job specifications exactly. He had learned quite early always to embody a great dollop of truth in any lie that you tell. As to Smith's fate, he felt it better to say that he had been neutralised in the line of duty. He left it to Windsor's imagination to interpret the precise meaning of that word.

The man was shocked.

"But his German was perfect." He paused. "And he told us about the decoy sites he'd been discovering."

"I believe his mother was German but he was born in Britain. Who better to know of the location of these sites than a man working for MI5?"

"He was very convincing."

"He was an actor at some point in his career. He was playing a part . . . but he was rumbled."

Windsor took another sip of tea. "I have to say, Geoffrey, that we had a right old conflab about the pair of you."

"And came to the right decision, I hope?"

"We did. It was unanimous in the end."

Stokes had a thought. "I don't suppose he made an appearance after that night, did he?"

"No. It was the fact that he high-tailed it out of here

when he heard you were due to arrive, that put the tin hat on it."

"I'm sure. He would not have wanted the confrontation. He said he was with the *Abwehr*, I believe. I could have exposed that as a lie within seconds and then he would have been at the mercy of . . . what, a dozen or so of us?"

They both laughed. Stokes breathed a silent sigh of relief.

"So, Reg, what have you been up to?"

The cell had been quiet, as Salter had requested. Their plans to start fires at various key sites across the city had been shelved. The emergence of both Smith and Salter had shaken them up.

Stokes laughed.

Windsor spoke again. "But now, I think we can continue. One of our members has photographs of some RAF bases . . . and at least one of them has a decoy site nearby."

Stokes' heart lifted. "That's good news. And I am glad you have decided against setting fire to factories. I don't think that was a good idea. My employers have a great appetite for decoy site information though."

The newsagent's eyes lit up. He went on to tell Stokes of what he called 'returning' members who were very mobile and would be pleased to have the Leeds cell back again as a focus for their efforts. 'Returning from the woodwork', Stokes thought.

They both relaxed into more social conversation as they finished their drinks. From Windsor, how he and his misguided cronies felt the war was going; from Stokes, news of the *Führer*'s plans for a 'thousand-year Reich' as well as other flights of fancy that he knew would appeal. He soon brought these to a close as he remembered how he must not be seen as an agent provocateur and should avoid being sucked into that. Knight had been at pains to point out that it would ruin any court case, if it ever got that far with any of these chaps.

They parted on extremely good terms. Stokes had effectively cemented the bond between himself and the cell. He was looking forward to receiving what they would now avidly collect for onward transmission to the *Abwehr*.

He made a mental note to bring a *Kriegsverdienstkreuz* medal with him the next time he visited Leeds. If only he had not had the recipient's name engraved on the obverse of the last one, awarded to Peter Armitage - late of Hull - he could have recycled it.

HE CALLED in at the police station that he had used on his first visit to Leeds. He wanted to bring Knight up to speed. He answered after just one ring.

"It's Stokes."

"Ah! And what are you up to? What news on the Rialto?"

Stokes remembered that this was Knight's witty, literary codename for the Siemens-Schuckert factory. "I thought I was banned from ever going there again?"

Knight laughed. "I'm teasing you." He paused. "I hope you haven't, my boy."

"Wesley can rot in hell as far as I'm concerned. No. I've been renewing my acquaintance with the misguided of Leeds."

More laughter from the other end. "That sounds rather like one of the lonely-hearts club clients. Signed - Misguided of Leeds." Knight felt he was being too jocular and that maybe Stokes was not in the mood for hilarity. "I'm sorry. Do carry on. What gives?"

"Just rebuilding bridges, really. The damage that Wesley

almost did in Leeds has been repaired, thankfully. And it sounds as if that particular cell may turn out to be quite fruitful. Remind me to pick up some of those medals the next time I'm in town, would you?"

"That good, eh?"

"I think so. That's the story on Leeds. Seeds planted, awaiting a bountiful harvest. In the meantime, I'm going to pop up to North Shields, if that's OK with you? While I'm in the north."

"Why? It wasn't so long ago that you couldn't wait to see the back of the place."

"Just to tie up some loose ends."

"That's fine with me. And, as it happens, there's a bit of a kerfuffle just a bit north of that. Scotland, in fact. Can't give you any meat on the bone just yet. But it could be quite big."

Stokes was intrigued but knew better than to press matters once he had been told there was no meat on the bone. That was Knight-speak for 'I know but I can't tell you yet.'

"Very well. You can get me on my regular North Shields phone number at the police station if you need me."

There was a short silence, presumably while Knight was checking to see if he had the number, so Stokes was the one to cut off the call.

"Speak soon."

CHAPTER 62

S tokes' regular digs in Bedford Terrace, North Shields had a room available so he dumped his suitcase and took the short walk to the police station. Sergeant Harris was at the desk.

"Ah, Mr Stokes. Welcome back. I thought we'd seen the last of you." He dropped his voice. "Don't tell me you've got another case up here?"

"No. I wanted a quiet word with Frank Metcalf. I'd like to see him at home though, rather than the shop."

Harris pursed his lips. "I'm afraid that's your only option. Mr Metcalf has closed the shop for the duration."

Stokes was surprised but he felt he knew what was coming.

"More vandalism, I'm sorry to say. All windows and doors are boarded up now. They've ceased trading."

"Word about Ernest and Freddie got out, did it?"

The sergeant nodded. "I think they were seen when they left here. And some folk put two and two together and got five." He turned and looked down the corridor. "Although, I wouldn't rule out loose tongues here, either, if I'm honest. It's a small town, Mr Stokes."

"I'm sorry to hear about the damage to the shop. I take it that Ernest and his uncle are still in Durham Prison."

"As far as I'm aware. Frank Metcalf may know more about that." Harris wrote the man's address on a slip of paper and handed it to Stokes. The sergeant gave him directions.

"Oh, and I'd be very pleased if you could pop in after you've spoken to him. Just to bring us up to speed, like?"

"Of course. As long as there's a cup of Geordie tea available."

"Why aye, man."

Stokes waved as he left the police station. He laughed to himself. He was now quite fluent in the Geordie lingo. He loved its musicality.

His spirits started to flag on the drive to the Metcalfs' house. He went via the shop in Nile Street. What he saw saddened him. If there was a pane of glass still intact, he could not see it.

The whole facade and the door were boarded up. Someone had been kind enough to daub the word NAZIS in red paint on the boards. The lettering above the frontage had been removed. All that remained was the faint outline of the original name - M E T Z G E R. Just as it had looked in 1915. He shook his head. He got the feeling that life was more circular than linear. He sighed.

Frank opened the front door at the first knock. He was surprised to see Stokes standing there, as if immediately seized by dread that his nightmare was still not over, but he was courteous and civil, and invited this harbinger of doom into his home.

As they sat in the living room and Frank called his wife through to meet their guest, Stokes looked him over. He looked gaunt and at least ten years older. Like the owner of the factory, and his friend, William Wilkinson, he was one of the many unseen victims of the factory tragedy.

Frank introduced his wife. "Hanna. This is Mr Stokes."

She obviously knew the name from what Frank had told her of his visit to the shop and the search of the flat. She looked morose and drawn. He doubted this was her normal appearance. They both sat, staring at Stokes. Hanna had a handkerchief at the ready. Frank just looked as if he was prepared for the worst. The MI5 man broke the silence.

"I haven't come here to add to your pain. I've spoken to Sergeant Harris and I've driven past the shop . . ." Hanna gasped. "So, I know what you have been through."

Frank spoke up. He gestured to himself and Hanna.

"*We* have done nothing, Mr Stokes. We have been good citizens . . . *British* citizens, for many years. But now we are being punished for what my idiot brother and my foolish son have done." Hanna sniffled. "The people in this town now hate us. And I can understand that. Really, I can . . . but . . ."

Words failed him. He put his head in his hands. Stokes reached across and put a hand on the man's shoulder.

"I don't know how much you know about how this all came to pass." He paused. "It was not entirely Freddie and Ernest's doing."

Frank looked up and nodded. He was angry. "I know. Jan. That Dutch Nazi cousin of ours."

At this point, Stokes sensed that they did not know the full story and he wanted to give them that information.

"Indeed, I saw his letters to Freddie but that's not who I mean. Have you been able to visit Ernest and Freddie in Durham, by the way?"

Frank looked at his wife. She was shaking her head. There were tears in her eyes.

"No. I believe we have to ask for a permit but we have not done so. I went to see Sergeant Harris. I understand their cases will go before a tribunal in order to decide their fate."

Stokes was surprised they had not visited. He was not sure which of them had made that decision. Frank, probably. He spoke directly to the man.

"I'm not sure about that, myself. If you want my opinion though, I think it might be better for all four of you if you could visit. Once their fate is determined, then things will happen very quickly."

Hanna looked pointedly at her husband, which confirmed Stokes' judgment on whose call it was not to go to Durham. Frank returned her look. Maybe there was a softening of his views.

Stokes broke the silence. "It wasn't actually Jan that I was referring to earlier." He paused for a few seconds. "The chap who delivered the wireless and later collected it - was a German spy. He was the one who sent the original message about the factory to his masters in the *Abwehr*. That contact, though, was engineered by Jan who, as you so rightly say, seems to be in the pocket of the Dutch *Gestapo*. Ernest and Freddie were victims of this spy's keenness to please his masters in Hamburg. They were duped."

Frank looked shocked. Hanna seemed somehow brighter, as the fact that there was a third guilty party involved in the whole sad story, somehow diluted the family's guilt. Stokes could not tell them the complete story of

Wesley. He simply wanted to plant the seed that Ernest and Freddie were not one hundred per cent to blame for the raid on the factory.

"All I can tell you is that this man led us a merry dance over several weeks."

Hanna spoke for the first time. "Is this man still at large, Mr Stokes?"

"He has been apprehended. And I can tell you that Ernest was very helpful in giving us information about him." That was a bending of the truth. Ernest *had* given them chapter and verse but most of it was already known. Stokes also neglected to mention that the spy was now once more 'at large', as Hanna had put it.

His hunch that Frank and Hanna were not aware of the machinations behind the whole affair, was correct. In fact, they had had no contact at all with the pair since they took flight in Frank's car immediately after the bombing.

Stokes was not sure if his visit had done the couple any good but they certainly looked less wretched than they had when he arrived. He was pleased. He changed tack.

"I was sorry to see that the shop is boarded up, Frank."

"Yes. And I am afraid it is permanent. We have made the decision to move away, Mr Stokes. We have family in Bradford in the same business. Soon, those who are vandalising the property will tire of their game and the premises will be sold - at a much-reduced price, of course. Our friends, the Grubers . . . do you know of them?"

Stokes nodded. "Yes, I read about them in a batch of press clippings that we found in the flat."

"Yes. Freddie has shown them to me on several occasions. Well, they will keep a watching eye on the place and the police have been very good. They agree that this criminal damage has to stop. And I believe there is to be a piece in the *Shields Daily News* about it. Similar to the ones that you have read recently, I would imagine." He paused. "What I do not understand is why my brother, Freddie, my son, Ernest, and this German spy were all so keen on the *Luftwaffe* bombing the factory. They make lemonade there, for goodness' sake."

Stokes had been dreading that question.

"I'm afraid I cannot tell you that, Frank. All I can say is that there was some perverted logic to it." He paused. "But I do not think they imagined, for a minute, that what they did would lead to the factory being bombed."

"I still don't understand?"

"It is known by some in the immediate area that there was a constant naval presence in the factory for some days before it was bombed. More than that, I cannot say."

Frank was stunned. Stokes saw a light go on.

"*Um Gottes Willen.*" It was the first time he had heard Frank speak German. It was a simple statement of shock. "But those who are steadily demolishing my shop do not know this, do they?"

"I think not. The vandalism is, I'm afraid, simply because you are German - or of German heritage, at least - and the bomb that killed about one hundred people was also German. It's a question of scale too." He paused. "I would just say, though, that neither Ernest nor Freddie thought that there would be any loss of life at all."

He was not sure if this information was making them feel better or worse. At least, though, they were better informed and now had the means to make sense of it all. He felt it was time to leave them. He stood and thanked the couple for their time.

Frank led him to the door. He shook hands with Stokes and said one last thing.

"I will go to see Sergeant Harris tomorrow and see if we can get a visiting permit. No matter what I think of the pair of them, Ernest is Hanna's son as well as mine."

He smiled faintly and closed the door.

STOKES WALKED to the car and manoeuvred it so that he was facing the town. Just down the road, he spotted the familiar figure of Lizzie Fenwick. He pulled in alongside her and rolled the window open.

"Mrs Fenwick?"

She smiled. "Oh, Mr Stokes. Wasn't expecting to see you."

Stokes laughed. "No, I don't expect you were. Are you on your way to see the Metcalfs?"

"Yes. I have something to tell them." She beamed at him and raised her eyebrows.

He did not want to pry. "Ah, I see. I have just come from there. I've been bringing them up to speed with the whole sad story. I won't keep you now but please tell them that you have spoken to me and that they can pass on the information I gave them."

Lizzie seemed taken aback. "Oh, yes. Thank you." She stood for a few seconds and then gave a small wave. "Goodbye, then."

He watched her walk through the Metcalfs' gate and knock on the door.

STOKES CALLED into the police station, as promised. Harris was in the same position he had been in just an hour earlier.

"Ah, Mr Stokes. How did it go with the Metcalfs?"

As he waited for the reply, he gestured to a passing

bobby to arrange two teas. Stokes sat on a stool at the counter.

"I'm not sure, but they know a little more now. And I think they will shortly be dropping in to arrange a visiting permit for Durham."

The sergeant looked pleased. "I wondered about that. I'll ring the prison later to see what needs to be done."

The tea arrived. Stokes spent the next ten minutes filling the policeman in on his visit. The sergeant made all the appropriate reactions and was in tune with Stokes about the injustice of the vandalism. He promised that all was being done to curtail it and he had been interviewed - as an unnamed police spokesman - for the newspaper piece that was coming out soon. Stokes reflected that it may well turn out to be a double-edged sword. He also suspected that any disclosure of the scale of the factory incident would come up against the public censor.

Their conversation over, Stokes asked the sergeant if he could make one last call to London.

"Of course. I'll ring the number. You know where to go."

Stokes took the call in what was now being seen as his office.

"Albert. How goes it?"

"All is well. Not much to report. I was just wondering if I'm coming back to London. You did vaguely mention Scotland the last time we spoke."

"Ah, yes. Forget that. The individual is en route to the Tower as we speak."

Stokes was surprised. "A high calibre individual, then?"

Knight laughed. "There's only one higher. Anyway, call in when you get back, old son. I'll reveal all then. Speak soon."

. . .

HE RETURNED to the desk and thanked Harris for the constant use of the office and telephone. They shook hands.

"Well, if you're ever in this neck of the woods again, Mr Stokes, you know where we are."

Stokes smiled and drew a card from his wallet. He handed it to the man.

"You know by now what line of business I'm in, Sergeant. If ever you suspect that there is anything I need to know about, please give me a call. This war is not just being fought by our armed forces." He paused. "I sometimes think that's what Churchill meant when he said 'we shall fight them in the fields and in the streets'. He wasn't just talking about Germans."

Harris thought about that for a moment and nodded sagely. "I'll certainly do that. In the meantime, 'mum's the word', eh?"

They both laughed, remembering the wordplay from their search of the flat above the shop.

"Indeed. You haven't seen me." Stokes started to walk away then turned. "Gan canny, mind."

Stokes could still hear the policeman's laughter as he got into his car.

CHAPTER 63

Howard Wesley made it into the Siemens-Schuckert factory at Brentford without any trouble.

It was not a particularly warm welcome. Although he was remembered and his *bona fides* not doubted, his very Englishness was now working against him. He was informed that he was making some of the 'left-behind' agents uncomfortable. They were German to a man, as Grosskopf had told him they would be. He did his best to get alongside them but his efforts were unsuccessful.

He transmitted a message to Otto under a new code-name of VOGEL. It was German for 'bird', and he was confident that his opposite number in Hamburg would understand the implication. He had flown. He also knew that Otto would recognise his fist and the message. Put succinctly, it was a request to trigger his escape plan - *Unternehmen Blauer Tiger.*

. . .

THE FIRST REPLY from Otto Ziegler was not as good as he had hoped. It was basically 'sit tight' pending further instructions. No mention of paratroopers storming the gates and whisking him away. More worryingly, no timescale, and life at this factory was exceedingly boring.

He was disappointed. At the end of a performance, he liked to enjoy the roar of the crowd, the plaudits, the ego-stroking. It was beginning to feel as if he had crawled over red-hot coals for the last few weeks in front of an empty house. He was deflated.

But then, a few days later, there came a second message. It stirred his blood. He may not be back in Hamburg very soon but he could be back in the field before he knew it. Wesley chuckled to himself at the literary contortions that Otto must have had to put himself through in concocting sections of the message. Such was their near-telepathy though, that he understood it implicitly.

He had no idea of the 'why' or the 'how' but having heard the whispers going around Siemens-Schuckert, he thought he knew the 'who'.

A very senior Nazi official had landed in Scotland and Hitler wanted him back.

HISTORICAL NOTES

Handler is a mix of fact and fiction, truth and invention, reality and artifice. All that can be taken as stone-cold certain is that there was a world war which started in September 1939 and ended - in Europe, at least - in May 1945. I feel compelled, however, to enlighten those readers who really need to separate the fact from the fiction. So, here it is.

The North Shields lemonade factory bombed at midnight on 3/4 May 1941 belonged to the family business founded by my great-grandfather, William Arthur Wilkinson. When it was hit by a single bomb from a 'lone raider', 107 people perished in the public shelter beneath. It was one of the largest losses of life from a single bomb during what became known as the provincial Blitz.

My great-grandfather died in January 1924 but I chose to extend his life by seventeen years in order to bring simplicity to the narrative. The company remained in family hands until the early 1960s.

Most of what I know of the tragedy has been gained from my good friend, Peter Bolger, whose book, *North*

Shields 173 – The Wilkinson's Lemonade Factory Air Raid Disaster, is an authoritative work and essential reading on the subject. If your interest is further piqued by what was a virtually unchronicled major tragedy, then I can also recommend Peter's comprehensive website - www. northshields173.org (North Shields 173 was the telephone number of the factory.)

Czech RAF Flight Sergeant Augustin Preucil stole Hurricane MkI A-PA, W9147, from RAF Usworth in September 1941. His full story can be found in *Prototyp Zrady* by Czech father and daughter historians, Jan Nemeček and Daniela Nemečková. No English translation exists but, thanks to a Czech friend, I was able to gain insight into Preucil's tale. Again, I tinkered with time by bringing the date of the heist forward a few weeks, thus moving it closer to the factory bombing.

The stolen fighter ended up in an aeronautical museum at Moabit, Berlin. According to modern German sources, work was carried out in summer 1943 to evacuate the collection and to transport exhibits out of harm's way to Poland - then part of the Third Reich but subsequently behind the Iron Curtain. The Moabit museum eventually fell victim to air raids in November of that year. *(source: Der Tagesspiegel, 21 September 2010).*

Hurricane A-PA is not listed in the Polish Aviation Museum's collection in Krakow so we must assume that it was either 'lost in transit' or was destroyed when Moabit was bombed. Interesting to note, though, that Krakow does have a Spitfire MkXVI-E. This variant did not enter service until October 1944 so it was not from the Moabit museum. I surmise that it may have been gifted to the Polish nation by the RAF in gratitude for their service in WW2.

The story of Preucil's theft of the Hurricane did not come to light until 2003. Amateur aviation historians – Richard Chapman and Roy Nesbit – were intrigued by a photograph which showed A-PA on display in the Moabit museum. By checking the aircraft serial number and markings, it was easily traced back to Preucil's last flight from RAF Usworth. His disappearance was written off as a training accident. The whole dirty tale and the scale of the Czech airman's treachery was eventually unravelled and is recounted in the aforementioned *Prototyp Zrady*.

The bulk of what you read about Preucil is, as far as anyone knows, true. That includes his relationship with Sunderland girl, Muriel Kirby. They did, in fact, marry in July 1941 – a union which I did not feature in the narrative. Muriel's friendship with Lizzie Fenwick is fabricated, as Lizzie is fictional. However, William Arthur Wilkinson did have a younger brother, Joe, who also had a lemonade factory in Sunderland, where I found Muriel a job.

Muriel was eventually able to contact her late husband's family after the war but it was a case of 'good news, bad news'. Augustin was alive but due to hang by decision of a Czech Extraordinary People's Court. His treachery had caught up with him. He died at the end of a rope in Prague in April 1947. His widow subsequently remarried in 1952 but remained firmly convinced of Augustin's innocence right up to her own death in 2005.

The site of RAF Usworth is now occupied by the large and sprawling Nissan factory. The *Three Horseshoes* pub still exists, albeit under its recent re-incarnation as *Rustica Trattoria and Inn*. On what would have been the site perimeter, there now stands NELSAM (North East Land, Sea and Air Museums) – www.nelsam.org.uk. It houses many exhibits, the star attraction being Avro Vulcan XL319, one of only a few surviving examples. NELSAM is now the only historical link to aviation at Usworth.

Accounts of the bombing raids in Hull in May 1941 are largely accurate. The city was literally pounded during the early years of the war. Restrictions regarding censorship bestowed upon Hull the soubriquet of 'a north east coastal town'. Wartime suppression of so much bad news also explains why the Wilkinson lemonade factory tragedy is not widely-known beyond Tyneside. Morale was everything.

The Punch Hotel on Queen Victoria Square still stands – adrift in an ocean of new development. At the time of writing in August 2021 it is largely unchanged, both inside and out. As the book relates, the then landlord, Fred Wallis, and five members of his immediate family died in the shelter of the Prudential building just yards away. The Punch Hotel itself survived that night - the only damage being a single broken window. It remains intact and undamaged.

The present owners, I was gratified to see, have framed words and a photograph on the bar, informing punters of the ultimate sacrifice made by the Wallis family on the night of 7/8 May 1941. This was just four days after the North Shields factory tragedy and in strikingly similar circumstances – a basement shelter.

Q-sites – or decoy sites – did exist. Their purpose was to deceive German bombing crews as to the exact location of their target. Cherry Cobb Sands was one of a few around the Hull/Humber estuary area.

The North Shields German pork butcher family – the Metzgers, anglicised to Metcalf – is pure make-believe. The only German pork butcher family that I could discover in the town were the Grubers who are mentioned in Freddie's reading of a press report, which is genuine. Both sides of the Tyne, however, were well-represented by pork butchery enterprises, many of which seem to have come from the same region of Germany in the late nineteenth century.

Another German pork butcher family on Tyneside was the Egners. Frederick George Egner was Town Clerk for the Borough of Tynemouth for many years before, during and after WWII, and would have overseen the aftermath of the factory tragedy. He was awarded the OBE in the New Year Honours of 1946. In a strange quirk, he was almost certainly related to my old Headmaster, William Edward Egner, at South Shields Grammar Technical School for Boys, whose parents were also pork butchers. He served in RAF Intelligence during the war and was also honoured with the OBE, in 1974.

I could find no evidence of any Fifth Columnist cell in North Shields of either English or German heritage. No slur is intended to any naturalised Germans of the time, many of whom, as can be seen from *Shields Daily News* articles of the time, fought in the Great War on the side of the British.

I also apologise for any offence caused to the many brave and valiant Czech and Polish RAF pilots who fought in WW2. Preucil's story is true, Gierczak is fictional.

Albert Stokes is based upon a real character, whose name was Eric Arthur Roberts. His role in rooting out and 'containing' many would-be Fifth Columnist cells and 'lone shark' Nazi sympathisers, was legendary. His true identity was not revealed until October 2014 with the release of information from the National Archives.

The notion that he posed as 'Hitler's man in London', that he carried German ID and presented his 'clients' with badges and medals bearing Nazi insignia may seem preposterous. I am secretly glad that it is not. It happened. So convincing was he in his alter ago, that he kept the streets clean of most Fifth Columnist activity throughout the war.

Information regarding the Double Cross operation, known as XX or the Twenty Committee, is also accurate. Any genuine German spies were either turned by XX, to act as double agents against their German masters, or had their lives terminated with the aid of a rope and a trapdoor. It was the perfect complement to Roberts' operation.

Maxwell Knight and Lieutenant-Colonel Robin 'Tin Eye' Stephens also existed in the roles which I have described. As did Oliver Strachey, a cryptographer at Bletchley Park.

Kriminalinspektor Oskar Fleischer was head of the Gestapo in Prague. Known to be a vicious, violent man whose interrogations at Petschek's Palace were savage, he gained the title of 'the butcher of Prague'. Given that the German word 'Fleischer' actually means 'butcher', it was most appropriate. He managed to escape capture after the war and was many times rumoured to be living 'somewhere in West Germany'. Nazi ranks had closed around him. His date and place of death are therefore unknown but, given that he was born in December 1892, I think it safe to assume that he is no longer with us.

The eponymous handler, Howard Oswald Wesley, his *Abwehr* Hamburg contacts, Otto Ziegler and *Major* Dieter Grosskopf, and the North Shields Fenwick family are all inventions. The Hull birdwatcher-cum-Fifth-Columnist, Peter Armitage, and Freddie's Dutch cousin, Jan Visser also never drew breath. Nor did the ill-fated Polish airman, Tomasz Gierczak.

Air Marshall Sir William Sholto Douglas, Air Vice-Marshall Trafford Leigh Mallory, Squadron Leaders Paddy Green and Johnny Kent, Winston Churchill, Chief Constable Blackburn were all real people. So too were *Obersturmbannführer* Lages and *Sturmbannführer* Harster, of the *Sicherheitsdienst (SD)* in Amsterdam. The latter pair were involved in the death of over 100,000 Jews in the Holocaust, including Anne Frank.

Anyone else named, you can assume, is fictitious.

It is almost beyond doubt that the bombing of the Wilkinson lemonade factory was a random attack. North Shields had suffered a number of raids before that – and indeed afterwards – but none with the massively tragic consequences of the single bomb that demolished the three-storey factory and devastated a community.

As regards the heist of a Hurricane from RAF Usworth – just a few miles from North Shields – I needed to fabricate little. I merely bent the dates by a few weeks. Everything else was gained from the only authoritative work on the matter – *Prototyp Zrady,* by father and daughter historians – Jan Nemeček and Daniela Nemečková. It is a shame that the book exists only in the Czech language. Preucil's story does not stop with the delivery of the Hurricane into Nazi hands. He died with blood on his hands.

The inspiration for *Handler* was the thought – expressed by many on various forums I have read – that Preucil could not have acted alone. He must have had a 'handler' – someone on the ground to ensure that he carried out his task. It is my belief that the existence of a 'handler' is infinitely more likely than the idea that there was top secret naval work being carried out on the top floor of the lemonade factory.

The two events, though – factory and fighter heist – were so close together, in both distance and time, that it is not sufficiently beyond the realms of possibility that they were linked. The possibility of a 'handler' proved too great a temptation. This book is the result.

ACKNOWLEDGEMENTS

I owe a debt of gratitude to many people – without whose contributions of information, knowledge and expertise, this book would not have seen the light of day.

David Penny, friend, fellow-author and a real whizz at the intricacies of publishing independently. Were it not for him, my words would simply never have been read. Nor would I have been aware of ALLi (Alliance of Independent Authors) in which is contained all that an aspiring independent author needs to know.

www.davidpenny.com

www.allianceindependentauthors.org

Sara Starbuck, my developmental editor. My first draft - where words were simply thrown at the page in no particular order – must have been a nightmare to read. (Think monkeys, typewriters and *War and Peace*!) Her nuggets of advice and encouragement were invaluable. Many months later and just minutes before I was wheeled down to have a heart pacemaker implanted, I read her feedback on the second draft. Already blissfully high on pre-op sedation, it sent me to another level. They could have severed my head, ripped it from my neck, dropped it in a bucket and I would still have been smiling.

Peter Bolger, friend, author, historian – and unrivalled expert in everything related to the Wilkinson's lemonade factory tragedy which features in this novel. His factual book on the subject, *North Shields 173 – The Wilkinson's Lemonade Factory Air Raid Disaster*, is a seminal work. Anyone at all interested in discovering more would also be well advised to visit his comprehensive website – www. northshields173.org.

Jan Nemeček and Daniela Nemečková, Czech father and daughter historians. Their book *Prototyp Zrady* told me all I needed to know about the renegade Augustin Preucil. Sadly, there is no English language version of the book so additional thanks are due to George Strass, a Czech speaker, who helped me out with the translation of certain sections.

Paul Schofield, of Hull. He kindly showed me around the various sites of WW2 interest in the city and was extremely informative. And all for the price of a coffee!

Ann Ulyatt, also of Hull, for her agreement to my use of her family history, relating to the Hull air raids on the night of 7/8 May 1941. The tragic story of the Wallis family is still displayed on the bar of the Punch Hotel in Queen Victoria Square.

Doug Spratt who pointed me in the direction of the Grubers. They were pork butchers in North Shields, of

German descent, and would have known my fictional family of similar background. That information was extremely useful.

I hereby apologise for any errors or omissions and will endeavour to rectify them on any subsequent reprint.

ABOUT THE AUTHOR

Terry Wilkinson is the emerging author of a series of novels set in World War II. They are a blend of fact and fiction and follow the experiences of English-born German spy, Howard Wesley, and his nemesis, MI5 agent, Albert Stokes.

Handler is the first in that series. The second - working title *Sleeper* - will see the light of day in late 2022.

Terry lives in Marske by the Sea in the north-east of England. He is quite old by biblical standards but still has most of his marbles. He has had a chequered career which spanned a broad spectrum. At one extreme, he was a stockbroker and survived the stockmarket crash of 1987, which wasn't his fault. At the other, he was a taxi driver for a few years, where he also survived a crash, which was not his fault either.

His portfolio of employment then culminated in fifteen years of touring schools with his own theatre company along with regular street theatre appearances. As his school reports used to say - 'Terry is very easily distracted'.

Having exhausted most means of gainful employment, he now lives to write. Discovering very soon that he had neither the time nor the patience to go down the (once) conventional route of mainstream publishing, he is taking the independent way.

Terry wants to write what he would love to read. He hopes you do too.

Find him on www.terrywilkinson.co.uk where more will be revealed. And, apparently, he blogs on www.terrydwilkinson.com.

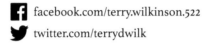

facebook.com/terry.wilkinson.522
twitter.com/terrydwilk

Printed in Great Britain
by Amazon

67087379R00303